NIGHT OF THE
WATER SPIRITS

BARBARA BISCO

Black Lotus

blacklotuspublishing.com

ISBN: 978-0-9560276-1-0

Typeset in Goudy by Lawrence Mann
Printed and bound in Great Britain by
CPI Cox and Wyman Ltd.
Reading, Berkshire, RG1 8EX UK
Registered under the Companies House Act
Number 2,196,742
www.cpibooks.co.uk

Published by
BLACK LOTUS PUBLISHING LTD.
25 Belsize Crescent
London, UK NW3 5QY
Registered under the Companies House Act
Number 5,928,807
www.blacklotuspublishing.com

Black Lotus has been registered as a Trade Mark
with the UK Patent Office

A CIP record for this book is available
from the British Library

Papers used by Black Lotus Publishing are natural, recyclable products made from
wood free paper. The Manufacuring processes conform to the FSC environmental
regulations of the country of origin.

MIX
Paper from
responsible sources
FSC® C014728

BARABARA BISCO caught her first glimpse of Thailand from the deck of a China Siam Line freighter as it steamed up the Chao Phrya River toward Bangkok in 1960. She quickly fell in love with the beautiful country and when, a year later, she had to leave, she went to the Erawan Shrine and asked the god, Phra Bhram, to bring her back to Thailand. He has brought her back to Bangkok many times since, once on a Fulbright Scholarship in 1968 and twice for two-year postings in 1980 and 1985 with her husband and daughter. During those four years, Barbara worked as a volunteer at the National Museum in Bangkok.

Barbara has a degree in anthropology from Harvard University, and a Ph.D. in Economics from the Southeast Asia Program at Cornell University where she met her husband, a nomadic economist.

Barbara is author of A TASTE FOR GREEN TANGERINES, a novel set in Indonesian Borneo, "a sizzling escape to a richly drawn other world... a book about finding yourself in the most unexpected of places". Her short stories have appeared in various books and magazines.

Barbara and her husband now live in London but Phra Bhram continues to pull her back to Bangkok for visits.

FOR MY HUSBAND AND DAUGHTER

CHAPTER 1
BANGKOK, 1958

'Daddy, Daddy, did you bring it?'

'The surprise from America?' laughed William Duncanson, setting down his cases. 'Of course I did.'

'Where is it? Let me see.'

'Right here,' William said, pushing forward a blond boy with pale green eyes who gazed around the room with reluctant curiosity, 'an American cousin for you to play with. His name's Teddy and he's looking forward to staying with us for a while.'

'Is that all you brought?' Panida cried, in disbelief.

'Isn't that enough?'

Tears of disappointment welled up in her dark eyes. 'But you told me on the phone you were bringing me something wonderful.'

'And that's exactly what I did,' he insisted, and turned to greet his wife.

Panida gazed through angry tears at this unwelcome boy. He was a little taller than herself, with blond hair and a face like the jack of diamonds on her mother's playing cards. How could her father have promised her a fabulous toy and then brought this horrible cousin instead?

Teddy did not take a corresponding interest in the

eight-year-old girl with honey coloured skin and black hair who was staring at him with such hostile eyes. Instead, he let his gaze sweep around the strange room, taking in its rattan furniture, its whirling ceiling fans and its funny windows that didn't have any glass in them and made up his mind that he wasn't going to stay here a minute longer than he absolutely had to.

His uncle's wife, who looked like a grown-up version of the little girl but who seemed friendly, spoke to him in funny sounding English and offered him something to eat.

He wasn't hungry.

'Panida, say something to your cousin,' her father ordered. 'Don't just gape at him.'

She mumbled something incoherent in Thai.

'Speak English,' William snapped. 'How can you expect Teddy to understand Thai when he's only barely off the plane? Take him out to the garden and show him around. I bet he's never seen a gibbon before.'

'It will probably bite him,' Panida said.

'Not as hard as I'm going to bite you if you don't behave yourself,' growled her father. 'Now go.'

'Do you like gibbons?' Panida asked him, when they were outside.

'No,' he replied. He didn't know what a gibbon was but he was sure that if this nasty girl liked them, he wouldn't want to have anything to do with them.

The bright afternoon sun was beginning to fade and the gibbon was getting sleepy. Panida lifted it down from its tree house, undid its chain and held it in her arms like a baby; the little creature twined its long furry arms around her and snuggled up against her.

'You'd better stay away from him' she told Teddy rudely. 'He likes me but he doesn't like strangers.'

'That figures,' he shot back. 'It probably thinks you're just another monkey.'

And with that, he trotted off to have a closer look at the fetid green canal that bordered one side of the garden.

'It isn't a monkey, it's an ape, Daddy says so,' she called after him. 'You don't know anything.'

Teddy paid no attention.

After a few moments of feeling rather forlorn, Panida perked up at the thought that her father always brought her sweets as well as a present when he came back from a trip. Telling herself that he surely wouldn't have forgotten, she put the sleepy gibbon back in its tree house and went inside in search of him.

To her surprise she found that the living room was empty. That was funny, she thought, where had Mummy and Daddy gone?

She went over to their bedroom door, pushed it open

and peered in. Her father was standing very close to her mother and handing her a small velvet box. That was a good sign, she thought. If he had remembered to bring a present for her mother he would surely have brought something for her too.

Her parents jumped apart when they heard the door scrape open and neither of them seemed very glad to see her.

'Did you bring me some sweets, Daddy?' she asked.

'I'm sorry, love. I did have some for you but Teddy got hungry in Tokyo Airport so I let him have them. You don't mind, do you?' And without waiting for her reply, he added, 'Run along now, there's a good girl. Go outside and play with your cousin. He's come all the way from America to see you.'

'I don't want to.'

'Well, do it anyway. Your mother and I are going to take a nap now.'

Panida stood her ground in obstinate silence.

'You have no hope of growing up to be as beautiful as your mother if you have a pout on your face and the manners of an orangutan,' William declared; and, taking her firmly by the shoulders, he steered her out the door and closed it firmly behind her.

She heard a loud click as her father turned the key in the lock.

'Let me in, let me in,' she cried, pounding on the door with angry fists.

There was no response from inside. She couldn't even hear them talking so eventually she gave up.

She thought about going round to the outdoor kitchen and talking to the maids while they grated coconut, peeled fruit and chopped vegetables for the evening meal. Usually she enjoyed that but somehow she didn't feel like it today. She didn't feel like playing either; so, for lack of anything better to do, she wandered out to the decrepit wooden bench near the canal. It was shielded from view by a low fence covered with luxuriant vines and purple orchids, which made it a good place to go when she wanted to think about things. It was a nearly secret spot, her special place, and one of the best things about it was that nobody else ever went there.

But today she could hardly believe what she saw. That dreadful boy was there, sitting on her bench, just as if her secret place belonged to him. He was staring at the canal.

'This water's disgusting,' he said when he saw her. 'Look, it's got green slime all over it.'

'You can get typhoid from dirty water,' she warned him. 'Lots of people do, especially foreigners. Their temperature goes up and up until it gets so high they turn purple and smoke comes out of their toes. You'd better go back to America before that happens to you.'

'Don't I wish,' he replied, huffily.

'Why don't you then?'

'I can't. Mom and Dad were in a car accident.'

'Are they dead?'

'Dad is. Mom's in the hospital with lots of casts and bandages and things.'

'Is she going to die, too?'

Teddy grimaced. The question gave him a hideous feeling that he was about to cry. Quickly turning his head and looking down so she couldn't see his face, he caught sight of a small lizard near his foot. On impulse, he picked it up and threw it in her face.

The creature scrambled up into her hair; in her frantic effort to shake it off she missed her step, lost her footing and toppled backwards into the greenish, blackish water of the stagnant canal.

Teddy started to laugh but then a terrifying thought struck him. Maybe she'd drown and he'd go to jail, get the electric chair. He hurriedly reached down to pull her out, but she bit him so hard that blood streamed from his fingers. Drops of red could be seen in the water.

The next few days were lonely and desolate ones for Teddy. A sort of armed truce, born of dire threats from his uncle, was in force between the two cousins. William was nice to him when he emerged from his study and his books, but that didn't happen very often. Most of his time seemed to be spent preparing lectures for some university with a funny sounding name.

In any case, seeing Uncle William made Teddy feel happy and sad at the same time, because he looked so much like his father. But where his father had been easygoing and full of fun, his uncle was gruff and stern.

Panida's mother tried to be kind, but the problem was that Panida was always following her around and talking to her in Thai whenever she was at home. She was out a lot though. She would usually wait until Uncle William went out and then she would dress up and go out too.

Although he would rather die than admit it, there were times when Teddy wanted to cry with homesickness. He kept thinking about his dad, wondering if he was really alive in some kind of heaven and looking down watching him. He kind of hoped he was, even though the idea sort of gave him the shivers.

When it came down to it, he decided, a lot of creepy things went on in Thailand. For one thing, people were always talking about ghosts and spirits. There was even a house for spirits in a corner of the garden, which either Panida or her mother took flowers and incense out to everyday. Sometimes they put rice out too although, for the life of him, he couldn't figure out what good that would do the spirits. And a couple of nights ago things had got even more weird. The family across the street had actually set a table on their balcony and put a bowl and a plate and a glass for some dead grandfather on it, even lighted a candle for him; at least, that was what Panida's mother had said they were doing. Back in the States dead people were dead and live people were alive; it was all very clear who was who and what was what – but here, things got all jumbled up. Dead people came to dinner and spirits lived in gardens and live people? Well, they certainly didn't behave the way people did at home.

Teddy's life took a turn for the better when school started. It was an international school and everyone there spoke English and did things pretty much the way they did back in Connecticut. The only trouble, and it was actually a big trouble, was that it wasn't very easy to make friends. The kids who were in the thick of things, the popular ones, all went to each other's houses after school and had mothers who took them swimming at the Sports Club. The rest of the kids, the ones who were totally out of it like himself, had mothers like Panida's, who expected them just to sit around the house after school. She even seemed to think he could play with Panida, a kid who was only eight, and – even worse – a girl. Never mind the fact that he couldn't stand her. It was hard to believe the ideas that some people got into their heads.

There was another problem, too. Teddy didn't really like to admit to himself, much less to anybody else, how much he missed his own mother. After all, he wasn't a baby anymore. He'd be thirteen in a few months and she would be out of the hospital by then. Everybody said she was going to be perfectly all right. He had no trouble remembering this in the daytime but sometimes at night he had terrible dreams. He'd see her lying on something very hard and very white, all wrapped up in dreadful bandages and covered with blood. Then he would wake up trembling and soaked with sweat and sometimes even have to run into the bathroom and throw up.

He had a ghastly dream like that in the early hours of the morning when it was just beginning to get light; so, instead of trying to go back to sleep afterwards, he unlocked the front door and went out and sat down on one of the veranda steps to think about things. Everything was quiet except for a persistent sound of *tokay*, *tokay*, *tokay* that was coming from somewhere near his right foot. Looking around, he saw an orange and green lizard a bit like the one he had thrown at Panida. He watched with fascination as its throbbing neck moved up and down with each fresh vocalisation.

Who was it calling to, he wondered, and why didn't people like lizards? Why did they always want dogs who would follow them everywhere and make them feel important, or cats who would... but he couldn't think what cats did, except sit around and wait for their dinner? He liked the glorious independence of a lizard.

He became so absorbed in watching the creature that he didn't notice the appearance of his uncle until a heavy scent of whisky assaulted his nostrils.

A very drunk Uncle William, looking as if he had been up all night, sat down on the step beside Teddy.

'I want you to stay away from women,' he told his nephew sternly.

Teddy could not have been more surprised if the orange and green lizard had stood up and started reciting the multiplication tables.

'Women are the devil,' William continued, and seemed about to go on in this vein when he stopped and peered at Teddy. 'I don't suppose you've had much experience with women yet.'

'Well, there's a girl back home,' Teddy lied.

'Avoid her like the plague,' advised his uncle. 'You know what girls will do to you, don't you?'

'Yeah, I've been around a bit,' said Teddy; he was warming to the idea of a man-to-man discussion, and wanted to make an impressive show of things.

'Then you know what women are after.'

Teddy nodded.

'Money,' asserted his uncle. 'Oh, they'll talk about love and they'll put on a damn good show about sex but all the time they've only got one thing on their fetid little minds:

money, and how to get more of it out of you.'

Teddy was about to protest. The only woman he really knew was his mother and she wasn't like that. Then he reminded himself that this wasn't a conversation about mothers, it was about women. That was different. He gave a low groan, as if he too had been the victim of sexual assaults by mercenary women. The resulting sound came out more like a gargle, but his uncle didn't appear to notice. His attention had been diverted by a furious little figure storming out onto the veranda, looking like she had been crying.

'It's your fault,' shouted Panida. 'You drove Mummy away. We were happy until you came back from America.'

'God damn it! Your mother runs off with a rich slimy lover and you think it's my fault? Well it's not my fucking fault and if you weren't still a baby you'd know that. Just take care you don't grow up to be like your mother – that's all I can say.'

'I will grow up like her. I'll grow up exactly like her. It will be easy-peasy because everybody says I look like her already.'

Her father glared at her; then, in a voice that almost sounded as if he were sober, he said: 'No, my dear, you're not going to grow up like her. I'm going to see to it that you don't. And if my present state of inebriation leads you to think you can ignore what I'm saying, you are making a

11

serious mistake.'

Then, getting unsteadily to his feet, he announced, 'And now I'm going to shake up the cook and get her to make some coffee.'

When he had gone Teddy, moved enough by the situation to put the usual state of warfare with his cousin aside for the moment, said, 'Maybe your mother will come back. After all, she didn't die or anything.'

'I don't think she ever liked Daddy very much,' Panida reflected, feeling the same unspoken call to a truce and sitting down on the step beside him. 'Mummy and I always had more fun when he wasn't around.'

'Maybe she won't like this new guy very much either,' Teddy suggested, 'and then she'll come back.'

Panida considered this possibility and brightened a little. 'Perhaps,' she agreed, but it wasn't enough to overcome the lonely empty feeling that seemed to be lodged in the pit of her stomach.

In the days that followed, Panida tried to compensate for the void her mother's departure had left by seeing to it that everything went on – as much as was possible – in the way it always had. She spent a lot of time with the maids because they spoke Thai and did everything the Thai way. She refused to speak English to her father and she solved the language problem with Teddy by not talking to him at all. She saw to it that fresh flowers were placed in front of the bronze Buddha image in the living room everyday and insisted on being the one to take the daily offerings out to the spirit house in the garden. She got up very early so she could be the one to offer food to the saffron-robed monks who stopped at the front gate each morning, a privilege her mother had always reserved for herself. Doing these things made her feel that if her mother came back she would be pleased with her; and, if she didn't? Well, she would have to try even harder to be as much like her as possible.

The weeks crawled by until the festival of Loi Kratong, the night Panida thought was the most magical of the year. It was the one when the banks of Bangkok's flowing canals and majestic Chao Phraya River teemed with life and their waters shimmered with lights from a multitude of candles.

As sundown approached Panida put on her best dress and inspected her Kratong for the hundredth time. Its banana leaf base had been shaped into a perfect boat and piled high with flowers, incense, and a candle. She had gone with one of the maids to buy it that morning and the venture had been especially exciting because her father, who had no idea how much a kratong should cost, had given her enough money to buy three of the biggest and most beautiful ones available: one for herself, one for her father and one for Teddy. She had even had enough money left to buy quite decent, though slightly smaller, ones for the maids. And each time her eyes fell on the glorious floral display that decorated her own, an excited tingling sensation ran all the way down from her neck to her toes.

It had been mid-morning by the time she had brought the kratongs home and even later by the time she got to school (not that she cared about that) – so Teddy didn't see his until that afternoon.

'What's that?' he asked, without much curiosity.

'An offering for the water spirits.'

'Why do you want to offer them anything?'

'To ask their forgiveness for all the nasty dirty things people have been putting in the canals and rivers all year.'

'Weird.'

'No, it isn't. But you don't have to come, if you don't want to.'

'Come where?'

'Down to the river. Daddy's taking us. He promised. And we're going in a boat.'

Teddy's ears perked up. That sounded like fun. There was nothing weird about boats, and it suddenly occurred to him that some of the kids at school had been talking about where they were going and what they were going to do that evening. Apparently this Loi Kratong thing, or whatever it was, wasn't just one of Panida's off-the-wall ideas. It was just one of the crazy things people did in Thailand.

'I guess I'll go,' he said, trying to sound reluctant but actually not wanting to be left out of something that might be fun.

The banks of the river had turned into a humming throng of people, all clutching kratongs, by the time William, Panida and Teddy reached the Oriental Landing. The boat that had been hired for their group – an assorted collection of professors from Chulalongkorn University (mostly Thais but also a few foreigners and their families) – wasn't as easily accessible as William would have liked. They had to scramble across a number of other rocking vessels, the first one tied to the dock and the subsequent ones tied to each other, to reach their boat. William was less than happy when he saw how many excited children were scampering over the deck but he wasn't a reliable counter of the younger generation. Ten of the little horrors invariably seemed like a hundred to him. But with several of the prettier secretaries already in the boat, along with a copious stash of Singha Beer and Mekong Whisky, he didn't let the presence of the little bastards depress him for long.

Teddy's interest immediately gravitated to the food supplies. There was rice, of course – didn't these people ever get tired of it, he wondered for the thousandth time – several poisonous-looking curries that had weird things floating around in them, and lots of snacks. These didn't look too bad but he knew from past experience that most of them would probably have hot chillies in them. He congratulated himself on his foresight in stowing a bunch of chocolate bars away in his pockets.

In the meantime Panida had been busy examining the array of kratongs lined up in the centre of the boat. She wanted hers to be the biggest and the most beautiful, and to her delight it was. At least, she thought so anyway.

When everybody was on board, the boat was detached from its moorings, steered out into the middle of the river and set on its course upstream. Panida and Teddy, along with most of the other children, crowded up to the front of the boat to catch the full force of the fresh breezes.

As darkness fell, this proved to be the best place to watch the river coming to life, with more and more kratongs drifting in the currents, the flames from their candles shimmering like dancing points of light on the murky water.

Panida, for whom this was the most beautiful night of the year, was completely caught up in the enchantment of it all – and even Teddy admitted that it was kind of nice.

It took them nearly two hours to reach their destination: a small, darkened temple surrounded by thick jungly vegetation. The passengers tumbled out onto a rickety wooden landing and, kratongs in hand, began to light the candles and incense and set the little floats adrift in the river.

Panida was afraid of matches so she looked around for her father to light hers. But, as he was at the far end of the dock lighting a candle for an attractive woman he had met on the way upriver, she settled for getting Teddy to do it instead. Then, finding a dry place to leave her shoes, she splashed down the wide temple steps, placed her kratong carefully in the river. Pressing her palms together, she raised her hands to her forehead in a brief prayer to the water spirits.

Teddy, uncertain what to do, watched Panida for a moment and then followed her down the temple stairs and put his kratong in the water.

'Make a wai,' she prompted.

'What's that?'

She repeated her gesture. 'It's a sign of respect. It's what you do when you ask the water spirits to forgive you for all the bad things you've done all year.'

He resisted the idea at first but when he saw that some of the other foreigners were doing it, he decided he might as well go along with it. Feeling rather self-conscious, he pressed his hands together in a hasty and none too graceful version of Panida's wai.

No sooner had he done this than he was overcome by a sudden panic. Was he going to be struck by lightning for praying to a bunch of spirits, he wondered? He waited; to his horror, he heard a low rumble of thunder in the distance... but no vengeful bolt of electricity shot out of the sky to strike him dead. Relieved, he turned his attention back to what was going on around him.

Panida seemed intent on watching the progress of her kratong. At first it merely drifted with the current; but then, caught by a sudden gust of wind, it gathered momentum and sped swiftly out toward the centre of the river where the stronger breeze soon extinguished the tiny flame from its candle.

Gradually the other passengers from the boat finished putting their kratongs in the water. They lingered on the riverbank, the adults talking and drinking, the children kept happy with sugary drinks and gooey sweets.

Panida and Teddy, for lack of anything better to do, began exploring the temple compound, treading gingerly across its broken and uneven paving stones until they came to the heavily lacquered entrance of the largest building. It was closed and locked. Disappointed, they turned to several of the smaller structures, but they proved equally inaccessible. So, spotting a wooden platform with railings, benches and a high pointed roof that Panida called a sala, they settled for climbing on that.

'What do you suppose this is for anyway,' Teddy wanted to know.

'It's for people to sit around and rest on when they come to the temple,' Panida explained, thinking that this was obvious. She didn't feel at all like resting now, though. She wanted to explore some more – find something exciting – so she jumped down and ran around to the back of the locked building.

Teddy had just caught up with her when the creaking of a door caught his attention.

'Watch out,' he whispered, 'someone's coming.'

They stopped and listened but no one came. The door seemed to be swinging in accordance with some rhythm of its own. Teddy's curiosity was aroused so he pushed it farther open; with Panida pressing up against him for reassurance, he peered into the cave-like darkness of the interior. A large bronze Buddha, reflecting a streak of moonlight, glowed in the darkness and seemed to draw them toward it.

At first everything, apart from the strangely swinging door, seemed quiet. Then a rustling noise from the direction of the image gave the impression that it was coming to life. Panida, now terrified, grabbed Teddy's hand – and, although he wouldn't have admitted it, a shiver ran down his own spine. The next thing he knew, a green and orange lizard scurried out from behind the Buddha; it ran toward Panida and scrambled up her leg before leaping off and disappearing out the door, pursued by another creature of similar size and colouring.

'Beautiful,' Teddy exclaimed as his eyes followed them into the darkness. Then, conveniently forgetting that he had been pretty nervous himself just a moment ago, he turned to Panida and said, 'There's nothing to be scared of.'

Nevertheless he wasn't quite so sure that he wanted to poke around this place anymore; there was something creepy about it. So he added, 'Maybe we'd better get back to the boat. Uncle William might be looking for us.'

Panida didn't protest, so they made their way out through the swinging door. Teddy, giving it an apprehensive look as they went past, saw with relief that its movements were due to a loose hinge rather than to anything supernatural. They made their way back to the river as quickly as the uneven paving stones allowed, but their progress was slowed by the need to keep a careful watch on where they stepped. As a result, it wasn't until they actually reached the landing that they realised the boat was no longer there. It was already well out into the middle of the river. They stared at it in stunned disbelief, scarcely able to take in the fact that they had been left behind.

'But Daddy couldn't have gone off without me,' Panida cried, 'he just wouldn't.'

She didn't know that William (flushed with generous doses of Mekong Whisky and realizing for the first time since his wife had left him that there were other attractive women in the world) had seen a blond boy and a dark haired girl sitting in the bow of the ship, their faces to the wind – and had assumed that his paternal responsibilities had been fully carried out.

'What will we do?' Panida sobbed, when frantic efforts at shouting and waving had failed to attract any attention at all.

'Don't worry,' Teddy said, with considerably more confidence than he felt. 'When Uncle William figures out we're not on the boat, he'll come back for us.'

'But it's dark and I'm cold,' Panida wailed. A gentle breeze, combined with a hefty dose of fear, chilled her tropical blood.

Teddy was at a loss for suggestions.

'Hungry, too,' she added.

This was a problem for which he had a solution. 'Come on,' he said, showing her his supply of chocolate bars. 'Let's go back to that sala place and have a midnight feast.'

Under the circumstances this seemed like the best thing to do.

'This is the first time I've ever had a midnight feast,' Panida said as she licked the gooey remains of a Bounty off her fingers.

'We have them all the time in the States,' bragged Teddy, who had just devoured his third.

'In the snow?' asked Panida, convinced that America was one step away from the Arctic.

'It doesn't snow all the time. It gets really hot in the summer. That's when I go to camp and we have midnight feasts. But,' he added in the interests of honesty, 'we really just have them sometime before midnight. Anytime after dark is OK, and we sit around a campfire singing songs and toasting marshmallows.'

This required some explanation to fit in with Panida's experience of the world, so Teddy found himself telling her all about life at camp. He concluded with one of the scary stories the older boys used to terrorize the younger ones. Unfortunately, he had just got to the most blood-curdling part when the onset of a light drizzle brought a cry of alarm from Panida.

'You're not afraid of a few drops of rain, are you?' Teddy asked, scornfully. 'We won't get wet here anyway. There's a roof.'

'It's not the rain,' Panida protested, 'it's the ghosts.'

'You don't really believe in that stuff, do you?' Teddy laughed. 'Don't you know there's no such thing as ghosts?'

'Oh, yes, there is,' Panida cried. 'My mother's seen them lots of times, she told me so. And other people have seen them too, especially on rainy nights. That's when they come out. Can't you hear them? Just listen.'

Suddenly a little less sure of himself, Teddy listened but

he didn't hear anything that sounded very ghostly. It was mostly just croaking frogs and buzzing insects and in the distance some barking dogs and screeching cats. Not, he reminded himself, that he knew what kind of noise a ghost would make.

'I don't hear any ghosts,' he said firmly.

'I do,' Panida said in a frightened voice. 'But perhaps they're not calling to you. That's why you don't hear them.'

'That's OK with me,' he said, getting a little nervous in spite of himself.

Panida grabbed his hand. 'Don't let them get me,' she pleaded.

'What makes you think they want you?'

'Don't you know?' she asked in surprise. 'Calling to me means they want to come and get me. They want me to die.'

'Bullshit.'

'No, it's not. The spirits got one of the maids next door that way. On rainy nights they used to call to her from the trees outside her window, and then one day she took a candle into the bathroom because the light wasn't working and right away there was a bang – and by the time they carried her out she was all blue and dead. I know. I saw her.'

'Why would the ghost have made a bang?' Teddy asked, beginning to be interested in spite of himself.

'It didn't. There was a leak – just a tiny one – of gas from the hot water heater and the candle made it go bang and that's when the spirits got her. Then the monks came and said prayers and sent the spirits away.'

'A gas leak and a lighted candle will do it every time,' declared Teddy, who had learned about things like that at school. 'You don't need help from a bunch of ghosts.'

'But don't you see? It was the bad spirits that made it all happen. Everybody said so.'

'Even Uncle William?'

'He's a foreigner,' Panida replied. 'They don't understand things.'

Teddy was about to object when a strange sound, high-pitched and eerie, caught his attention. It seemed to be coming from the trees and for some reason it gave him a distinctly queasy feeling in the pit of his stomach.

That's crazy, he told himself, it can't be ghosts or spirits. There's no such thing.

Yet the fact remained that something weird was happening to him. He wondered if the crap Panida had been spouting could be getting to him.

She heard it too and, moving closer to him, tightened her grip on his hand.

'Watch what you're doing, you're about to push me off the bench,' he grumbled, although he was only pretending to complain. Abandoned in this dark creepy place, filled with animal sounds and possibly ghosts, the nearness of another human being – even if it was only Panida – was somehow comforting.

They both listened as the haunting, vaguely unearthly sound persisted. Teddy returned the pressure on Panida's hand.

The worst was yet to come.

A quick gust of wind blew a nearby palm frond aside and revealed two piercing eyes, round and unblinking, watching them through the rain.

Too frightened to move or to speak, they could only sit still and stare back at the… but that was the terrifying part. They didn't know what it was.

After a while the breeze died down, the frond fell back to its previous position and the eyes were once again screened from view by the protective greenery.

Teddy felt his blood run cold. But, thinking about what John Wayne or Humphrey Bogart would do, he said, 'I'm going to see what those eyes are attached to.'

Panida's terror increased. 'Oh no, don't,' she cried. 'It will come get you and take you away and then I'll be here all by myself.'

'If it's going to get me, it will get me,' declared Teddy.

With some difficulty he detached himself from Panida's grasp and made his way toward the spot where the eyes had been. Then, mobilizing his courage, he reached up, touching the end of the palm frond and moving it to one side. The flapping of massive wings that ensued made him draw back in alarm but not for long. With a shout of relief and delight – one that convinced Panida he had gone mad – he realised that their supposed ghost was merely an owl.

'It's OK,' he called as the powerful wings carried it off into the surrounding foliage, 'there isn't any ghost, just a plain old owl.'

'I don't believe it.'

'I tell you, I saw it. I know what it was.'

'A ghost could make itself look like an owl,' she maintained.

Totally exasperated, Teddy decided that it just wasn't possible to reason with girls. Not with Panida, anyway.

'You know what kind of ghosts we have in America?' he asked in an effort to jolly her along.

'No, what?' she sniffed, without much interest. Nothing that far away could be very frightening.

'Halloween ghosts; you take a sheet and cut two holes in it for eyes and then you tie it around your neck with string or something and go trick or treating and try to scare people.'

Panida scowled.

'But you can really only scare little kids,' he admitted regretfully.

'I would never do that,' she said.

'Scare little kids, you mean?' he asked, surprised that Panida was suddenly being so kind-hearted.

'No. It's terribly, terribly dangerous to make fun of the spirits like that.'

'What's dangerous about it?'

'The spirits won't like it. They'll be angry and do horrible things to you, perhaps make you sick and die.'

'Can't you understand? There's no such thing as real ghosts and spirits.'

But Panida couldn't – or, in Teddy's view, wouldn't – understand, so eventually he gave up and changed the subject. Talking about Halloween had made him think about home and he found himself telling her about the football team at school and about his butterfly collection and even about the icy Sunday afternoon when he and his dad had built a snowman together.

Gradually Panida became convinced that the owl-ghost wasn't going to come back; she began to relax and take an interest in Teddy's stories about life in that strange faraway place. And he found that telling someone about home, getting her to understand what it was like (or trying to, anyway), was so wonderful that he almost forgot about the plight they were in. He talked on and on.

By the time a much sobered and contrite William realised the frightful mistake he had made, arriving in the boat to take them home, Panida was absolutely certain that this boy who wasn't afraid of ghosts or spirits was the bravest boy in the world. And Teddy found that it was kind of nice, having someone around who knew a few things about his old life (a life that was now so achingly far away). Even though Panida was only a girl, he decided that she was OK.

The days and weeks passed more happily now. The holidays came and Teddy thought it was pretty funny to have an orange tree for a Christmas tree.

'It comes already decorated,' Panida said, pointing to the colourful fruit that hung from its branches. He admitted she had a point.

By January Teddy had made more friends at school, including a couple of boys whose mothers didn't seem to mind taking him along when they went swimming at the Sports Club after school.

Another thing that was going great was his lizard collection. He was building up an interesting collection of different sizes, colours and markings in the garden; it was keeping him so busy that he had to let Panida help catch insects for them and feed them.

His own food was another thing that didn't seem as bad as it had at first. All that rice and garlic and those funny-looking root things – Panida didn't know the English name for them but somebody had said that one of them was ginger — and chilli peppers so hot they made you feel the inside of your mouth was on fire... they didn't seem so weird to him anymore. He was even getting so that he didn't mind some of it. And when people spoke Thai around him he actually got the gist of some of it so he didn't feel so left out of things anymore.

Panida's determination to be as much like her mother as possible continued undiminished; abetted by a disinterested father and servants who were eager to please her, she gradually slipped more and more into her mother's role in the house, directing the maids and generally seeing that things were done the way she wanted.

Teddy, watching her giving orders to one of the maids about cleaning the spirit house, made the pleasant discovery that this was one more way in which his life in Thailand was upside down and backwards. At home the grown-ups told the children what to do but here it was just the opposite. He and Panida, the children, told the grown-ups, the maids, what to do. Not that he actually told them very much — it was mostly Panida — but he had managed to make it clear to the gardener that no one was to mess around with his lizard collection. Of course, he couldn't help enjoying this odd turn of affairs and sometimes when he thought about his mother lying in a hospital bed back in the States he felt a little guilty about how much he was getting to like it here.

Gradually a bond, borne of the shared experience of being alone together in an adult world, was forged between them. It became stronger than either of them knew.

Near the end of April Teddy received a letter from his mother telling him of the plans she had made for his home-coming. She also told him the date, shortly after the end of the school term, that had been set for it.

Teddy was wild with excitement when he first read it, but as the time drew nearer his enthusiasm diminished. Of course, he was extremely glad that his mother was OK again. The problem was that she might not realise he was thirteen now and not a kid anymore. He couldn't have her doing things like telling him to drink his milk or sending him off to bed or – heaven forbid – reminding him to pee before they went out somewhere or other crap like that. And he had a nagging feeling that it was going to be an up-hill struggle.

When his last afternoon in Bangkok came around, Panida moped around the garden with a forlorn expression on her face. Teddy, making the rounds of his lizard collec-tion, was closer to sharing her feelings than he would have liked to admit.

'You're sure you won't forget to feed them,' he

admonished.

'I won't.'

'Every afternoon.'

'I know,' she said, wondering how he could think she needed to be told. Then, after a moment's hesitation, she asked, 'Are you sad?'

'No way,' he said, having seen enough movies to know that tough guys like John Wayne and Humphrey Bogart didn't spend their time moaning about being sad. 'It'll be great to be in the States again.'

'Are you ever coming back here?'

'I don't know, probably not.'

'Do you want to?'

'I guess so, maybe sometime.'

Panida, seeing her father hurrying down the veranda steps and going to the car, called out, 'Daddy, where're you going?'

'The Erawan bar.'

Then, noticing Teddy, he remembered that it was the boy's last day and wondered if he should make some effort on his behalf. But what? That was the problem with children. He never knew quite what to do with them.

'Hop in the car,' he said, seizing on the inspiration of the moment. 'The two of you can have an ice cream in the Erawan tea room while I meet this chap in the bar. I won't be long.'

31

Taking no chances on missing a treat in one of the steamy city's few air-conditioned places, they were in the car almost before he had finished his sentence.

When William had parked the car in front of the Erawan Hotel, he handed Teddy enough money for at least six ice creams and said, 'Meet me in the bar in about an hour.'

Panida and Teddy scampered out through the main gate of the hotel and around the corner to the tearoom. As they passed the shrine to the four-headed god, Phra Bhram, Panida paused, pressed her palms together and raised them to her forehead in a wai. Then, eager for their promised treat, they made their way through the crowd of pedestrians, vendors and beggars outside the shrine, and fell happily into the heavenly coolness of the tearoom.

Once inside, they ordered enormous ice creams. After Teddy had scraped his own dish clean and finished Panida's for her, they found they still had time and money left over. Knowing that William wouldn't be ready to take them home yet, they wandered back out to the pavement to see what – if anything – was going on.

They found that musicians, hired as a votive offering by a rich petitioner, had started playing inside the shrine; they drifted toward it, pressed their faces up against the encircling iron rails and peered in. Lights from a multitude of candles flickered in the now rapidly falling dusk, the air was thick with incense and the scent of jasmine from a thousand floral offerings permeated the area.

'Let's go in,' Panida urged.

'Why? It's just as good here.'

'If we go inside we can ask Phra Bhram to bring you back to Bangkok.'

'Can't you ask him from here?'

'I could but it's better if we go inside, that way we can take him offerings.'

'You can if you want. I'm not going to.'

'Why not? You said you wanted to come back sometime.'

'I said I might want to.'

'That's almost the same and Phra Bhram is very powerful. That's why everyone comes here when they want to ask for something.'

'I don't go in for that stuff.'

'Never mind, just come with me and I'll ask.'

Unable to think of anything better to do until his uncle was ready to take them home, he agreed and started to go in.

'Wait,' Panida said, catching hold of his arm, 'we have to buy our offerings first.'

And, after leading him over to an old woman who was selling things on the side of the pavement, she selected a bundle of incense sticks, two rings of jasmine flowers and a packet of saffron coloured candles. She argued briefly about the price of each and demanded that Teddy hand over some of the leftover cash from the ice creams.

'Do we really have to buy that stuff?' he exclaimed, loath to see money that could be spent on chocolate wasted on such things.

'Of course we do and we need an elephant too,' she said, drawing him over to another mat where different sizes of wooden elephants of were laid out in neat rows. A heated argument ensued (Panida wanted to buy the largest one they could possibly afford and he wanted to keep most of money back for chocolate). Eventually they settled on one that left a few baht – although not nearly as much as he would have liked – in reserve for what he considered better things.

Teddy had passed this shrine a hundred times without paying any attention to it but this was the first time he had actually gone inside. He found himself drinking everything in, from the mountains of jasmine flowers that infused the air with their scent, to the dancing flames of the yellow candles, to the sandalwood smoke that rose from the incense sticks.

Noticing that his eyes were following some of the rings as they drifted up toward the heavens, Panida whispered, 'It carries people's prayers to heaven and it will carry ours there too.'

Although he was sceptical about this, he could feel that his usual resistance to anything strange or mystical was melting away. He watched Panida place her ring of flowers on top of the many others already at Phra Bhram's feet and carfully put her elephant down at his side. She had trouble with her incense stick though. In spite of her best efforts to light it, it kept going out. Teddy took it from her, lit it and placed it along with other sticks of incense in front of the image. Then they both stepped back and Panida lifted her hands in a wai to the god.

'Make a wai,' she told him in a loud whisper.

Teddy glanced out at the surrounding pavement to make sure none of the kids from school were going by just then. They'd think he'd flipped his lid. Luckily though, he didn't see anyone he knew – so he hastily made the required gesture. Of course it wasn't that he actually believed any of it, he assured himself... still, you never knew.

Their nearness to the image made the sandalwood smoke seem stronger; as be breathed in more of it, a curious feeling of light-headedness overcame him. Things that wouldn't have seemed remotely plausible before he came to Thailand began to seem possible.

'I do want to come back, I really do,' he murmured, not

so much to Panida as to the four headed god who seemed to be peering into his very soul through the flickering candlelight.

INTERLUDE

Dear Teddy,

How are you? One lizard got away but the others are fine.
I don't think Mummy's ever coming back. I have a new
mother. I don't like her.

Love,
Panida

November 1959

Dear Panida,

How are the lizards? We dissected a frog in class today. I've decided not to go out for football. I might get some kind of head injury and I want to save my brains for important work.

As ever,
Ted

September 1960

Dear Teddy,

How are you? Daddy's latest girlfriend is an American. She hasn't quite moved in but almost. I pretend I don't speak English. School is harder this year. There was a snake in the kindergarten room today.

Love,
Panida

May 1961

Dear Panida,

I feel really sick. I mean like I'm going to throw up. Mom is actually going to MARRY the revolting turd she has been seeing. They're going to live in California, thank God. It can't be far enough away for me. I'm going to Andover in the fall and I will spend Christmas with Gran.

As ever,
Ted

November 1961

Dear Teddy,

Daddy's girlfriend is all right. She is called Christie. She is an anthropologist and she loves Loi Kratong. We went down to the river as usual. Daddy says I have to go to England to boarding school next year.

Love,
Panida

Dear Panida,

I've been working on my project for the Science Fair all weekend. It is on monitor lizards. I would explain it to you but it would take too long. I hope you like boarding school. It can be a bit rough sometimes but it's really not too bad.

As ever,
Ted

November 1962

Dear Teddy,

It is very cold in England. My best friend is called Catherine. She thinks it is horrid to be in a school where there are no boys. I hate all boys except you. The food here is disgusting. We have beans on toast every Wednesday. The worst thing in the whole world is playing lacrosse.

Love,
Panida

P.S. The other girls call me Panda.

February 1963

Dear Panda,

I'm going absolutely crazy. Between practicing for the fenc-
ing team, rehearsing for Macbeth (I'm Banquo), and doing
extra stuff in the biology lab, I am seriously overworked.
There are other things too like college applications to fill
out and they are really a bitch. Mother wants me to go
to Harvard but I think it is too full of greasy grinds to be
any fun. Charlie (he's my roommate's brother) goes there
and he says Radcliffe girls are the ugliest girls in the world.
After all these rehearsals for Macbeth I've been around
enough witches to last me a lifetime. I'm going to go to
Yale IF I GET IN.

As ever,
Ted

April 1965

Dear Teddy,

You will never guess what happened. Catherine was caught DOING IT with Samantha's hunky brother in the music room. She was expelled that very afternoon and her parents had to come and get her. At least, she won't have to revise for her O levels anymore. I'm doing ten of them but will probably get a U in physics.

Love,
Panida

P.S. They did it under the piano.

February 1966

Dear Panda,

Great news! John and Tim (the two gorillas I've got for roommates) and I are going to Europe this summer. They want to go climbing in the Alps and sailing in the Med but I see myself drinking absinthe in decadent cafes in Montmartre. After all, why go to Europe to be healthy and boring? I can do that in the good old USA. It's debauchery and vice that turns me on.

I don't know if I'll have time to get over to England but if I do it might be kind of fun to get together. Can you ever get out of that prison you call a school? If you can, maybe we could check out the Natural History Museum together.

As ever,
Ted

P.S. I'll be in Europe June 7th–Aug 15th.

September 1967

Dear Teddy,

SURPRISE! SURPRISE! I got 5 As, 4 Bs and 1 C on my O levels. Samantha can't believe I deserved even a semi-respectable grade in physics. I can't believe it either.

The summer with Daddy and Christie and Alexander was great. Alexander is walking now and is the fattest, naughtiest, most adorable little boy in the world. He talks a lot too but the new maid said the most dreadful thing – that Alexander's Thai is better than mine. She says that I speak it like a foreigner while he speaks it like a Thai. I cried after that. I don't feel at home in Thailand anymore but I'm not sure I really feel at home in the UK either. Perhaps I should spend the rest of my life in airplanes.

Love,
Panda

February 1967

Dear Panda,

Christmas vacation was great. I spent it with Lisa's family in New Hampshire. They don't make a big fuss about how we're too young to get married the way my mother does. In any case we're waiting until after graduation so what could be a more normal time than that to get married?

Mom is having a fit because I refused to apply to medical school. I did pre-med just to keep her off my back and all that biochemistry will be useful in whatever I end up doing but I draw the line at spending my whole life poking around in people's insides and hearing about their aches and pains. The thought revolts me which means I wouldn't make a very good doctor. I'm trying to get a fellowship or an assistantship in a lab so I can do a PhD in zoology.

You see what a loyal guy I am? I haven't forgotten my first love, the scandalous scaly lizard.

As ever,
Ted

CHAPTER 2
OXFORD, 1968

White flecks of sleet swirled through the rain as Panda, waiting in front of the Oxford Union, scanned the muffled faces of the people passing by.

'Teddy?' she said, tentatively to someone who looked surprised and hurried on.

Several other possibilities approached but disappeared into the building without any sign that they were looking for anyone.

Perhaps he won't come, she agonized as the wintry day grew bleaker; perhaps he's forgotten. Don't be so silly, she told herself, he's only five minutes late. Of course he will come. Nevertheless she couldn't help feeling impatient. It seemed like such ages since that glorious afternoon they had spent together in the Natural History Museum, an afternoon made possible by her skill in fantasy and forgery. The signature at the bottom of the typewritten letter requesting that she be allowed to go into London for tea at the Savoy with an elderly aunt had ostensibly been her father's.

It had been risky of course but she hadn't been caught and the chance to see Teddy again had been too tempting to resist. She hadn't seen him since their time together in

Bangkok but he had grown up with her in her imagination and, when the girls at school had talked and giggled about their boyfriends, she had used wishful thinking as a substitute for reality and had told them all sorts of stories about herself and Teddy. Still, his letters, short and infrequent though they were, had been real and she had lost her virginity in the arms of a green-eyed boy with an engaging smile who reminded her of Teddy.

She was drawn from her reverie by the sight of Teddy hurrying along the pavement toward her and was suddenly overcome by indecision. Should she throw her arms around him with undisguised enthusiasm or play it cool and be a bit distant?

He solved the problem for her by enveloping her in a giant bear hug, saying, 'Hey, it's great to see you.' Then, holding her away from him, looking her up and down, he added, 'You've grown up and I must say you haven't turned out all that badly.'

'Did you expect I'd have turned into some kind of a witch?' she returned with a laugh.

'I wouldn't have been surprised. You were a pretty vicious kid you know, nearly biting my hand off the first day we met.'

'I was hoping you had forgotten that.'

'Never. Listen, is there any kind of pub or place that's halfway warm around here? I'm a Californian now and this weather is freezing me out.' Then, noticing that shining crystals of sleet were glistening in her hair and she was shivering, he pulled off the long woolly scarf he was wearing and wound it around her neck. 'Here, you need this more than I do. After all, you've been a tropical creature from day one.'

'I don't feel much like a tropical creature anymore,' she said with a touch of regret in her voice. 'All these years in England have changed me.'

It wasn't long before they were ensconced in the warmth of The Red Lion. After telling her briefly about a herpetology conference he had just been to in London, Teddy launched into an account of his life at Stanford.

'The trouble is that everyone takes this graduate school stuff so seriously,' he said. 'Undergraduate life at Yale was a picnic in comparison. I mean I get practically zero chance to see anything of this famous California lifestyle. Of course labs are pretty much the same everywhere but I really drew the short straw when research assistantships were handed out. I swear, the slave driver I've been assigned to would make Dracula seem like a nice guy. He doesn't give a rat's arse about the fact that I've got a full load of course work to do on top of all the crap I have to do for him. I mean if he were even halfway human it might occur to him that I'd like time to have a few beers or get a little sleep once in a while. God knows why I have an apartment; I'm never in it. And if you can believe it, I barely got the bastard to give me a few days off at Christmas.'

'Where did you go?'

'New Hampshire again, with Lisa's family.'

'That must have been fun.'

'It had its moments.'

'What happened in the other moments?'

Teddy grimaced. 'Well, you see Lisa and I – well, it's all kind of complicated. You know we were planning to get married right after graduation.'

'What made you change your mind?'

'A lot of things; she began making noises about how she didn't ever want to get married; you know, all the usual rubbish about not letting her life become mired housework and diapers and that sort of thing. I think at that point she was still hoping to be accepted in a corps de ballet somewhere, but now it's pretty clear that's not going to happen.'

'Why? How can you be so sure?'

'Didn't I tell you? Some careless bastard dropped a heavy suitcase on her foot when she was going through Boston airport and broke her toe – the big one on her right foot. That was over a year ago and the bone still refuses to heal properly. The doctor says that it probably never will. For most people that wouldn't be the end of the world, but for a ballerina not to be able to dance in toe shoes... well, that's a career stopper if ever there was one.'

'Poor Lisa, she must be really gutted.'

'She is but she's managed to find a few consolations.'

'Such as?'

'Such as another guy.'

'How do you know?'

'She just announced it one day; said she was "sort of half in love" with somebody else so that pretty much threw cold water on any wedding plans.'

'Then how come you still spent Christmas with her family?'

He shrugged. 'It turned out that Mr. Somebody Else was only a quarter or an eighth in love with her so that put an end to that. She claimed that it had all been an idiotic mistake but at least it had made her realise how much she loved me. And to tell you the truth, I had fallen off the straight and narrow a couple of times myself; so I wasn't in any position to take the high moral ground. Anyway our relationship is pretty much back on track now but we haven't done anything as drastic as setting another date for the wedding.'

'Are you still in love with her?'

'The trouble is, I'm not really sure. We don't have a lot in common, if that matters. I had never been to a ballet in my life before I met her, and she has yet to see a lizard she considers worth taking a second look at — but there really does seem to be something to this notion that opposites attract. And there are actually things we both like to do, like going ice skating or to the theatre or even just taking in a movie, although getting something to eat afterwards can be tricky.'

'What's tricky about that?'

'In spite of the toe, she still thinks of herself as a dancer; they have to keep themselves super slim you know, so she basically doesn't eat. And I feel like a prime glutton if I pig out on a giant hamburger with all the trimmings and a couple of bottles of Bud while she makes one glass of white wine last for hours and barely manages to eat half a leaf of lettuce. On the other hand she's a beautiful girl and if skipping the calories means getting right down to the main event... well, other guys would think I was crazy to complain.' And reaching for his wallet, he added, 'I've got a picture of her here if you want to see it.'

Curious to see what a girl who interested Teddy would be like, Panda took it from him. One glance was enough to convince her that Lisa wasn't the right girl for him. She didn't lack for anything in the looks department; she had large blue eyes, cheekbones to die for and straight blond hair that was drawn back into a long ponytail. But there was a delicate, almost saintly, air about her that was completely at odds with anything she would have expected in a girlfriend of Teddy's. Panda could easily imagine that if that pale yellow hair were allowed to hang loose,

Lisa would look like one of those angels that you saw on Christmas cards, telling the Virgin Mary that she was going to have a rather extraordinary baby.

The trouble with that beatific image was that an angel probably wouldn't string her boyfriend along while she had a fling with somebody else. So it seemed there were a few things about the lovely Lisa that didn't quite add up.

Still, it was easy to see why Teddy didn't spend a lot of time worrying about how much or how little they had in common. Lisa was drop dead gorgeous – and surely he must have realised by now that girls who gazed fondly at lizards were few and far between.

'The thing is,' he continued, 'there's a girl who works in the lab at Stanford; she's Chinese, Chinese-American I mean. I don't know her very well yet but I have a feeling that that's going to change and...'

He trailed off, not knowing exactly how Panda would react.

'And what,' she asked, although it wasn't hard to guess.

'Well, I can't help wondering if I'm really cut out for this monogamy thing. Am I just the kind of guy who'll do a little fooling around no matter who I marry or is this girl in the lab a sign that I shouldn't marry Lisa?'

'All men play around,' Panda said dismissively, 'lots of them do anyway. You probably won't be any worse than most so you might as well go ahead and marry Lisa. She looks a bit too angelic for you, but apart from that you probably won't do better.'

'You're awfully cynical for a kid.'

'I'm not a kid anymore. And I'm just being realistic.'

'I shouldn't be laying all this on you, anyway,' he continued. 'It's just that I'm usually the kind of guy who knows what he wants, and this indecision about marrying Lisa is driving me round the bend. I promise you, I'm not in the habit of ranting on about my personal life like this. But she's coming out to California for spring break – assuming Dracula can be bludgeoned into giving me a few hours off, that is – and I pretty much need to sort out how I feel about things by then. But that's enough about me. How about you? How's Oxford treating you?'

'It's great. I can't imagine any place I'd rather be.'

'After that prison of a school you were locked up in, I guess almost any place would look pretty good.'

'It wasn't a prison. I rather liked it, actually – once I got used to it.'

Teddy's mind flew back to the afternoon when she had managed to escape from the place and they'd prowled the cavernous halls of the Natural History Museum together. It had been a beautiful day in late June shortly before the end of term and they had sat on the museum steps talking and eating ice creams for ages afterwards. If she hadn't been such a kid, to say nothing of the fact that she was his cousin, he would almost have suspected that there had been a teasing invitation in her dark eyes. Well, that just showed how a few years at Yale could warp your mind.

Fortunately – at least, it was going to be fortunate for some other guy – she wasn't jailbait anymore. 'Any exciting boyfriend in your life these days?' he asked her.

'No one special.'

Teddy tried not to look too pleased.

'By the way – do they have any food around here?' he asked, abruptly changing the subject. 'I'm starving, and I've got to catch that bus to Heathrow at half past nine.'

'You can't think about going yet,' she protested. 'You just got here.'

'I know. But Dracula will string me up by the balls if I'm not back in that lab by nine o'clock on Monday morning.'

Resigning herself to the fact that his visit was going to be short, Panda took him to her favourite restaurant. It was a small place just off Carfax.

'Is there anything special you'd like?' Teddy asked, after scanning the wine menu.

'No, you choose – I'm no expert. It doesn't go with our food, you know.'

'You mean Thai food?'

'Of course.'

'I'm surprised.'

'Why?'

'You were just a kid when you first came here, your dad's a Brit and you sound as English as the queen. How come "our food" isn't roast beef and Yorkshire pudding by now?'

'Going to school here isn't the same as living here, you know. I certainly don't look very English; I'd need a peaches and cream complexion for that. Everyone here just automatically thinks of me as a foreign student. To tell you the truth, I think of myself that way too.'

'Well, you do look Thai,' he acknowledged.

'I look like my mother,' she said. 'Although in Bangkok most people figure out that I'm Eurasian.'

'How do they do that?'

'I'm taller than most Thai women and my nose is higher, more like an English nose – a few things like that.'

'Does it bother you?'

'My nose? Not really.'

'Not your nose, you idiot. It's a Class A nose. I mean not being thought of as British? Do you mind about that?'

'No, I mind more about people at home not thinking of me as really Thai. But I suppose the truth is that I don't one hundred percent belong anywhere.'

'Nonsense,' he declared. 'It's the teenage years that are the formative ones. And you've spent yours here so you've got to be more British than Thai by now. This is clearly the place where you really belong.'

Panda looked doubtful.

'I know what'll clear the matter up,' he said.

'What?'

'An English boyfriend; a beautiful girl like you isn't going to be without one for long. Even these Oxford types must look up from their books once in a while – and when they see you… Well, some lucky bastard is going to persuade you that he's the best of the bunch; then it won't be long before I find a gilt-edged wedding invitation in my mailbox.'

'Don't be too certain of that,' Panda said.

'Don't tell me you're not planning to invite me; that will never do. I've got to have a chance to check him out before you make any rash promises about loving and obeying.'

'That's not going to happen.'

'It had better not,' he declared. 'How did we get onto this subject anyway? There isn't a specific bridegroom panting at the church door, is there?'

'Definitely not. It's just that we were talking about where I wanted to belong, that's all.'

'That's OK then. Anyway – somewhere between the engagement ring and the first baby, you're going to decide that you want your life to be here.'

'Perhaps,' she said, with a notable lack of enthusiasm. 'We'll see.'

And as the question of belonging really seemed to trouble her, Teddy changed the subject and launched into an account of his own plans for the future. 'You see if I can just get a post-doc –'

'What's that?'

'A post-doctoral research grant,' he explained, 'for when I finish my degree. Then I'd be able to do some really interesting stuff on monitor lizards.'

'Good heavens – you never change, do you?' she said. 'But it sounds great. As long as you don't expect me to feed them for you.'

'Don't worry,' he said; then, as she betrayed no signs of going comatose (most girls had to be rushed home with a sudden headache, or suddenly remembered that they would be busy for the next fifteen Saturday nights whenever he started talking about lizards), he launched happily into a detailed account of the anatomy, the territorial range and the lifecycle of the world's largest lizards.

By the time they left the restaurant so much sleet had become mixed with the rain that Panda slipped and would have fallen on the icy pavement if Teddy hadn't put his arm around her to steady her. And, since the danger of a broken bone didn't diminish as they went along, he kept his arm where it was. Any good Yale man would have done the same thing, he told himself. Fortunately, she didn't seem to mind – quite the opposite, if the way she nestled into the curve of his arm was any indication.

For a moment he almost wished that he could change his flight and not have to get on that bus for Heathrow, but then his better judgment prevailed. It was a damn good thing he had to be in that lab on Monday morning, he told himself. Just because Panda wasn't jailbait anymore didn't mean that she wasn't a bit young for him to be messing around with. Moreover, she was his cousin; there were certain kinds of thoughts he really shouldn't be having about her.

By the time they got to Gloucester Green and found the coach for Heathrow, the air was thick with tiny flecks of sleet. They sparkled in Panda's hair and covered the ground in a wintry white. In spite of the cold they made him think of another night, when tiny sparkling lights had seemed to dance about her in the surrounding darkness.

'You'll never guess what I was thinking about just now,' he said.

'You'd better tell me then.'

'Remember that night when Uncle William got drunk as a skunk and left us at that abandoned temple?'

'On Loi Kratong? Of course, I remember.'

'I'd tell you something, except I know you'd laugh.'

'No, I won't.'

'Promise?'

'I promise.'

'I still think about that night sometimes, and about you. Not as that crazy kid with the water spirits anymore but transformed into a beautiful girl with something incredibly alluring and magical about her.'

Then, feeling that the wine might have tricked him into saying too much, he turned and hurried onto the waiting coach.

CHAPTER 3
NANTUCKET ISLAND, 1970

As the ferry pulled up to the dock, Panda searched the waiting crowd. She hoped Teddy would be there, but when she didn't see him she put her disappointment aside and made her way down the gangplank.

'Panida?'

'Aunt Betty?' she asked in response, and quickly found herself in the embrace of a middle-aged woman with blond hair and Teddy's green eyes.

'Teddy and I have been dying for you to stop off and see us on one of your trips back to Bangkok,' she said. 'Of course we're not exactly on your way – but once you're in a plane what difference do a few more miles make? How's your wonderful father? I absolutely adore him for the way he took charge of Teddy after the accident, taking him back to Thailand and all that. I was completely broken in body and spirit, you know, and of course Teddy's poor father was... but we won't talk about that now. Then there was that ghastly business with my second husband. What a mistake that was. The divorce was nothing short of vicious but that's all history now. I do hope your suitcase isn't getting too heavy because we have an enormous trek ahead of us to get to the car. Those fiends in human form at the police station practically send you to Alcatraz if you park anywhere near the ferry.'

Panda assured her that her case wasn't too heavy and happily found that Aunt Betty's 'enormous trek' wasn't really much more than a short walk.

'We think all this is very quaint,' Aunt Betty told her, as the car bounced over the cobblestones on Main Street. 'But after England you probably won't agree. Of course, our little place is out at Madaket. That's just a cluster of houses really, at the very tip of the island.'

Aunt Betty continued chatting as they left the town behind them and turned out onto the open moorland. 'Teddy and Lisa are coming tomorrow. Just a little secret between you and me – but I don't know why he ever married that girl. She's so thin she's barely there at all. Practically lives on black coffee and broccoli, and she's always having miscarriages. What I can't understand is why she is so eager to have a baby when Teddy's still in graduate school and she is doing some course – teacher training, I think, somewhere. Her parents are insisting on it. I don't think she's a bit interested in it but they think she should have a reliable occupation, one that doesn't depend on her silly toe. Can you imagine having your career prospects hang on your big toe? It's too ridiculous. But if you ask me, she doesn't care about anything except ballet, not even about Teddy, at least not as much as she should but then what can I do? I'm just his mother.'

There was a momentary pause as she swerved to avoid annihilating a group of cyclists; then she went on, 'Teddy's so eager to see you. I do think it was sweet the way you two wrote to each other for so many years.'

The theme of how amazing Teddy was, punctured by occasional references to Lisa's many inadequacies, continued to dominate her chatter as they drove across the windswept moors to Madaket.

'This is our place,' Aunt Betty said as she drew up in front of a grey-shingled cottage. 'It's very small and simple but I can't sell it because Teddy loves it. It belonged to his grandparents, you see, and he spent a lot of happy holidays here when he was a child.'

It's not her sort of place at all, Panda thought; it's easy to see why she doesn't like it. Thank goodness Teddy is coming tomorrow. I hope I like Lisa. The fact that Aunt Betty clearly doesn't is a good sign.

Panda found that she did like Lisa – sort of. At least she didn't have a specific reason not to like her. The trouble was that she couldn't quite connect with her somehow. She discovered this the next morning when Aunt Betty had pressed Teddy into service accompanying her on numerous errands and left her daughter-in-law and her niece to chat in a rather desultory fashion as they washed up the breakfast things.

It didn't take them long to get around to the one subject they had in common: Teddy.

Lisa talked easily about the books and movies he liked, his favourite baseball team and what he wanted to do with his life – but this led her to a subject that appeared to depress her. 'Monitor lizards,' she said, glumly. 'He's obsessed with them.'

'Is that so dreadful?' Panda asked. 'I mean, it's not like he's keeping one in the back garden, is it?'

'No. But the problem is that the best places to work on them are West Africa and Southeast Asia and he already had to give up a chance to do his PhD thesis in Indonesia because I was pregnant. He was awfully nice about it but I know how much he wanted to go. Still, what could I have done about it? After all, babies are more important than lizards.'

Panda had to agree with this – but she couldn't resist pointing out, 'People do have babies in those places, you know.'

'Of course they do. But the thing is, I've already had one miscarriage – and I feel that's a sign that I'd better be super careful if I ever want to carry a baby to term. That's why I'm not going to swim while we're here even though...'

'You mean you're pregnant? How exciting!'

'No, no,' said Lisa, hastily. 'It's just that… Well, there's always just a tiny possibility, isn't there? And a little time before you actually know? Of course it's going to be agony to just sit around and watch everybody else having a good time in the water. But the waves are so strong and unpredictable here – I don't want to risk having one of them hit me really hard in the stomach or knock me off my feet and send me crashing down onto the sand.'

'No, of course not,' said Panda, who didn't much like the idea of being bashed about by the waves and thrown down on the sand either. At Hua Hin, the beach of her childhood, the waves had lapped against the shore so gently that even as a small child she had been able to play safely at the water's edge. Here at Madaket it was different. The waves looked alarmingly high.

'You won't mention this to Teddy though, will you?' Lisa said, realizing she had given away a little too much to someone she had just met. 'He gets very nervous at the idea of becoming a father. He just doesn't see how wonderful it would be and I don't want to worry him. Anyway, I have this really bad cough, leftover from the bronchitis I had a couple of months ago – and he somehow got the idea that I don't want to swim in this icy water (it really is Arctic) because of that. I didn't actually tell him that but since he seems to think it, well…'

She shrugged.

'No, of course I won't say anything,' Panda assured her.

As soon as Teddy was back from the errands with his mother he changed into his swimming togs and plunged into the water.

'Come on in,' he called to Panda – who, at his urging, had put down the book she was reading and ventured out to the beach. In Thailand everyone avoided the midday sun and only splashed in the water in the early morning or late afternoon.

With some trepidation because the waves looked huge, she went down to the water's edge, allowing the icy water to swirl around her toes. 'It's freezing,' she cried, drawing back with a shiver.

'Coward,' he shouted back. 'You'll warm up fast enough when a few big ones start knocking you around.'

This was exactly what she feared would happen and she didn't relish the thought. Teddy, seeing this, grabbed hold of her and pulled her out to meet the waves as the rolled into shore.

During the next few days he showed her how to dive through the waves and – something she thought was even more fun – how to turn her body into a human surfboard and catch an enormous wave at just the moment it would send her hurtling in toward the beach. It was all quite terrifying at first. But after a bit of practice, she began to have a thrilling time.

'I really envy you,' Teddy said, one afternoon when he and Panda had stretched out on the beach to catch their breath between waves.

'Whatever for?' she asked, astonished.

'Going to Thailand next week. God, I wish I could get on that plane and go with you.'

'I heard you had to turn down a fellowship in Indonesia.'

'Did Lisa tell you that?'

Panda nodded.

'I'm amazed. It's been a rather tense subject between us.'

It was Panda's turn to be surprised. 'She didn't sound tense when she talked about it. She seemed to think you didn't mind all that much.'

'Well, she's wrong, as usual. She wouldn't see that I minded about something unless I threw a fit and started bashing her over the head with a club – but that's not exactly my style. I can't seem to live up to the expectations of my caveman ancestors.'

'That's too bad,' observed Panda. 'Lisa might actually prefer the caveman treatment to…'

'Good God – you're not one of these women who enjoy letting guys bash them about, are you?'

'Heavens, no. It's just that I'd really hate it if someone was doing to me what you're doing to Lisa.

'What I'm doing to her?' he exclaimed, incredulously. 'What she's doing to me, you mean – ruining all my chances to do field work just so she can gestate some horrible little embryo that, if it manages to be born at all, will probably grow up to be a second Idi Amin or Attila the Hun or –'

'Oh, do shut up. Then I can tell you what a total fathead you're being. You've lost all sense of proportion. Lisa loves you a lot more than you deserve and your monitor lizards aren't going to become extinct tomorrow. You can go hobnob with them some other time.'

'Not necessarily. My chances of getting a research grant became extinct yesterday.'

'Rubbish – you'll have other opportunities.'

'It's not rubbish. But in any case, if Lisa does manage to stay pregnant for the full nine months at some point – do you really think she is going to take her darling little Attila off to some steaming jungle where his dear little intestines might possibly suffer from the water? I very much doubt it. She'll find some excuse, one that might even include producing a precious little Caligula to play with darling Attila. Then I'll never get to do any field work.'

Panda started to object but he waved for her to be silent.

'I can just see myself ten years from now, trudging dejectedly home to my three bedroom mortgage in some dreary suburb...'

'People in the suburbs don't trudge, they drive,' Panda pointed out.

'Don't interrupt. Where was I? Oh yes, dragging myself home from my dead end job in some second rate lab to face the screaming household of juvenile delinquents I've sired. Each one clamouring for new shoes for his – or possibly her – little cloven hoofs. That's what Lisa would like.'

'It's what you deserve, the way you're acting. And if they do have little cloven hoofs, it's perfectly obvious that they will have inherited them from you.'

'Totally untrue,' he declared, waving a sandy foot in the air. 'See?'

'What is true is that you're trying to make Lisa into some kind of monster when her only crimes are that she loves you and wants to have a baby.'

'Well, my only crime is that I don't want to be loved, at least not like that. It's stifling. And I don't want my plans messed up by the appearance of some squalling brat.'

Panda, thoughtfully piling sand up into something vaguely resembling a castle, didn't say anything for a few minutes. Then she suggested, 'If you went away for a while, gave yourself a little room to breathe, would that make things any better?'

'Maybe,' he shrugged. 'But anything like that is completely impossible.'

'Why?'

'Lack of funds.'

'If you could scrape up the price of a ticket to Thailand you could stay with us for a few weeks and see how the lizard population there is getting along. Indonesia isn't the only country that has them, you know.'

'It's the only place that's got komodos.'

'Got what?'

'Komodo dragons.'

'Have you started reading fairy tales?'

'No, I'm serious. They're among the oldest species in the world, and the most interesting – to me, at least.'

'Is that what your thesis is on?'

'It was going to be, but I had to change my topic because of the impending arrival – or so we thought – of Attila.'

A cloud of gloom came down over his usually cheerful face and Panda began to lose sympathy. 'If you're just going to sit there wallowing in self-pity,' she said, 'I'm going for another swim. I don't feel sorry for you at all.'

It was clear to Teddy that nobody understood him, so he sat disconsolately on the beach and watched Panda playing in the waves. She had caught on pretty fast, he acknowledged, getting the best ones at the critical moment, stiffening her body into a human surfboard just the way he had shown her: letting it take her speeding in toward the shore, then managing to come up for air before it slammed her down on the sand.

From where he was sitting he could catch occasional glimpses of the excitement sparkling in her eyes as she pitted her wits and her newly acquired skill against the power of the waves. His mind's eye fleshed out the scene with a picture of her lithe body moving like a mermaid beneath the surface.

He'd have to watch out for her, he thought, play the big brother and see that no womanizing bastard took advantage of her. The problem was that he didn't know how he was going to do that when he was in California and she was in Thailand. 'Fuck,' he muttered under his breath, 'that's just not going to be possible.'

God, Panda had certainly hit it right on the mark when she claimed he was feeling sorry for himself, he realised. But then, didn't he deserve to? What a mistake it had been to marry Lisa. The fact that Panda was right about what a nice person she was – he could see that for himself – just made matters worse. He wished she'd attack him with a kitchen knife or screw the plumber or do something that could get him out of the relationship without having to feel guilty about it. Well, fat chance of that. He might as well wish a Komodo dragon would knock on the door and politely hand him an enormous research grant. Even a stingy one would be welcome at this point.

There was one option open to him though. He could let Lisa find out about Nancy Chan. She might divorce him then, but that would be a shitty way of going about it. Anyway he had a feeling that that little episode was just about over. Nancy was getting fed up with the role of 'the other woman', and when it came down to it he couldn't understand why she had put up with it for so long. She deserved better; that was for sure. In any case, even if Lisa did find out, she'd probably cry and go around grief stricken for a while and then end up forgiving him.

In the meantime, he'd better make Panda get back in closer to shore. She had gone out beyond the last breakers and she wasn't the strongest swimmer in the world. She clearly didn't realise how treacherous the undertow was around here.

Leaping to his feet, he strode down to the water's edge and called, 'Come back, stay closer in.'

She either didn't hear him or she deliberately ignored him, he wasn't sure which. He shouted again, louder this time. 'You're out too far. Come back.'

This time she waved back at him, laughed and actually went out a little farther.

Refusing to let her flout his instructions like that, Teddy swam out to get her and bring her in – forcibly, if necessary.

He had just managed to come within a few feet of her when his plan was made easier by a large wave that picked them both up; it sent them careening toward the shore before depositing them, gasping for air, in the shallow water near the beach.

Panda reacted quickly, standing up and rubbing the salt water from her eyes before the next wave could cut off her breath, only to be confronted with another threat, one that came not from a monster wave but from Teddy himself. Before she quite realised what was happening, he had grabbed her, turned her around and was holding her in a vice-like grip while he gave her a sharp spank on the appropriate part of her anatomy.

'That's for not coming back when I said you were out too far,' he declared. Ignoring her squeal of outrage, he was about to administer a second correction on the same spot when he felt the sand slipping away from under his feet. Another wave, more powerful than its predecessor, knocked them both down, scrambled them around, swept them up onto the beach and left them – he still holding her and lying half on top of her – stranded on the sand.

He realised that he had lain there just a moment longer than necessary; then, getting up, he saw Lisa's face in the window.

'It's absolutely absurd to think I could have the slightest interest in Panda in that way,' Teddy insisted when he was alone with Lisa that evening. 'She's my cousin, for God's sake. That's one step away from a sister. We lived in the same house together when we were kids. Anything like that would be completely incestuous, a real biological no-no.'

'Nonsense. You weren't in the same house together very long and in any case that was ages ago. You've hardly seen her since then. And she certainly doesn't seem like a member of the same family as you – much less like someone who's incestuously close.'

'She seems that way to me,' Teddy insisted stubbornly.

'Nonsense.'

'It's not nonsense. We kept in touch, writing to each other and all that.' Then, seeing that this line of argument wasn't getting him anywhere, he changed tactic. 'Could you be attracted to your cousin Tommy?'

'Of course not. Nobody could be attracted to Tommy.'

'You just think that because he's your cousin.'

'I think that because he's a pimply-faced adolescent idiot.'

'That sounds like a very cousinly point of view to me,' Teddy declared. 'I bet some teenage Jezebel is dying to get him into the backseat of a car.'

'And is that what you're dying to do to Panda?'

'Honestly Lisa, give me a little credit. If I found Panda the least bit attractive – which I don't – I'd have something considerably more grown up in mind than the back seat of a car.'

'Oh do tell,' she scoffed. 'I'm dying to know what sort of place you would like for the ideal extramarital rendezvous.'

'I haven't the slightest idea what I would like because I'm not interested in any extramarital rendezvous.'

'Is that really true?' Lisa asked, her eyes suddenly filling with tears. Then pulling herself together, she said, 'I'm sorry. I don't know what's the matter with me these days. I always seem to be on edge.' And winding her arms around him, she added, 'I guess I just love you too much'

Teddy, unable to think of anything to say to this, settled on kissing her instead.

During the next few days Aunt Betty kept them all so busy with preparations for the beach party she was planning – 'just a little festive send-off for Panda on her last night with us' – that they had time to think of little else.

'We'll let everyone go for a swim first,' she said, thinking out loud. 'Then they can warm up with picnic cocktails and steak sandwiches. You won't mind building the fire while the others are swimming, will you Teddy darling? There'll probably be a few ex-boy scouts in the group who'll pitch in and help. You know how they are about rubbing two sticks together. They absolutely adore it.' And, turning to Panda, she explained, 'It gets quite chilly here after the sun goes down, even in the summer.'

Invitations were issued and accepted with enthusiasm. Everything augured well for an enjoyable evening until the morning of the festivities. To Aunt Betty's dismay, the day dawned remarkably cold and cloudy, even for Nantucket.

'If it rains tonight I'll kill myself,' she announced at breakfast.

Her life seemed increasingly at risk as the morning progressed. A light sprinkle began to fall about eleven and turned into a serious rain while they were having lunch. It reverted to something like a drizzle while Lisa and Panda were doing the washing up and then: 'It's a miracle,' cried Aunt Betty joyfully as she detected a few thin rays of sunshine in the sky.

The weather was on its best behaviour by the time the first guests arrived. The braver ones changed into their swimming suits and headed for the water while their less intrepid friends gravitated to the fire Teddy was trying to get started.

Aunt Betty was busy encouraging everyone to help themselves to drinks and snacks when a middle aged-couple and their drop-dead gorgeous son, Mike, arrived and claimed her attention.

'You must be absolutely thrilled to have Mike with you for the whole summer,' Aunt Betty told his parents. 'Teddy barely arrives before he leaves again.' And casting a baleful look at Lisa, she added, 'That's what happens with a married son.'

'Yes, he's going to be the leading man at the Straight Wharf Theatre this summer,' Mike's mother replied. 'We're so pleased about it. Even though,' she lowered her voice, 'it means we have Oberon with us, too. I do hope you don't mind our bringing him with us this evening.'

'Oh no – we're delighted,' Aunt Betty said, assuming the owner of the preposterous name (but what would you expect from theatrical people?) was a friend of Mike's.

It was only when an enormous sheepdog bounded down the beach, shook itself, scattered sand all over everyone, and then made a dash for the steaks, that she realised Oberon wasn't a human guest. She was just about to ask her friends to take the animal away when a stern reproof from Lisa, a burst of laughter from Panda and a string of curses from Teddy interrupted her; she saw Oberon racing triumphantly along the beach with a thick steak in his mouth.

'Get him!' Aunt Betty called to Teddy. 'Don't just stand there, hurry.'

By this time not only Panda but Lisa and Teddy were doubled over with laughter.

'What the hell,' Teddy said when he could manage to get the words out. 'Let him enjoy it.'

'Mike,' Aunt Betty said, thinking the owner of the beast might at least try to help. 'You're not a statue, are you? Do something.'

Mike responded with a shrug. 'It's no use. Oberon's a terrific runner. Nobody can catch him if he doesn't want to be caught.'

It wasn't easy for Aunt Betty to keep herself from slapping the nonchalant expression off Mike's handsome face, but she controlled herself by turning to Teddy and scolding him for his slowness in making drinks.

Teddy was struggling to keep himself from telling his mother off when Oberon, remembering where that delicious steak had come from, came dashing back across the beach, jumped up first on Mike and then on Panda, and showered them both with wet sand.

'Down boy, down,' Mike ordered. But Oberon, who didn't consider muddy paws a problem, paid no attention.

'Oh hell,' Mike said, rubbing a splotch of dirt off of Panda's swimming suit, 'he's gotten you all dirty.'

'That's all right,' Panda replied. 'I'm going in the water in a few minutes. That should take care of it.'

'I wish I could do that,' the actor said regretfully, 'but that water's freezing and I can't risk getting a cold. We open next week and with a part like mine – I'm the romantic lead, you see – it would be catastrophic if I sneezed my way through the big seduction scene. Or through any scene, for that matter.'

'Don't you have an understudy?'

'Yes. But – just between you and me – his performance really isn't up to scratch. Of course, I'm stretching myself a bit to do it because I'm really a Shakespearian actor. But I like to dabble in modern comedy now and then, just to keep myself as versatile as possible. And when I do, I feel an obligation to raise the standard of the company as a whole.'

Teddy, tending the steaks, had the ill-luck to be within earshot of this exercise in self-aggrandizement and felt like being sick. Nevertheless he soon had a roaring fire going, drinks flowing and a delicious smell of roasting meat wafting through the air.

The latter kept Oberon in close attendance on the food supply. Mike and Panda hovered nearby too, laughing a lot and taking turns feeding him juicy bits of steak. To Teddy's irritation, Mike was making a big deal about how he had always been fascinated by Thailand and was absolutely dying to go there; all a total lie, he was sure.

The swimmers didn't stay in the icy water very long. The waves were particularly strong that day and were delivering a strenuous pounding to anyone within their reach. A little bit of this rough treatment was enough to make the temptation of food, drinks and warmth irresistible. Before long, everyone had clambered out and was gathering around the fire, enjoying the results of Teddy's bartending efforts.

The only person who wasn't enjoying the party was Teddy himself. He was annoyed with his mother; she seemed to expect him to pour the drinks, build the fire, cook the steaks... in short, to lead a life of penal servitude while she waltzed around the beach in an age-inappropriate black bikini and diaphanous orange sarong. She must be freezing, he thought – and it serves her right.

Panda, he fumed, was being even more infuriating, talking to that self-centred little prick Mike (Narcissus would be a better name for him) as if he were actually capable of saying something interesting. Couldn't she see what a phoney the guy was? And the maddening thing was that he was keeping Panda so busy answering questions about temples and beaches that, as far as being any help where the food or drinks were concerned, she was worse than useless. Of course, he could understand the bastard zeroing in on Panda as the most attractive woman at the picnic – what guy wouldn't? But it was galling to have to stand there flipping steaks around and watch it. And when it came to giving him a hand with the million and one things his mother wanted him to do, Lisa wasn't much better. After cooking a few steaks the smoke had sent her into such a paroxysm of coughing that she had rushed off into the house.

When the last of the steak sandwiches had been eaten and everyone was busily putting marshmallows on long sticks for toasting over the fire, Mike suddenly exclaimed, 'Hey, where'd Oberon go? With his sweet tooth, I can't believe he'd take off when there're marshmallows to be had.'

Everyone obligingly looked around but saw no sign of the dog.

'I think it went that way,' said Aunt Betty, vaguely waving her hand toward a cluster of houses farther down the beach.

'We'd better go look for him then,' said Mike, pulling Panda up from the blanket she was sitting on. 'Come on.'

Teddy scowled at them through the darkness, toasting a marshmallow he didn't really want; he put it down without eating it and poured himself a whisky instead. He was thinking what a boring group of friends his mother had when Mike's parents cheered him up by announcing their intention of leaving. The only problem was that Mike and Oberon weren't back yet.

'I'll go find them,' Teddy volunteered, eager to hasten their departure.

'Oh, thank you,' said Mike's mother gratefully. 'Oberon is such a trial. Sometimes I think the entire household revolves around him.'

'And whose fault is that?' laughed her husband. 'You're the one who lets that happen.'

'I know,' she admitted ruefully. 'I'm a slave to that animal.'

'Well, he'd better get back here fast,' declared Mike's father. 'A wind's blowing up and I think it's going to rain.'

Teddy was also noticing the wind as he hurried along the beach. Clouds were covering the moon, making the night exceptionally dark and like an idiot he hadn't brought a flashlight with him. If it hadn't been for the white caps splashing up at the water's edge he would have had no idea where he was going.

Why the hell had they gone so far, he grumbled? What a nuisance that fucking dog was.

After what seemed like ages, a ray of light enabled him to distinguish two figures standing at the water's edge a little way ahead of him. One of them, presumably Mike, was holding a torch and focusing its beam on Oberon who was bounding out of the surf with a stick in his mouth and a look of triumph on his face.

'Good boy,' Teddy heard Mike say and watched him relieve the dog of the stick and throw it back into the breaking waves.

Oberon joyfully bounded after it.

'Hey Mike, your mommy says it's your bedtime,' Teddy

called as he came up to them. 'Everyone's been looking for you.'

Mike gave a quick laugh, pretending to think this was very funny, and then yelled, 'Come on, Oberon – drop the stick. We've got to go.'

Oberon either didn't understand or didn't like what he heard. Determined to carry on playing a little longer, he refused to surrender his treasure and instead took off at top speed down the beach with it.

Fortunately, in Teddy's opinion, he chose to do this in the direction of the picnic.

'Goodbye, it's been great talking to you,' Mike shouted at Panda as he dashed off after Oberon.

'What a stupid dog,' observed Teddy.

'Not at all,' Panda argued, 'he's really very clever. Didn't you see how he got his way?'

'Well, he's a pain in the ass,' Teddy grumbled, even though he usually liked dogs. 'They both are. In any case, we'd better head back. It's starting to rain.'

No sooner had he said this than the clouds that had been hovering overhead since early morning unleashed the full force of their contents. A torrential downpour drenched them both in seconds and kept them from seeing anything that was more than a few feet away.

Seizing Panda's hand, Teddy said, 'Quick, there's a house not far up the beach. We can go there.'

They ran the short distance in record time but the place proved to be all locked up and they had no choice but to settle for the minimal shelter they found under the roof of its wide veranda.

'What if the people who live here come home?' Panda asked.

'Oh, that'll be all right. They know us. They'll invite us in. And even if they didn't, it would take some real bastards to send us packing on a night like this.'

Panda shivered and pushed her dripping hair back from her face. 'I feel so much colder when I'm wet,' she said.

'This is summer, for God's sake. How did you ever survive the winter in England?'

'I didn't go out in the pouring rain wearing nothing but a wet t-shirt and a soggy swimming costume.'

'Well, this shouldn't last much longer,' Teddy predicted optimistically, 'and I'll make you a hot rum punch when we get home. That should warm you up.'

In an effort to illustrate the heat-generating effect this would have, he put an arm around her, just in a brotherly sort of way of course, and began vigorously rubbing her up and down. After all, he couldn't just stand there and let her freeze to death, could he?

He hadn't expected her to turn in the circle of his arm and press up against him, honestly he hadn't, and after that he didn't know quite what he had expected but somehow both her arms were around his neck and her hips were moving against his in a way that was driving him crazy and making the most sensitive part of his anatomy spring into mid-season form.

Of course he kissed her; what else could he do? He was human, wasn't he? All that brotherly nonsense completely slipped his mind as he ran his hands up and down the outside of her wet t-shirt. Then somehow the t-shirt wasn't there anymore. She was left with just her bikini and that was like wearing nothing at all. Damp and virtually naked in his arms, she was responding to his touch as if she had been waiting for him all these years.

He didn't need to worry though, he assured himself. She would surely stop him before they went too far but she wasn't stopping him yet. Actually her fingers were unbuttoning his shirt, her lips were on his chest, her leg was wrapped around his thigh and her hand was sliding down inside his swimming trunks, thoroughly annihilating the vestigial remains of any brotherly thoughts he may have had. He didn't think about the fact that she was his cousin, the next thing to a kid sister; he didn't think at all. Feeling was all that mattered, the feeling of Panda: no longer the little girl of the water spirits but now grown up and in his arms. He pulled her down onto the wooden floor of the veranda and plunged into her.

'Oh God, Panda,' he said when the power of thought

and speech returned to him and the realization of what they had just done flooded over him. 'I promise this will never happen again.'

CHAPTER 4
AROUND THE PACIFIC, 1970

Teddy's words – 'I promise you it will never happen again' – rang in Panda's ears as the flight droned on. Her thoughts gyrated back and forth between guilt that she had let it happen even once and a dizzying desperate hope that it would happen again. And deep down she knew that she hadn't just let it happen, she had done everything she could to encourage him. Even now, the memory of it pulsated through her with such intensity that if he had been sitting there beside her, membership in the mile high club might have gone up by two.

But he wasn't there and it would probably be years and years before she saw him again. By that time, if Lisa had her way, there would be a household full of little Attilas keeping a thoroughly domesticated Teddy firmly glued into life in some California suburb. The picture made her laugh… but at the same time it brought home the fact that he was right about that night in Nantucket. It must never happen again.

'I promise you, Lisa,' she murmured almost aloud. 'You have nothing more to worry about – not from me, anyway.'

Panda wondered whether Lisa suspected what had been going on with that girl in the lab, and if that was the reason she was so eager to have children at a time that was clearly inconvenient for Teddy's career. Did she think a family would convince him to spend more time at home, bind him to her and to a lifestyle that she wanted even if he didn't?

If that was the theory she was going on, Panda had serious doubts about whether it would work. Teddy clearly wasn't going to be an easy man to be married to, she was sure of that. Still, Lisa might be just the sort of woman who would be able to handle him: someone who would play the devoted wife most of the time, humouring him in everything that was trivial while making sure she got what she wanted when it came to things that were important to her. If that were true – and it seemed likely that it was – Panda couldn't help feeling a reluctant admiration for Lisa, even hoping that she and Teddy would have lots and lots of little Attilas together.

Yet, as the plane droned on through the Pacific night, Panda fell into a light, and then into a deeper, sleep: one where dreams and longings, fears and doubts played tricks on her memory and created their own reality. And she was on the beach in Nantucket again and the only other person in the world was Teddy.

BANGKOK, 1970

Almost before Panda was ready to leave the dream world of the flight, it was time to change planes in Hong Kong. Then a few hours later she was stepping out into the hot, humid air of Bangkok where the fragrance of jasmine flowers, the stench of open sewers and the aroma of garlic fried in coconut oil spoke to her of childhood and told her she had come home.

As always she greeted her father, stepmother and little brother, Alexander, with the undemanding affection that characterized their relationship. It was Thailand itself rather than the individuals in her family that aroused her most intense feelings.

She revelled in the sight of the brightly coloured temples that dotted the roadside, their walls of mirrored glass sparkling in the setting sun. She liked the idea that they were designed to reflect the images of any evil spirits that might be approaching – spirits so hideous and malevolent they would turn and flee in horror when they caught sight of their own appearance. Then she frowned, wishing her reaction hadn't been so English.

Yet as the car, driven badly by William, raced along, she continued to think like a foreigner, regretting the Chinese shop houses that were springing up on land that used to be rice fields and sending the water buffalo into history. But her nostalgia for the Thailand of a decade earlier was pushed to the back of her mind when they reached the frantic swirl of activity that was downtown Bangkok. Dusk was falling and the glittering night of the city's naughty pleasures was waking up, sending the fruit markets and the silk shops of the respectable daytime into sleep. But it was this daylight city that was the one she recognized and she was relieved to see that it had changed so little.

Lights from the veranda of their old house were shining on the purple orchids along the garden fence but leaving the stagnant remnants of the canal in merciful obscurity when the car finally turned into the driveway. Two servants, graceful in their brightly coloured sarongs and thin white blouses, greeted Panda at the door. The ancient gardener, who seemed to have fewer teeth each time she came home, picked up her two cases, padded into her room with them and set them down next to the large Victorian wardrobe.

Panda loved the moment at the beginning of each holiday when she first walked into this room. After a quick glance around to make sure that nothing had changed, she rushed to the bed and hugged the wise but slightly grumpy looking teddy bear who was always on the pillow waiting for her. She felt that something of her little girl self lingered in that room; and, if she could just re-connect with her and somehow weave her into the fabric of her grown-up, almost English self, she would know who she was.

Panda slept deeply and dreamlessly that night and woke the next morning to see a small face peeking in at her door.

Alexander was always fascinated by this curious half sister. She was much too old for him to think of her as a real sister and she always brought him presents and took him out for ice creams – things that real sisters didn't do. He knew that from his friends at school who had sisters. They were more likely to throw you out of their room, snatch your sweets and not let you play with their silly toys. He wouldn't like to have that kind of sister, but Panida was all right.

'Hello,' she said cheerfully, 'you'd better come in and close the door or you'll let all the air conditioning out.'

He hesitated, needing time to get used to her again.

She repeated her instructions, this time in Thai. It was a funny sounding Thai, he thought. It didn't come out quite right so he opted for English instead.

'There was a snake in the kitchen this morning,' he announced, 'a little green one about that long.' He held his chubby none-too-clean hands nearly a foot apart, 'but it's gone now.'

'What happened to it?'

'It went away.'

'That's good.'

'Don't you like snakes?'

'No.'

'Why not?'

'They're ugly and they can be dangerous.'

Alexander pondered this bizarre attitude while Panda took a shower and got dressed. Then he followed her into the dining room and sat at the table while she drank her coffee. She was almost down to the last sip when one of the maids went by with a tray of fresh flowers, rice, and incense for the spirit house in her hands.

'Oh, let me take it,' Panda cried.

'Only Thai people do that,' Alexander said reproachfully.

She felt as though he had hit her and she had to control a strong desire to hit back. But he's just a child, she told herself firmly, he couldn't have any idea how a comment like that would tear me up. He didn't mean it badly. Nevertheless, her voice was unusually stern when she said, 'I'm Thai too, you know.'

Alexander wasn't entirely convinced. She almost looked like she was Thai, he thought, but when she said anything in Thai there was something strange about the way it came out.

'In any case, bringing flowers to the spirit house makes me feel that I'm really home. You can come with me if you want.'

94

He seemed to think this was a good idea and trotted along beside her.

'You see, they don't have spirit houses in England,' she added conversationally.

'Where do the spirits live?'

'I'm not sure. I don't think they actually live anywhere.'

Alexander didn't like the sound of this. He wanted the spirits to have nice houses so they would stay in them and he would know where they were.

Panda didn't seem bothered about it though, he thought, as watched her take down the previous day's offerings. She replaced them with the fresh ones and pressed her hands together in a wai.

He made a wai too and then, still uneasy about the idea of spirits wandering around just anywhere, he was struck by a new possibility. 'Don't they have spirits in England?' he asked.

'Some people believe they do; but not everyone. Not most people, anyway.'

'Do you believe in them?'

'Not when I'm in England.'

'Do you here?'

'Sometimes,' she returned vaguely. 'I'm not sure.'

'I believe in them,' Alexander said solemnly, 'except when I'm at school.'

'Perhaps there aren't any spirits at the International

School,' she suggested.

Alexander considered this. It seemed reasonable. 'Maybe not,' he agreed.

In the afternoon Panda took an offering to Phra Bhram at the Erawan Shrine. She had visited the image at the beginning and the end of every holiday since she had first left for school in England. She had been more frightened than she had wanted to admit on that last day in Thailand so long ago, and had gone to ask Phra Bhram to bring her home again. He had done it. That meant, of course, that she had had to go and thank him when she came back. She had really believed in him then and been confident of his power to help her.

Now, although a visit to the shrine and become an intrinsic part of coming home, she had gradually over the years in England stopped believing in him… more or less. Ghosts and spirits and gods with extraordinary numbers of arms and heads weren't taken seriously there, and after a while she had begun to see them differently.

Yet whenever she was back in Bangkok, she found her old ideas and beliefs reasserting themselves. It seemed that the influence of the nonmaterial world was everywhere here, permeating every aspect of life. But it was in the flower-strewn enclosure of the Erawan Shrine that she felt these mystical forces most keenly. And it was here that she found it easiest to pick up the thread that bound her to her child self and to bring a sense of continuity to her life.

When she came home from the shrine she found her stepmother curled up on the rather threadbare sofa, surrounded by piles of books and handwritten notes.

'Don't you ever feel like chucking all that academic stuff and just relaxing?' Panda exclaimed.

'No,' Christie assured her. 'I relax too much as it is; that is, if you can call looking after Alexander relaxing.'

'You can't,' Panda declared. 'He never stops asking questions, not even when he's running around screaming or being a dinosaur or tearing the house down in one way or another.'

'Don't I know it,' Christie agreed. 'But after going to all that effort to get a degree in anthropology, I feel I really should do something with it. I mean, I'm living here in Thailand anyway with the anthro all around me, for God's sake. So it would be a real waste not to.'

'What're you writing about this time?'

'The opium trade up in the tribal villages, the Meo mostly, north of Chiang Mai.'

'Aren't you asking for trouble, getting into a subject like that?'

'Not really, I'm just dealing with traditional uses and trading patterns; you know, easing old people out of their aches and pains and that sort of thing. That stuff doesn't hit the international market so no huge sums of money are involved and nobody cares too much about it.'

'I still think you ought to be careful,' Panda warned. 'After all, wasn't some foreign woman killed up there last summer?'

'Yes, but that was by bandits,' Christie returned, 'the sort of thing that could happen anywhere; like in Philadelphia, for example. I swear the walk from my apartment to my classes at the University of Pennsylvania was more dangerous than any place I've been in Thailand.'

Panda was thoughtful for a moment and then asked, 'Do you ever smoke a bit of opium yourself? Is that why you're doing this?'

Christie looked shocked. 'Good heavens, no.'

'But aren't anthropologists supposed to be – what do you call it – participant observers?'

'Definitely not in this case,' Christie said firmly. 'If you saw the people I'm talking about, the ones who've been on opium a long time; they just lie around in clouds of sweet smoke and they're not much more than living corpses. There's no other way to describe them – so this is definitely one case where the participant observer thing doesn't apply.' She paused for a moment, frowned, and then continued thoughtfully, 'The only way I'd ever touch the stuff is if I knew I was dying anyway. Then I think I might be tempted to go out in a beautiful dream.'

'Out where?' asked Alexander, coming into the room holding a paper cone filled with chunks of pineapple topped with salt, sugar and chillies; he left a trail of sticky sweet juice along the floor behind him.

'Eat that in the garden please or we'll have ants all over the place,' admonished Christie, and quickly went off to get the maid to clean up the gooey mess.

Panda followed Alexander outside.

'Do you want some?' he asked, proffering the paper cone and getting a splotch of pineapple juice on her dress.

'Thanks, I was about to take a shower anyway,' she said, spearing a chunk with a wooden stick. This was the only place where people knew how to eat pineapple, she thought, as she savoured the sweet, salty and fiery taste. God, it was to good be back.

The days passed in a sun-splashed haze of familiar people and places. It was hard not to think about Teddy though. Whenever she saw a lizard hopping around the garden or climbing on a wall inside the house, a picture of the thirteen-year-old Teddy flashed into her mind. But that was all right, she told herself, that child didn't exist anymore. It was the grown man who mustn't be allowed into her thoughts.

She was strict with herself in the daytime but she was helpless when he strode into her dreams at night and it took a serious effort to push him away when she woke up in the morning.

CALIFORNIA, 1970

Teddy was making a similar attempt to put Nantucket out of his mind – when, in the final days of summer, he found himself once again pacing the waiting room of San Francisco General Hospital.

God, how I hate these places, he thought, as he tried to shake off the image of Lisa being wheeled away on that ghastly stretcher thing. This miscarriage, although earlier in the pregnancy than the previous one, had been distinctly worse. He didn't want to think about it. He took out a cigarette, lighted it and belligerently vented his feelings by blowing smoke at the 'no smoking' sign.

Almost instantaneously a starched and angry figure was by his side.

'Can't you read?' the nurse snapped, waving at the sign.

'No,' he said in a voice heavily laced with mock regret.

'I suffer from severe mental retardation complicated by intermittent fits of homicidal mania that can only be controlled by nicotine.'

'I hope you don't think you're being funny,' she retorted. 'Put that thing out immediately.' And after lingering just long enough to watch him do it, she disappeared through a door marked STAFF ONLY.

Teddy resumed his pacing and looked at his watch. Fuck, he thought, it was only fifteen minutes later than when he last looked. How time crawled by in this sterile soulless room.

About a hundred years later – or so it seemed – he finally heard the doctor's voice say, 'Mr. Duncanson?'

'How is she?' he blurted out.

'Good news,' the doctor said. 'Your wife will be out of the anaesthetic in a little while and home within a few days.'

'Thank God,' he mumbled, a flood of relief sweeping over him.

'However,' the doctor continued, 'there are some women who just aren't cut out to have children. I'm afraid your wife is one of them.'

'You mean she can't ever –'

'I never like to make definite pronouncements about things like this. I've had a few surprises in my time but in your wife's case I would say it is highly unlikely that she will ever carry a child through to term.' Looking at Teddy with kindly sympathy, he added, 'I hope you're not too disappointed. There's always adoption, you know.'

With that, the doctor hurried off down a labyrinth of white corridors. Teddy, after visiting a still very groggy Lisa, sang to himself as he walked through the San Francisco drizzle to his car.

We're free, he thought as he drove back to Palo Alto: free from those horrible hospitals, free from the ghastly miscarriages, free from the menace of a house full of screaming brats. He'd have the old Lisa back, the lovely girl he had married, the girl who looked like a Botticelli angel – but who, when it came to a romp in bed, displayed an unmistakable appreciation of earthly delights.

What a nightmare the past twenty-four hours had been, he thought. There was nothing like seeing someone semiconscious in a pool of blood to make you realise how much you cared about them. Sure, his relationship with Lisa had gone well beyond the honeymoon stage, but that had to happen to all marriages. It was just a question of how long it took and what kind of relationship you had in the end.

Well, he'd try to shape up; he'd be a better husband in the future, get home a little earlier, take her out to dinner more often, and make an effort to notice what she was wearing... He'd tell her how great she was looking, things like that.

And without any kind of pregnancies or babies to worry about, she might even change her mind about going some-place like Africa or Southeast Asia where he could work on monitor lizards. It was too late to change his current research topic and apply for a grant to do a field thesis; but he could try for a post-doc next year, maybe even get one to work in Indonesia. If he presented it to her as a sort of second honeymoon it might appeal to the romantic side of her nature. After all, she still had that dreamy and passion-ate quality he loved about her; a quality that had so nearly been lost in all that crap about babies.

God, he thought, as the prospect of Indonesia took hold in his mind; they had about a million different species of lizard there. He'd go wild. And maybe they could even stop off in Thailand on the way and see Panda if she hadn't gone back to England by then.

Panda – hell no, bad idea; he had to forget about Panda. He couldn't understand why he kept thinking about her. After all, they had just had sex that one time, to say noth-ing of the fact that she was only a kid and his cousin to boot; it was adultery, pederasty and incest, all in one fell swoop. For a moment he wished he were a Catholic. The thought of going into the confessional and laying that on some parish priest was too marvellous for words. He imag-ined playing it up for all it was worth, not mentioning that his 'child victim' was actually twenty-years-old and that the incest bit had only involved a first cousin.

Anyway, all that was ancient history. From now on he was only going to think about Lisa, he promised himself. Then he pulled the car to a stop in front of a liquor store, went in, and selected a bottle of champagne for when she came home.

'Can you put a pink ribbon or pink paper or something around it?' he asked.

'This ain't Valentine's Day, mister,' growled the man behind the counter. 'Your girlfriend will just have to drink it like it is.'

'It's not for my girlfriend, it's for my wife.'

The man looked shocked, apparently considering this a waste of good champagne.

When Teddy got home he put the bottle in the refrigerator, mixed himself a scotch and soda and settled down to enjoy it – but the place seemed damn lonely without Lisa. He wondered if she had felt that way about it when he had been at the lab till late – or when he had said he was at the lab but was really somewhere else. When he thought about it, it wasn't any wonder she had wanted a kid. She must have needed some noise and clutter around the place to keep it from seeming like a morgue.

Well, things were going to be different from now on, he resolved.

CHAPTER 5
BANGKOK, 1970

The last thing Panda wanted was for things to be different. For the moment at least, she was glad to let Thailand reclaim and reabsorb her; and that's what it was doing when, after a lovely swim in the pool at the Sports Club, followed by a fresh lime and soda on the surrounding terrace, she heard a vaguely familiar voice say, 'Panida?'

Turning she saw an old friend, a boy – well, he was a man now, actually – with a face so round that William used to claim that the Almighty had created him by putting the point of a compass on his nose and tracing a perfect circle around it. Like herself, he had been sent to England for much of his education and had often come swimming here during the school holidays.

'Thanit! I didn't know you were back,' she exclaimed in English, now the best language for both of them. 'Are you living here now or just here for the summer?'

'Living here, working for my dad,' he replied, with a noticeable lack of enthusiasm.

'You don't sound very happy about it.'

'Just between you and me, I'm not.'

'Why are you doing it then?'

'The whole family would be up in arms if I didn't. You

know what Thai families are like – or perhaps you don't. After all, you don't have one.'

It was Panda's turn to look glum. 'No, unfortunately. I wish I did.'

'Don't wish it,' he said firmly. 'You've no idea what it's like.'

'I know it would make me feel that I really belonged here,' she replied.

'And you don't?'

'Sometime I almost do but other times I feel totally outside Thai life.'

'You don't know how lucky you are,' Thanit said. 'I'd give a good deal for the chance to feel like that.'

'But if I don't belong here, where do I belong?'

'How about in the UK?'

'Not really, I mean sometimes I feel I belong there but then I pass a mirror somewhere and I'm startled by how different I look, nothing like the people around me. Oh, school was a bit of a cocoon, university is too – so I haven't experienced any of the horrible racism you read about. But, even after all these years, people still introduce me as their friend from Thailand.'

'Why shouldn't they?'

'No reason really, except that it keeps me from feeling that I belong there. Everyone thinks I look Thai, and the really absurd thing is they expect me to be the local expert

eyes and freckles on her nose.'

'An English girl then.'

'Scottish.'

'And your parents don't approve?'

'They'd go ballistic if they knew. The idea of a foreigner in the family, perhaps even redheaded grandchildren – it would be the end of the world for them.'

'Why not go ahead and marry her and let them see that the world actually goes on?'

'That's not as easy as it sounds and anyway I couldn't do that to Fiona.'

'Do what?'

'Bring her here and try to get her to fit into a Thai–Chinese family like mine. One of my uncles has five wives and eighteen children, for God's sake. How do you think a nice Scottish girl would feel about that?'

'He can't have all those wives,' protested Panda. 'It's against the law.'

'It's not against the custom,' Thanit explained, 'and that's what's important.'

'But how much could your uncle's life possibly matter to her?' asked Panda, exasperated at what she saw as a silly excuse.

'A lot. We're all part of the family business, you see. I'm part of it now and indirectly she would have to be part of it too. Everybody's life matters to everybody else because we're all part of a single economic entity.'

'But does that have to dominate your entire life?'

'Absolutely. You see, the business and the family are everything to each other. The family lives for the business and the business exists totally for the family. It's the temple in which the family gathers to worship the great god Money. Bringing offerings of more money, and passing money on to our children after we die, gives us our reason for living.'

'My father's head of the business,' he continued, 'and he thinks nothing of knocking on my brother's door at two o'clock in the morning to discuss some business problem. And if my brother happens to be making love to his wife at the time, that's no excuse for keeping the old man waiting. Can you picture a Scottish girl being happy in an environment like that?'

'No,' Panda confessed. 'I can't.'

'The complete and total submersion of the individual in the group,' Thanit continued, 'is the hardest thing for me to accept when I'm back here in Thailand. There's no way I could subject Fiona to it. And the thing is, Western notions of individualism are a constant threat to a family like ours. Any slight crack in the fabric of family authority could start a deluge that would wipe us all out.'

'Aren't you exaggerating a little?'

'I don't think so. There is a family empire built on

paternal authority and mutual obligations and dedicated to the accumulation of wealth. Nobody involved wants to risk losing the status and power that go with that wealth; nor do they want to risk losing all the little trinkets that it buys. So the thumb screws are put on anyone who shows even the remotest signs of defecting.'

'Do you think of defecting?' asked Panda.

'Believe me, I've thought about it a lot.'

'And?'

'And I've made my decision,' Thanit said firmly. 'Now all I have to do is come to terms with it – but it's not easy. Sometimes I feel that I'm absolutely being torn in two.'

It was Panda's turn not to be very sympathetic. If he wanted to choose money over love, she told herself, let him suffer.

Nevertheless – as the days passed, Thanit's situation kept running through her mind. She couldn't quite believe that he was the sort of person who would be obsessed with money and greed. Perhaps he hadn't merely opted for money, she reflected, perhaps his choice had been based on loyalty, on family and on an acceptance of the way of life into which he had been born.

The more she thought about it, the more she wondered about what kind of life she, Panida or Panda, had been born into. And this was the question that was bothering her when, near the end of the summer, she met Sonchai

Kaewsonthi.

Panda often went to the Sports Club with her father, Christie and Alexander on Sunday afternoons, and it was there that she first noticed him. He was sitting alone at the bar; this struck her as unusual because Thai people never seemed to go anywhere alone. Of course, he could just be waiting for someone, she reasoned; or he might not actually be Thai. He looked it – sort of, but not completely. His features were Thai but his build was unusually thick and stocky for someone in this part of the world, and his mop of thick hair was extraordinarily bushy. All in all, there was something about him that made her think of a large thirsty bear.

He was back again the following Sunday; but this time, after sitting alone at the bar for a while, he was joined by a man who looked to Panda like he might be English.

'Isn't that Alex Carter?' asked Christie, when she caught sight of him.

'Who? Where?' William demanded.

'At the bar with that shaggy looking fellow.'

'Good God,' exclaimed William, 'Alex! I haven't seen him in ages. I heard he was... well, somewhere, I don't remember where. I'll go get him, shall I?'

He was back a few minutes later with both Alex and the thirsty bear in tow. Introductions were made and chairs were moved so the newcomers could be included in their group. The bear sat down between Christie and Panda. As they asked him about himself, he answered their questions in fluent American English.

He was essentially an artist, they discovered, but was currently supporting himself as a photographer for *The Bangkok World*. Of course that meant he could only paint in his spare time but fortunately he had managed to accumulate enough work for an exhibition that he was going to have in a couple of weeks. And as if remembering all the things he had to do before he would be ready for it, he soon made an excuse and left.

A few days later Panda ran into him in the lobby of the Oriental Hotel and asked him how the preparations for his exhibition were going. 'Where did you say it is going to be?' she added.

'At Sinlapakorn University, starting a week from Friday.'

'I'd like to see it,' Panda said, suddenly deciding that she would.

'I didn't know you were interested in art,' he replied, looking surprised.

'I'm not any kind of expert, if that's what you mean.'

'No, I just meant – the thing is, sometimes I think I'm the only person in Bangkok who cares about art.'

'How in the world did you come up with an idea like that?'

'By going for months at a time without meeting anyone else who's interested in it.'

'Perhaps you just move in the wrong circles,' she suggested.

'I guess that's it,' he agreed, smiling at her in way that lit up his black eyes and softened his craggy features. It gave her a strong feeling that, if given half a chance, she might really like him.

When the exhibition opened, Panda went to it. She actually knew very little about art, had never known any artists before and had certainly never given any thought to how much a picture might reveal about the person who had painted it. Yet as soon as she stopped in front of the first picture she was struck by the relationship between the painting and Sonchai himself.

The brush strokes were forceful and heavy without being sombre, while the colours – bright primary ones – gave an element of childish playfulness to the quirky and often whimsical forms depicted. It seemed, she reflected, almost as if the artist had been taking the world by the tail and tweaking it a few times – mocking it while stopping short of reviling it completely. And in spite of the clear influence of the European expressionists on the style, Thai elements were there too, visible in such things as the curve of fingers on a hand, the juxtaposition of colours on a background and the rising spire of a stupa. It was, she suspected, Sonchai himself transferred from flesh and blood to paint and canvas.

'What's your reaction?' he asked, coming up behind her.

Panda panicked, wondering why no words apart from 'nice' and 'interesting' came to mind.

'You don't like them,' he said glumly.

'No, that's not true,' she protested. 'I like them enormously. I just don't know how to talk about art, that's all.'

His face glowed with pleasure. 'You don't need to talk about it,' he declared. 'It's a purely visual medium. Most of the people who try to say clever things about it are just pretentious dilettantes.'

Panda laughed. 'Are you always so hard on people?'

'No harder than they deserve.'

Panda didn't try to argue. Instead she let him lead her around the exhibit, sometimes just stopping and standing quietly in front of a picture, other times going into great detail about what he had wanted to convey and how he had gone about it. By the time they reached the last one Panda felt that she had come to know more about him in an hour than she discovered about most people in weeks. And he felt that he had given more of himself to her than he had given to anybody in… he didn't know how long.

'You must be thirsty after all this,' he said, when they had finished making the rounds. 'Thammasat is just next door, as you probably know, and at this time of day most of the students will have gone home so we should be able to get a table next to the river.'

The cafeteria at Thammasat University was simple and a bit decrepit. Its long wooden benches and tables testified to decades of student use, but it was shady and cool and its open sides allowed a soft breeze to waft in from the Temple of the Dawn across the river.

'You must have studied abroad,' Panda observed when they sat down with their drinks, 'your English is so good.'

'My father was in the Foreign Service so I just went to school wherever we happened to live, mostly Canada and Singapore. Then when we moved back here – I was in the ninth grade by then – my parents put me in the English section of Ruam Rudee School. I guess they thought they might go abroad again but they didn't.'

'Did you stay here for university too?'

He nodded glumly. 'Sinlapakorn,' he said, 'the fine arts university.'

'Well then, I don't know how you can say you don't know anyone who's interested in art. You must know squillions.'

Sonchai shrugged. 'I used to. Well – not millions, but some. That seems like a long time ago though. What I meant was that I'm never around anyone like that now, not since I've been working for *Bangkok World*.'

'Isn't photography a form of art? Sometimes, anyway?'

'Not news photography.'

'Still, it must be interesting working at the *World*.'

'It has its moments. In any case, it's better than grinding my life away in some office. I couldn't stand that. And I'd starve if I tried to make a living from my painting.'

'Did you ever consider going abroad? France or Italy perhaps, to study art?

'Consider it?' he exclaimed. 'I wanted to do it so badly I could taste it. But my father wanted me to study economics. Can you imagine? Nobody with a soul could possibly study economics. I refused to do it so they refused to send me overseas. It was as simple as that. So I ended up staying in Thailand and going to Sinlapakorn.'

'And your family didn't mind if you studied art as long as you did it here?'

'They minded like hell. But I didn't let that stop me.'

Remembering her conversation with Thanit, Panda said, 'I thought if you were Thai – with a real Thai family I mean, not one like mine – then defying your parents on something like that just wasn't an option.'

'That's pretty much true. But I've got this crazy great aunt – crazy-wonderful, I mean – so I decamped and went to live with her. Actually, she's not really my great aunt. She was my grandfather's first wife. My grandmother was his second.'

'And you get on with her better than with your grandmother?'

'I never met my grandmother. She was Hungarian, you see; and she went back to Europe. My grandfather met her in Vienna when he was studying there. He brought her here and – after her initial shock at discovering that he already had a wife – she and Auntie actually became friends. Maybe it was sort of an alliance against my grandfather, I don't know. Anyway, my father was born and my grandmother stuck it out here until my grandfather took a third wife. That was too much for her. She gave the kid, my dad, to Auntie and went back to Europe. I've no idea what happened to her after that.'

'Couldn't you go to Europe now?' Panda asked.

'With what *Bangkok World* pays me, you must be joking. I could no more save up the price of a ticket – plus a few months spending money – than I could fly to the moon. Anyway I don't care about it so much anymore. My life's here now.'

By the time they finished their drinks and started along the Sanaam Luang Park toward Sinlapakorn, the setting sun was turning the fantastical spires and rooftops of the Temple of the Emerald Buddha into a glistening spectacle of colour. They hadn't gone very far when Sonchai stopped, waved his hand over the surrounding area and exclaimed, 'Just think about it. The royal palace, the most sacred temples, the art museum, the theatre; a priceless heritage – all within a few steps of where we're standing right now. The very soul of Bangkok is here and so is the soul of everyone with any Thai blood in his veins. And that includes you and me.'

It seemed to Panda that he was proclaiming his feelings about Thailand in a very un-Thai way and she wasn't sure whether to let herself be caught up in his rhetorical fervour or not.

'Think about the Sunday market,' he continued. 'When it opens here on weekends, you can just feel the vital life force of the Thai people surging through the crowds.'

Panda wasn't at all sure she could. 'What I can feel is that you have a strong mystical streak,' she said.

'You must have one too because you're half Thai and it's in your blood. You can't get away from it. After all, it's there in your mother's people, isn't it?'

She shrugged. 'I wouldn't know. I haven't seen them since I was small. They live somewhere up near Chiang Mai and I don't think my dad gets on with them.'

'Keep it that way if you can. You'll be better off.'

'I thought you couldn't live in Thailand without a family,' she said, once again thinking of Thanit.

'You've got it all wrong,' he returned. 'You can't live in Thailand with one – at least not if you care about having any control over your own life.'

Panda looked at him in surprise.

'You're like me,' he continued, 'Thai and not Thai. We're the ones who can see Thailand with the clearest eyes. We're close enough to it to know it and to understand it in a way that no foreigner ever really can. The feelings we have for it are in our blood – yet we're always at a little bit of a distance from it, never totally a part of Thai life. This sharpens our perceptions and keeps them uncluttered by too much emotional involvement or attachment.'

'It seems to me that you're seriously involved and hugely attached,' she observed.

'In my own way, I suppose I am,' he agreed. 'You'll find that you will be too, if you give yourself half a chance. Why don't you come back when you finish university – that'll be next year, won't it? – and live here again, get involved with the life here. I'll show you the Thailand of the free spirit, something not many other people here even realise exists.'

'Not a bad idea,' Panda laughed. 'Who knows, perhaps I will.'

The next day a letter came from Teddy. She tore it open and read:

Dear Panda,

I'm trying like hell not to think about you. That's why I haven't written sooner. Great as it was, we've both got to forget about that night on the beach in Nantucket.

The good news is that we're not under the menace of any more Attilas. Lisa had another miscarriage, a monster one this time, and it seems to have put an end to her baby fixation. It was a bit naughty of her to have let me think she was on the pill when she wasn't but in the end it didn't make any difference so I'm not going to worry about it. She is very unhappy right now so I have been trying to cheer her up by plunging into the good husband routine. She just doesn't understand what a God-awful father I would have made.

If you think of me at all, which I don't deserve, just think of me as the world's greatest bastard.

As ever,
Ted

P.S. If you answer this send it to me at the lab. The address is on the back of the envelope. T.

Panda dashed off a reply without bothering about how much of it was actually true.

Dear Teddy,

No need to worry that I'm thinking about you because I hardly ever do. I have decided that when I finish university I'm going to come back here and make my life in Thailand. That means we probably won't ever see each other again.

Your cousin,
Panda

CHAPTER 6
CALIFORNIA, 1971

'Hurray,' shouted Teddy, waving a letter in his hand, 'I got it. Oh National Science Foundation, I love you, I love you, I love you!' And he demonstrated his excitement by picking up one astonished lab assistant after another and whirling them in the air.

'Put me down,' one of the white-coated girls cried, making a frantic effort to keep her test tube upright. 'Have you gone crazy?'

'Yes, crazy in love with the king of all lizards. Komodo dragon, here I come.'

'There's going to be a murder around here,' growled one of Teddy's colleagues, 'if you don't watch what you're doing.'

'Feeling homicidal, are you?' cried Teddy, picking up a ruler and brandishing it like a sword. 'Okay, on guard!'

'Don't be an idiot. What does the letter say?'

'A year in Indonesia, tickets for two, inadequate research budget – but

that's pretty much inevitable. And a meagre living allowance, about enough to feed two medium sized cats for a week – but who cares about that? I'm off to see the dragons.'

Lisa's response to the news was considerably less enthusiastic. What about her teaching job, she wanted to know? She had already signed her contract for kindergarten starting in September. And where would they live once they got to Indonesia? And did anyone there speak English?

'Details, details, details,' protested Teddy, clamping his hands over his ears in exasperation. 'Everything will work out, just wait and see. What the hell are you doing with that skillet?'

'Getting ready to bash you over the head with it.'

'That's OK then. I was afraid you were going to cook something with it.'

'I am – chicken with bamboo shoots. I thought you liked it. Aren't you hungry?'

'Good God,' he exclaimed, horrified. 'Chicken cut up into horrible little pieces on a night like this! You must be joking. This is a night for champagne and oysters, filet mignon and artichokes.'

'That may be,' she replied, tartly, 'but we don't happen to have those things in the refrigerator at the moment. All you'll find in there is a piece of leftover chicken, a few alfalfa sprouts from the salad last night and some carrots. But luckily there's a can of bamboo shoots in the cupboard, so we can manage.'

'Completely unacceptable,' declared Teddy. 'Throw that damned skillet out the window and put on that new dress you bought the other day. The dream of my life is about to come true and I'm going to take my gorgeous wife out on the town to celebrate. We'll start out at the Top of the Mark, feast on lobster and wash it down with Moet. And when we're utterly satiated we'll go down to Fisherman's Wharf and dance 'til dawn. Then I'll bring you home and throw you on the bed and ravish you like you've never been ravished before.'

This prospect brought a lively sparkle to Lisa's eyes – one that inspired a preliminary ravishing, before they both put on fresh clothes and went out for the best evening they had had in a long time.

Preparations for a year abroad, particularly the defence of his thesis in front of a panel of his professors, proved to be more daunting than Teddy had anticipated. It went well but, as had happened to many of his fellow PhD candidates, he was ordered to do a number of revisions.

'My God, we'll never get out of here,' he grumbled at each day's delay. But Lisa, who was in no great hurry to arrive in Jakarta, took advantage of the delay to enrol in an eight-week summer course in Indonesian.

'You won't be able to finish it,' Teddy predicted when she told him about it. 'We won't be around long enough.'

'Perhaps not,' she agreed as she thumbed through her

new copy of *Mastering the Indonesian Language*. She had perfected the art of knowing when to listen to him and when to ignore him.

It was late September by the time Teddy finished his final revisions and could get down to the business of making departure plans.

At least that was what Teddy was starting to do when Lisa dropped her bombshell about spending a month in Japan on the way. Not just a weekend – not a week – a whole damn month.

'Don't you see, it's the chance of a lifetime,' she explained patiently. 'It'll cost absolutely nothing for the ticket because it's a free stopover on the way to Jakarta. And I'll have a place to stay that won't cost anything at all.'

'Where?'

'With Sally and Phoebe.'

'Who the hell are they?'

'You should know; I've talked about them often enough. They're the ones I did that team teaching thing with last semester. They're going to be at the International School in Tokyo this year and they said I could stay with them anytime. I've always been fascinated by Japan –'

'No, you haven't,' he interrupted. 'This is a totally new thing.'

'It's not new. I've been interested in Japan since I was

a teenager.'

'Bullshit. I haven't heard you even mention it for ages.'

'That's because you either go comatose or change the subject when I do.'

'I do not,' he protested. 'That would be excruciatingly bad manners.'

'You said it.'

'Well, I just can't just take a month away from my work to see a few cherry blossoms and that's that.'

'Nobody's asking you to.'

Teddy stared her. She was becoming more astonishing every minute.

'But you just said –'

'Of course, if you want to come too, that's great. I just assumed you'd be too busy. I want to spend the first couple of weeks in Tokyo and then travel around a bit on my own. It'll be fun doing it like that, a real adventure, and afterwards I'll meet you in Jakarta. In the meantime you can be finding us a place to live and settling in.'

Teddy looked doubtful. 'I'm going to have a thousand things to do from the instant I get there. I won't have time to do any of that finding or settling in stuff.'

'Well, I'll look for a place when I get there – after my month in Japan. In the meantime, you can sleep in the Komodo enclosure at the zoo, since you love them so much.'

No uprising of the slaves ever caught their masters more by surprise.

Teddy felt injured and unappreciated. He had wanted to stop in Bangkok for a couple of days to see how his uncle was doing and meet his little cousin Alexander – and of course to see Panda, if she happened to be there – but he had had dropped the plan because he realised Lisa wouldn't like it.

He couldn't figure out how she had got the idea there might be something going on between him and Panda. But she clearly had, even though that week in Nantucket they had been so careful to avoid each other whenever she was around.

Of course, the last thing he wanted to do was to hurt Lisa. He was sure she had never had a clue about Nancy Chan or Mary Hargrove. In any case, that little episode with Mary had been so brief it hardly counted. It was just that a guy needed someone new sometimes to keep up the excitement. Sex with the same woman all the time, no matter how great she was – it just got to be kind of routine after a while.

He wished Lisa would understand that but he didn't hold out much hope. She should have married a more home-and-slippers type of guy – a lawyer or a banker; someone who wanted to come straight home after work, walk the dog, help the kids with their homework, then watch a game or something on television. There were lots of them out there – guys who would have loved Lisa's meat loaf and chocolate chip cookies – but he just wasn't one of them. And Lisa would have to accept it.

Then it occurred to him that Lisa actually was accepting it. This little Japan thing wasn't serious, just a momentary rebellion – the sort of thing any spirited girl might do, and he admired her for it. Nevertheless he had to admit that he was amazed she had even thought of going off on her own like that, especially at a time when he would need her to find a house and get them settled in Jakarta. Well – it just showed how much confidence you could have in a woman.

Still, Lisa wouldn't really go through with her little threat, he told himself. She was probably about to get her period, that was all. She always got a little edgy then. The best thing to do was to humour her for now and let everything sort itself out.

Teddy did humour her and things did sort themselves out – Lisa's way.

They took the flight to Tokyo together and then – and he didn't believe it until it actually happened – he stood in the transit area and watched her disappear towards the immigration lines for arriving passengers.

During the month that followed he got two postcards from her from Tokyo: one from Kyoto and one from a place called Beppu. She said she was having a good time but he didn't think it could really be true. This made the postcard from Kobe saying that she was staying on for another week barely creditable. Had she been kidnapped, he wondered, or had she lost her mind?

JAKARTA, 1971

Teddy met Lisa at the airport with a bunch of lavender orchids when she finally arrived.

'God, it's great to see you,' he said, enveloping her in an enormous hug that astonished the observers. Indonesia was a country where public displays of affection were rare.

'I thought you'd never get here,' he continued, brushing off a throng of boys who were vying for the job of carrying Lisa's cases. 'You can't imagine what I've been going through trying to find a place for us to live. Rents are astronomical in this town, way beyond anything possible on our meagre stipend. I was getting pretty desperate, I can tell you, when I came across this really great guy – a professor at the University of Indonesia. He told me the pavilion of his house was for rent.'

'The what?'

'The pavilion – a smallish house built on the side of the main family home. It's meant for the eldest son, I think. Lots of these Indonesian houses, the older ones anyway, have them. This one isn't half bad. It's not the biggest place in the world but it's got masses of flowering plants all over it and bird cages in the garden and a maid who pops in every day to clean and wash the dishes.'

Lisa tried to protest that she didn't like the idea of keeping birds in cages but stopping Teddy in mid-flow was no easy task.

'I've got to admit the furniture is pretty awful though,' he confessed. 'Lacquered with some kind of nasty shiny stuff and covered with weird carvings of God knows what. But the good news is that the landlord's cook is stirring up an Indonesian meal in your honour – some kind of goat meat curry. Anyway it smelled great when I left the house, so I hope you're hungry.'

Teddy's enthusiasm was boundless and he carried on talking non-stop as their dilapidated taxi (the oldest and least comfortable vehicle Lisa had ever been in) rattled and groaned through the steaming midday heat.

Lisa wondered when she would be able to squeeze in a carefully selected word or two about her time in Japan, but he seemed too preoccupied with his own life to be interested. And of course she did want to hear about the house... But when he started rambling on about the lab

131

facilities, his Indonesian colleagues, the possibilities for doing fieldwork, the distinctive characteristics of hundreds of different species of lizards... then, she became seriously annoyed. Why wasn't he ever capable of thinking of anyone but himself?

During dinner – a sort of curry, not as good as the Indian ones she'd had – Teddy went back to the subject of lizards. It was monitor lizards this time, and over coffee on the terrace afterwards he narrowed his focus down to komodos.

Lisa began to have a disconcerting sensation that she was invisible – or possibly that she wasn't there at all.

'And they're not just on Komodo Island, you know. You can find them on the western tip of Flores and on –'

Suddenly she simply had to make him acknowledge her existence, no matter what it might cost her later.

'I had an affair in Japan,' she remarked, as casually as if she had been telling him about a lovely piece of silk she had bought.

'Yeah right,' he laughed. 'Did I tell you that komodos can swim? That's presumably how they got –'

'You don't mind then?'

'Mind what?'

'Mind my having an affair.'

'Sure I'd mind – but you're kidding, aren't you?'

'I'm not actually. His name is Hisato Nakamura and I

met him at the Golden Temple in Kyoto.'

For once, Teddy was speechless.

'I was sitting in the garden, just sort of absorbing all the peace and beauty of the place when he started talking to me,' she continued. 'I think in the beginning he just wanted to practice his English. He explained a lot of things about the temple to me and' – she flushed like a schoolgirl – 'he was really good looking, tall for a Japanese and with kind, intelligent eyes. I couldn't help being drawn to him and he seemed to feel that way about me. After we left the temple we went to a coffee shop together and then to a little place where we sat on tatami mats and drank lots of tiny cups of sake and ate broiled eel on rice. He said it was a Kobe specialty. I didn't think I'd like it, but I did. Anyway, we talked and talked; and somehow, the more we talked, the more we had to say to each other. Then he suggested going dancing, so we did – and it was great.'

'We both knew we wouldn't have a lot of time together and if things didn't happen quickly, they wouldn't happen at all. So after we had seen each other a couple of times we went to an onsen – that's what the Japanese call a hot spring resort, up on Mount Rokko. Well you know – or maybe you don't – the thing to do in an onsen is take a bath, so that's what we did.'

'Together?' gasped Teddy, not troubling to conceal his amazement.

'Yes, you see onsens have lovely rooms that open on to their own little garden with a big bath tub and –'

'Good God, you don't have to go into every detail.'

'Sorry. The important thing is that we spent the whole weekend there and after that – well, we saw each other whenever we could.'

'Are you in love with him? Are you telling me you want a divorce?'

'No, I don't want one – not unless you do. It all seems like a dream to me now. There was something not quite real about it even at the time. It was so totally removed from anything else in my life. Looking back on it now, I can scarcely believe it really happened. Anyway, it's over.'

A silence that was nearly palpable hung in the air between them for what seemed like a century, and then Teddy reached across the table and took her hand. 'You're not going to keep on doing that sort of thing – having affairs with men you meet on exotic vacations – are you?'

She laughed softly. 'No, I don't think so. I'm not really that sort of person.'

'I don't want a divorce,' he said. 'I've missed you like hell these past few weeks.'

And, pulling her up from her chair, he led her into the bedroom for a ravishing that rivalled – or perhaps surpassed – the one in San Francisco the night they had gone dancing at Fisherman's Wharf.

As the weeks went by they gradually settled into life in Jakarta. Teddy was untroubled by the oven high temperatures, the bloodthirsty mosquitoes, the jam-packed buses, the cinder black pollution, or the doubtful hygienic character of the spicy food. He saw only flowering trees, smiling people and – most important of all – a profusion of lizards.

Lisa's attitude toward their new environment was more temperate. She liked exploring the markets and practicing the Indonesian she had learned during the summer, but she didn't take to the food at all. The spices upset her stomach and the muggy heat of the rainy season oppressed her. Worst of all, for the first time in her life she felt lonely.

Her life had always been full and active; but now, when she said goodbye to Teddy in the morning, she was faced with a completely unstructured day ahead of her. It was true that she had a vast city and a whole new culture to explore, but doing it entirely on her own wore thin after a while. Jakarta wasn't as visitor-friendly as the cities in Japan had been, and she found that the heat exhausted her. She always went out somewhere – if only to the market – in the morning; but she would come home before lunch and spend the hottest part of the day reading the *Jakarta Post*, wishing there were more English books available, or sometimes just thinking about the various turns her life had taken.

Now and then she even let herself wonder about Alicia,

the baby cousin she had played mother to for an entire summer and had come to think of as her very own. After all, she had had almost sole care of her, even though she had only been twelve at the time.

It had all come about because her father, who taught American history at a small college in New Hampshire, had been invited to give a course at a university in Australia. And her mother, not wanting to miss out on the adventure, had gone with him. Aunt Sylvia and Uncle Howard had come to stay with her, bringing little Alicia with them. The plan had been for Uncle Howard to commute to his law firm in Boston while Aunt Sylvia would look after both her baby daughter and her niece, but it didn't exactly work out that way. Aunt Sylvia, who was only twenty-three – much younger than Uncle Howard – was very chic and beautiful, hated housework and took no interest in her niece. She didn't even seem to like her baby very much. She preferred spending her days going to exercise classes, shopping and having lunches with people she met during her efforts to keep fit. She was more than willing to leave the bottles and the nappies and all the rest of the baby care to her helpful niece.

Playing 'mommy' to little Alicia had been so absorbing that she had barely thought about ballet at all, and for the first time in her life had actually skipped some of her classes at dancing school. Then, almost before she knew it, September had come and everything had seemed to happen at once: her parents came home from Australia, her school started, and Aunt Sylvia and Uncle Howard got ready to leave.

She would never forget the moment when her mother had wrenched Alicia from her arms and given her to Aunt Sylvia. As she had stood there and watched them get in the car and drive away, the longing for a baby of her own, one that nobody could take away from her, had been born.

When her mother had pointed out that ballet and babies didn't go together, she had turned a deaf ear and had ignored the suggestion that she should make up her mind about what she really wanted. Things would sort themselves out, she had told herself – and in fact, that was what had happened. Throughout her teenage years ballet had taken up more and more of her time, her energy and her thoughts; and, as she had become more realistic about what pregnancy and baby care would do to a dancer's career, her inclination to have her own little Alicia had gradually faded until – one heavy suitcase and one fractured toe that refused to heal properly had put an end to everything.

The physical pain had been nothing compared to the agony of giving up the dream she had worked so long and hard for. She didn't know how she would have coped with it if it hadn't been for Teddy. And for the possibility of making her other dream – that of having a baby of her own – a reality.

She knew she shouldn't be letting herself dwell on past disappointments; it was just that the difference between Teddy's life here and her own was so enormous. His life was so active and interesting – if you liked lizards, anyway. He was busy. He met people. He was doing work he loved while she was hard pressed to fill the endless hours of the days. She would have had to be a saint not to feel a little envious.

The one thing that saved her sanity was that Teddy liked to bring friends or colleagues to the house in the evenings. They would have drinks on the terrace and then go out for dinner in the lively commercial area known as Blok M. These contacts with people who spoke English always refreshed her – and would, albeit briefly, restore her naturally positive outlook on life.

One evening Teddy invited a fellow herpetologist at the University of Indonesia (Tony Mathews) and his wife Ann over for drinks.

Ann taught second grade at the International School; and when she discovered that Lisa was also a teacher, she launched into an account of the latest troubles to befall the school. The most critical of these was that the fourth grade teacher had come down with malaria.

'I didn't realise that was a problem here in Jakarta,' Lisa said, slightly alarmed. 'I haven't been taking the pills.'

'That's OK,' Ann assured her, 'you only need them if you go to Pelabuan Ratu, or anywhere on the south coast for that matter. But Betty just came back from a weekend there and she must have been bitten by an anopheles mosquito. So now the search is on for a replacement. And it isn't as easy as you might think to find a qualified teacher – English speaking, of course – who is willing to do it.'

Lisa applied for the job the next morning and on the following Monday she was in the classroom, slipping easily into the new routine. The curriculum, with very few modifications, was just what she had been trained to teach in the States, the children were bright and the discipline problems were few. Reinvigorated by the sense that she had a reason to get up in the morning, she was in her element again.

Teddy was less enthusiastic about her new job because it meant that she couldn't go to Flores and some of the other eastern islands, including Komodo, with him. He was going to go on the missionary boat (no booze, they had said, but he didn't suppose they'd check his suitcase) and he would be gone for two months.

Would she be all right in Jakarta by herself, he wondered? Wouldn't she be lonely? Didn't she want to chuck the job and come with him?

She told him emphatically that she did not. The very thought of being on a rocking boat with nothing but Indonesian food to eat made her want to throw up.

Teddy felt a little guilty about leaving her but there was just no way he could come all the way to Indonesia and not go to Komodo Island. And if they met in Bali at the end of his trip, he reasoned, that should sort of make up for going off and leaving her alone all that time. And why did he always have to feel guilty about things when he was around Lisa, anyway?

In spite of the new job, Lisa did feel lonely when he was gone. Teaching had never tired her in America but here she felt completely dragged out at the end of the day. At first she put it down to the heat – but then, a ghastly suspicion crept into her mind. She had felt a little like this during her brief and ill-fated pregnancies. She hadn't had a period for a while, but they had been so irregular since her last miscarriage that she hadn't thought much about it. In any case, it was almost impossible for her to be pregnant again. The doctor had told her that after she had lost the last baby – and he had seemed so sure about it that she hadn't bothered about any precautions when she was in Japan. Not that it really mattered; because if, by some miracle, she really was pregnant, the baby was almost certainly Teddy's.

The next day she went to a local clinic and had a pregnancy test. Just as she had predicted, the results were negative. She could only think how silly she had been to have imagined they could have been anything else.

The hot humid days passed in slow succession. Then one morning a button popped off her shirt while she was getting dressed; looking in the mirror, she could see that she had put on a little weight. Well, what could she expect when she continually filled up on cookies and chocolates? Not to mention the delicious Indonesian version of peanut brittle she had discovered in a little kiosk near their house. The problem was that, apart from a few snacks, she just didn't like the local food. Not only was it too spicy for her, but almost everything was cooked in the strong smelling and horrible tasting coconut oil. The very thought of it turned her stomach.

Fortunately she had always kept herself ballerina-thin – too thin in Teddy's view – so a few extra pounds weren't really a problem. And Teddy might be right; they might make her look better so she didn't make much of an effort to cut back on her distinctly unhealthy diet.

Predictably her clothes continued to get tighter until, as she was relaxing in the teacher's lounge at school one afternoon, the art teacher came over and said, 'You know, I still have a bunch of old maternity clothes taking up room at the back of my closet. I'll be glad to give them to you if you want.'

'But I'm not pregnant,' Lisa exclaimed with a valiant attempt at a laugh.

'Oh, I'm terribly sorry,' her generous colleague replied; looking embarrassed and a bit sceptical at the same time.

'It's just that I've been eating a lot of sweets since I've been here and not getting any exercise. That's why I've gained so much weight. I sort of knew it was happening but I didn't bother about it very much. Still, if I'm actually looking pregnant I guess I'd better go on a diet.'

'Oh, don't pay attention to anything I've said,' the art teacher urged. 'I didn't know what I was talking about.'

'Don't worry about it. I promise it's fine,' Lisa assured her; she laughed, pretending to think it was a good joke.

The next day she went to a different clinic and this time the test came out positive. The doctor estimated that she was about five months pregnant – although, of course, he couldn't pinpoint the timing exactly.

In spite of the heat, Lisa broke into a cold sweat. It was about five months ago that she had been in Japan.

'You are not happy?' the doctor asked when he saw the expression on her face.

'No,' she replied with a grimace. 'I'm not.'

'You very happy when you hold baby,' he assured her. And when she didn't seem convinced, he added, 'Remember, five months very late for abortion.

Much dangerous.'

Abortion, she thought as she left the doctor's office. It was incredible that anyone who had wanted a baby as much as she had needed to be cautioned against an abortion. And it was silly too because everything was going to be fine. She was certain – well, almost certain – that the baby was Teddy's. It simply had to be!

Less than a week later Lisa met Teddy on the terrace of a small hotel nestled in a grove of tall coconut palms beside a white sand beach in Bali. He was waiting for her there, a glass of something long and wet and icy on a bamboo table beside him – but he knocked it over in his eagerness to throw his arms around her.

When he pressed her to him, he was immediately aware that something was different. 'Hey, have you, of all people, actually put on a little weight?' he exclaimed, sounding pleased. 'You must've started to like Indonesian food.'

'Some of it,' she said, wanting to postpone her revelation as long as possible.

Yet a little later Teddy suggested a swim, and she knew the moment of truth had come. He would have to be blind not to figure things out when he saw her in a swimming suit. After all, it had only been the lack of a full length mirror in their little pavilion in Jakarta that had allowed her to remain blissfully ignorant of her condition as long as she had; that, and not wanting to come to terms with even the remotest possibility of having a baby who couldn't possibly be Teddy's.

'Actually I still hate Indonesian food,' she said, deciding to bite the bullet.

Teddy wondered if he had heard her correctly.

'I mean, I haven't gotten fat – at least that's not the main thing. I'm pregnant.'

'But the doctor said –'

'I know. But doctors can be wrong, can't they?'

'Not very often.'

'Often or not, this seems to be one of the times.'

Studying her figure, he couldn't argue. 'I guess so,' he said, glumly. 'How far along are you?'

'Three and a half or four months, I think. The doctor wasn't quite sure.'

Lisa had too truthful a nature to find lying easy. But she had decided that since the baby was most likely Teddy's, it was better to keep any troubling little doubts about its paternity to herself.

After overcoming his initial aversion to yet another pregnancy, Teddy accepted this one with considerably more equanimity and grace than he had the others. They were in Indonesia now, where he wanted to be, doing what he wanted to do – so a baby didn't seem like such a threat to his freedom and his future anymore. They'd just pop the kid into one of those baby backpacks and go ahead with whatever they wanted to do, no problem. What the hell, he thought – it might even be kind of cute.

Anyway, with the prospect of a glorious vacation in Bali ahead of them, why was he wasting his time thinking about babies?

The week surpassed his expectations. They swam in the warm clear water in front of the hotel, wandered through Hindu temples where doll-sized houses shaped like pagodas waited for the arrival of the gods, and watched as extraordinary creatures with manes like lions danced out their battles against terrifying witches. They ate delicious meals in lamp-lit courtyards under the stars and Lisa found that she was no longer bothered by the spicy food. Then they would saunter back along the beach to make love in their thatched-roof cottage beneath the waving coconut palms.

And Lisa, like many of the most talented liars, came to believe her lie… almost.

A little less than four months later Lisa gave birth to her baby, took one look at its little Japanese face and felt that her life was over. Too devastated to cry, she lay back against the pillow and stared blankly at the ceiling.

The doctor tried to hide his surprise but the nurses made no effort to suppress their giggles.

When the evidence of the birth had been washed away and the baby had been placed in the curve of Lisa's arm, Teddy was allowed into the room.

One glance at his wife told him that something was very wrong. And when he looked at the baby he knew what it was.

Utterly stunned, all he could do was gasp, 'Good God!'

Lisa said nothing. What was there to say?

'You must have known all along,' he blurted out.

'I wondered. But of course – I didn't know for sure.'

'If you couldn't go a whole month without sex, couldn't you at least have found some Caucasian guy to screw around with?'

Lisa reached her hand out toward him. 'I'm sorry,' she murmured, 'so terribly, terribly sorry.'

'Fine, great – what good is that going to do?'

'None, I guess.'

'We might be able to put the little brat up for adoption,' Teddy said, 'but it's going to be one hell of a mess.'

Lisa instinctively enclosed the tiny form more closely

in her arm. 'No,' she said, firmly, 'he's my baby. I can't do that.'

'If you're suggesting that I go through life as the cuckold father, you're out of your fucking mind. It isn't a role I'd particularly enjoy, thank you very much.'

'I wouldn't expect you to play that role.'

'Oh, have you another one in mind? If so, your imagination is one hell of a lot better than mine.'

'I'm just being sensible, that's all. I'll take the baby back to the States and we'll get a divorce and we won't need to see each other anymore. That way you can get on with your life and none of your friends ever need to know about it.'

'I see you've thought it all out.'

'God, yes,' she admitted. 'I tried to convince myself that it wasn't going to happen this way and most of the time I succeeded – sort of. But there were times when I didn't and I couldn't keep the ghastly nightmares away.'

'But you never thought of letting me in on your little secret? Why the hell not? You must have known I'd find out eventually.'

'I didn't know that. I desperately hoped the baby would look like you and I'd never have to tell you that I hadn't been sure. The horrible thing is that I love you and I don't want to lose you. I absolutely hate the idea of getting a divorce but I can't give up my baby.'

'It's too bad you didn't think of all that before you let Mr.. Kamikaze swoop in and score,' he said. And, too angry to utter another word, he flung himself out of the room.

When Teddy got home he opened a bottle of whisky and was just settling in to an evening of solitary fury when he heard Tony and Ann Mathews at the front gate.

Christ, he thought, was this the evening they were coming for drinks and then going to the Senayan Sate House for dinner? Fuck, it probably was.

'Sorry we're late,' Ann apologised. 'The electricity's been off at our house – in the whole neighbourhood for that matter, since three o'clock this afternoon. And Tony couldn't find his car keys in the dark. He's so disorganised and he never puts anything in the same place twice.'

With a colossal effort, Teddy pulled himself together and offered them a drink.

'Where's Lisa?' Ann asked, surprised that she didn't see her.

'In the hospital,' Teddy said.

'The baby,' Ann exclaimed. She was about to say 'how wonderful' when the look on Teddy's face made her swallow her words. Clearly something awful had happened.

'Is Lisa having trouble?' she asked. 'Is the baby –?'

'Dead,' Teddy replied, grasping at the first thing, short

of the embarrassing truth, that popped into his mind.

Both Ann and Tony were full of sympathy, but Toby just mumbled something vaguely appropriate while Ann wouldn't let the subject go.

'What was the problem?' she asked.

Shit, thought Teddy, but then remembered a colleague in the lab back home who had had a kid that hadn't made it. 'A hole in the heart,' he lied.

'Oh, poor Lisa,' Ann murmured, devastated for her friend. 'I'll go see her first thing in the morning.'

'Oh, you mustn't do that,' Teddy said in alarm.

An expression that was at once both hurt and puzzled crossed Ann's face and Teddy knew he had to justify his reaction somehow.

'She's been sedated, a really heavy dose of something,' he told her, casting about wildly for a plausible explanation. 'She was hysterical. It's the disappointment, you see. She wanted the baby so badly. The doctor says she mustn't have visitors until he gives the OK. I'll let you know as soon as you can see her, I promise.'

'I can imagine how hard this must be for her,' the tender-hearted Ann said. 'Some people – generally the ones who would make the best parents, like you and Lisa – have such trouble having babies. And then others... well, just look around you at all these poor people who have a baby every year even though they don't know where tomorrow's lunch is coming from for the children they already have. It's dreadful.'

Teddy growled something in agreement and firmly changed the subject.

Ann came back to it over dinner. 'There's nothing more heartbreaking than an unwanted neglected baby,' she declared. 'Fortunately, Indonesia is one of the few countries where it is still relatively easy to adopt.'

She went on at great length about an orphanage in Suryabaya where a friend of hers had had a good experience adopting. But eventually the two men, neither of whom found the subject remotely interesting, managed to bring the conversation around to the more compelling topic of the unexplained variability in the metabolic rate of a newly discovered species of frog.

Teddy spent the next evening alone, getting very drunk and wondering what to do next. God damn it, he would have sworn he could have trusted Lisa not to make him a laughing stock in front of the entire world. If the kid just didn't look so fucking Japanese, he'd be tempted to close his eyes to the fact that it wasn't his. After all, he wasn't one of those men who wanted to have a son as a way of getting some kind of immortality. He didn't give a shit about that sort of thing. Anyway, kids were women's toys, so why not let Lisa have her baby? And they could carry on with their life together except – fuck, fuck, fuck.

The next day Teddy had such a colossal hangover (practically life-threatening, he thought with a groan) that going to work was out of the question. After tossing and turning and trying to sleep as the bedroom got hotter and hotter (the electricity was off in their area today) he decided that a swim might make him feel better. And with this hope in mind, he set off for the pool at the American Club.

Fifty laps followed by a club sandwich and a beer (nothing like the hair of the tail, he told himself) beside the pool actually did make him feel considerably better. He ordered a coffee afterwards, lit a cigarette and took a look around him.

He had never been there on a weekday before and he wasn't much impressed with what he saw. The place was full of women and small children too young to be in school, but none of the women were much to look at. Lisa was better looking; and probably brighter too, than any of them. It was hard luck to have to give her up just because some squalling brat had arrived in the world. Sure, she hadn't exactly been a saint during her little stopover in Japan – but who was he to climb onto a high moral plane? He knew how little these things could mean. It was just that it was so damn hard to imagine Lisa going in for that hello/goodbye kind of sex.

A slim blond woman at the next table caught his attention. Not only was she prettier than the others – she broke into a particularly lovely smile when a little tot who looked Indonesian trotted over to her. She lifted the little fellow onto her lap and began feeding him something out of a bowl while she continued her conversation with her friend.

'Oh yes, the Surabaya orphanage is the best,' she was saying, giving Teddy the astonishing experience of hearing about it for the second time in less than twenty-four hours. 'And you know, even with all the legal fees, it costs less to adopt a baby in Indonesia than it does to give birth to one in the States. Isn't that incredible?'

Teddy jumped into a taxi and within minutes he was bursting into Lisa's room at the hospital.

'How's Mitsubishi today?' he asked jauntily.

'If you mean the baby,' she returned coldly, 'he's fine.'

'And you?' he asked, perching on the bed.

'Not too bad.'

'Listen,' he said, 'I've had an idea – one of such genius that no one who knows me would ever credit me with it.'

A wave of exhaustion swept over Lisa. 'I'm not listening to any more of your ideas, not ever. My life is a shambles. I don't know what I'm going to do about it, but one thing

I'm absolutely certain of is that it's not going to include any more revelations about lizards.'

'But –'

'I'm not listening,' she cried, something close to hysteria suddenly getting the better of her. 'And if I ever hear another word about your ghastly reptiles, I'm getting out of this bed and taking my baby and running out on the street and I don't care what happens to me. I'm going home, back to a country I understand, back to a place where I belong. I'm –'

And, most un-Lisa-like, she broke into a torrent of sobs.

'Shhh,' Teddy murmured, reaching over and putting his arms around her, 'just lie back down and let me tell you my idea. It has nothing to do with lizards, I promise you, and if you don't like it we'll forget it.'

He pushed her gently back onto her pillow and went on to explain, 'It's about Mitsubishi. We'll just tell people we adopted him. It's incredibly easy.'

'Could we?' Lisa's face sparkled with delight for a moment and then it fell. 'But everyone knows I was pregnant – not only the people here but my parents and just about everyone I know back in the States. Unfortunately I've been on a massive letter-writing kick.'

'That's no problem,' he said confidently. 'We'll just tell everyone the baby died and you were so broken up about it that we adopted Mitsubishi.'

'But it's not as if he were an Indonesian baby,' Lisa pointed out.

'Do you really think people are going to figure that out? I mean he looks Asian, doesn't he? And lots of Indonesians have Chinese blood. Tell the truth now, if you were looking at two babies and one of them was half Japanese and the other was half Chinese, would you know which was which?'

'No,' she replied, actually beginning to let herself think such an outlandish scheme might actually work. But how about the people we know here? How will we explain finding a baby and arranging an adoption so quickly?'

'Easy,' said Teddy, inventing quickly. 'We'll just say the doctor brought it to us. He knew how unhappy you were about losing your baby and at the same time he was worried about this unwanted kid he had just delivered. Not only was it illegitimate but – to make matters worse – it was half Chinese and half European. The father was nowhere in sight and the mother's family, the Chinese side of things, were refusing to have anything to do with it. The good doctor knew it would be headed for an orphanage unless he could turn two bad situations into one good one by bringing the baby to us. That makes sense doesn't it?'

Lisa nodded. She didn't know whether it made sense or not but she didn't care who believed it and who didn't. The only important thing was that she wasn't going to lose Teddy – her darling wonderful Teddy. He was going to stay with her and her baby. What other man would do that when the baby so obviously wasn't his? And what other man would be capable of dreaming up such a wildly preposterous story and actually making it sound credible? She must be the luckiest woman in the world to be married to Teddy.

'The pavilion has been damned empty without you,' he admitted, leaning over and kissing her, 'and it's made me think about a few things.'

'Like what?'

'Like how great it is that men don't get pregnant.'

They both laughed.

'You see,' he continued, 'and you've probably guessed, I've kind of strayed a couple of times myself. I promise you it didn't mean anything,' he added hastily, 'but I did feel guilty about it. Now, thanks to Mitsubishi here, we can start out again, this time on a level playing field, just the two of us.'

'There're three of us now,' Lisa pointed out.

'Silly,' he said, unable to think of babies as people – but he didn't argue.

'There's just one thing though,' she said.

'What?'

'Would you stop calling him Mitsubishi?'

'What should I call him then?'

'I don't know, something ordinary like John or Paul or Bill.'

'Too boring,' he declared. 'We must be able to do better than that. Let's go for something like Darwin or Wallace or Leonardo or maybe Linnaeus?'

'We could call him Leonard,' Lisa replied, trying it out on her tongue.

'That'll do,' Teddy agreed, and rapidly lost interest in the subject.

His thoughts flew back to what he had just told Lisa about his relationships with other women, that they hadn't meant anything. Well it was mostly true – true, except for Panda.

CHAPTER 7
BANGKOK, 1973

The floor to ceiling windows of the Anglican Church on Sathorn Road were thrown open and a smell of freshly cut flowers filled the air.

The crowd inside waited expectantly.

Panda, her blue-black hair grazing the shoulders of her white silk dress, held her father's arm and listened for the first strains of the wedding march. Sonchai and the best man took their places near the altar. The organist poised her fingers above the keys. Then, as Mendelssohn's clear notes rang out, Panda and her father began their walk down the aisle.

How handsome Sonchai looks in his dark blue suit, Panda thought, taking in every detail of his appearance from his carefully combed hair to the tie she had helped him choose, to the well-pressed crease in his trousers that ended just above his toes. His toes! She could scarcely believe her eyes as she gazed at the ten exposed appendages. Yet there they were, clearly displayed between the thongs of a pair of leather sandals. It beggared belief! Living like an artist, defying convention... being a free spirit was one thing, getting married in sandals was quite another.

'Dearly Beloved, we are gathered together,' the vicar began.

'You toad,' Panda whispered as she took her place beside him.

The vicar looked horrified but carried on, 'in the sight of God to unite –'

'Those sandals; how could you?' she whispered in a voice loud enough to be heard in the first few rows.

'I like them,' returned Sonchai.

The vicar went on, his tone laden with disapproval, 'for better, for worse, for richer, for poorer –'

'With those sandals, it's going to be for the worse,' Panda persisted.

This was too much for the vicar. He paused and, with barely suppressed indignation, murmured, 'I don't think we should continue this service.'

Oh God, groaned Panda, thinking of the wedding guests, the presents, the garden at the Oriental Hotel all set up for the reception… (We can't call everything off now. We can always get a divorce later if we want to. In any case, he's an artist, isn't he? What can anyone expect? And I really do love him. Most of the time, anyway).

Stop the service, Sonchai thought with astonishment. Why should they do that? Just because Panida was making a silly fuss about his sandals? Women were like that. They cared about funniest things. It was best just to ignore them

– but maybe the vicar didn't know that.

'No, no – do go on with it,' he urged. 'Panida's a little nervous, that's all.'

'Yes, that's it,' she agreed. 'I wasn't quite myself a minute ago but I'm fine now.'

The vicar didn't believe her but decided to take the easy way out.

'God forgive me,' he murmured under his breath, then went on with the rest of the service.

The organist, who had overheard the little spat at the altar, quickly managed to pull herself together. She launched into the triumphant chords of Lohengrin while the vicar, glad to see that at least some measure of peace seemed to have been restored between the bride and groom, was relieved that the most distressing wedding ceremony he had ever performed was over.

Panda was trying to keep her eyes averted from Sonchai's toes as they went back down the aisle. Then, the astonishing sight of Teddy amongst the guests drove everything else from her mind.

'I can't believe you're really here,' she cried, when she managed to get him to herself for a few minutes at the reception. 'I told Daddy there was no point in even sending you an invitation.'

'Well, he sent one anyway and I came straight from the airport.'

'But how –'

'Easy, I just hopped in a cab, showed the driver the address on the invitation. It was written in Thai, thank God, and he took me right to the church. I just have one small bag so –'

'I didn't mean that, silly. I meant coming all the way from California –'

'Oh, you can thank the Rainforest Research Organisation for that. They love to have conferences in exotic places. I shouldn't knock them though. They not only sent me to Indonesia for a few weeks, they got me to my favourite cousin's wedding on the way home. Of course, you might not want to thank them. I'm being conceited, as usual.' And waving his champagne in the air, he added, 'Maybe you'd better cut off my supply of this stuff.'

'You've always been conceited – but that's all right. I'm used to it,' she said with a laugh. 'But why didn't you let us know you were coming?'

'I didn't know myself until the last minute. Then things worked out. A field trip was cancelled and some meetings were called off and I saw that if I made a dash for the airport... well, here I am.'

'Great! How are Lisa and the baby? I nearly fainted when you wrote that you'd gone in for adoption. I thought a baby was the last thing you wanted.'

'It was but I kind of lost that battle. And I have to say, Leonard's not a bad kid. And he keeps Lisa occupied.'

'You're happy then – the three of you?'

He shrugged. 'As happy as most people, I guess. But what the hell, I should be more enthusiastic about wedded bliss when I'm talking to a new bride.'

'Don't bother. I've just decided I don't like being a new bride.'

'Yeah, I sort of noticed that during the ceremony.'

'Was it that obvious?'

'I thought it was about to become the most interesting wedding I'd ever been to. It was a great disappointment when you and Sonchai reverted to happy couple mode.'

'You seem to be treating it all as some sort of joke,' she said, slightly put out.

'It's the way weddings should be treated,' he maintained. 'What are they after all but community circuses, complete with some poor bastard who is going to be sacrificed to a lion, or rather a lioness? The crowd puts on its best clothes and best smiles to witness the spectacle. Then after the victim's doom has been sealed, the tribe on the side of the lioness invites everyone around for feasting and rejoicing. So why aren't you happy, my dear cousin? This is supposed to be a day of triumph for the lioness. Is your prey by any chance giving you indigestion?'

'Certainly not.'

'He's not balking at playing the role of the sacrificial Christian?'

'He's not feeling sacrificial, thank you very much, and he doesn't feel like a Christian, I know that. He's a Buddhist.' She hesitated. 'Much as I hate to admit it, I expect he would agree with you about weddings being circuses.'

A shadow passed across her face and Teddy felt contrite.

'Jesus, what a bastard I'm being. I didn't come here to make fun of your wedding. I swear I didn't. I'm really sorry.'

'Don't worry,' she said, trying for a moment to sound like this was the happiest day of her life; then, realizing that she wasn't succeeding, she said: 'it's just that everything's gone wrong today, that's all.'

'Come on then, tell old cousin Ted what's the matter. Why don't you like being a new bride?'

'I feel like I'm being tied up in chains.'

'That's not exactly how brides are supposed to feel. Can you be a little more specific?'

'It's the wedding ceremony and everything that goes with it. Things like not being able to just walk out of the relationship if I want to because of all the possessions that would have to be divided up and the divorce courts that would have to be dealt with and... oh God, I can't even bear to think about it.'

'You're not supposed to be thinking about it at your wedding reception,' Teddy pointed out.

'Why ever not? If Sonchai can think about getting married in sandals, why can't I think about a divorce?'

'Honestly Panda, those sandals aren't all that big a deal,' he said, laughing. 'If you marry an artist you've got to expect that sort of thing. They're all a little crazy or they wouldn't be artists in the first place.'

'Yes but it all seemed different before we got married – just light-hearted and fun. And we did love each other, I know we did. I suppose the difference is that I knew if I got fed up I could always throw a few clothes in a bag, get in a taxi and go back to Daddy and Christie's.'

'Well, I take your point but I still think you're making too much of the sandals. You're marrying a man, not a suit of clothes.'

'I know it's trivial. And I suppose I'm being really shallow and petty – but it's not just that.'

'Oh? What is it, then?'

'It's the feeling that I'm trapped by law courts and possessions.'

'May I ask you something?'

'Of course.'

'Why did you marry Sonchai?'

'I told you, because I love him.'

'Then why didn't you just keep on loving him without getting married? After all, you could have thought of these possessions and law courts a little sooner.'

Panda considered this for a moment and then said, 'I suppose it was because I wanted a commitment from him and –'

'Very nice, great idea,' Teddy interrupted. 'Typical feminine logic. You want a commitment from him but as soon as it's a question of a commitment from you, you start complaining about being tied up in chains. That's not exactly a level playing field, if you ask me.'

'I hadn't thought of it that way,' Panda admitted. 'The thing is, I've been thinking about going back to England and looking for a job there because I can't see any future for me here in terms of a career. But if I'm going I should go soon, not wait until I'm ninety-five, so I don't want to hang around here forever just to see where my relationship with Sonchai is going. Can you understand that?'

'I think I can – and it seems to me you're just using the poor guy. I'm surprised at you, Panda. I didn't think you'd do that sort of thing.'

'You colossal hypocrite,' she cried, her face turning pink with outrage. 'Honestly! Giving me a hard time about being nice to Sonchai after the way you've treated Lisa!'

'The way I've treated Lisa?' he repeated, shocked. 'I've been a damned good husband to her.'

'No you haven't. You've lied to her and cheated on her. Don't try to tell me that night in Nantucket was the only time. I bet you've done a lot of playing around with a lot of women. You obviously don't love her anymore and you've been horrible to her about wanting to have a baby, something that any woman –'

'Hey, wait a minute,' he interrupted; he was now as angry as she was. 'No man in the world could have been better about his wife wanting a baby than I have.'

'Rubbish.'

'I swear to you – it's the truth.'

'Just how were you so great about it, I'd like to know?'

'I'll tell you then. We didn't adopt Leonard. He's Lisa's child by a Japanese lover.'

This revelation startled Panda into silence.

'So,' he said. 'Do I get the Husband of the Year Award or not?'

'Definitely not. You got exactly what you deserve from Lisa. And she has my total admiration for giving it to you.'

'Lucky I never looked to you for understanding,' he said, huffily. 'And I might add that if you breathe one word of this to any living soul, I'll be on the next plane across the Pacific to wring your treacherous little neck and hasten your arrival down in the fiery regions below.'

A picture of Teddy, sword in hand, dressed rather like Superman, flying across the ocean seeking revenge... it made Panda burst out laughing. 'If you're not careful I'll pull you down to those fiery regions with me. There's no question that you'll be allowed in. Anyway, here comes Sonchai. Have you had much of a chance to talk to him yet?'

'Panida, everyone's been looking for you,' Sonchai scolded when he reached them.

'I didn't know you cared about "everyone", darling,' Panda replied tartly. And, seeing her old friend Thanit a short distance away – she left the two men to enjoy – or not to enjoy, each other's company.

Teddy, wondering briefly what you talked to an artist about (and deciding you talked about art), approached the subject from the angle that interested him.

'Are lizards much used as fertility symbols in Thai art?' he asked.

'No,' Sonchai replied, wondering if this new cousin had all his marbles.

'The reason I'm asking is that you see them a lot in the woodcarvings from Borneo and I think a stylized lizard would be a great basis for the World Wildlife Organisation's new logo; you know, tie in beautifully with the idea of saving endangered species and all that,' Teddy explained. 'I've just been to a conference there… well, in Jakarta actually, not in Borneo. And there was a woman there – a designer, an artistic type like you – from some company in London.

She was working on a new logo for them. We sort of got to know each other and I tried to persuade her about the lizard thing but I didn't have much success. What do you think? I'd like an artist's opinion.'

'I'd have to see it before I could say anything,' Sonchai replied, hoping his mother wouldn't find out about the insanity in Panida's family. She was very concerned about heredity and it would certainly upset her.

To Sonchai's relief, Christie soon saved him from any further conversation with the crazy cousin.

'I'm sorry Teddy – I'm afraid I'm going to have to take Sonchai away from you. He and Panida (wherever she is – oh, over there with Thanit and his wife) need to cut the cake,' she said. 'I want to hurry things along a bit in case William ends up celebrating a bit too much.'

'I'll go tell her,' Sonchai volunteered.

Christie gazed after him as he made his escape. 'I really hope they'll be happy,' she said, sounding rather doubtful. Lowering her voice to a confidential tone, she added, 'Sonchai is very sweet, but – just between you and me – I sometimes wonder if he's quite right for Panida.'

'Is anybody exactly right for anybody else?' he returned.

'I suppose not. But then most people don't make it quite so obvious during the wedding ceremony, do they?'

He couldn't deny that – but Christie was reassured once everyone had gravitated to a trellised area at the side of the garden to watch Panida and Sonchai cut their splendid wedding cake. They really did look like they were very much in love, she thought, either that, or her stepdaughter had greatly improved her acting skills since they'd left the church.

But Panda wasn't acting. She was drinking in the scene in front of her: the beautiful garden with the water lapping up along the river's edge, the crowd of faces – mostly Thai but with a liberal sprinkling of foreign ones – and she was revelling in the sense of belonging they awakened in her. This was her world, her own custom-made combination of Thailand and England, and Sonchai was an intrinsic part of it all. He understood this half-and-half world. It was as necessary to his existence as it was to her own. And as Sonchai's hand covered hers to press the silver knife down through the snowy icing on the cake, she thought, we're a couple, we're together in front of all these people, together in front of the world for always – and I love having it this way.

She was so thrilled to discover that she really was in love that when she came across Teddy helping himself to what she suspected must have been about his hundredth glass of champagne (and looking rather disgruntled) – she only reminded him that people were supposed to look happy at weddings, then left him to deal with his ill-humour alone.

He had been part of her childhood, she told herself, and then the hero of her schoolgirl fantasies. But those days were long past; that little girl didn't exist anymore. She had grown up and turned into a woman who had just married the one man in the world who was perfect for her.

Yet, later that night as she slept with one of Sonchai's arms thrown casually over her, the breezes from the Gulf of Siam wafting into the room, an image of Teddy flickered through her mind. It lingered near an open shutter and then disappeared beyond the outer reaches of her dreams.

CHAPTER 8
BANGKOK, 1975

A sandy coloured gibbon called Uan swung down from his favourite rambutan tree in the garden, loped over to Panda and performed several feats of acrobatic excellence for her benefit before settling down to watch her sipping her morning coffee. He liked Panda. She often played with him and could be depended on to laugh whenever he successfully slipped out of his chain collar and evaded the gardener's efforts to catch him (for a while, at least, although the fellow always got him in the end). He also enjoyed parting her thick hair and looking for interesting mites in her scalp. He hadn't actually found any yet – but he had an optimistic nature and didn't let this deter him from further searching.

Another thing that endeared Panda to him was that she frequently gave him special treats and it looked like this morning was going to be no exception. There was a large bowl of fruit on the table and when she finished her coffee she took an orange and held it out to him.

'Now don't throw the peels all over the garden,' she admonished.

Uan refused to let these instructions cramp his style. He felt that the large garden with its assortment of outbuildings was his personal playground and there were only two places in it that he assiduously avoided. The most important of these was the main house, a formidable place where the matriarch of a large Thai–Chinese family, a real dragon lady in Sonchai's opinion (and apparently in Uan's too, as he always avoided her), presided over her vast array of daughters-in-law, grandchildren, poor relations and servants. Uan could tell that she didn't like gibbons and knew she was the one who ordered the gardener to put him back on his chain whenever he managed to escape for an unfettered romp through the trees and bushes. Small but almost as alarming was the building at the back of the compound, where the gardener lived; Uan avoided that too, even though the man brought him food and sometimes played with him.

Uan had just finished eating the orange and was just coming over to have a look through Panda's hair when Sonchai – his face, his hands and his clothes all splattered with green paint – came out of the room he used as his studio.

Panda barely noticed. He was usually splattered with something when he was working.

'The light keeps flickering,' he complained. 'We've got to get Her Majesty to have that big tree trimmed back.'

'She's probably holding court right now,' replied Panda, waving her hand in the direction of the dining room in the main house. 'Her minions usually get their instructions for the day around this time. Why don't you go ask her?'

'I hate asking her. It's too demeaning. You do it.'

'Why should I do it?' objected Panda. 'You're the one who wants it done and it's just as demeaning for me.'

'Good God, you're not going to become like one of those bossy American wives, are you?'

'Thai women aren't exactly doormats either,' she pointed out.

'They take care of things around the house though.'

'The tree's not around the house. It's around your studio.'

Sonchai glared at her for a moment and then his eyes fell on the coffee pot.

'If I want a cup of that, I suppose I'll have to pour it myself,' he grumbled.

'No,' she replied, coolly. 'I don't mind pouring coffee. I do mind petitioning Her Majesty.'

Panda reached for a cup. 'Why don't you just give the gardener a bit of money and tell him to cut back the tree? The chances are that no one will ever notice. And if they do, it won't matter. It'll grow back in a couple of months.'

She was about to hand him the coffee when Uan, deciding he had been patient long enough (and that it was time for the sort of roughhouse Panda wasn't any good at), leapt on Sonchai. Seizing a lock of his bushy hair, he did his best to pull it out by the roots.

'Get this animal off me,' ordered Sonchai.

'Come on, darling, come over here,' Panda said, coaxing the animal with a laugh.

Uan ignored her, so she went over, slipped one arm around his furry waist, and – with her free hand – gently detached his fingers from Sonchai's hair.

Uan enjoyed this attention and obediently allowed himself to be carried away; this uncharacteristic docility evaporated, however, when he saw the gardener coming to put him back on his chain. In a flash of limbs and fur he leapt out of Panda's arms, scrambled to safety in the highest branches of a nearby rambutan tree, and – from there – called down taunts and insults at the hapless fellow.

'I'm glad he gets away sometimes,' Panda said.

'Well, he'd better keep out of my paints,' Sonchai growled, although he secretly shared Panda's feeling.

'Damn – the gardener's getting reinforcements,' Panda lamented, as another boy approached.

'Don't worry; that's just Sompun with the mail.'

Several letters were deposited on the table.

'I hate mail,' said Sonchai, glaring at the envelopes.

'That's strange, most people like it.'

'I can't imagine why. Letters always interrupt you just when you're doing something interesting. And they're always trying to get you to pay something or go somewhere or do something. They're horrible.'

'This one can't be horrible,' Panda said, picking up an envelope with an American stamp on it. 'It's from my cousin Teddy.'

'Who?'

'My American cousin. You met him at the wedding, remember?'

Sonchai looked blank for a moment before he twigged. 'Oh the crazy one,' he said.

'He's not crazy. Whatever made you think he was?'

'I can't remember, just something he said at the wedding.'

'That's hysterical.'

'Why?'

'Because he thought you were crazy too. He thinks all artists are.'

'Silly fellow,' Sonchai muttered; then, not much interested in cousin Teddy, he went back into the studio.

Panda opened the letter, and read:

Dear Panda

Incredible news! Lisa and I are coming to Bangkok. I'm going to do a two-year stint, with a possible one-year extension, at the Institute for Tropical Biology there. I can't begin to tell you how much I'm looking forward to it. There is a slight problem though. Lisa is worried that Leonard, who is nearly three, might not find Fisher Price toys, a Montessori School and English speaking playmates in Bangkok, and she is convinced that he will suffer permanent brain damage without these stimulants to his budding intellect. She is also worried about intestinal parasites lodging themselves in his precious little insides. Plus there are a few other things that might make her dig in her back feet and refuse to come, but I can't think of them at the moment.

So can I ask you a colossal favour? Would you write to Lisa about the intellectual environment and hygienic conditions that would await a pampered, over-protected American toddler in Bangkok? And without actually lying, could you make it all sound as positive as possible?

Hugely looking forward to seeing you and old Uncle William, also Christie (I really liked her, by the way) and that crazy artist husband of yours.

As ever,
Ted

P.S. Better not make your letter too positive or she'll

figure out that I put you up to it. Thanks again, Ted.

Panda laughed as she was folding up the letter but then she became serious. Poor Lisa, she thought, if anyone ever married the wrong man, she did. She really should leave him and find someone else to marry – a man who would want a comfortable house in a leafy suburb and who would like the idea of filling it with lots of children. Then she remembered Lisa's baby – or rather the naughty escapade that had produced that baby – and decided there must be a side to her that she hadn't seen yet. There had to be, not only because of the Japanese lover but because Teddy had been attracted to her in the first place.

Wondering what she could say to ease Lisa's fears about coming, she realised that a little research would be required. She hadn't a clue about playgroups or nursery schools or anything like that, but Christie would surely know – so she would stop by there after work.

Panda always enjoyed going 'home' (as, much to Sonchai's annoyance, she insisted on calling it). She liked being in the old house again, having a chat with Christie, seeing what Alexander was up to and exchanging a few words with her father. Her relationship with him remained as cool and distant as ever, but she had concluded long ago that that wasn't necessarily a bad thing. Some men just weren't cut out to be television-style daddies, that was all there was to it. He had given her a good education, a step-mother she was enormously fond of and a home where she could always go, so she had a good many things to thank him for. There had even been a point a few years ago when she would have said the best thing her father had given her was a baby brother – but recently Alexander had turned into such a little beast that she wasn't at all sure he was an asset to the family. Feeling that a good boarding school might sort him out, she had repeatedly urged her father to send him to England; but Alexander had said he didn't want to go. Christie had taken his side and that had been that.

'I got a letter from Teddy today,' Panda told Christie when they were comfortably settled with cold drinks on the veranda.

We did too,' Christie replied, happily. 'He sounds like he's really excited about coming out here.' Then after hesitating for a moment, she added, 'I suppose we should ask them to stay with us until they find a place to live.'

'I don't see why you need to,' Panda replied, doubtfully. 'This house isn't really big enough; at least, it would be awfully crowded.'

'I think we could manage, though – as long as they

didn't stay too long. Teddy and Lisa could have your old room and we could put their little boy in with Alexander.'

'Poor little boy! Nobody should have to share a room with Alexander.'

'You're always so hard on him,' Christie said, reproachfully.

'No more than he deserves. You're his mother so you don't see what a menace he's turned into.'

Christie was about to protest when a pimply face, followed by a hand, appeared at the door and hurled something small and grey at Panda. It landed in her lap, turned a couple of summersaults and then scurried away on tiny rodent feet.

'You little horror, you'll be sorry for this,' she cried, leaping up from her chair and chasing Alexander into the house. She caught up with him just as he was trying to close the door of his room on her, grabbed him by the ear and administered three sharp slaps on his well-padded backside.

When she came back to the veranda her eyes were sparkling with fun. There was nothing like a tussle with Alexander to make her feel like a child again – a feeling she found wonderfully exhilarating.

'You know, I'm not sure I like being grown-up,' she told Christie.

'Why? What's the matter? Is it your job or is it Sonchai?'

'Oh, the job's fine. I'm doing most of the interviews for the magazine myself now, and Sonchai's been teaching me a lot about photography. Enough, hopefully, to have a fair shot at starting a separate "Beautiful Home" section soon.'

'Great,' Christie exclaimed, then added with less certainty, 'you know, I've been wondering – but it's not really something anybody should ask –'

'You're not just anybody. Ask me whatever you want.'

'Well, how are you and Sonchai getting on these days? Sometimes I get the feeling things aren't quite right with the two of you.'

'Sometimes I get that feeling too. A lot of times, actually,' Panda said, with a semi-successful attempt at a laugh. 'I don't know whether it's because I had ridiculously high expectations about marriage or because Sonchai isn't so easy to live with, not to say absolutely maddening half the time, or…'

'No one can live with an artist,' growled William, coming through the front door, tennis racket in hand. 'It's impossible. I don't know why you didn't figure that out before you married him. He's a nice enough chap though. I quite like him.'

Then, having no wish to hear about his daughter's marital problems, he hurriedly asked, 'Are you two coming along to the club?'

'I don't think so,' replied Christie. 'Panida just got here.'

179

'Suit yourselves then. I won't be home before eight, though.'

'Artists aren't the only people who are hard to live with,' Panda observed as her father climbed into the car and rattled down the road. 'I swear, you deserve a medal.'

'Hardly,' Christie said, with a laugh. 'William's pretty easy to handle once you know him. And in any case, isn't that pretty much what marriage is all about? Learning to live with somebody, I mean.'

'I thought it was supposed to be a bit more than that,' Panda said, ruefully. 'Maybe you read too many novels,' Christie suggested.

'Perhaps,' Panda began, almost agreeing with her for a moment – then changing her mind. 'No, I can't accept that. Marriage has got to be more than just making some kind of accommodation with someone. That would be so drab and boring absolutely no one would ever get married.'

'Not necessarily. And it might have something to do with the fact that so many people get divorced when the truth dawns on them. It's only if they're looking for the same kind of life or if they want to watch their children grow up or –'

'Grow up into animals like Alexander,' exclaimed Panda, half-laughing. 'That can't be fun.'

'It's a lot of fun and you know it. You play with him enough. And in any case, he won't be ten-years-old –

almost eleven- forever. You'll like him again when he's sixteen or seventeen.'

'Try twenty-five, or maybe seventy-five.'

'OK, twenty-five,' Christie agreed. 'The important thing is that the kind of love that comes from a shared life and shared experience is the only kind of love that really means anything. The other kind, the Hollywood romance kind, is just for school girls to dream and giggle about.'

'Haven't you forgotten something?'

'What?' Christie asked, surprised.

'The grand passion; it does happen, you know.'

Panda wondered (as she said this) what role – if any – a grand passion had played in Christie's life. Surely it couldn't have been with William.

But Christie gave away no secrets, responding only with a dismissive laugh. 'I thought we were talking about marriage,' she said. 'If you want to talk about grand passions, fine – but that's a different subject. I agree that they can happen but they burn themselves out; and they don't have anything to do with marriage.'

'I'm not so sure about that,' Panda said thoughtfully. 'After all, some people do marry their grand passion, don't they?'

'In America and Europe they do,' Christie agreed, 'that's why the divorce rate is so high. Then as soon as the person they married begins to seem a little less attractive, they scream "mental cruelty" or something equally vague and ambiguous and go running off to the divorce court. Here in Thailand people are far more sensible. They generally marry for family connections or for money or for a suitable bloodline for the grandchildren – so the divorce rate is a lot lower.'

'That's what my friend, Thanit, says,' replied Panda, thoughtfully.

'Doesn't anybody ever eat around here?' complained Alexander, coming out onto the veranda. 'How can I do my homework if I'm so weak from lack of food that I can't open a book?'

'Don't you ever think of anything except your stomach?' demanded Panda.

'Right now I'm thinking about my legs and how feeble they are,' he replied. 'I can feel them getting weaker and weaker and I don't think they can support me much longer.' With that dire prediction, he collapsed onto the veranda floor and lay there writhing about and screaming: 'Food! Food! I need food!'

'I'd better get him something to eat,' Christie said, looking at her watch. 'I didn't realise how late it was. Actually, why don't we all have a bite to eat? I don't see any point in waiting for William. Heaven knows when he'll be home.'

Christie went off to the kitchen to tell the cook she could put dinner on whenever it was ready; and Panda, seeing her chance to get a little revenge for the mouse incident, leapt down on Alexander, pinned him to the floor and began tickling him mercilessly up and down his sides and on the stomach.

His screams of 'Food! Food!' soon turned to 'Help! Help!'

Unfortunately for Panda, he was getting quite strong – and it wasn't long before he was able to free himself from her grasp and escape to the protection of his mother.

'Panida tried to kill me,' he told her solemnly.

'It's what you deserve after throwing that mouse at her.'

'What would I have deserved if it had been a rat?'

'Never mind that. Right now you deserve to have your hands and face washed so you can have your dinner.'

This was not at all the reply Alexander wanted to hear. He considered what he could do to make his feelings on the subject known, but then decided that any sort of dramatic protest might delay the arrival of the nourishment he so desperately needed. So he settled for chanting 'Women are the devil' as he trotted off towards the bathroom, instead. He had heard his father say that just last week and he liked the sound of it. It put women in their place, he thought. Of course, he needn't really worry about women because he was going to be a mercenary on the Cambodian border when he grew up. And there wouldn't be any female relations to tell him to wash his face and hands there.

'Women are the devil' continued to be his favourite refrain for the next few months. He used it so much, that even his mother began to think that Panda wasn't altogether wrong in calling him a little beast.

It was only with the greatest difficulty that, several months after hearing Teddy's news about coming to Bangkok, Christie managed to clean Alexander up enough to go to the airport with Panda. The plan was for them to meet Lisa and Teddy and their little boy while she – free of the unhelpful presence of her son (he seemed to bring bedlam and chaos wherever he went) – would have a chance to get the house ready for the new arrivals. William, she knew, could be relied upon to incarcerate himself in his study until it was time for his lecture, and do nothing to help or to hinder the proceedings.

I really shouldn't be here, Panda thought to herself as she and Alexander waited for the plane to pull up to the gate.

How silly, of course I should be here, she told herself a minute later. I have to be here. Alexander can't drive (thank God; the streets of Bangkok will become a total disaster area the day he's old enough to get behind a wheel). Daddy is giving a lecture and Christie has lots of other things to do. If I didn't meet them, who would?

Her thoughts were interrupted by a triumphant hoot from Alexander.

'I think I see them,' he cried.

'You can't. The plane hasn't come to a stop yet.'

'You must be looking at the wrong one. See those people over there,' he said, pointing to a wrinkled blond man, a weather beaten woman and a gangly boy. 'I recognize Teddy from when he was here before.'

'Fathead. That man is positively ancient.'

'But you said Teddy was even older than you and you're almost ancient. We're studying about ancient Egyptian mummies at school and I saw a picture of one that looked just like you.'

'And I saw a gorilla at the London zoo that made me think of you – except that he was smarter and better looking. There's the right plane, over there; the one that's just opening its doors.'

A few minutes later the passengers started filing down the steps and she caught sight of Teddy's blond head in the crowd. Barely suppressing a cry of excitement, she waved until he saw her and waved back.

'Daddy's car should be in an antique shop,' Panda explained once they had miraculously squeezed themselves and all their luggage into it, and were sputtering out of the airport. 'How was the trip? I hope you're not too exhausted.'

'I hate these long flights,' Lisa said, 'but Leonard held up very well. And we stopped in Hong Kong for three days so we're over the worst of the jet lag now.'

'Are you more or less reconciled to the idea of living here now?' Panda asked her. 'Not dreading it too much?'

'Ted's thrilled about it,' Lisa replied, 'and as long as Leonard can handle the adjustment, I don't mind. Your letter made a big difference. I felt much better about everything after I got it. And of course the really lovely one from Christie, inviting us to stay with them until we find a place, was wonderful too. It is so incredibly nice of her – your father, too – to do that. I just hope we won't be too much trouble for them.'

Panda made a point of talking to Lisa instead of Teddy on the way home, and it soon became clear that Lisa's favourite subject was Leonard. By the time they turned off Sukumwit Road into the lane leading to the house, she felt she knew every detail of the little fellow's life history.

Teddy was unusually silent, contenting himself with reabsorbing the passing sights and smells of Thailand while Alexander, in a rare display of helpfulness, occupied himself with pointing out water buffalo and other things that he thought might interest Leonard.

There was nothing disappointing in Christie's hospitality. She liked Teddy, was curious about Lisa and had a natural way with children, so there was nothing artificial in her welcome. She soon had them settled them with cold drinks on the veranda. William, eager for a restorative after his lecture and glad to see his nephew again, soon joined them. And a reluctant Sonchai – who still felt that families, whether his or Panda's, were best avoided – managed to put in an appearance half way through dinner.

'I hope you'll find you like Thai food,' Christie said, as she passed a hot and sour salad followed by what looked to Lisa like a spicy curry around to everyone except Leonard. 'But I had the cook make some fried chicken for him and possibly for you as well.'

'I'll just try a little of the curry with a lot of rice,' Lisa said, remembering the Indonesian food she had struggled to keep down when she was pregnant.

'Don't worry, there's plenty of chicken,' returned Christie, encouragingly. 'And just a fruit salad for dessert.'

Lisa's not at all like Panda's description of her, Christie thought. She had expected her to be very thin and ballerina-like, not softly rounded and maternal. Had the nine months of eating for two before Leonard's arrival made her give up on eating like a dancer, she wondered? In any case she suspected there was a lot more to Lisa than Panda had led her to believe.

With an effort Christie turned her attention back to the conversation that was going on around her. William had launched into a discussion of one of Bangkok's favourite topics: the mysterious disappearance of Jim Thompson a few years earlier.

'He's the American who revived the Thai silk industry,' Christie explained for Lisa's benefit.

William scowled at her. He didn't like being interrupted.

'I met a very interesting woman at lunch today,' he continued. 'She was a close friend of Thompson's and was with him in the Cameron Highlands the weekend he vanished. She's convinced he fell into an animal trap; says there were lots of them around, put there by the tribal people. I asked her if she had any time for the theory that he was eaten by a tiger, either in or out of one of those traps – but we agreed that tigers were too clever to fall into them very often. What do you think?' he asked, turning to his nephew.

Teddy had only been half-listening (barely that, actually). Instead he had been wondering why Panda looked so different now, much taller and thinner than when he had last seen her. No, he told himself, she couldn't be taller. It must be that she was just thinner – or maybe it was that she was holding herself taller. That could be it. In any case there was an exotic quality about her now, combined with a new sophistication which the university student he remembered from Nantucket hadn't had. It was intriguing... oh, hell – his uncle was asking him something.

'What was the question?' Teddy said. 'I'm afraid I didn't quite get it. My mind was on the food and how good it was.'

'I was asking what you think about it,' his uncle repeated testily. 'You're a naturalist of sorts, aren't you? What's your opinion? Are there enough tigers left in the Cameron Highlands to give any credence to the theory that Thompson was eaten by one?'

'It would explain why his body was never found,' interjected Panda, 'so I think it was highly likely.'

'I really don't know anything about it,' declared Teddy, restraining himself from adding that he also didn't care. 'But I think that if someone were eaten by a wild animal there'd be a few fragments of bone and clothes lying around. I'm no expert on tigers but I'd be surprised if any of them had been taught to clean their plate before they left the table.'

'I don't agree at all,' put in Sonchai, who had joined them by this time but had effectively tuned out everything the lunatic cousin had said and was disputing Panda's tiger theory.

'Oh, does Thailand have finishing schools for well-bred young tigresses?' asked Teddy, who didn't take to Sonchai with any more enthusiasm now than he had at the wedding. 'What a good idea.'

What in the world made Panida so fond of this nut case, Sonchai wondered irritably, before going on with the subject that interested him.

'Anyone who lived in Thailand as long as Jim Thompson did would surely know enough not to go roaming around the jungle by himself,' he said. 'Not to mention the fact that he had been to the Cameron Highlands often enough to know better. He must have been kidnapped, either by the CIA or the KGB. It's the only explanation that fits, and that should put an end to all these wild theories.'

Lisa, not remotely interested in this Jim something-or-other, was trying to reconcile the dreadful things Ted had said about Panda's marriage – namely that it had been a terrible mistake and that her husband was some kind of lunatic – with the fact that Sonchai seemed like a really intelligent man, totally sane and very attractive. And when that lock of jet black hair fell down over his forehead, as it seemed to do every five minutes, it made her want to reach over and smooth it back for him. And she couldn't help thinking that, far from making a mistake, Panda had done very well for herself.

'Some people think he had a deliberate arrangement with the CIA to spirit him away and give him a new identity,' Christie said.

'Why would they do that?' asked Alexander.

'To keep the KGB from getting him,' William explained. 'He might have been a counter-spy.'

'Or a double agent,' suggested Sonchai.

Although Panda shared the widespread interest in Jim Thompson's disappearance, Teddy and Lisa seemed more engrossing at the moment. Lisa, she thought, actually looked much prettier now that she wasn't so desperately thin. She looked happier, too. Panda wondered whether that was because she finally had the child she had wanted so badly or whether it signalled an improvement in her relationship with Teddy. Had he actually stopped playing around with other women and turned into the home-and-slippers husband Lisa really should have married? That didn't seem too likely somehow. And in any case, was that what she really wanted? What had happened to Lisa the dancer anyway? Wasn't that the Lisa Teddy had married? Where and why had she disappeared? And was it altogether surprising that, when he thought he had married a free spirit, he strained at the leash when he found himself married to a suburban yummy mummy?

Well, she couldn't worry about other people's marriages, she told herself; her own was enough to be concerned about. It amazed her that Sonchai was actually here this evening. He hated family things so much. She found herself wondering just how she actually felt about Sonchai.

Did she really love him? Silly question – of course she did. Living with him would have driven her mad by now if she didn't. She suspected Teddy wasn't easy to live with either, possibly even worse than Sonchai. At least, as far as she knew, Sonchai didn't fool around with other women – not yet, anyway, although it was probably just a matter of time until he did. That was what you had to put up with if you married a Thai man. But then perhaps it was the same with men everywhere; they were all bastards when you came down to it.

Alexander brought her attention back to the subject of Jim Thompson.

'I think a tiger ate him,' he was saying. He illustrated his point by making clawing motions with his hands, biting motions with his teeth and roaring sounds that were as much like those of a big cat as he could manage. Unfortunately he turned and roared directly at Leonard, who was sitting next to him.

Leonard burst into tears and threw himself into his mother's lap. 'I don't want to be eaten by the tiger,' he sobbed. 'I want to go home.'

'I'd better put him to bed,' Lisa said, scooping him up and darting a furious glance at Alexander.

At the door of the room he was expected to share with Alexander, he became hysterical. Screams of 'I don't want to sleep with the tiger, I want to go home' reverberated through the house until the sound of a closing door indicated that Lisa had put him to bed in her room to soothe him.

Christie and Panda rained reproaches down on Alexander while William, Teddy and Sonchai – in silent accord – escaped to the peaceful atmosphere of the veranda for a brandy and coffee.

It was a relief for everyone except Teddy when the new arrivals were established in a house of their own on the eastern edge of the city. But he had enjoyed revisiting the scenes of his childhood: seeing the maid take rice and flowers to the same spirit house that had intrigued him so long ago, watching the descendants of the same lizards that had originally captured his imagination climbing on the veranda rail and chatting with Panda when she dropped by to talk to Christie or to fight with Alexander.

The more he saw of her, the more the different facets of her personality began to intrigue him. When she was with her little brother she was the child he remembered: playful and quick to anger, but equally ready to laugh or to tease. She didn't seem to have changed much in regard to her father either. She was cool and a bit distant with him: always polite, never intimate, giving nothing away. And he was more or less the same with her – if you could substitute gruffness for politeness. But it seemed that it was Christie who drew out the real Panda: someone who was warm and friendly, open and casual in a way that he wished she would be with him. After all, hadn't he practically been a big brother to her, if you didn't count Nantucket? He wondered what she was like with Sonchai. Pretty damned passionate, he expected, but then quickly reined in his imagination. He wasn't going to let himself think about that. Maybe it was actually a good thing that she treated him the way she did, always joking, never taking him seriously, keeping him a little bit at a distance. He hadn't actually seen her with Sonchai since the night they arrived; and, as she hardly ever mentioned him, it was all too easy to let the fact that she was married slip his mind.

Fortunately his work at the Institute was becoming very absorbing. And the good thing about lizards, one of the many good things, was that he never had to worry about what they were thinking or feeling. The larger ones would be focused on having you for lunch if they got the chance, and that was that. The smaller ones would be thinking about finding lunch elsewhere. In the unlikely event that they suffered from stress or rejection, they kept it to themselves. They were all so wonderfully simple – not like Panda. He wondered if anyone could really be as complicated as she was, or whether he was just imagining all those different aspects to her character. Probably the latter, he told himself. Lisa often told him he was letting his imagination run away with him. Lizards were damn lucky, he thought, they had no imagination at all. Maybe in his next incarnation, if he had one, he could come back as a lizard.

He gave a vigorous shake of his head, in an effort to rid himself of this thought. What the fuck had gotten into him, he wondered? He had only been back in Thailand three and a half weeks and he was beginning to think about things like reincarnation. It must be Panda's influence – although after all those years in England he guessed she didn't go in much for that stuff anymore. In any case, he wouldn't be seeing so much of Panda now that he and Lisa were settled in their own house. And that might not be altogether a bad thing.

Lisa was also glad when they were in their own house but she quickly found that life was a great deal harder in this unfamiliar and often baffling country without Christie's continual help. And she missed seeing as much of Panda, too. She had shown her around Bangkok whenever she had had a little free time, and been someone to laugh and have fun with.

It was so silly, Lisa reflected, to have thought she didn't like Panda, to have even been a little jealous of her. Maybe there had been some reason to feel that way in Nantucket but that certainly wasn't true anymore – not now that

Panda had such an attractive husband.

Sonchai was very kind too. He had been so welcoming that afternoon when, at the end of a shopping trip to Sam Peng Lane with Christie, they had dropped in on him. She'd had Leonard with her of course, and while she'd loved the narrow crowded street with its array of gold shops and cloth merchants, he had seen nothing nice about it and had soon become hot, tired and difficult. That was when Christie, who seemed to have a solution for everything, had suggested that – since they weren't far from Panda and Sonchai's place – they could go by and let Leonard play with the gibbon.

Panda was at work when they got there but Sonchai, who had been in his studio painting at the time, had stopped what he was doing, found the gibbon and offered them tea in the garden. Then he had taken them into his studio to see some of his recent work and Lisa had been astonished at the emotional power that emanated from the canvases. She couldn't help feeling a little sorry for Panda, though. She wouldn't want to be married to a man who spent so much time painting naked women. One good thing about lizards – the only good thing she could think of – was that they didn't take off their scales and lie around looking seductive, the way Sonchai's models did.

Panda, however, wasn't concerned about the nude models. She knew what Sonchai was like when he was painting. He was utterly absorbed in his creation, and the only function of the model was to make that creation possible. In any case, she reasoned, Bangkok was so full of tempting opportunities for straying husbands that a few models with no clothes on would hardly make any difference.

Panda had tried not to let herself think too much about the fact that most Thai men – the ones who had enough money anyway – went to massage parlours, where there was a good deal more on offer than just a massage. She more or less accepted the fact that going to such places with their friends and colleagues was an evitable part of male social life. She knew that a few wives rebelled and threw fits of jealousy over it, sometimes with disastrous consequences, but most of them came to terms with it in the end. She sometimes wondered how she would react if, or when, she was faced with the same situation – but then pushed the thought out of her mind. There was a chance, wasn't there, that Sonchai was too individualistic to be pushed into that sort of thing for social reasons, and too sensitive to seek it on his own account?

Yet Panda was forced to think about it one afternoon when she came home from work and found Suchida, the youngest of the daughters-in-law on the compound, sitting on a stone bench under a large bougainvillea tree. She had a book in her hand but clearly wasn't reading it; she looked like she had been crying.

When they had first moved in, Sonchai had been adamant that he didn't want to get involved with the landlord's family. Dealing with his own relations was hard enough, he claimed. He didn't need anyone else's meddling in his life. And as Panda was equally averse to the idea of interfering neighbours, she readily agreed that keeping their distance was a good idea.

However, when Suchida had approached her saying that she wanted to practice her English, Panda had found that she couldn't be quite as detached as Sonchai would have liked. Suchida had not only read English literature at Chulalongkorn University, but she had actually been one of her father's students – so she didn't feel she could just dismiss her out of hand.

It didn't take long for Panda to realise that Suchida wanted more than just someone to practice English with. She wanted a friend and confidante outside of her normally expected network of fellow students – someone who would be a link with the world she had experienced all too briefly when, after finishing at Chulalongkorn, her parents had sent her to spend a year in England. Her cousin had already been there, studying at a language school near Cambridge, and the family had thought it would be nice if the two girls had each other for company. It had been more than nice, it had been heaven; at least – until her parents had found out about the blond-haired, blue-eyed boy she was seeing, and had made her come home immediately. Then, as a further precaution against an unsuitable son-in-law and the arrival of an unwelcome grandchild, they had quickly chosen a husband for her.

'It wasn't really an arranged marriage,' Suchida had told Panda. 'Our families introduced us, but that was all. We found we had so many things in common and so much to talk about that... well, we fell in love.'

'And,' she'd added with a smile that was both shy and wistful, 'as you can see, he is very good looking.'

Yet Panda noticed that, as time went on, Suchida's smiles became fewer; then came the afternoon when even her careful make up didn't succeed in concealing the unhappiness beneath it.

Suchida made a valiant effort to appear cheerful when she saw Panda coming into the garden. She put down the book she was reading and quickly started telling her about a new place she had found to buy silk. Then, when she had exhausted that topic, she told her about the little maid who was pregnant. But finally the thing that was really bothering her came out amidst a flood of tears. It was the new ruby ring her husband had given her the previous evening.

'But that's wonderful,' exclaimed Panda, mystified by Suchida's reaction. 'It seems like he's always giving you jewellery lately.'

'No, no, it doesn't – he isn't,' Suchida protested.

'But how about those beautiful pearl and ruby earrings? Didn't he give you those just a few months ago? And then there was the Buddha on a gold chain for your birthday – don't forget that.'

'I suppose. Yes, he did,' Suchida acknowledged sadly.

'What do you mean, you suppose? You know he did. What's the matter? I thought you loved gorgeous jewellery.'

'Oh, I do,' sobbed Suchida, completely breaking down and telling Panda the whole story. 'I did not know it at the time but he started giving me jewellery when he started going to massage parlours. He told me it didn't mean anything – being with those bad girls there, I mean. He said if he didn't go his friends would laugh and say he was afraid of his wife. He promised me he loved me but he had to go those places. He said all men go. If he does not go, he will not have friends. But when he is out too, very late, I think about him there with another woman and I go crazy. I love him so much. It hurts me like someone is cutting me with a knife. Sometimes I think I cannot stand it.'

Panda was speechless, not knowing what she could possibly say that would be comforting, so she just reached over and gently smoothed her friend's hair.

If Sonchai is doing the same thing, she mused – for the

first time letting herself think that he very likely was – why aren't I as torn up about it as she is?

Suchida seemed to read her thoughts. 'Perhaps Sonchai is different, not like other Thai men,' she said. 'Perhaps he does not do bad things.'

'Perhaps not,' Panda agreed. 'At least, not yet.'

Later that evening Panda mentioned Suchida's unhappiness to Sonchai.

'Who is she?' Sonchai asked.

'You know, Ahrtit's wife.'

'For God's sake! Don't get involved in their family squabbles,' Sonchai exclaimed. 'Between my family and yours I'm drowning in families already.'

'I can't imagine why. You hardly ever see either of them.'

'Hardly ever is too often.'

'Anyway, I'm not involved. Suchida was telling me what was bothering her and I listened, that's all. She is upset because Ahrtit has started going to massage parlours.'

Sonchai, who had no interest in Arthit's sex life – or any other part of his life – paid no attention. 'What happened to today's *Bangkok Post*?' he fumed. 'Have you seen it anywhere? I've got to keep up with what the competition is doing.'

'It's on the desk. Suchida really loves him, you know.'

'That's nice,' he replied absently. Then opening the paper, he exclaimed, 'Good God, they've got a picture of Khun Sa's camp on the front page. How do you suppose they managed that?'

'Managed what?' asked Panda, whose mind was still on what Suchida had told her.

'Getting into that place,' Sonchai said impatiently. 'It's got be the very epicentre of the drug trade, for God's sake. The whole thing beggars belief.'

'You wouldn't ever do that, would you?' persisted Panda. The more she thought about straying husbands the more likely it seemed that Sonchai was, or would soon be, one of them. But then, hadn't she known all along that that was the price she would have to pay for marrying a Thai?

'Of course I would, I'd go like a shot,' returned Sonchai, wondering how Panda could be oblivious to the fact that every photojournalist in Bangkok would kill for a chance to get a picture of Khun Sa.

Panda, outraged at his unashamed reaction, could only stammer, 'But I thought –'

'It's the excitement of the thing,' Sonchai went on to say, still not realizing that they were talking at cross-purposes. 'You know that I can't stand routine. It drives me crazy when things go on the same way day after day. I'm not going to put my life into a straightjacket for God's sake, so don't try to nag me into doing it.'

Panda, convinced that they were still talking about massage parlours – and that being married to her was the straightjacket in question – seized a bronze ashtray that was on the coffee table and hurled it across the room at him. 'Well, you can stop worrying about straightjackets right now,' she cried, 'because from this moment you're free and so am I.'

Sonchai staggered backwards. The meaning of her words dawned on him just as the heavy ashtray landed full force on his chest. 'Have you gone crazy?' he asked, in astonishment. 'What have I done?'

'You bastard, how can you possibly ask?'

'I can ask because a flying missile just about wiped me out. What the hell has got into you anyway?'

'Oh, nothing much, it's just that I'm ever so slightly annoyed to learn that my husband has to go to brothels in order to have a little sexual excitement in his life, that's all.'

Sonchai looked at her as if she had just flown in from Mars. 'Brothels?' he demanded. 'What the fuck do brothels have to do with Khun Sa?'

'I don't know and I don't care. Nothing, I suppose. But you just said you –'

'I certainly didn't say I went to brothels because I don't. They're slave markets. Whatever gave you the idea that I did?'

'Massage parlours then. The services are the same, aren't they?'

'I don't go to those, either – at least, not for years. And never very much.'

'But you just told me you would. You said you'd go like a shot because just having sex with me would make you feel like your life was in a straightjacket.'

'I said no such thing,' retorted Sonchai, looking completely baffled. Then he burst out laughing. 'I was talking about going up to Khun Sa's camp, you idiot. I'd go there like a shot if I got the chance and so would every other newspaper guy I know. To hell with the danger! I certainly didn't mean – life with you, a straightjacket? God, no! With your moods it's more like a rollercoaster – but that's one of the great things about it.'

'My moods?' argued Panda. 'How about your moods? You're the one who has moods.'

'Maybe I do. And you know what I'm in the mood for now?' Sonchai said, putting his hand up under Panda's skirt and pulling her toward him.

'Wait a minute,' she protested, pushing him away. 'I want to know about the massage parlours first.'

'I told you, I don't go to them.'

'Yes, but can I believe you?'

'Of course you can. What do I want with some bought

and paid for sex? It's boring,' he declared, kissing her and undoing the zip at the back of her dress.

Then it got stuck.

'Damn this thing – it's worse than a suit of armour.'

'Good.'

'Don't tell me you're still angry about the brothels I don't go to.'

'It's not that,' she said, dismissing his protest with a laugh. 'But I can't take my dress off here. What will the maid think?'

'She's nowhere in sight.'

'She might come in.'

'We'll go in here then,' he said, pulling her into the bedroom, breaking the recalcitrant zip and making fervent love to her. It was over before she really got started – but, fairly certain that another round would follow, she wasn't disappointed. She just let herself drift off into a light doze until, feeling his kisses progressing farther and farther up her inner thighs, she gave herself up to the slow and sensuous pleasure of a second go. And the good use he made of the lessons he had received from the professionals when he was a teenager convinced Panda that there was something to be said for being married to a Thai man after all.

CHAPTER 9
BANGKOK, 1976

'That was Christie on the phone,' Panda told Sonchai. 'She's planning a birthday party for Daddy.'

'I'll be working,' he returned crisply.

'But I haven't told you when it is yet.'

'Never mind. Whenever it is, I'll be working.'

'But this is going to be just your sort of party,' protested Panda. 'Lots of booze. And it's going to be at Tom Fennel's place upriver. Christie says he has a great little Thai -style house right on the water with nothing but jungle behind it.'

'That's not possible anywhere near Bangkok,' Sonchai growled.

'It's not near Bangkok. It's about an hour and a half upriver by long-tailed boat.'

'And even longer if the motor breaks down,' Sonchai added, on her behalf.

'Don't be such a grouchy old pessimist,' Panda cajoled, going over and perching on the arm of his chair. 'I admit Christie's "jungle" is probably just a handful of trees – but the boat isn't going to break down. At least, that's not very likely. And what is certain is that any party for Daddy is going to be a very wet one. I promise you the whisky is going to flow like Niagara.'

Sonchai realised that he had overlooked this aspect of the situation. Not only would there be plenty of booze but William always drank good Scotch whisky – not the cheap Mekong stuff that was all that idiots who worked on *Bangkok World* could afford. Maybe he'd better go after all, he decided.

When the day arrived, William, Christie and most of the guests – the ones who lived in the foreign enclave around Sukumwit Road – gathered on Oriental Landing to board the three long-tailed boats that had been hired to take them upriver. A few of the people invited, including Panda and Sonchai, lived in the pleasant but less fashionable area not far from Sanam Luang; they gathered at Elephant Landing and waited to be picked up there.

'Happy birthday, Daddy!' Panda called as the boat drew up to the landing. A moment later she spied Alexander and hurled a hairy rambutan fruit at him but missed. Then, grabbing Sonchai by the hand, she climbed on board, making her way over and around numerous baskets of provisions (for what promised to be a truly sumptuous picnic) to find a seat next to Christie.

Despite the tropical sun, it was blissfully cool on the river, and Panda gave herself over to enjoying the passing scene. When she was in Bangkok, it seemed as though the old Thailand – the Thailand she had known as she was growing up – was rapidly fading into oblivion. Yet here on the river those old ways, the truly Thai ways, seemed to be flourishing; and she sat, watching as traditional house-boats chugged along with the family laundry billowing out the back; hapless children being dangled over the side to relieve themselves in the murky water.

Three-sided houses along the banks – their fourth wall open to the river like a proscenium stage – gave Panda ample opportunity to view the happenings inside. She exchanged stares with wrinkled grannies whose mouths were stained blood red from chewing betel; watched younger women busy washing their clothes and their dishes in the mud brown water at the river's edge; smiled at the sight of naked children splashing in their watery play-ground; and gazed at the men bending strips of bamboo into fish traps, mending nets and working on their boats.

Panda revelled in the timelessness of the scene, enhanced as it was by the luxuriant palm trees along the riverbank, the vines and lianas growing just behind the houses and the lush vegetation that gave the illusion of jungle, concealing the neatly spread out rice fields just beyond the deceptive curtain of green.

Eventually the three boats arrived at their destination, a three-sided house much like the others they had passed on the way. An arthritic caretaker, followed by a woman with more wrinkles than teeth, came out to greet them. Everyone pitched in to help carry the vast quantities of food and drink up to a wide veranda at the front of the house; and, before long, everyone was relaxing with icy drinks and chilled fruit.

Teddy glanced over in Panda's direction just in time to see her slip off the all-enveloping man's shirt she was wearing and pull off her jeans. Good God! What the fuck is she doing?, he thought as – with feelings that were anything but cousinly – he watched her emerge in a handkerchief sized blue top and a skimpy blue shorts.

Not wanting to make an idiot of himself by staring at her, he hastily turned away and started talking to two anthropologists; they were friends of Christie's he guessed, who were standing nearby. He told himself that nobody should have to watch Panda take off her clothes unless there was a warm bed or a cold shower nearby.

It was a relief when three other women, younger and prettier than the anthropologists, clustered around him and started telling him how great it would be if he joined their little theatre group. They were about to cast a Noel Coward play, they said, which would be put on in April. Teddy, his mind still on Panda, heard himself making a number of promises he had no intention of keeping.

She broke into his field of vision a few minutes later

taking Sonchai a glass of something that looked like a whisky and soda. Teddy noticed with exasperation that the stupid bastard didn't look very happy. What a dumb arse he must be, thought Teddy, who found it hard to imagine any red-blooded man being anything but over the moon, faced with a half-naked (no – ninety-five percent naked) Panda bringing him a drink. And why the fuck did she have to drape herself over the veranda rail in that sensuous way, just to talk to her husband? Especially when the fathead didn't deserve her?

His still eyes on Panda, he would have allowed his thoughts to ramble on in this vein if he hadn't felt small fingers tugging at his trousers. Glancing down, he saw to his annoyance that Leonard was trying to get his attention.

'Daddy, Daddy,' he was saying.

Teddy still had trouble realizing that word was meant for him. 'What do you want?' he asked, making an effort not to show his irritation.

'I want to show you something.'

'What?'

'Over here,' urged Leonard, taking his hand.

'OK,' Teddy agreed, and reluctantly allowed Leonard to lead him over to the veranda rail.

'See,' the little boy said proudly. 'A lizard.'

'Oh, that's just a gecko,' Teddy replied testily. 'They're everywhere.'

Leonard's face fell with disappointment. He had so wanted to show Daddy something wonderful. Then maybe Daddy would like him.

He had actually done his father the rather dubious favour of bringing him over to Panda and Sonchai – but he got no thanks for it.

'You know, Leonard's really cute,' Panda said, looking him up and down.

'Do you think so?' Teddy asked, surprised.

'Don't you?'

'I guess so.'

'He looks more like he's Panda's kid than yours,' put in Alexander, who was supposedly passing around a platter of spring rolls but eating most of them himself.

Leonard gave him a baleful look. He wanted to look like his daddy.

'It's quite startling to see you being so helpful,' Panda told Alexander. 'Have you had a brain transplant or some-thing?'

Alexander stuck his tongue out at her.

'He doesn't really look like Panda,' said Sonchai, after examining the child's face for a moment. 'It's just the slightly western cast to a basically Asian face that's kind of similar.'

'That's what I mean. He looks like Panda,' contended Alexander; and, popping another spring roll in his mouth, he trotted off to pass the few remaining ones around.

'There you are,' Lisa cried, rushing over to Leonard. 'I've been looking for you everywhere.'

'I was with Daddy,' he announced proudly.

'Thanks for watching him,' Lisa said gratefully. 'I was helping Christie sort out the food.' Then turning back to Leonard, she asked, 'Would you like a banana, darling, or would you rather have a sandwich or maybe a carrot?'

'I want a candy bar,' he replied.

A prolonged discussion of the merits of these alternatives ensued and – although Sonchai didn't actually listen to it – he became increasingly intrigued by the changing expressions on Lisa's face: overwhelming tenderness and love alternating with flickering shadows of impatience and at times even exasperation.

It was the interplay of these latter emotions, the ones that were never portrayed in the faces of traditional Madonnas, that interested him. They brought to life the complexities of mother love, raising it above the mundane, the instinctive and the sentimental. It seemed to Sonchai that there was a whole world of light and love and human failing in Lisa's face – a world he suddenly felt compelled to capture and set down on canvas.

Neither Panda nor Teddy, their attention totally focused on each other, paid the slightest attention to the passing expressions on Lisa's face.

'Is the Tropical Biology Institute turning out to be more or less what you hoped?' Panda asked.

Sonchai, who was not remotely interested in hearing the answer, drifted off.

'More, definitely; the herpetology section is pretty damn exciting actually,' Teddy replied. 'They're expanding the lizard section, as opposed to snakes and frogs and turtles and the like, and I'm getting a chance to work with ones that have never been studied in any detail. So I'm having a real field day.'

'Lucky you. I wish I could be so enthusiastic about my job.'

'I thought you really liked it.'

'Part of the time I do,' she admitted. 'The interviewing is fun and I like writing the articles but there's a lot of deadly dull stuff along with it. Still, if it doesn't kill me it should be good experience; I hope so, anyway.'

'Well, hang in there. It sounds like it will be worth it in the end.'

'Perhaps. Although when you come down to it, it's not actually going to get me anywhere – at least not here in Bangkok.'

'Why not?'

'Because there are so few English language periodicals here. And my Thai – the reading and writing part – isn't really up to doing much on a Thai one.'

'That's a bitch.'

'Plus it doesn't help that I'm working for the editor from hell. I swear she glories in making my life as miserable as possible. I try to get back at her whenever I can, but there is only so much I can do without getting the sack.'

'Well, just don't go doing something idiotic like packing it in and having a baby instead.'

'You're a fine one to tell me that! You seem to have made a great success of the daddy thing. Leonard obviously adores you.'

'Weird, isn't it? Not that I would put it that strongly. Still he does seem to like me. I can't imagine why.'

'Perhaps he just wants a father – even if it's only you.'

'I never thought of that.'

'That's no surprise. You don't spend a lot of time thinking about him, do you?'

'Not as much time as I spend thinking about you.'

'Well, you should. He's your son, isn't he? I'm just a cousin.'

'I don't exactly think about you as a cousin.'

'What then? Just as someone you happen to run into here and there?'

'Now you're being absurd. I think about you as someone I got caught in the rain in Nantucket with.'

'That seems like a dream to me now,' Panda said, with a soft laugh. 'Like something that never really happened.'

'That's funny,' he said with no sign of laughing. 'It's my favourite reality – after monitor lizards, of course.'

'Thanks a lot.'

'Well, at least they don't go around in show-stopping blue shorts, draping themselves seductively over veranda railings like you do. You might think about following their example – because you're driving me crazy.'

'Am I really? How lovely!'

'It's not lovely at all. It's hell.'

'I'm quite enjoying it, actually.'

'There's a word for girls like you,' he warned.

'Perhaps – but you wouldn't want to use it about your cousin, would you?'

'You'd better keep reminding me about this cousin thing,' he said. 'It keeps slipping my mind.'

William, who was doing his rounds as host, overheard this last remark and said, 'You must be more forgetful than I am – and that's saying a lot these days – if you can forget Panda is your cousin.' And seeing that Teddy's glass was empty, he added, 'Here, we'd better do something about that drink of yours. Christie's threatening us with some food pretty soon.'

'I'd better go and help her,' Panda said, and darted away toward the kitchen area at the back of the house.

Christie and Lisa were in the throes of setting out a massive spread of cold ham and chicken, hot and sour oyster salad, sticky sweet crispy noodles, sliced pineapple, hairy rambutans half in their outer shell, as well as small (but delicious) bananas, pink custard apples and an enormous birthday cake. The ancient caretaker and his wife wandered amongst the guests refilling glasses of cool white wine.

By the time the groaning tables of food had been ravished; the candles on the cake had been lit and Alexander had asked why there were only ten of them when Uncle William was fifty-seven-years-old – justice had also been done to the supplies of wine, gin, whisky, and beer. Darkness had fallen over the river, and there was general agreement that the party had been a brilliant success.

'Come on,' Sonchai urged Panda. 'Let's make a move while there's still room in the first boat.'

'But we can't go yet,' she protested.

'Why not? It looks to me like the party's over.'

'You go if you want to. I'm going to stay and help Christie clear up.'

Sonchai hesitated. The day hadn't been as deadly as he had expected and there was still an inch or two of whisky left in some of the bottles. But he had a picture he wanted to work on the next morning and he didn't want to be too hung over.

'You won't mind if I go then?' he said, more as a question than a statement.

'No, go ahead,' she replied, relieved to see him leave while he was still tolerably sober.

When Leonard, whose impatience to be in the first boat rivalled Sonchai's, was told that he wasn't going to be in it, he reacted with the predictable petulance of a tired child.

'But I want to go in that one,' he sobbed over and over again.

'We'll go in another one, darling, and it will be just as nice,' said Lisa, unwilling to go before she had helped Christie pack the remnants of the picnic into hampers.

'Here, hand him down to me,' called Sonchai, who was already in the boat and assumed that Lisa would be jumping down after him.

Instead, one of the other guests obligingly picked Leonard up and passed him down to Sonchai.

This was not what Leonard had in mind. Admittedly he was getting his way about the boat – but he wanted it to be with his mother, not without her. Being picked up by a virtual stranger and forcibly given over to someone he barely knew was not what he had been thinking of. He screamed and shrieked and kicked as if he were being stabbed by a dozen knives.

The idea of taking sole charge of Leonard – even for

five minutes – never occurred to Sonchai, who would have been appalled at the idea. 'Come on, jump in,' he shouted to Lisa over the colossal racket Leonard was making. 'I'll give you a hand.'

Lisa – faced with the choice of leaving Christie and Panda to do the clearing up without any help from her or abandoning Leonard to the care of heaven only knew who – did the only thing possible. With a flying leap, she managed to get into the boat just as it was pulling away from the dock.

'Ted,' she called as soon as Sonchai had helped her right herself. 'Tell Christie –'

Unfortunately the sound of the motor, with the help of some additional sounds from Leonard, drowned out what he was supposed to tell Christie. Teddy contented himself with giving her a wave and turning his attention back to the other people still on the veranda.

Christie, William, Panda, Alexander and Teddy, along with a few friends, had been left to pack up the plates and dishes and to finish off the wine and whisky (although Alexander's contribution to the latter part of these tasks had to be carried out well away from his mother's eagle eye).

Eventually the remaining guests were bundled off in the second boat and only the family, along with the now empty picnic baskets and bottles, was left to return in the third one.

'Let's stay here all night,' suggested Alexander, who had begun to notice that his head was spinning around in a rather unsettling way, and that for once he wouldn't mind a little nap.

'There aren't any beds or mosquito nets,' Christie pointed out.

'I don't care. I'll sleep on a mat like they do,' Alexander declared, waving his hand in the direction of the caretaker and his wife.

'I'd like a comfortable bed, thank you,' put in Panda.

'Do you think Lisa will be all right?' Teddy asked Christie, feeling a little guilty about not going with her.

'Of course she will,' Christie assured him. 'The Bates live near you and so do the Firmans. One of them will take her home.'

When everything worth taking back to Bangkok – mostly dishes plus a few bottles that still had a few inches of interesting stuff in them – had been loaded onto the third boat and everyone had jumped in, the boatman pulled the chain to start the motor. It made an encouraging noise for a moment and then everything went quiet. He pulled again – and this time the promising noise lasted an even shorter time before the motor sputtered into silence.

'Damn, it sounds like the blasted thing is out of petrol,'

growled William, casting a baleful look at the boatman. But, as there was a decent amount of whisky left in some of the bottles, he wasn't too bothered. Christie could send the old fool (jerry can in hand) to search for more fuel, he thought, as he settled himself back into the most comfortable chair for a pleasant nightcap. Christie was wonderful. She could always handle everything.

Alexander, thinking that running around might be a good way to stop the unpleasant spinning sensation in his head, tried chasing butterflies for a while – but it didn't work. That whirring sensation just seemed to get worse. Then he got the brilliant idea of looking for Mars in the wonderfully clear night sky. But, as lying down was obviously the best position for doing this, he didn't manage to stay awake long enough to find it.

Christie found a mat in one of the two back rooms and lay down to let the pleasant tiredness from a successful party lull her into a light sleep.

Panda, feeling the effects of more fresh air and white wine than she was used to, was about to trip over her unconscious brother when Teddy reached out and prevented a disaster.

'Thanks,' she said, steadying herself. 'I was just going to see if there was another mat in the room with Christie.'

'On a beautiful night like this?' he exclaimed. 'What a waste!'

'But it's late.'

'Not really. Anyway, just look at the stars. You can really see them out here away from the city lights. I was going to try and find Mars and show it to Alexander – but then he saw his mother looking daggers at him and went shooting off.'

'Why would he do that?'

'I don't know. Maybe he was afraid of getting a telling off for all the swigs he took from those not-quite-empty whisky bottles. I think he managed to put away quite a bit. Anyway – never mind about that. It's far too beautiful a night for you to share it with Christie.'

He emphasized this point by putting his arm around her and trying to pull her toward him as he continued his search for Mars.

Panda drew away. 'I have to think of Sonchai,' she said simply.

'Why?'

'For the same reason you have to think of Lisa.'

'I can forget Lisa, for a little while anyway.'

'I know you can. But I'm not like you.'

'You forgot about me when you married him,' Teddy said. 'Now it's only fair that you forget him for a change.'

'What do you mean, saying I forgot you?' she demanded, indignantly. 'Of course I forgot you. What was there to remember?'

'You know very well what there was.'

'Yes, I know – one night on a beach with a man who was married to somebody else. Putting that out of my mind was the best thing I could possibly have done.'

'But you haven't forgotten, have you?' he said, making another attempt to pull her toward him.

Panda, in her effort to elude him, banged into a nearby chair, sending a metal ashtray that had been left on it clattering to the floor.

The noise woke William. He sprang up and barked, 'What was that?' Then, seeing Panda and Teddy, he demanded, 'Are you kids fighting again?'

'We're not children any more, Daddy,' Panda reminded him.

'Then stop acting that way. How can I have a little kip when you're making all that racket?'

'Sorry, Daddy,' Panda apologised; then, sharing the same memories, she and Teddy both doubled up with laughter.

'Remember how furious you were when I threw that lizard at you?' he said with a grin.

'I got back at you though, didn't I? I bit your hand 'til it bled.'

'You always were vicious, even then.'

'No I wasn't. I was just acting in self-defence.'

'No apologies then?'

'None whatsoever.'

'Have you no feelings?'

'Not for you anyway.'

'That's a lie.'

'Perhaps – but what if it is? Sometimes a lie is better than the truth.'

'Are you kids determined to keep me awake all night?' William growled from his chair.

'Sorry, Uncle,' Teddy said.

Panda, ignoring the interruption, persisted. 'Can't you get it through your thick head that I love Sonchai and I want to keep on loving him and that you're not helping?'

'Sure you do. But you love him the same way I love Lisa, and that's not enough for you anymore. Nor, as you well know, is it enough for me. You're just trying to pull blinders down over your eyes.'

'Rubbish! You don't know anything about how I love Sonchai. I would never love anybody in the terrible way you love Lisa.'

Stunned, Teddy demanded, 'What's so terrible about it?'

'You just use her.'

'I do what?'

'You use her love to enslave her. She does everything for you and you just rake it all in as though you deserved it. That is, if you notice at all.'

'What the hell do you mean, just raking it all in?' he demanded angrily. 'I'm the one who works ten or twelve hours a day making a living for us while she just sits around the house and plays "Mommy", for God's sake.'

'Oh! It's so noble of you to give your slave a little food and shelter,' she jeered. 'But even the lowliest ones won't be around very long if you don't.'

'And I suppose your love for Sonchai is all very noble and self-sacrificing,' he replied with equal sarcasm.

'I'm not saying it is. But at least I haven't enslaved him; quite the opposite, actually. Come to think of it, I'd do well to take a few lessons in that from you.'

'From me?' he laughed. 'Now that really is a crazy idea. If I had a clue how to enslave anybody I'd start with you.'

'Well you wouldn't succeed. Nobody is going to enslave me.'

'I wish I could say the same.'

'Can't you?' she asked, surprised.

'No. You may not know it but you've got me so that I'm not thinking straight. I can't get you out of my mind. I'm falling desperately in love with you, Panda.'

'That's too bad. Because I'm falling out of love with you.'

'Then you do love me,' he said, finding unintended meaning in her words.

'I love Sonchai,' she declared firmly.

'Maybe, maybe not. But you're not in love with him. That's different.'

'No, it's not. Not with me, anyway.'

'Tell the truth – has sex with him ever been as great as it was on the beach in Nantucket?'

'Yes, lots of times.'

'You're lying again and it won't work. I know you too well.'

'You don't know me at all. We've hardly seen each other since we were children.'

'We wrote to each other all those years and thought about each other.'

'I never thought about you,' she returned hotly.

'You should have your mouth washed out with soap,' he retorted angrily. 'We wrote to each other, we thought about each other and we saw each other whenever we could. Admittedly that wasn't very often, but when it did happen it was vivid and intense.'

'If it was so intense, why did you marry Lisa?'

'You were still a kid. I was too, for that matter – and I thought the way I loved Lisa was the whole show. Now I know better.'

'A pity you didn't twig a little sooner.'

'Well, I might remind you that you didn't "twig" – if you want to put it that way – quite soon enough either. Otherwise you wouldn't have married Sonchai. I really do believe you when you say you love him. I understand that kind of love. I love Lisa that way too. And, God knows, I don't mean to treat her the way you say. Why the hell do you think I didn't get a divorce when Leonard was born? I certainly had grounds. Damn good grounds, most people would say.'

'If I had a gold medal,' she said, pretending to look around for one, 'I'd pin it on you.'

'Sorry. I didn't mean to go on about Lisa's little indiscretion. That's beside the point. What I'm trying to tell you is how much I love you and want you.'

'It's too late.'

'No, it's not. Let's go somewhere after we get back to Bangkok tonight.'

'No.'

'Tomorrow then, meet me tomorrow.'

'No.'

'Then the day after or next week or the week after that. Tell me when.'

'In my next incarnation perhaps, if you're lucky.'

'Is it impossible for you kids to be quiet,' barked William, coming to life for a moment and then dosing off again.

'Listen,' Teddy whispered, pressing Panda as close to him as possible, 'I've got to see you. Let me take you to lunch tomorrow – everything on the up and up, I promise.

It'll just be lunch with your old cousin Ted. You can't say no to that, can you? I'll even pry that hoodlum, Alexander, out of school and bring him along as evidence of my high minded intentions if I have to – although I'd definitely rather not.'

Panda laughed. 'I'd rather not, too.'

'It's settled then. I'll meet you at the Maneeya Lotus Room at one o'clock,' he declared.

Panda was protesting that it wasn't settled at all when a loud spluttering from the boat's engine forced a change of subject. 'That must be the boatman, back with the petrol,' she said. 'I'll go tell Christie.'

Teddy gave Alexander a shake. 'Come on, you rascal, look alive,' he ordered.

There was no reaction.

'If I have to carry you onto that boat I'll tell your mother about all the whisky you've been chugging down.'

This threat was sufficiently dire to penetrate Alexander's consciousness and he managed to stagger to his feet.

Teddy hurried on ahead of him, determined to make it down to the boat landing before either his drunken uncle or his idiot cousin did. He wanted to make sure that neither of them toppled into the river while they were getting into the boat because he'd sure as hell be the one who would have to jump in and haul them out. A raging case of typhoid from that turgid water was the last thing he needed.

Almost as if on cue, Alexander tripped on the rim of the boat, missed his step – and would have fallen in, if it hadn't been for Teddy's iron grip on his arm.

After ascertaining that Christie didn't need much help, Teddy watched in amazement as William, with an agility that was extraordinary for his age and state of sobriety, leapt into the boat.

Panda was the last one to get on board; this suited Teddy very well as he envisaged them sitting together in the back of the boat, well out of Christie's line of vision. But it didn't work out that way. Panda thwarted his plan by going directly to the front and sitting there. He tried to follow her but the boat lurched forward just as he was passing his uncle and he was thrown off balance.

'Watch what you're doing or you'll find yourself in the water,' William exclaimed. 'And I don't relish the prospect of getting you out.'

Teddy was supremely thankful that his uncle had no way of knowing that, just a few minutes before, he had had the same thought – only with their roles reversed. He mumbled something about being more careful and continued on in the direction of the prow. Unfortunately, once he got there he wasn't so sure it had been a good idea. The seats there weren't really seats at all, more like uncomfortable wooden benches built for much smaller people. But he managed, with some difficulty, to cram himself onto the same narrow wooden plank as Panda. The problem was that he couldn't find any place for his right arm; after a moment's indecision he flung it along the back of the seat, almost touching Panda but not quite.

'There're other seats, you know,' she pointed out helpfully.

'I like this one.'

'Suit yourself then,' she said; and, determined to ignore him, she settled back to enjoy the cool river breezes. If she realised they were blowing long wisps of her hair across Teddy's face, she gave no sign of it.

He was acutely conscious of it, though – and it was only the likelihood that Christie's eyes were on them (she was sitting somewhere near the middle of the boat) that made him keep his arm on the back of the seat. Otherwise he would certainly have closed it around Panda. He hadn't been so well chaperoned since he'd been a teenager on his first date, he thought with a silent groan. This trip back to Bangkok is going to be torture. Yet gradually the beauty of the river scene, wrapped in the drowsy stillness of the night, began to work its magic on his mind; as they drifted past trees, houses and temple spires, all silhouetted against the night sky, he forgot about Christie and the others in the boat. He and Panda were alone, racing through a windblown adventure to – he didn't know where. It didn't matter. Only the moment counted.

Somehow he was certain that she too was caught up in the enchantment of the darkened river. He no longer felt a need to touch her. It was enough that they were riding together through the night and the wind and the fantastical world along the riverbanks.

I wish we would never get to Bangkok, Panda thought. I wish Teddy and I could just fly through the darkness forever – or perhaps be washed up on some magical island and never ever leave it. If Christie and Daddy and Alexander were washed up there too, that would be all right. And the boatman could be there. He's such a wise-looking wrinkly old fellow, a bit like an owl. And of course there must be all sorts of strange new species of lizards for Teddy to –

Suddenly the boat bumped up against the wooden pilings of Elephant Landing and the trip was over.

'Teddy darling, you'll help Panda find a taxi, won't you? We'll wait for you here,' Christie said.

'Sure,' he replied, bringing himself back to reality with an effort, 'but don't wait. I'll see her home, make sure she gets there all right.'

Panda, no longer under the spell of their ride down the river, saw immediately that this was a very bad idea. 'No need to do that,' she said. 'I'll be fine.'

William didn't agree.

'Good idea,' he told Teddy approvingly. 'Go with her,

that's much better.'

'You're all treating me like a child,' Panda protested.

'You're my child,' returned William, in a rare display of paternal feeling that made Panda laugh.

'Well, happy birthday, Daddy,' she said. 'Goodnight Christie, it was a great party.'

And passing Alexander, she added, 'Goodnight, beast.'

'I didn't want that ride to end,' Teddy said when they were in the taxi.

'Neither did I.'

He leaned closer to her and started to put his arms around her but she drew away. 'We're back in the real world now,' she said, 'and I'm going home to Sonchai.'

'It's not too late to change your mind about that.'

Shaking her head, she murmured, 'I can't.'

'You'll be quiet then, won't you? Promise me that, at least.'

She gave him a quizzical look.

'Don't wake Sonchai up. Don't have sex with him tonight.'

'Don't worry,' she said softly. 'I wouldn't want to.'

'And you won't forget tomorrow; one o'clock at the Lotus Room.'

'All right. I'll be there,' she said, wondering just what had possessed her to agree to go.

A moment later the taxi pulled up in front of her

garden gate; she hurried inside before she found herself agreeing to anything else.

CHAPTER 10
BANGKOK, 1976

It was actually five minutes to one when Panda and Teddy met, as neither of them had wanted to be late; and they were almost formal with each other in their determination – Panda's, anyway – to behave as 'just cousins'. They talked about their work and about the delights and frustrations of living in Thailand almost as two strangers would have done. All in all, they were so successful in keeping anything personal out of the conversation that Panda had no problem agreeing to meet him again.

They had lunch together twice the following week and three times the week after that – and it was on the last of the these occasions that Sonchai came to the restaurant with four Japanese reporters.

'Don't look so upset,' Teddy said when the five men had had sat down at a table across the room. 'You aren't doing anything you shouldn't. Why would Sonchai mind your having lunch with your cousin?'

Panda had to admit that he had a point – one that was confirmed a few minutes later when Sonchai noticed them and nodded and smiled.

'Go over and say hello,' Teddy urged.

'Should I really?'

'Of course – don't be an idiot.'

'Why don't you do it?'

'Sonchai and I hardly know each other. It wouldn't be natural for me to go leaping up and rushing over to him.'

Panda considered this. 'Yes – but why should I rush and leap?'

'Because you're his wife. Wives are supposed to leap. It's in the marriage contract.'

'Not in mine,' returned Panda hotly.

'Yours is barely legal. You nearly walked out on Sonchai three feet from the alter, remember?'

'Don't remind me.'

Taking another glance over at Sonchai, she could see that he was absorbed in an animated discussion with his companions. 'I don't think there's any need to barge in on their lunch,' she said. 'Why don't we both just say hello on our way out?'

'Suits me.'

They ordered coffee but Teddy, realizing that Panda wasn't enjoying hers, folded up his napkin and said, 'Let's go. I don't know why being in the same restaurant with Sonchai is bothering you so much – but it obviously is.'

'Wouldn't it bother you if Lisa came in?'

'That's different.'

'Why?'

'She has a suspicious nature and – if I'm being honest –

234

I've got to admit she may have something to be suspicious about.'

'Then doesn't Sonchai?'

'No. His wife is being an irreproachable ice goddess.'

Teddy paid the bill and they crossed over to Sonchai's table. He stood up, greeted them cordially and looked like he was about to make introductions; but Teddy cut him off.

'I don't want to interrupt your lunch,' he said. 'And in any case, I have a busy afternoon ahead. I'm afraid I've got to go.'

'So do I,' said Panda, and escaped as quickly as she could.

Everyone looked relieved.

'There, what did I tell you,' Teddy exclaimed, when they were outside. 'He wasn't upset, was he?'

'No, not at all,' she replied, relieved that it had gone so well, though slightly annoyed that Teddy understood her husband better than she did.

'Let's not go back to work right away,' Teddy suggested.

'I've a lot to do and –'

'Fuck it. Say you sprained your ankle or fell into a canal; you've done that before, so you must be pretty good at it by now. Or claim to have been kidnapped by a crazed rickshaw driver. Tell them anything. I feel like going some-where, doing something. Labs are the same everywhere and I want to do something that reassures me I'm really back in Bangkok. After all, this place is a part of you and always will be; so I want it to be part of me, too – more than just a few childhood memories, that is.'

Panda wavered for a moment and then confessed, 'Actually, I was just going to stop by Wat Benjamapohbit on my way back – I want to see where my Thai exam's going to be. Would that do for a Thai experience? Do you want to come with me?'

'Great. Although for the life of me I can't see why you need to take a Thai exam.'

'I told you – I went to the British School when I was small so I never learned to read and write Thai very well. But now, living here as an adult, it's awful being semi-literate. I hate it.'

'OK. I can see that having a few lessons might help – but why bother with take an exam?'

'Why not? Passing it – if I do – will give me a sense of accomplishment. So I might as well have a go.'

'It just seems like doing things the hard way. But if it makes you happy, why not? Come on, let's check out this scene of self-imposed agony.'

Wat Benjamapohbit, known to English speakers as the Marble Temple, was gleaming in the afternoon sun, its tiers of undulating red tile roofs shining in reflected brilliance, when their taxi pulled up in front of it.

'The Lord Buddha is this way,' Panda said; and, showing him into the temple's inner sanctuary, she knelt down in front of an imposing bronze image, pressing her palms together in a wai.

Much to Teddy's surprise, she actually appeared to be praying.

'Hey, do you really believe in all this?' he gasped a few minutes later, when they were crossing a courtyard outside the sanctuary.

'Are you so surprised?'

'Flat out with amazement would be a more accurate way of putting it.'

'Don't you remember when we went to the Erawan Shrine and asked Phra Bhram to bring you back to Thailand?' Panda replied. 'We both believed it then.'

'Not me.'

'Yes, you did. For a while, anyway.'

'Maybe but we were just kids then. That doesn't count.'

'I suppose "maybe" is the way I feel about it all now,' she mused. 'If you stay in Thailand very long it's hard not to be drawn in by it.'

'I think it'd be pretty easy,' Teddy said firmly.

'For you, perhaps,' she acknowledged. 'Anyway let's go find out where my exam's going to be.'

This proved to be no easy task. None of buildings that

dotted the temple compound looked like a particularly likely spot; and, as sleeping through the hottest part of the day was one of the few luxuries allowed to a monk, no one was around to ask.

Eventually an old man who worked in the temple came up and – speaking to Panda in Thai – asked her what she was looking for.

When she told him he said he would not only show them the room where the exam; but, if they liked, he would take them to meet the abbot as well.

Panda hesitated. She didn't want to be rude but she really just wanted to find out where she would have to go in the morning.

'He can help you pass the exam,' the old man added.

Panda translated this for Teddy and added, 'I'm surprised the abbot even knows what's on the exam.'

'He probably doesn't. I bet he just wants some money.'

'How can you say such a thing?' exclaimed Panda, horrified. 'An abbot would never –'

'He's human isn't he?' Teddy pointed out.

'Not in the way you mean; he's an abbot.'

The distinction was lost on Teddy.

Panda turned back to the old man and, as politely as she could, declined his offer about meeting the abbot.

He seemed to think that she was being very foolish and repeated that the abbot could help her pass the exam.

She tried to explain that if she couldn't have the satisfaction of doing it on her own, there was no point in taking the exam at all; but she didn't get her point across very well. Then it occurred to her that if they actually met the abbot it would give Teddy a chance to see what a wise and holy man he really was – so she agreed.

The old man, looking very pleased (probably calculating the size of his tip, Teddy thought), took them over to a set of rickety wooden steps and indicated they should follow him up to a long narrow veranda.

It was Panda's turn to be astonished. This was clearly the monks' living quarters, a place she had never imagined she would be allowed to visit. But since their guide seemed to think it was all right, she climbed up after him.

Following his lead they soon found themselves in a shadowy room that appeared to be a sort of chapel. A large bronze Buddha held pride of place amongst a vast assortment of smaller images of the deity, all of which were illuminated by saffron coloured candles anchored in heavy brass holders. Smoke from long sticks of sandalwood-scented incense swirled around the feet of the central image while a collection of gilded trees lined the edges of the room. The only sound was the ticking of clocks – large clocks, small clocks, finely crafted clocks, simple clocks, all sorts of clocks – there to remind the worshipper of the transience of earthly things. Offerings of fresh fruit and flowers, as well as cone-shaped mountains of steamed rice, gave evidence of the devoted care accorded to these divine beings, whose spirits resided in the representations of themselves housed in the room.

It seemed to Panda that they had stumbled into a strangely compelling otherworld, one where the spiritual power radiating from the sacred images was so strong it was nearly palpable.

Teddy thought the place was just plain weird.

'Wait here,' the old man told them, 'and when the abbot comes you can ask him to help you pass the exam. You can also make a contribution to the temple if you like, but it is not necessary.'

Then, after imparting this advice, he disappeared in the direction of the monks' sleeping quarters.

Panda was glad that Teddy hadn't been able to understand the bit about the contribution. She would be happy to make one, but it would be hell to have to hear him say 'I told you so' afterward.

Hoping it wouldn't be too long before the abbot actually arrived, she made a wai to the main image of the Buddha and sank down on a straw mat to wait.

Teddy, glancing down at his watch and muttering something faintly obscene under his breath, joined her on the floor.

A few minutes later the abbot, looking kind and wrinkled and very, very old, came in through a side door. He was followed by a younger monk and they paid the appropriate respects to the Lord Buddha, chanting something that Teddy supposed must be some kind of prayer; then they sat down facing the visitors.

'Give him your offering,' whispered their guide, who had slipped in at the back of the little chapel.

Panda hastily rummaged in her handbag for an appropriate sum, telling herself what an idiot she had been for not having had it ready sooner. When she found it, she went over to the holy man on her knees, occasionally dropping down on her elbows for balance, in what Teddy later described as 'the crab walk'. Then as soon as she was in front of him, she raised her hands to the tip of her forehead in a wai of deepest respect before placing two crumpled hundred baht notes on the mat in front of him. It was, she knew, forbidden for a monk ever to take anything directly from a woman's hand.

With a slight motion of his hand the abbot indicated that his acolyte should pick them up.

'Now explain who you are and ask him about the exam,' prompted the man who had guided them there.

Panda still couldn't believe the abbot would give her any useful information, but she didn't want to offend the nice old man who had brought them there. So she explained about the exam – said that she was very worried about it, and asked if he could help her.

The abbot listened, nodded, and, after intoning a blessing, took a copper amulet from his robe; placing it on the mat in front of her, he indicated that she should pick it up. There was no need to explain the significance of the gift. She knew that it was intended to help her pass the exam.

Teddy sort of got the idea of what was going on; but, of course, he had no confidence in the power of the charm so he was horrified to see that the abbot was motioning for him to come forward next. Worse yet, he had a ghastly feeling that he was expected to resort to the same preposterous crab walk she had used and would have refused (if, that is, he hadn't been fairly sure that any perceived slight to the holy man would mean the end of his chances of getting anywhere with Panda).

I can't believe I'm really doing this, he thought, as he sat in front of the saffron robed figure and listened to whatever gobbledygook was being chanted.

The abbot then presented him with an amulet similar to the one he had given Panda and indicated with a nod that their private interchange was over. With relief, Teddy reversed his crab-like gait and went back to sit next to Panda.

After a final blessing the abbot and his attendant withdrew.

'You see, I told you he would help you,' their guide said

triumphantly. 'Now you will certainly pass.'

Panda thanked him and the guide, warming to her appreciation, asked, 'Would you like to have your fortune told? One of the monks is very good at seeing into the future.'

'No,' Teddy said promptly when Panda translated this; but he could tell she was agreeing to something. Whatever it was, he didn't like it. 'It's all just hocus pocus and you know it,' he insisted, 'another way of ripping us off.'

'Nobody has asked for any money at all,' she retorted hotly; and, now seriously annoyed, she let the guide lead her down to the far end of the narrow balcony.

It was on the tip of Teddy's tongue to point out that just because the subject of money hadn't come up yet didn't mean that it wasn't going to – but he restrained himself. Faced with the choice of following them or charging off in a huff, the former seemed like the better alternative.

The fortune-telling monk didn't keep them waiting long. Emerging from the dark recesses of the building with a pencil and a scrap of paper in his hand, he immediately set about the business at hand. After quizzing Panda about the day, the time and the place where she had been born and making elaborate calculations on his bit of paper, he said, 'You left home when you were twelve or thirteen.'

Panda nodded. 'Yes, that's true,' she said, remembering that she had been eleven when she had first gone to

England to school and figuring that was close enough.

A rather grumpy Teddy had joined them by this time, so she translated for his benefit.

'You went many places,' he continued, 'going very far, very much alone.'

Again she nodded.

'You married when you were twenty-four.'

That's almost right,' she said encouragingly. 'I was twenty-three.'

'No,' he maintained, holding fast to his original calculation, 'you were twenty-four.'

'He's just guessing,' Teddy said dismissively when Panda related the small mistake.

Not liking the way he had said this, she leapt to the fortune-teller's defence. 'But twenty-four is awfully close,' she protested, 'and he got the bit about leaving home almost right too.'

'He just got a couple of lucky hits,' Teddy declared.

The monk didn't understand much English; he knew enough, though, to semi-guess the gist of their conversation – and an angry expression crossed his face. He checked his calculations again and then repeated, 'Twenty-four.'

Panda suddenly understood and broke into a smile. 'You are right,' she admitted. 'I should never have questioned you. I was thinking in terms of English counting.'

'He's using Thai counting for his calculations,' Panda

explained, turning to Teddy. 'It's the same as Chinese. You're one the first year of your life so I was really twenty-four when I got married.'

The monk showed no interest in her apology. He had known all along that he was right. Instead he continued to study the numbers on the paper and then looked up and gazed thoughtfully at Panda.

'You have troubles now,' he said, 'but in two years you will be happy, at least for a while. You will have two children.'

Panda tried to press him for more information but he was either unwilling or unable to reveal any more. Instead he looked enquiringly at Teddy, who instantly made it clear that he did not want to have his fortune told.

Worried that the monk might take offense at Teddy's brusque manner, Panda hastily thanked him for her fortune and offered a donation for the temple. It was declined, so she simply made a wai and led the way down the shaky staircase to the courtyard below.

'Why were you so adamant about not having your fortune told?' Panda asked, as they made their way toward the temple gate. 'You could see from what he told me that he's really good.'

'Like I said before – he just got lucky, that's all.'

'But that's not all. Telling me the exact age when things happened to me can't be just luck.'

'Well, if it isn't luck, it gives me the creeps. Either way, I don't like it. Come on – let's get out of here.'

He hailed a taxi and told the driver to take them to the Erawan Hotel.

'Why are we going there?' asked Panda, surprised.

'I need a nice normal drink in a nice normal bar after all that mystical superstitious stuff. I can't believe the way you've let yourself be bamboozled by it all.'

'I haven't been bamboozled and there's nothing superstitious about it,' she declared furiously. 'Buddhism is a religion, a very beautiful one, and its traditions and practices are not superstition. And if people, with the sensitivity of a cockroach, can't understand it or relate to it – that's just too bad. Too bad for them, anyway.'

'Jesus, I've been compared to some of the lower species of pond life before but never to a cockroach. I hope you realise this is a first,' he said, laughing (but secretly rather hurt).

'How long have you been in Thailand anyway?' she demanded.

'Long enough to know there is a lot of stuff here that just doesn't make any sense.'

'To you perhaps,' she said scornfully.

'OK, explain a few things then. How about starting with the way our little session with the abbot just now is going to help you pass the exam.'

Her fingers instinctively closed around the amulet. 'You can't possibly expect me to explain something like that in a short taxi ride.'

'This one isn't going to be short. Look at the traffic, it's terrible.'

It was a long trip, and the fact that Panda – still furious at his attitude in the temple and now further incensed by his flippancy – refused to speak to him for the rest of the way made it seem even longer.

After what seemed like ages, the taxi pulled up in front of the Erawan Hotel. But by the time Teddy had paid the driver and managed, with some difficulty, to extract the change from him, Panda was nowhere in sight.

She probably went on into the lobby, he told himself; it'll be cooler in there. But when he went in he didn't see her. After checking the bar and the garden terrace he decided that she must be in the ladies' room, so he gave a passing maid two baht to go in and see. But when she came out she reported that no one was there.

Then, remembering the power Panda had always attributed to the Erawan Shrine, he decided to have a look there. It was just the sort of place she was likely go if she was upset – as she apparently was.

Confident that he would find her there, Teddy strolled out the gate of the hotel and over to the outer perimeter of the shrine. More people than usual were there, crowding the pavement and peering into the sacred precinct while strains of music wafted through the steamy afternoon air. Teddy, glad for his height, peered over the heads of the other viewers and saw that some sort of classical dance was being performed, presumably in honour of the four-headed deity he remembered so vividly from the last day of his childhood sojourn in Bangkok.

Panda would know what it was all about, he thought. She was tall for a woman in Thailand so it didn't take him long to spot her bargaining for a ring of jasmine flowers. She didn't see him at first but after a moment or two she spun around and looked directly at him as if she had somehow felt his eyes on her. Then she pointedly turned her back on him, left the flower seller and went over to an old woman who had wooden elephants in a variety of different sizes spread out on a mat around her.

'Here, let me buy one for you,' Teddy said, when he had made his way over to her.

'No thank you.'

'Come on,' he urged, 'choose one.'

'I already have,' she replied, showing the vendor which one she wanted and starting to discuss the price.

Teddy, uninterested in bargaining over the tiny sum involved, handed the woman the amount she had asked for and tried to give Panda the elephant.

'Keep it yourself,' she said, brushing it aside and picking

up another one.

'What would I do with it?'

'Offer it to Phra Bhram, of course, to thank him for granting you your wish.'

'My wish?' he repeated, confused.

'Yes, don't you remember? You asked him to bring you back to Bangkok and he did.'

Teddy did remember. He also remembered that he had felt like a prize jackass at the time. 'I can't quite see myself doing that,' he said, putting the elephant down.

'You can just sod off then.'

'No, I want to stay here and watch the dancers.'

'Suit yourself,' Panda said. Turning her attention back to the elephants, she made a new choice, argued briefly about the price, and bought it. Then, after buying a packet of candles and incense sticks, she went into the shrine.

Teddy followed her with his eyes as she added her offerings to the mountain of similar ones already piled up at Phra Bhram's feet. Then, when it became clear that she wasn't coming back out any time soon, he turned to go; but the odd thing was, his feet didn't seem to want to carry him away. All he could do was stand there watching Panda as she watched the dancers until the sandalwood scented smoke from the incense, the perfumed air from the jasmine flowers, and the plaintive notes of the bamboo instruments exerted the full force of their hypnotic powers. Then it was as if he were a child again, standing in front of Phra Bhram with Panda, asking the deity to bring him back to Bangkok and really believing, at that moment anyway, that the gilded image could do it.

And Phra Bhram had done it. He was back in Bangkok, wasn't he?

Good God – what was he thinking of, he asked himself. It was the National Science Foundation that had brought him back to Bangkok by offering him a job here. That statue in the middle of the shrine was just a chunk of bronze. It hadn't done anything. Panda may have bamboozled him into going along with some of her superstitious nonsense about it – even half believing it, when he was a kid – but he was a grown man now and a scientist to boot. He was a rational human being. The supernatural wasn't his thing and never would be.

And as he stood there, listening to the strangely disturbing strains of the music played out on the unfamiliar pentatonic scale and watching the grace and beauty of the dancers as they acted out an ancient story (which everyone else in the crowd probably understood), he began to see the fence around the Erawan Shrine as a barrier, firm and impenetrable, between Panda and himself.

'Oh Panda, come back,' he wanted to cry. 'Don't go where I can't follow you.'

Almost as if she had heard him, Panda raised her hands

in a farewell wai to Phra Bhram and made her way through the crowd toward him.

'I'm surprised you're still here,' she said. 'I didn't think this was your sort of place anymore.'

Teddy, not at all sure it had ever been his sort of place, replied, 'But it's your sort of place. That's why I'm here.'

'It's beautiful, isn't it – the dancers and everything?'

He nodded. He had no trouble agreeing with that.

And in silent accord they turned their steps toward the destination they each had in mind: the Erawan Terrace, for a late afternoon gin and tonic.

CHAPTER 11
BANGKOK, 1976

Lisa, seated on a sort of dais in Sonchai's studio, asked, 'Are you sure you really want to paint me; and Leonard, too? I doubt if we can get him to sit still very long.'

'He doesn't have to. I'm not actually going to paint him.'

'Then why –'

'I want him here so you can watch him.'

She was mystified.

'It's the expression on your face – like a Raphael Madonna – that I want to capture. But you have to be looking at Leonard for it to be there.'

Lisa thought he was mad, but didn't want to say so. She didn't understand how he could want to paint her, no matter what kind of expression she had on her face – especially not now when she had gained nearly five pounds and felt so fat. She had never let that happen before. The problem had been the food when they were staying with Christie and William. She had never known quite what was in it, and had been shocked when she had gone into the kitchen one day and seen how much oil the maid was blithely pouring into the pan. After that she had tried to eat less, but the last thing she wanted was to be rude about the food when Christie was being so welcoming and wonderful. She just couldn't do it, even if it meant letting the unthinkable happen – gaining weight.

Of course it wasn't really so unthinkable, she reminded herself. It had happened in Jakarta when she had been living on cookies and sesame sweets and she hadn't been very bothered by it. Of course there had been too many more important things to worry about then. It was different now though. In this city of beautiful women every extra pound made her feel like a heffalump in a forest of gazelles, and that wasn't a nice feeling at all.

She tried to explain some of this to Sonchai, but he only laughed and told her she was talking nonsense.

'A more softly rounded figure would be perfect for you,' he argued. 'It suits the Madonna image. Now if you'll just tip your head to one side – no, the other side – that's right. Bring your chin up a bit but don't take your eyes off Leonard – that's good: perfect. Now try to hold that expression. That's it, just what I wanted.'

He set to work and apart from the noise made by Leonard's model red Ferrari (a recent present from Auntie Panda) as it whizzed across the floor and crashed into the opposite wall, the room was quiet.

Eventually, however, Leonard's enthusiasm for his new toy began to wane. Looking around for something interesting to play with, he remembered the gibbon, and trotted out to the garden in search of him.

Lisa started to call him back but Sonchai cut her off, saying, 'It's OK, I'll just need him for a few minutes today. Let him play anywhere he wants to for a while. And don't worry, the gardener's out there. He'll keep an eye on him.'

Lisa, a bit uncertain about the gardener, started to protest; but then thought the better of it, and relaxed. In any case, Leonard reassured her by popping in from time to time to report on the various antics of the gibbon.

At first Lisa tried to curtail these interruptions, fearing they would disturb Sonchai; but he said, 'Talk to him all you want, just don't move.'

She didn't... and she discovered that it was quite fascinating to watch Sonchai as he worked: mixing the various colours on his palette; screwing his face into an expression of frustration whenever he had trouble getting an effect he wanted on the canvas. Even better were the times when he ran his fingers through his hair and threw back his head in triumph because something – she would have loved to know what – had gone his way.

The time passed more quickly than she would have imagined; before long, the session was over and the maid was bringing them tea in the garden.

'How do you find enough time for your painting when you're working full time on *Bangkok World*?' Lisa asked.

'For a start, I don't see much of my wife.'

'That must be hard.'

'Yes, but we manage. We each have our own life.'

Lisa considered this for a moment. 'Maybe it's better that way,' she said doubtfully.

She thought about this possibility again when she had finished her tea (and, after tearing a reluctant Leonard away from the gibbon, was on her way home). Would it be better for Teddy and me, she wondered?

As the sittings continued and the portrait progressed, Lisa began to look forward to them with greater eagerness.

Conversation with him hadn't been easy in the beginning. After all, they had little in common and he clearly wasn't the sort of person who had much patience with small talk. Yet the more she watched him painting, the more questions she wanted to ask him about his work, about his life, about all sorts of things; and he never seemed to mind answering them, over the inevitable cups of tea in the garden after he put down his brush.

'How can you be so involved with what's going on at the *Bangkok World* and care so much about things like getting into Khun Sa's camp when painting is your real love?' she asked him one day.

'No problem,' he said. 'There isn't any conflict except

maybe in terms of time.'

'But time must be very important to you,' she said. 'Although that's not exactly what I meant.'

'What, then?'

'Well, aren't artists totally single-minded when it comes to their work? – Their painting I mean? I thought everything else had to give way to it.'

'Maybe I'm just not a real artist then,' he said regretfully.

'Oh, you know that's not true. Anyone who sees your work knows how good you are.'

He smiled. 'Thanks. I just wish there were more people like you around.'

Lisa didn't know what to say so she merely toyed with a bougainvillea petal that had wafted onto the tea tray.

'Sometimes I feel like I'm two different people,' Sonchai mused. 'I get terribly caught up in anything I do. Anything I like, that is. When I'm painting, the rest of the world could vanish and I wouldn't even notice, much less care. Absolutely nothing else counts, not people, certainly not things –'

'Not even Panda?' Lisa interrupted before she could stop herself.

'Not even Panda.'

To Lisa's relief, he gave no sign of minding the question or of feeling guilty about his answer.

'I suppose it's because painting is so completely absorbing,' he continued, 'it's impossible to be thinking about anything, or anybody else, when I'm doing it.'

'Does it work the other way too, when you're at the *World*, I mean? Do you forget about painting then?'

'I try to but it doesn't always work. There are times when I can't get an unfinished picture out of my mind. It keeps calling me back and I can't concentrate on anything else. Generally though, when I put down my brushes I manage to close the door on that world. Then my other world, the world I share with my wife and the *Bangkok World*, takes over for a while.'

'Only for a while?'

'That's right.'

'What brings you back to the world of painting?'

'Instinct – the same thing that brings me up for air when I'm under water. It's just something that's absolutely necessary for my existence, that's all. There is no way I could survive without it.'

'But the photography – couldn't you somehow make that part of your art?'

Sonchai burst out laughing. 'Not a chance! They're two completely separate things. Painting is for my soul, photography is for my stomach. But they're each an essential part of my life in this world and each one feeds and stimulates the other. After all, the body has no meaning without the soul, you must agree about that; and the soul is housed in and nurtured by the body. They each draw their dynamic force, the force that is life itself, from each other. So you see – when I'm wallowing in the mire of photojournalism I'm actually nourishing my soul by absorbing the experiences that one way or another are going to come out in my painting.' He broke off, looking embarrassed; then he asked, 'Am I making any sense at all? Do you know what I'm saying?'

'I think so. I sort of envy you actually.'

Sonchai looked astonished. 'Why?'

'I wish I had a grand passion in my life the way you do, some means for the expression of my soul. If I have a soul, that is.'

'Not have a soul!' exclaimed Sonchai, genuinely shocked. 'Of course you have a soul. It's your soul that I'm painting.'

'You may find that you don't have a picture then,' she laughed.

'Impossible,' shouted Sonchai, jumping up in his excitement. 'Come into the studio. No, don't finish that tea. You must look at the picture right now.' And taking her by the hand, he pulled her inside and didn't let her go until she was standing in front of the unfinished portrait.

'Is that a painting of someone without a soul?' he demanded. Then answering the question himself, said,

'No, it clearly isn't. The soul shines in the eyes; it is reflected in every contour of the face. You don't have to believe in a standard theistic religion, you know, to be convinced that you have a soul and that the people and animals around you have souls.'

'Hold on a minute,' Lisa laughed. 'I have a hard enough time believing there's anything nonmaterial in human beings. If you want to include the dogs and cats and the lions and tigers you lose me completely.'

Sonchai grimaced. 'You're a prisoner of the Judeo–Christian way of thinking,' he said. 'You're taught that God made man in his own image and put the animals there to serve him – and for some reason you cling to that idea for dear life. But look around you; try seeing the world as Buddhists and Hindus see it. You'll have a much wider, more comprehensive, view of things; one that takes in the fact that we're all in this world together with the same need to eat and breathe and mate... all caught up in the same cycle of birth and death and rebirth.'

'I'm afraid that's a bit difficult for someone like me to believe,' Lisa replied.

'I don't know why. It seems so obvious –'

'Mommy, Mommy!' Leonard cried, running into the studio. 'The gibbon took my red fire engine. He's half way up the tree with it and he won't give it back.'

'I'm afraid you'll just have to let him keep it until he

decides to bring it down or drop it,' Sonchai said.

'But it's my fire truck. I want it back,' Leonard maintained stubbornly.

'Well – let's see if we can find the gibbon and persuade him to bring it down,' Lisa said, taking him by the hand and going back into the garden.

Unfortunately Uan proved to be a very hardhearted creature. They had almost given up hope of persuading him to relinquish his treasure when they heard a voice – one that sounded American – calling 'Hey, Sonchai!' from just outside the gate.

'I lost your phone number,' the visitor, John Smith, said after the gardener had let him in. 'I've had one hell of a time finding your house. I've got to talk to you. You haven't got a beer around anywhere, have you?'

'Sure, have a seat. What's up anyway?'

'I've been talking to those Japanese guys; you know, the ones who were up in Khun Sa's camp. At least, I've been talking to one of them – the one who speaks passable English – and I've pretty much fixed things for us to get up there. Are you on?'

'Of course, I'm on. How the hell did you manage it?'

'They're willing to cut a deal; take the two of us along with them in exchange for us letting them in on the CIA–Cambodia story.'

'Does that include all of them?'

'No, the deal is two for two.'

'You don't think having a couple Japanese guys with us while we're prowling around the Cambodian border – maybe even making a few quick forays across it – is going to call too much attention to us, do you?' Sonchai asked. 'You know the American authorities are none too eager to let reporters – even US ones – into the area. They certainly wouldn't like the idea of the Japanese getting hold of the story. I mean if anything goes wrong –'

'Nothing is going to go wrong. But if by any chance we did get picked up and were in a bad spot – there'd be a lot to be said for having it a genuinely international team. In fact, I thought we'd get Gunthe – you know, that Swedish guy – to go along too.'

'OK,' said Sonchai, who had been after the Khun Sa story for a couple of years and was willing to go to just about any lengths to get it. 'If that's the deal, I'm with you.'

'Sonchai, Sonchai!' Leonard called, running over to him, followed at a distance by his mother. 'I've got my truck. Uan was nice. He gave it back.'

'This is my wife's cousin, Lisa,' Sonchai explained, 'and her son, Leonard.' Then indicating his friend, he added, 'John here – he's a stringer for CBS News in the States.'

After chatting for a few minutes, John turned to Leonard and said, 'Hey, let's see that fire truck you've got.'

Leonard was more than delighted to show it off and the

two of them remained absorbed in its wondrous capabilities until Lisa, looking at her watch, saw that it was time to go.

'Thank you for being so nice to Leonard,' she told John as they said goodbye. 'You certainly have a way with children,'

'I like kids,' John returned. 'They relax you and take your mind off the idiocies of life.'

When Lisa, with Leonard in tow, came back for another sitting a few days later, she found that John was staying with Sonchai and Panda until his new place was ready.

He played with Leonard and the gibbon for almost an hour during her sitting, and had tea with them in the garden afterwards.

'Can the nice man come to our house?' Leonard asked his mother in a whisper loud enough for both John and Sonchai to hear.

'Why yes, I hope so,' Lisa replied.

'When?' Leonard persisted, knowing that when his mother was vague about anything she usually meant 'no'.

'Well, let's see,' she said, running her mind over her calendar for the upcoming week. Unless Teddy had something planned for the weekend that he had forgotten to tell her about, they were free. 'Could the three of you –

including Panda I mean – come to dinner on Saturday?'

'Sure, that sounds great,' John replied, enthusiastically.

'If Panda hasn't made any other plans,' Sonchai replied, wanting to give himself a little wiggle room.

'Can Uan come too?' Leonard begged.

'He goes to sleep at six o'clock,' John explained. 'All gibbons do.'

'Why?'

'They're smart. They know that if they stay up too late they won't feel like playing and having fun the next day, so they start getting ready to go sleep as soon as the sun begins to go down. Then by the time it's dark they can't keep their eyes open so you have to play with them in the daytime.'

'I like to stay up late,' Leonard announced proudly.

'You're not a gibbon, dear,' his mother pointed out; and, taking him firmly by the hand, she said goodbye.

Teddy was surprised and not entirely pleased later that evening when Lisa said, 'I've invited Sonchai and Panda and a friend of Sonchai's to dinner on Saturday night. I think we might invite Christie and William too.'

'What's this sudden craze for family togetherness?'

Lisa was taken aback. 'What do you mean? I thought you were very fond of them all. Well – maybe not Sonchai.

But the others.'

'I am. But that doesn't mean I want to spend my Saturday night playing happy families. Especially not with some boring friend of Sonchai's who barely speaks English in tow.'

'His friend's an American.'

'What's he doing with an American friend?'

'Why shouldn't he have one? He probably has dozens. He works on the *Bangkok World*, you know.'

'Well, that rag isn't exactly known for having reporters who can string a proper sentence together in any language.'

'You're in a horrible mood this evening,' she said. And in a rare moment of sarcasm, she added, 'is it your period?'

'Don't be revolting.'

'I'm just trying to be sensible. Anyway, you know you like Christie. And I thought you were always really glad to see Panda. I promise you, Sonchai's friend is really nice. Sonchai never talks much when he's in a group, so what's the problem?'

'You said you didn't want to have people to dinner until we got a better cook.'

'I didn't want to.'

'Then why did you take it into your head to invite my entire family tree?'

Lisa felt it would be wiser not to mention that the

original suggestion had come from Leonard. That wouldn't improve Teddy's attitude at all. It was funny, though, that Teddy didn't even want to see Panda. It had been a couple of months since he had seen them all – not since the party upriver.

Something must have gone wrong at work today, she decided. He'd been keeping really long hours lately, poor darling; and you couldn't do that forever in this stifling heat without getting thoroughly exhausted.

'I just felt like inviting them but I can postpone it if you want. I haven't called Christie and William yet.'

'Never mind,' Teddy grumbled in a manner not at all in keeping with his usual cheerful self. 'I'll live with it.'

Live with it? Teddy thought – I can't wait. But I can't stand it either. The very idea of being in the same room, at the same dinner table, with Panda and Sonchai and Lisa was almost more than he could stand. He shouldn't have to endure it but there just wasn't any good reason he could give for refusing to go through with it.

Maybe Panda would think of something and they wouldn't come, he thought hopefully. She had been nervous enough when they had been at the restaurant together and she had seen Sonchai. The problem – damn it – was that she actually had nothing to hide whereas he... well, he certainly had his real feelings to hide, but he would just have to manage it somehow. He would just have to pull himself together, sit at the dinner table, and play the genial host. The only good thing about it was that with any luck he could keep refilling Sonchai's wine glass until he was too sozzled for any sex when he got home.

Lisa was busy trying to placate Leonard when the guests arrived. He had been fractious and difficult ever since he had realised that John wasn't coming solely to play with him but to spend his time talking to the grown-ups. In desperation she had finally told Leonard that he could stay up until everyone came and then spend ten minutes ('but only ten, dear, no more than that') showing John his toys.

She was quite touched a few minutes later at how cheerfully John put down his gin and tonic and allowed himself to be led off by Leonard. He actually looked pleased that the little fellow wanted his company.

Lisa kept a sharp eye on her watch nonetheless – and, after the allotted time had passed, went to rescue her guest. She found him sitting on the floor with Leonard, surrounded by the upturned contents of the Lego basket.

'Darling – it's time for John to come back and finish his drink now,' she said.

A howl went up from Leonard. 'But we're building an Eiffel Tower,' he protested.

'Just let us finish the foundation,' John said, 'and I'll be with you in a couple of minutes.'

Leonard, who had only the vaguest sense of time, relaxed into a happy smile at this reprieve; and John, who had a habit of losing track of time when he was enjoying himself, settled back to their construction work.

More than half an hour passed before John had his drink in his hand again.

Christie, sitting next to him, took the opportunity to broach a subject that had been worrying her. 'Panda told me that you and Sonchai were talking about going up to Khun Sa's camp next weekend,' she said. 'You aren't really going to do it, are you?'

'I hope so. We will if we can.'

'But isn't it going to be awfully dangerous?'

'I doubt it. Khun Sa's got enough on his hands without antagonizing foreign governments by shooting reporters.'

Christie didn't think this sounded very convincing. 'But they're ruthless up there,' she said, 'not only Khun Sa but the KMT and all the others involved in the drug trade. If you're not careful you could get caught in some very nasty crossfire.'

'Who are the KMT?' asked Lisa, joining in the conversation.

'The remnants of the old Kuomintang army from China,' John explained. 'They've been up there around the border areas since 1949 and at this point they're Khun Sa's main competitors.'

'Good heavens! You can't want to go up there then,' Lisa said.

'But I do,' John insisted. 'I want to go where the stories are. And the bigger they are and the harder they are to get at, the more kudos I get for pulling one off – if I do pull it off. It's just the nature of the beast when you're a foreign correspondent.'

'Then why don't you do something else for a living?' Lisa asked, not liking to think of anyone as nice as John taking chances like that.

He laughed her suggestion aside. 'No way,' he said. 'I've wanted to be a foreign correspondent ever since I was a kid. The trouble is, it's a tough racket to break into. The best I can do at the moment is patch a living together as a stringer for CBS. It's all pretty much catch as catch can though. You see, they only pay me when I can produce a story for them – and even then it's pretty meagre.'

'That's awful,' Lisa exclaimed. 'They should treat you better than that. Do you really have to put up with it?'

'It's pretty much that or small town USA, writing articles about Mrs. Waldo's cat getting stuck up a tree. Or Mr. Jones kicking the bucket at the age of ninety-two and leaving five thousand dollars to the public library. That's the generally accepted route into the newspaper world, but I'd hate it. I want to get to the exciting stuff right away.

The problem is that no newspaper or wire service is going to put me on the payroll until I've got a track record in the business – so that leaves me pretty much delving into my own pocket if I want go where the good stories are. I just hope I'm going to be able to make it into the big time that way. The problem is, my pockets aren't very deep.'

'How do you manage then?' Lisa asked.

'Odd jobs mostly. Sometimes I sell a story and a couple of times I've taken groups of tourists trekking or shooting the rapids up in the north. Actually I've sold a few stories from those trips to travel and adventure magazines. So one way or another I'm managing to put it all together.'

'But how long are can you keep it up?' Christie asked.

'I've blocked out three years for my great adventure and I've still got two to go. If things work out and I get hired as a correspondent for a paper or for one of the news services or networks I'll be the happiest man alive. If not, I'll go back home to Charleston and settle down knowing that at least I've had more excitement in three years than most people have in a lifetime.'

'You're not married then, I take it,' Christie said.

'Not at the moment.'

And although Lisa quite liked John, she could have killed Teddy for choosing that particular moment to offer him another drink as this effectively cut-off any further revelations about John's marital situation. Teddy, in characteristic fashion, launched into an account of the various lizard species they could expect to see in the area near Khun Sa's camp.

When they were all seated around the table Teddy cast a furious look at Lisa. Why the hell had she put Christie on one side of him and Panda on the other? Christie would surely notice if he spent too much time talking to Panda. On the other hand, if he scarcely talked to Panda at all Christie would probably figure out that something was up. God, women were a pain sometimes. The starfish had the right idea: just divide yourself in two when you wanted to perpetuate the species. Of course, those poor guys probably didn't get many kicks that way – and, in any case, that wasn't an option for human beings. He'd just have to settle for the next best thing: keeping women well out of his life for everything but sex. It wouldn't be all that easy but he'd do his best.

He noticed that down at the other end of the table William was saying something to Sonchai about the Thai military. Great topic, he thought – military stuff was just what he was looking for because it always cut the women out. And tonight it offered an additional advantage. One of the few books he had read on Thailand, other than those of particular interest to herpetologists, was one on the role of the military in Thai politics. A colleague back at Stanford had given it to him to read on the plane and, because the flight had been practically endless, he had actually finished it. Now he felt he could hold his own in a conversation about it.

It turned out that the book was highly controversial and precipitated an animated conversation amongst the men around the table. Sonchai had strong opinions on the subject but hadn't read that particular book, so Teddy promised to lend him his copy.

Lisa was relieved to see that Teddy seemed to be enjoying this dinner (which he had been so unaccountably opposed to), but she was a little disappointed that all the talk about the armed forces had kept her from having much of a chance to talk to John. When she had planned the seating she had decided to be a little selfish and put him next to her – but it hadn't done much good. The military had marched in and driven her out.

She decided to wait and see what she could do when they all went out on the veranda for coffee. John had such a kind sensitive face, she thought, not at all like the reporters in movies. And he wasn't flip and animated like Teddy. He didn't say ridiculous things and expect you to think they were funny. He was just serious and rather quiet, she decided, but with a touch of humour in his clear blue eyes. She liked that. She liked a lot of things about him – so many, in fact, that by the time the cook brought out the coconut ice cream topped with crème de cacao she could sense alarm bells ringing in her head.

Was she on the verge of making a fool of herself over him, she wondered, panic suddenly setting in. She mustn't let that happen. When she was pregnant with Leonard she'd vowed that there weren't ever going to be any more flings in her life. In any case, she felt older now and less attractive. And in this country of beautiful women how could a good looking single man like John possibly be interested in her? Well, that didn't matter. She had Leonard and Teddy. What more could she want?

Yet somehow, when they had all moved out to the veranda, Lisa found herself sitting a bit apart from the others, talking to John.

'The language here is really a bear,' John told her as she sipped her coffee. 'I thought I'd be able to pick it up just from hearing it around me but I've been here nearly a year now and haven't made much progress.'

'It's the tones that put me off,' Lisa said. 'I'm not very musical and I don't think I could ever get them right.'

'You have to be a second Caruso to put a Thai sentence together,' John agreed. 'Still, I'm going to try my damnedest. Yesterday I signed up for a course at AUA.'

'What's that?'

'The American University Alumnae something or

other. They have Thai classes for foreigners and I'm going to give it a try. Why don't you sign up too? If you're interested, that is.'

'It might be useful,' Lisa said, doubtfully, 'but I have to think about Leonard, you know. I can't just go off and leave him every day.'

'Can't he go to playschool or something in the morning? My kid wanted to go when he was Lenny's age.'

Lisa was surprised. 'I didn't know you had children,' she said.

A mask came down over John's face. 'Just one and I don't see him anymore.'

'That must be awful,' Lisa said, instinctively reaching for his hand.

He nodded – and it was, she felt, almost as if a fleeting moment of intimacy was being shared between them.

Had Teddy noticed, she wondered when the instant had passed and she'd dropped his hand. A hasty glance in his direction set her mind at rest. He seemed to be too absorbed in his conversation with Panda to have paid any attention to her.

She didn't hear him murmur in Panda's ear, 'This has been the most ghastly evening of my life.'

'But it's been a lovely evening,' she protested. 'You must have led quite a charmed life if all your other evenings have been even better.'

Ignoring this, he said accusingly, 'You never told me Sonchai was going away at the end of the week.'

'It never occurred to me that you'd be interested.'

'You can't mean that.'

'Why ever not?'

'Spend a night with me while he's away,' Teddy urged.

'No.'

'He'll never know,' Teddy persisted.

'That doesn't matter. I'll know.'

'Damn right, you'll know. I'll make sure it's a night you'll never forget.'

'Even if I wanted to, which I don't –'

'Which you do,' he argued.

'I don't know what gives you that idea. But, in any case, I can't. I'm going to Malaysia that weekend.'

'Cancel the trip.'

'No.'

'Postpone it then.'

'Out of the question.'

'OK. I'll come with you, then.'

'You can't. I have to work. I'm doing an article on the Cameron Highlands, the area where Jim Thompson disappeared.'

'I thought all that happened years ago.'

'It did but people are still talking about it. There are all sorts of theories about how it could have happened.

Remember how Daddy wouldn't get off the subject the evening you arrived?'

'Come on, Panida,' Sonchai said, coming over to them, 'it's time to go. I've got to work tomorrow.'

William, overhearing this, announced that he was ready to go home too, and soon everyone was thanking Lisa for a lovely evening and saying goodnight.

Teddy was standing on the veranda watching them all go when Sonchai's car spluttered to a stop. Panda leapt back out, darted past him into the house, and then quickly reappeared with the book on the Thai military for Sonchai.

Pausing for just an instant beside Teddy, she murmured, 'I lied, sort of. The evening was hell for me too – except for those moments when I felt that the only other person in the room was you.'

'Hurry up,' Sonchai called, 'I don't want to wait here all night.'

And Panda dashed into the waiting car.

CHAPTER 12
MALAYSIA, 1976

Teddy flew to Penang on the Friday following Lisa's dinner party, took the ferry over to Butterworth and hired a car with a driver to take him up to the Cameron Highlands.

Had Panda gotten his telegram, he wondered, as the car hiccupped once or twice, backfired and then started up the steep winding road. And, if she had, what was her reaction? Would she be there to meet him?

He had phoned her office before he had left Bangkok, found out where she would be staying and left a message for her to meet him at a place called Foster's Smokehouse (which Christie had mentioned once). He remembered that she had said that it was a great change from Bangkok – and, thinking it sounded like a nice place to take Lisa (Panda didn't have to know that part) he had looked it up in a travel book. Apparently it was some kind of lingering remnant of an Edwardian hill station run by an ancient and un-repatriable Brit who hadn't quite noticed that the days of the Raj were past. Fires were lit in huge stone fireplaces to take the chill off the air in the evenings; fresh scones were served with clotted cream and strawberry jam at teatime; drinks were available from a well stocked bar for the asking and succulent joints of mutton, roasted to perfection, were on the dinner menu almost every night.

All that old colonial stuff gave him a second reason, after the romantic one, to take Panda there. More than just a way of getting her away from Sonchai and into bed (he could, with a little bit of luck, do that in a Bangkok afternoon) it would bring her back into the western world, the English world – although admittedly a rather old-fashioned version of it. It would get her away from that mystical Thai view of the world which she found so compelling and which he could never share.

Sonchai shared it, damn him. That was what bound her to him; or part of it, anyway. Of course, there was a question of loyalty too – of the horrible fact that she was married to him.

Loyalty was something he had never been very good at. Not that sort of loyalty, anyway. He supposed he should admire her for it but that wasn't easy to do under the circumstances.

In an effort to get his mind off this inconvenient aspect of Panda's character, he turned his attention to the passing scenery. All he could see was thick jungle on either side of the road; he had a feeling that there was something menacing about it. He had heard that you could lose your way in that dense greenness even if you were just a few feet away from a path or a village. God, he hoped Panda hadn't been seized with some kind of mad journalistic fervour – one that might drive her to take the pursuit of her story about Jim Thompson's death (or disappearance or whatever it was) a little too seriously. He didn't think she would try to follow some path the fellow might have taken into the jungle (possibly even do it alone), but he wished he could be altogether sure. He suspected she was capable of doing some pretty crazy things sometimes. But basically she was sensible… or was she?

Some of the accounts written by nineteenth century naturalists that he had read when he was a kid – they had good stuff about lizards in them – had reports of all this dense tangled vegetation playing strange tricks on the mind. Apparently the endlessly entwining branches and lianas could come to seem like a sort of trap, making it impossible to escape from the twisted snarl of green. Otherwise rational people could fall prey to wild hallucinations, nightmare fantasies that sometimes drove them mad when that happened.

Teddy put his head in his hands to shut out the sight of the jungly greenness that now seemed to press in from each side of the narrow road. He sent a silent message to Panda. 'Don't meet me tonight,' he thought, forming the words almost as if she could hear him. 'Go back to Bangkok, back to Sonchai, back to that crazy Thai way of looking at the world. It doesn't matter – nothing matters –

as long as you don't follow Jim Thompson into some kind of terrible oblivion in the jungle.'

He was so wrapped up in this imaginary scenario that he barely noticed a car careening down the road in the opposite direction.

Panda, far from being on the lookout for Teddy in any passing car, was trying as hard as she could to put him out of her mind.

How could he possibly believe she would just rush up to some hotel and meet him on command like that, she asked herself indignantly. There was no way she would do that. If she wanted to be unfaithful to Sonchai – which she didn't – she could do it in Bangkok. She wouldn't need to go to some remote mountain hideaway. After all, what she felt for Teddy was just… Oh God, there was no 'just' about it; it was everything.

Oh Teddy, why did you have to go and marry Lisa? she asked, almost aloud. Why did you forget me during all those years we were growing up? I know we were far away from each other – but it wasn't enough to make me forget you. And don't try to say that we can be together now, so it's all OK. It's not OK. You may not care what it would do to Lisa if she found out, but it would bother the hell out of me. And sooner or later she would find out. Secrets like that don't stay undiscovered forever. I know I didn't think about her that night in Nantucket – but I scarcely knew her then. Anyway, I'm older now and more capable of imagining how she might feel. And I'd feel like a cheating little rat.

Oh – I know you're not completely horrible. You don't want to hurt Lisa either. You just believe you can get away with it because that's what you want to believe; and because you know that in the long run it won't matter. Lisa will close her eyes and make your leash so long that you won't even feel it's there.

It's different with Sonchai. I do care what he feels. I admit I don't love him the way I love you – but I value what we have together and I don't want to risk losing a way of life that suits me for – for what? For a few nights, or perhaps a few afternoons, of great sex? No, it's not worth it. You're not worth it.

I'm glad you're going to be waiting for me at that hotel tonight, having dinner by yourself, going to bed alone. I hope you're disappointed and miserable. Suffer. You've made me suffer enough.

She's got to be here, Teddy thought as his taxi pulled up in front of the large Tudor style hotel. I know she'll be here.

He was full of confidence as he paid the driver and

went inside, but the air of stolid Victorian respectability that greeted him in the lobby made him wonder whether he had chosen quite the right place for the sort of night he had in mind. Of course, Panda wouldn't be meeting him here – if she did meet him – for the interior decoration. But the atmosphere put a slight damper on his spirits nonetheless.

After looking around and ascertaining that Panda wasn't anywhere to be seen, he went over to the reception desk.

'Has my wife checked in yet?' he asked, after giving his name and refreshing the clerk's memory on the subject of his reservation.

'No sir.'

'Well, show her up to the room when she comes.'

'Yes sir.'

He turned and followed a room boy up a flight of stairs, down a series of narrow corridors and into a room that unfortunately echoed the mood of old-fashioned respectability he had found in the lobby. Not even the large double bed, stiffly made up with a starched coverlet and unyielding pillows, looked ready to welcome of a pair of lovers.

Shit, Teddy said to himself. The only halfway romantic thing about this place was the view. It wasn't bad as long as you liked lakes (although he could do without them himself). Compared to the ocean, they just didn't have it – not that that would matter after dark. And it was already after four. If Panda didn't get here pretty fast he'd have to write off the seductive effect of the view.

He kept a sharp eye on his watch, expecting her to arrive at any moment. But when nearly half an hour had passed and there was still no sign of her, he began to get worried. Had something happened to her? Or could it be that she was deliberately leaving him here to spend a ghastly evening, and – worse – a night, alone? She wouldn't. Or would she? The hell of it was that she just might.

But he wasn't going to consider that possibility yet. He'd go out for a walk. That would get him out of this dismal room. And, who knew? Maybe he'd be able to figure out what it was that people saw in lakes.

He didn't.

Nevertheless the cool highland air was really great after the liquefying heat of Bangkok and he found himself actually enjoying his solitary wander along the deserted shore. He had to watch his step though, because the rim of the lake was made up of layers of soft shale that could slip away or break under his feet.

After a while it became apparent that the lakeshore wasn't quite as deserted as he had thought. An elderly lady and two girls who looked like they might be her granddaughters were amusing themselves at the water's edge.

The older girl, a pretty blond teenager with a layer of puppy fat around her middle and a heavy camera around her neck, was scouting out the best places to take pictures while the other girl, considerably younger, was playing with some of the broken bits of shale that dotted the water's edge.

Teddy nodded to the grandmother as he passed; and, in a voice that sounded distinctly Australian, she responded with a friendly comment about the beauty of the lake.

He hadn't walked on very far when a loud crunching sound, one that clearly came from pieces of shale sliding over each other, made him turn around.

There were screams and then a splash.

The soft surface of the rim had broken under the older girl's feet and she had tumbled into the water. She bobbed up for a moment and then – amidst wildly flailing arms – went under again.

'The camera,' Teddy shouted, running toward her. 'Drop the camera!'

Either she didn't hear him or she was too frightened and confused to take in what he said.

The younger girl shrieked and the grandmother held out both her hands in a vain attempt to reach the floundering girl.

Fuck, thought Teddy, chucking off his shoes and diving into the lake. A moment later he came up behind the girl and reached around her, intending to clasp her under the chin. But, too distraught to understand or cooperate, she turned and clutched him as hard as she could. Her weight, along with that of the heavy camera, dragged him down before he had a chance to take a deep breath.

It wasn't easy to shake her loose long enough to come up for air but a sense of panic gave him the strength to do it. Then, reaching one hand out to take hold of what looked like a rock, he held his other hand out to her.

She seized it and pulled herself up for a moment but the additional weight was too much for the brittle shale. It broke off in his hand and they both sank back under water.

Teddy's first thought was to get the camera out from around her neck but when he tried he only succeeded in choking her so he gave up and looked around for something else to hold on to. More shale was the only option so he reached for a bigger and hopefully stronger piece. Once again it broke off in his hands and they fell back into the water.

By this time the girl was too frightened to struggle and he managed to get the camera away from her. Over and over again he tried to find something strong enough to hold their weight but the farther out of the water he managed to pull them, the farther under the surface they fell when the piece of shale he was grasping broke off in his hand.

The smaller child ran off screaming for help and the grandmother kept trying to offer her hand – but he knew that if he took it he would only succeed in pulling her in with them.

There just had to be something – somewhere – that would be strong enough to hold them, he kept telling himself. And all he had to do was find it. The problem was, he was getting tired... fuck.

Panda tapped the taxi driver on the shoulder.

'Turn around,' she said. 'I'm going back – up to a place called Foster's Smokehouse.'

'You crazy, miss?' the taxi driver asked. 'That's just a few miles from where we started. We're almost at Butterworth now.'

'I know it seems silly, but I – I forgot something.'

'Return trip cost double.'

'You have to go back anyway,' Panda reminded him.

The driver was unmoved by this argument. 'Two ways, two fares,' he insisted.

'Alright, two fares then.'

She thought she heard him mumble 'crazy lady' as he turned the car around. But she wasn't sure; and, anyway, she didn't care.

Why am I doing this, she asked herself, even though

she knew the reason lay in the terrifying feeling that had overwhelmed her a moment before. She had felt as though the whole world had suddenly been plunged into darkness and there had been nothing but swirling emptiness around her. The air she had needed to breathe had turned to oceans of water and a deathlike chill was slowing the flow of blood through her veins.

Then the nightmare moment passed; but it left her with a longing for Teddy so intense that no rational considerations were of any importance. She had to go back. She had to see him. That was all that mattered.

The three-hour trip back up the winding road into the hills passed in a sort of daze.

Darkness had settled over the surrounding greenery by the time the rattletrap taxi drew up in front of the hotel. Without waiting for the car to come to a full stop, she leapt out and rushed inside. So intent was she on her frantic search for Teddy, she didn't even hear the angry driver shouting for his money.

The lobby was empty except for a slender Chinese man behind the reception desk. 'May I help you?' he asked, thinking she looked a little deranged.

'Yes, I'm looking for Mr. Edward Duncanson,' she replied, reading disapprobation in the man's face and making an effort to appear a little calmer.

'Mrs. Duncanson?' he asked, secretly feeling sorry

for that nice Mr.. Duncanson, having to put up with a demented wife.

She started to correct him but then caught herself and said, 'Yes'. It seemed funny to have her old name back, but it sounded right somehow.

'You will find him in the lounge,' the clerk told her, indicating a large room off to the left. He tried to give her some useful information about her key and her bag, but she was halfway across the lobby before he had quite finished his sentence.

Relief and happiness flooded over her when she saw Teddy. Clearly nothing terrible had happened to him. He was all right – more than all right, actually. He looked like he was thoroughly enjoying himself – and her initial relief was quickly replaced by a sort of bewilderment, then by a vague feeling of irritation at the thought that while she had been going through hell, he'd been sitting in a comfortable chair in front of a roaring log fire, a blanket over his shoulders, his feet propped up on a footstool and a glass of something that looked like champagne in his hand. A number of people were hovering around him, apparently bent on pressing more of whatever-it-was on him every time he took a sip; he looked more like a pampered prince than a man worried about whether or not his romantic rendezvous would turn into a very solitary evening.

Sensing Panda's eyes on him, he turned toward her,

gave her a welcoming grin and, direction. Grinning, he starting to get up, spilled some of his champagne in the process.

'What are you doing wrapped up in all those blankets?' she demanded, going over to him.

He laughed, and, turning to his adoring entourage, said, 'This is Panda'. Then, in deference to the Victorian atmosphere of the place, he quickly added 'my wife', before going on to introduce the grandmother, the parents and the little sister of the girl he had pulled from the lake.

Mayhem broke out as they all interrupted each other in their eagerness to tell the story of how the wonderful Mr. Duncanson had nearly drowned saving their dear Lavinia.

Panda looked around for the femme fatale who could have inspired this astonishing feat of courage and gallantry on Teddy's part.

'She's upstairs sleeping now, exhausted from her ordeal,' the girl's mother explained. 'She was so terrified, poor child. You simply can't imagine how much water she had swallowed! It is a miracle she didn't drown.'

'And she would have drowned too,' the granny put in, 'if it hadn't been for Mr. Duncanson, and for a clever young man from the hotel who knew all about artificial respiration.'

'But it was Mr. Duncanson who saved her,' stressed the little girl, not wanting her hero to have to share any of the credit. 'And he nearly drowned doing it. He was turning blue – a sort of bluish purple actually – and making terrible gasping sounds. Like this.' (Obligingly, she began to illustrate this with a series of rasping and choking noises.)

'Hey, I didn't sound that bad,' Teddy protested. 'Nowhere near.'

'Yes, you did,' insisted the little girl, who had a flare for the dramatic and went on to enhance her story. 'You sounded much worse than that – like a death rattle.'

'No way,' he laughed. 'I promise you I was very much alive.'

'You didn't look it.'

'You weren't there. You'd run off somewhere.'

'I was back by the time you finally pulled yourself out.'

'And dear Lavinia,' her granny reminded her – although neither the little girl nor anyone else was in danger of forgetting it. 'He pulled her out, too.'

By this time Teddy was beginning to feel restive. He wanted to have Panda to himself.

'Let's go upstairs,' he said, turning to her; and, amid a chorus of concern about how tired he must be and whether he would be all right, he finished his drink, threw off the blanket, and took Panda up to their room.

'I was afraid you wouldn't come,' he admitted when he had closed the door behind them.

'I wasn't planning to.'

'What made you change your mind then?'

Instead of answering, she asked, 'When did all this happen – this nearly drowning, I mean?'

'Don't pay any attention to what that kid said. She's got too much imagination, that's all. I was nowhere near drowning.'

'Never mind that; when was it?'

He shrugged. 'Three or four hours ago I guess, I'm not sure. I wasn't exactly looking at my watch. What does it matter anyway?'

'I was almost at Butterworth when I had the taxi turn around.'

'Good God! Talk about a last minute change of heart… What brought that about? Something must have.'

'I don't know. I can't understand it myself. I just felt a blackness wash over me and I couldn't breathe. Everything swirled around.' She hesitated for a moment, weighing her words. 'It was almost as if I were drowning.'

'Are you sure?' he asked incredulously. 'You're not just making it up?'

'Of course not, why would I do that?'

'Because that's exactly the way I felt.'

Panda didn't reply.

An uncomfortable suspicion dawned on him. 'You're not trying to claim that some kind of weird hocus pocus was going on – something that made you feel what I was feeling – are you?'

'I think I am, actually.'

'That's rubbish and you know it,' he said, harshly. 'That kid downstairs isn't the only one with too much imagination. You're giving her a damn good run for her money.'

'No, I'm not. I'm telling you what I felt at the time – that's all.'

'I don't believe it.'

'Don't believe it then. I don't care.'

'Well, I care. Because if you've had an attack of some kind of brain fever on the way up here, I want to know about it.'

'It wasn't an attack of anything. It was just a really strange feeling that I can't explain in an ordinary way.'

'Well, at least it got you here. For whatever crazy reason,' Teddy said, deciding there were times when it was pointless to try to have a rational discussion with Panda. 'And I'm glad of that.'

'Well, one of us is glad then – and it certainly isn't me,' Panda retorted. 'If I'd known how insulting you'd be, I'd be on my way back to Bangkok right now. I'm sorry I came. It was stupid, but it wasn't for any crazy reason. It was because of a very real, very intense, very terrifying experience, and –' She would have carried on in this vein but the ringing of the telephone stopped her.

'Who the hell can that be?' Teddy exclaimed, as he

picked up the receiver. 'Hello?'

'Mrs. Duncanson's taxi is still waiting to be paid,' said the voice at the other end of the line.

'I'll be right down.'

'Don't bother,' Panda retorted, when Teddy relayed the message. 'I'm leaving.'

Putting his arms around her and holding her firmly against him, he laughed. 'You're not going anywhere – not if I have to find a rope, or possibly a pair of stockings, and tie you to the bed post.'

'If you think that kind of fantasy is going to keep me here,' she said, struggling to evade his grasp, 'you couldn't be more wrong.'

'In that case, it looks like I'll have to cut off your escape route by paying off the taxi. But you just better be here when I get back because I'm going to make love to you in that bed tonight –'

'Not unless you give me dinner first. I'm starving.'

'Fair enough. I'm pretty ravenous too, thanks to my unexpected dip in the lake. But then I'm going to fuck you until you really do feel that you're drowning. Now, are you going to behave properly while I'm downstairs or am I going to have to knot the sheets and tie you up before I go?'

'Being tied up doesn't appeal to me very much.'

'Good, it would be a lot of trouble and would probably

mess up the bed.'

A few minutes later the phone rang again and Teddy's voice said, 'Can you come down to the lounge? Thanks to my little splash this afternoon, the old geyser who runs this place has told the bartender to give us drinks on the house.'

'Lovely – I'll just take a quick bath first.'

'Don't be long or I'll come up there and climb in the bath with you. And then we'll miss out on our drinks. We probably wouldn't get any dinner either. I gather they're not exactly flexible about eating hours in this place.'

'I'll be two minutes,' she predicted, optimistically.

'What were you doing going back down to Butterworth anyway?' Teddy demanded some twenty minutes later when they were settled in the lounge with tall glasses of gin and tonic in front of them. 'Why weren't you going to meet me here tonight?'

'Two reasons,' Panda replied, glancing around to make sure that 'darling Lavinia's appreciative family were no longer there. 'Lisa is one and Sonchai is the other.'

'I notice you put Lisa first,' he said.

'I had to put one of them first, didn't I? I didn't mean anything by it… Although, come to think of it, she's actually the one I'd feel the worst about hurting.'

'That's a surprise.'

'It shouldn't be. Sonchai is obviously less vulnerable than Lisa. He has more available diversions, but Lisa would probably be really hurt if she found out.'

'That didn't seem to worry you that night in Nantucket. What's brought on these new and improved moral scruples?'

'Growing up, I suppose. I'm not the totally selfish little horror I used to be. At least, I hope I'm not. And of course I'm a lot more likely to identify with the wronged wife these days.'

'Why, is Sonchai –'

'Probably. I'm not sure but it would be hard to find a Thai man who didn't play around. If he could afford to, anyway.'

'Doesn't that bother you?'

She shrugged. 'I try not to think about it too much. It's just the way things are if you live here. But now of course I'd love to find out definitely that he was going to massage parlours – because then I wouldn't have to feel guilty about being with you here.'

'That was pretty much the way I felt when I found out about Lisa's little indiscretion in Japan. It took the guilt away from any little fun and games I had had.'

'Oh,' she said. 'Is that what our night in Nantucket was – another round of fun and games?'

'Don't be absurd,' he said harshly. 'You know that's not true.'

'Is it?' she asked doubtfully. 'I hope so. But let's not talk about Lisa and Sonchai and marriages and awful things like that tonight. Just this once I want to forget them. Let's pretend that Foster's Smokehouse is the only place in the entire world – and nothing else and no one else exists.'

'Perfect.'

'Was that little girl right? Did you really turn blue and gasp and nearly drown?'

'Far from it,' he declared. 'Remember – you were the one with the drowning symptoms, not me.'

'Don't make fun of me,' she said, with a note of warning in her voice.

'I won't, I promise. How could I possibly want to make fun of the feelings – whatever they were – that brought you here?'

'I don't know. But I had a horrible feeling just then that you were about to manage it.'

'Then I'm really sorry.'

He frowned and seemed to be thinking hard about something, so Panda sat back and sipped her drink and watched him.

'You know,' he said after a while, 'there was a moment in that damned lake – after I'd pulled myself and that idiot Lavinia almost completely out of the drink and then fallen

even farther back under water about a thousand times –
when I did feel… I don't know quite what it was – exhaustion, perhaps, or maybe I was just desperate for oxygen. In any case, I'd swallowed so much water by then that I may have actually been spaced out enough to send you some kind of mental telepathy message. I can't believe I'm saying this, but –'

'Why not?'

'Because it's such a crazy idea.'

'No, it isn't.'

'Not in your world, perhaps.'

'You are in my world here,' she reminded him.

'That's funny. The whole reason I suggested this place was that I thought it would get you out of "your world", back into the Western world.'

'Why would you want to do that?'

'To get you into a world of rational thought and individual liberty – a world I can share with you.'

'Thai thought *is* rational. It's just based on different premises than Western thought.'

'This conversation is getting a bit much for me on an empty stomach,' he said. 'Let's find the dining room and get something to eat.'

'Good idea,' she said. 'But there's just one thing before we go…'

'Fire away.'

'When you were having so much trouble, falling back into the water and not being able to breathe every time you tried to get out – didn't you ever consider letting go of Lavinia? She must have added a lot of extra weight.'

'I certainly thought about it. At least, I did afterwards – when I was sitting by the fire soaking up all that lavish praise from her family, and they were plying me with hot chocolate that had a mega dose of brandy in it.'

'What do you mean, hot chocolate? I saw you waving a champagne glass around.'

'That came later. In the meantime I had more or less come to my senses and realised how great it was to be alive. That was when it dawned on me how close I'd come to making a grand exit. But the funny thing is that when it was all happening, I didn't think of letting go of her. I guess that was because I didn't think at all. She was just there and somehow I had to get us out. It must have been instinct or something. It certainly wasn't a rational consideration of the pros and cons of putting my life on the line for some chubby little teenybopper I didn't even know. If I had considered it that way – I'm afraid dear little Lavinia would be a beautiful memory by now. I hope that doesn't shatter any illusions you may have had about my heroism; I don't want to send you racing back down to Butterworth with that ratfink taxi driver.'

'If it's a choice between you and the taxi driver, I suppose I'll stick with you,' Panda said airily. 'But if it's a question of shattering my illusions – that's impossible, because I've never had any about you. I just love you for your horrible old self.'

'As long as you keep on doing that,' he replied with a grin. 'That's all I ask.'

The Australian family was already digging into their sticky toffee pudding by the time Panda and Teddy got to the dining room, but they called out a cheery greeting between bites.

Panda found it rather startling to be regarded as 'Mrs. Duncanson'. There was also something rather nice about having her old name back, although of course it hadn't been preceded by 'Mrs.' when she had had it. And when old Mr. Foster, stopping by their table for a chat, called her Mrs. Duncanson too, she decided that it was rather fun playing the role of Teddy's make-believe wife.

After Mr. Foster had moved on to talk other guests, Panda gave free rein to her sense of the ridiculous and held forth on the crimes and misdemeanours of their imaginary dog. Teddy joined in the playful mood – and what had started as a way of giving an impression of conventional respectability soon became a lively source of amusement for themselves. They shook their heads in disapproval over the paternity suit being served on their neighbour's fifteen-year-old son, and, in voices heavy with condemnation, speculated on the virginity (or probable lack thereof) of the nymphet who lived down the street.

When the waiter came to take the remains of the roast mutton away, Teddy asked, 'And how did you enjoy the dinner, Mrs. Duncanson?'

'It was delicious. You don't suppose they could make up one of those American doggy bags, do you? Rover would love it.'

'Those things are wasted on dogs,' he said. 'Why don't we give it to the kids? They might like something besides beer and Mars bars for a change.'

'Yes. You know, if we didn't have so many children, feeding them wouldn't be such a problem.'

'Do you really think ten's too many?'

'Oh no – I love being pregnant. We should be able to manage sixteen, at least.'

'I'll do my part,' he volunteered enthusiastically. 'I do hate to see you looking so slim. It's a real turn off.'

'You know, I heard somewhere that somebody claimed there were other things in marriage besides animal passion. Do you have any idea who could have said that?'

'None of my friends,' Teddy declared.

'None of mine, either,' Panda said firmly.

'Speaking of animal passion, I'm beginning to feel a

slight inclination for it right now.'

'Slight,' she exclaimed, outraged. 'If it's that slight, why don't you just call for a hot water bottle?'

'If you even think of making another suggestion as revolting as that, I'll –'

'You'll what?' she laughed, flicking off a dollop of treacle tart that had found its way onto the tip of his nose.

'I'll take you upstairs and tear off your dress and throw all your clothes on the floor,' he said, rubbing a lingering bit of treacle off his nose. 'And then I'll pick you up and fling you on that big double bed and teach you the difference between animal passion and hot water bottles.'

'I quite like the sound of that,' Panda replied.

It wasn't long before Teddy was carrying out his threats – or promises, as Panda would have it – lying naked on top of her and running his hands and then his lips over her entire body.

'Oh God, Panda. I've wanted you so much for so long. I've been going crazy with wanting you.'

'It serves you right,' she said, putting her hands on either side of his face and covering his neck and chest with kisses. 'Because I've been wanting you ever since I was old enough to know about wanting.'

His answer was to press his face into the long silky

strands of her hair and then to pull away and lift himself off her.

'I just want to look at you for a second,' he said. 'Make sure this is all really happening and impress this picture of you on my mind.'

And seeking the evidence of touch as well as sight, he ran his hand from her breast down over her abdomen and in between her legs – where he allowed a finger, followed by a second finger, to stray into the opening there.

'Somehow I don't have any problem feeling that you're real,' she murmured, moving slowly and rhythmically in response to his intruding fingers. She opened her legs, more than ready for another part of him to follow.

Yet instead of demonstrating the surge of libidinous urgency she expected, Teddy continued to lie several inches away from her, touching her only in the tantalizing passage deep inside her until, driven to distraction, she took the initiative herself and tried to move closer to him.

To her surprise he held her firmly away, saying, 'No, not yet, you tortured me long enough – sending me round the bend with wanting you while you played the virtuous ice goddess. Well, tonight is payback time. I can't do the icy, don't-touch-me stuff, that's for sure – but I'm not going to stop until you are wild with wanting me. I'm going to make you want me as much as I've wanted you. And I promise you, this is going to be a night you're not going to forget in a hurry.'

This threat, like the one he had made in the dining room, was not an idle one. Time and again Panda thought 'now, it will be now', only to find that it was merely his hands that were sending her into frenzies – hands that wouldn't let her rest, hands that renewed their caresses as soon as each pinnacle of excitement had retreated into a momentary lull.

'Please,' she whispered, after what seemed like an eternity of desire and rapture had passed. 'Please – now.'

'Panda – my darling Panda,' he breathed, as he finally plunged into her.

When Panda opened her eyes the next morning Teddy was standing naked in front of the heavy Victorian wardrobe, holding a fresh shirt by the sleeve and making faces at himself in a small cloudy mirror on the door. The room was chilly and she snuggled down under the blankets and watched him.

'Aren't you cold?' she asked, after a few minutes.

'Get up, you sloth,' he said, instead of answering. 'I'm starving.'

'No,' she replied, wiggling further down under the covers for warmth.

'No?' he exclaimed. 'Yes, I say.'

After a brief struggle in which the blanket was pulled off, she felt herself being picked up, carried into the shower and set down under a stream of cold water. She leapt out of range as quickly as she could but it wasn't in time to keep him from catching her and pulling her back.

'I'll turn the warm water on,' he promised and, reaching for the soap, he made a thick lather and rubbed it slowly over her.

'If we carry on like this we'll never get any breakfast,' he predicted.

'But I haven't had my turn yet,' she exclaimed, taking the soap from his hands and massaging it along his chest and then his abdomen.

She was about to continue further down when he stopped her and said, 'Don't. I don't think I can stand anymore.'

'Actually neither can I,' she was agreeing. Then she glanced down and saw a change in him that belied his words; she decided that if he could change his mind, so could she. Seizing him by his now very long, very hard dick, she dried him off and led him back to bed for one more romp before breakfast.

'I want to marry you,' Teddy said, over bacon and scrambled eggs, mushrooms and tomatoes.

Panda, spilling her coffee in surprise, asked, 'Haven't you forgotten something?'

'Like what?'

'Like the trifling little fact that we're both already married,' she said, doing what she could to mop up the effects of the spill.

'No, I haven't forgotten it. That's what I was thinking about before you woke up. God knows, I'm not blind to what a great person Lisa is. I care a lot about her – enough to have accepted Leonard's presence in our lives; that should tell you something. I just don't feel passionately about her the way I do about you.'

'Are you trying to say that you and Lisa don't…?'

'No, I'm not saying that. The fact is we do,' he replied testily. 'It's just that when I think of a life with her and then think of a life with you; well, there's no comparison. I know the direction I want my life to take and that means spending it with you.'

'And how long would it be before you were saying exactly that sort of thing again? Only it would be to some other girl, one you probably haven't met yet.'

'That's a rotten question.'

'No it's not. It's a very sensible question. Our kind of love – last night's kind of love – doesn't last. And then I would just be another Lisa waiting at home while you have affairs with other women, and I couldn't stand that. It's one thing if Sonchai plays around. Not that I particularly like it, but I'm not absolutely torn apart with jealousy over it. If it were you doing the same thing, I don't think I could bear it.'

'It wouldn't be like that, I swear to God.'

'Swearing doesn't mean anything.'

'Jesus! How can I convince you? Do I have to write you sonnets and love songs? I'll try if you insist, but they're bound to be so awful you'll shudder when you read them.'

'Perhaps you'd better skip them then.'

'Right – but can you give me a clue about what I can say or do to make you understand that I love you, and always will?'

'That's easy. Leave out the "always" part.'

'But it's true,' he protested. 'Last night was great – but if you think that's the only way I care about you, then you must have a brain the size of a chimpanzee's.'

'I can see that love songs and sonnets wouldn't be your strong point,' she said, laughing. 'You don't have a very romantic way of putting things.'

'Point taken. So let's be practical, then. There's such a thing as divorce, you know. You can't tell me you're happy with Sonchai. If you love me you can't be. So do you really want to spend the rest of your life with him?'

'Yes.'

'Why?'

'Because he's safe. He can't hurt me – at least, not very much.'

'Jesus, Panda! I never thought of you as someone who was afraid of life. Just the opposite, actually,' exclaimed Teddy, shocked at the very idea.

'Perhaps you don't know me as well as you think you do.'

'I know you better than you know you,' he returned crisply. 'And you're not like that.'

'Let's not talk about depressing things like marriage,' Panda said, reaching across the table and putting her hand over his. 'Let's just enjoy the morning. We don't have to leave until after lunch, do we?'

'I have a better idea. Why don't we stay on and enjoy the whole weekend? I guarantee I won't talk about marriage or the future or anything like that. Just give Sonchai a call and tell him you're swamped with work and can't make it back.'

'I don't have to. He's up in the north with the Japanese doing the Khun Sa interview.'

'Great. Then I'm the only one who's got to make a phone call. After that we can go explore the tea estates.'

'I haven't agreed to stay yet. Or haven't you noticed?'

'I've noticed,' he declared. 'But I'll stay on by myself if I have to. I'm not going back yet.'

She blew him a kiss across the table. 'I couldn't bring

myself to leave if you were staying.'

'And the truth is – I couldn't actually bring myself to stay without you,' he said with a grin.

CHAPTER 13

BANGKOK, 1976

Lisa almost felt like she was a teenager again, young and free and full of optimism, as she walked down the hall toward her first class at the Thai language school. Leonard had seemed quite happy to be left at the playschool and – while realizing that he was old enough to be away from her for several hours without any preliminary tears had been a bit of a wrench – it certainly had its advantages. To begin with, it was giving her this chance to learn a little Thai, something that should make her life in Bangkok considerably easier. She was really glad John had given her the idea.

She wondered if he would be there, too. Probably not, she decided. He might not even be back from that trip to the north he had been talking about; and, even if he were, he would probably be too busy to sign up for a class that met every morning for six weeks. It didn't really matter though. Of course it would be fun to see him but she certainly wasn't studying Thai just because he might be there.

'Hey there, Lisa, are you looking for the beginner's class?' a drawling voice behind her called. 'Somebody said it was the last door on the left.'

'John,' she said, turning toward the voice. 'How are you? How was your trip?'

'Pretty good, although I have to say it had a few hairy moments. If you've got a little time after class, I'll tell you about it. Maybe we can get ourselves a cold drink or something.'

'Great! I don't have to pick up Leonard until twelve.'

They found the right room without difficulty, took seats next to each other and spent the next hour wrestling with the nearly unpronounceable sounds and tones of the Thai language.

'I feel like a wrung out old rag after that,' John declared when the lesson was over. 'I don't think I'm ever going to be any good at this damn language.'

'It's certainly a lot harder than Indonesian was,' Lisa said as they made their way along the school's open corridor.

'You mean you speak that too?' John asked admiringly.

'A little. We spent eighteen months there around the time Leonard was a baby. That's where we adopted him actually.'

'I guess you're used to this climate then,' John said, taking out a handkerchief and mopping his forehead. 'Let's see if we can find something cold to drink. That classroom was like a furnace.'

'Good idea. I was roasting in there too.'

'I thought I'd gone to the end of the world,' John said, when they were settled with their drinks in a large shady coffee shop on the ground floor, and Lisa had pressed him for details about his trip. 'We had to use mules to get up to Khun Sa's hangout and I still haven't recovered from riding on the damn things. I swear, my leg muscles will never be the same. We didn't have any choice though, because there was no way we could get anything like a jeep or a land rover up those mountain trails; they were too steep and narrow. Anyway – after all that effort to get there, I got the surprise of my life when I saw Khun Sa's digs. You won't believe this, but he's got a house that looks like it belongs in an LA suburb: ranch style layout, air conditioning, television aerial sticking out the roof, you name it. I thought I was seeing things.'

'Good heavens! Does everyone in the camp live like that?'

'God no, it's strictly thatch hovels and mats on the floor for the troops. But you know what really killed me?'

'No, what?'

'Seeing all the boy soldiers. He has his own army, you know. And it was the sight of ten-year-old kids standing around leaning on their guns that really blew my mind.'

'How awful,' she agreed, horrified. 'But at least he can't be all that threatening if his army is made up of children. I mean I can't believe they can really fight.'

'Believe it. They know what to do with a gun – you don't need a college degree to have learned that. And they know that when it comes to the crunch they've got to fight or be wiped out. They're not Khun Sa's only protection though. He's got grown-up soldiers too, masses of them. They're small, like everybody else in this neck of the woods, but they're men. And they're strong as steel. I've arm-wrestled with a couple of them and I swear it was the most humiliating experience of my life. I was out of the contest in a matter of seconds. You see, Khun Sa takes them when they're seven- or eight-years-old and, if they live to grow up – which I bet a hell of a lot of them don't – they can stand up against anyone or anything. Except for possibly a machine gun.'

'They sound scary.'

'They scared the hell out of me, that's for sure. You can bet your bottom dollar I was glad to get out of that place. I think it'll make good copy back in the States though. The only trouble was that we didn't get anything out of the old boy that was really front page stuff – only background, you know; page three or four of the Sunday supplement, that sort of thing. Still – a real life story on the drug trade generally gets some attention somewhere; and, what with Sonchai's pictures – that makes it all very close up and personal. It should make a bit of a splash. There's hope anyway.'

'Of course there's hope – lots of it. I mean, how many reporters get an inside look at the daily workings of a camp like that?'

'Not too many, I guess,' he acknowledged. Then, glancing down at his watch, he finished his coke and reluctantly said that he had to go.

Without thinking much about it, they fell into the habit of having a cold drink together after the class, and there never seemed to be a shortage of things to talk about. Not only were John's constant attempts to 'harpoon the front page story', as he put it, a source of constant interest to Lisa; but the details of her life, which she viewed as far from exciting, never seemed to bore him.

'I moved into my new apartment on Saturday,' John announced at the beginning of the third week. 'I can't believe I stayed with Sonchai and Panda for so long. They were really great to put up with me. I'd thought I was just going to be there for a few days – but then I had to get out of my old place or sign another year's lease, and then it turned out to be more than a month before I could move into the new one. Still – as long as they could put up with me, I've got to say it's a place worth waiting for. One of those old houses on Sathorn Road with high ceilings and whirling ceiling fans and those old-fashioned shuttered windows that go all the way down to the floor and a huge balcony. It looks like the setting for one of Somerset

Maugham's stories. I can't wait for you to see it.'

'I can't wait for you to invite us.'

'I'm having some people over for drinks on Friday. Can you come – you and Ted, I mean? Sonchai and Panda have promised to come and I've asked a few people from the Foreign Correspondents Club as well.'

'I'd love to. I'll have to see if Ted has made any other plans. If not, we'll certainly be there.'

Teddy hadn't made any other plans but he was noticeably unenthusiastic about the housewarming.

'Who's John?' was his first reaction.

Lisa stared at him in amazement. 'You must remember John,' she said. 'He was over here for dinner just a few weeks ago – that time we had Panda and Sonchai, Christie and William too.'

'Was he? Well, he must have been pretty boring if I've forgotten him already.'

'Maybe you're going senile,' she suggested, annoyed at having John dismissed as boring.

'Very likely,' Teddy admitted glumly. 'I came across three grey hairs when I was shaving this morning, but I still don't see why we should waste our time on someone we can forget five minutes after we met him.'

'I didn't forget him,' Lisa protested. 'He's a lot nicer

than you seem to realise. He's in my Thai class and we usually have a cold drink together afterwards.'

'You must be pretty thirsty.'

'Why are you being so awful about him?' she exclaimed. 'I'm not like that about your friends.'

'OK – I'm sorry, really I am,' Teddy said, suddenly contrite. 'We'll go.'

'And you'll be reasonably polite once we get there?'

He looked shocked. 'Of course I will. Do you think I was brought up in the gorilla cage at the zoo?' he responded; and, feeling very unappreciated, he buried his troubles in the pages of the *Bangkok World*.

Friday arrived. And, after being reminded of the event, Teddy reluctantly showered and changed, and they set off for Sathorn Road.

'What a dump,' he exclaimed, as they pulled up in front of John's apartment.

'It's not! And anyway the atmosphere is fantastic – sort of like a Somerset Maugham novel.'

'Since when have you gone in for that sort of thing?'

'Since I first read his stuff.'

'And at what point in your life did that literary breakthrough occur?'

'A few days ago,' she admitted with a giggle.

Teddy didn't pursue the subject. His mind was on the fact that Panda was likely to be at this party and his interest in architecture and literature, never very compelling, fell away to zero.

He saw her the moment he entered the room. Wearing a blue silk dress that traced the outline of her figure with tantalizing accuracy, she was standing by an open French window chatting with a couple of guys – slimy newspaper types, he guessed.

Well, he wasn't going to play the idiot by vying with those creeps for her attention, Teddy decided; spotting Christie on the other side of the room he went over and started talking to her. The trouble was that, as a means of distracting himself, it didn't work very well. He found himself straining to catch the sound of her voice, and to put together bits of their conversation.

'Don't you think that's a good idea?' Christie asked.

'Yes, great,' he said, although he had no idea what she was talking about.

'Good. Then if Lisa agrees, I'll make the reservations.'

Shit, Teddy thought, what had he gotten himself into? Not another one of her ghastly little family parties, he hoped. He didn't know how much of that sort of thing he could stand. Still, he guessed he would just have to put up with it – at least, until Panda...

Christie had drifted off to talk to other people during

these ruminations; the guests moved around from one group to another and once again Teddy found his gaze fixed on Panda.

She looked back at him this time and her eyes were serious and troubled.

Does it bother her to be in the same room with me while all these people are around?, Teddy wondered. I hope so. I hope she can't think of anyone but me and that she's wishing I'd rush over and talk to her. Well, I won't. I'll be damned if I'll join that group of dickheads hanging around her. Far better to play it cool and let her come over and talk to me.

With that in mind, he resolutely struck up a conversation with a middle-aged woman who told him more than he wanted to know about her bridge group.

Why is Teddy ignoring me like this?, Panda wondered. It must be because Lisa's here. She is looking great this evening – better than I've ever seen her; ten years younger, too. And the way she's flirting with John! I hadn't thought she was interested in any males over the age of four – but I must have been wrong, very wrong. It serves Teddy right though… and sort of says something about her little indiscretion in Japan. There must be another side to her that isn't immediately obvious.

More people arrived and the room became quite crowded. Teddy's bridge playing friend was joined by several of her companions.

'This is Ted Duncanson,' the woman told her friends. 'He works with lizards.'

'I live with a reptile,' one of the women said. 'We celebrated our twentieth anniversary last week.'

'Why Susan,' another one said, 'how can you talk that way? Bryan is such a sweetie.'

Teddy drifted away. Almost as if he were watching himself on a screen, he found himself crossing the room toward Panda. Then he realised what he was doing and abruptly turned toward the bar instead.

'I don't stay anywhere for long,' a rough looking man with kind eyes was telling Panda. 'Fishermen never do. Of course, you probably don't know what a fisherman is.'

Panda made a disinterested protest.

'I fish things out of oil wells that have fallen in. That's why they call me a fisherman, see. Sometimes it takes an hour and sometimes it takes a month. You never know. There're times you get lucky and there're times you don't.'

This man is the complete opposite of Teddy, Panda was thinking. He looks sort of rugged and uncouth but he's probably a really nice person if you can get past the whiskers and the beer cans. He probably has a wife who waits for him at the kitchen table with something she just baked and they have a comfortable reassuring kind of life, a smothering kind of life. Perhaps Teddy and I deserve each other.

If he doesn't come talk to me in the next five minutes I'm going to go over to talk to him. After all, what's wrong with talking to your cousin at a party?

Teddy, after jostling against someone at the bar who turned out to be Sonchai, asked, 'How was your trip to that opium den?'

'Not bad. There weren't any dens, though. Khun Sa's no fool. He doesn't let his soldiers touch the stuff.'

'How about the rest of his mob?'

'They're all soldiers. They haven't any choice. Everybody except babies and women and old men, that is. And there aren't many old people. If a bullet hasn't gotten them before they're forty, dysentery or pneumonia probably has.'

'I saw you got a full page of pictures in the *Bangkok World*.'

'Let's say we laid the groundwork for the next visit.'

'You're certainly a glutton for punishment if you're going back again. It can't be an easy trek up into those hills.'

'It wasn't any problem really. We managed to take mules most of the way and it was great to be out in the open, away from all the Bangkok congestion and pollution.'

Teddy, who couldn't keep his eyes off Panda very long, could only think that anyone who liked the idea of exchanging her company – however briefly – for that of a lot of filthy mules and drug dealers must be out of his mind. But then, it wasn't the first time he had had serious doubts about his cousin-in-law's sanity.

He turned his attention back to what Sonchai was saying, only to discover that he was no longer there; so he contented himself with leaning against the bar, rattling the ice around in his glass and watching Panda out of the corner of his eye. She seemed to be caught in what had to be a deadly dull conversation with the woman who was married to a reptile and he considered going over to rescue her.

The truth was that Panda wasn't bored – because she wasn't paying any attention to what her companion was saying. Instead, she was wishing that Teddy would stop watching her, because she couldn't think of anything else while his eyes were on her. She just wished that all the other people in the room would magically disappear. As it was, she didn't dare look at him. But why shouldn't she? Just for a moment? No, it was too dangerous. It was heaven to think of him looking at her though. She hoped he wouldn't stop. She hoped...

Almost involuntarily, she turned toward him. For just an instant her dark eyes held his pale green ones, and the same promise of a smile lit up both their faces. Then she turned away again.

Lisa, feeling a wave of something like electricity in

the air, stopped talking to two women she knew from Leonard's playgroup. Glancing first at Teddy and then at Panda, she read their faces and knew in a flash of certainty that they were lovers.

For a moment she felt nothing. Then she was overcome with a simple sense of emptiness. What was the meaning of her life with Teddy? He was a father for Leonard; that was all. She remembered the searing jealousy that had swept over her in Nantucket when Teddy had been too interested in Panda. After that, there had been the terrible time in California when she had been sure that he was having an affair with someone (although she didn't know who). Well, she was drained of jealousy now. She simply couldn't feel that way anymore. And in any case – if it weren't Panda, it would be someone else; so she couldn't even feel any real animosity toward her, just a sort of indifference. As long as Leonard's life wasn't affected, it didn't matter. She could live with it.

Leonard... how she loved him. He had been difficult today though; he'd thrown one of his worst temper tantrums. Teddy often said he was spoiled and maybe he was right. And maybe, when she thought about it, Leonard wasn't really the only one who mattered. Shouldn't she matter too? She was still young and there was something awful about the idea of devoting herself completely to a child. It was as if her own life were over. But then, when she thought about it, maybe it was.

No, she told herself fiercely, it's not over! I won't let it be. I won't let Teddy consign me to a life where there's motherhood and nothing else. I'm still young. I want a man to love me and make me feel alive. And I want to love someone but I can't love Teddy any longer. There's really nothing left between us now, nothing but routine and habit... but I'm not going to let that be as bleak as it sounds. I'm going to enjoy the freedom it gives me, enjoy it to the fullest.

'Excuse me, I'm going to get another drink,' she said to the man who had been telling her his plans for producing freeze dried vegetables in Chantaburi. Finding John, she held out her empty glass to him.

'This was so good, I could use another,' she said, hopefully.

'That shouldn't be difficult,' he replied, taking her glass from her and leading her through the circle of journalists who were laughing and joking around the bar.

John joined in the repartee while he was refurbishing her drink, but she had an exciting feeling that he was talking just to her. Then Lisa noticed that somehow – she didn't know quite when or how – she and John had drifted out to the far end of the long balcony. And there was no doubt that his attention was focused on her alone.

Teddy was so absorbed in his own life that it took him a while to notice how understanding Lisa was being about the amount of time he was spending away from home. He would have expected her to complain – and he mentioned it to Panda one afternoon as they were lying in bed in the Erawan Hotel.

'Christie thinks Lisa's seeing a lot of John Smith,' Panda said, with a naughty sparkle in her eye. 'Perhaps that's why she doesn't miss you as much as usual.'

'That deadhead?'

'He's not such a deadhead. He's quite intelligent actually, and awfully nice.'

'Bullshit! He's about as interesting as a cod on a slab.'

'You just have a thing against him, that's all.'

'No I don't. Why should I?'

'Because, as I might remind you, Lisa happens to be your wife. You're jealous. Go on, admit it.'

'Don't be absurd. I'm not in much of a position to be jealous, am I?'

'No, but that probably wouldn't stop you.'

Teddy considered this for a moment. 'Does Christie really think they're having an affair?' he asked.

'Yes.'

'Does she suspect the same thing about us?'

'Probably. She hasn't said anything, though.'

'Jesus. Did somebody put a notice in the *Bangkok World*, or maybe the *Bangkok Post*? Does Sonchai know?'

'I don't think so. He doesn't act as if he knows, and I certainly haven't told him.'

'When are you going to tell him?'

'Never, if I can help it.'

'You've got to tell him.'

'Why?'

'You know damn well why.'

'No, I don't.'

'Either you're being deliberately obtuse or you're trying to drive me mad.'

'Neither,' she replied calmly.

'Good God, Panda!' he rasped. 'I can't stand it anymore – knowing you're his wife, knowing that he's touching you and making love to you. I just can't share you. The thought of it tears me apart at night when I'm not with you. It tortures me. You've simply got to tell him about us and put an end your relationship with him. I can't go on like this anymore.'

'But you have Lisa,' Panda objected.

'I know. And sometimes at night when I'm half crazy with wanting you, I make love to her. But then afterwards, when I realise she's not you, I feel so awful about it that I have to get up and have a drink and do some work until I can get the whole thing out of my mind.'

323

'But why should you feel so bad about it?' she asked, genuinely bewildered.

'Because it makes me feel like some kind of rapist.'

'Why? You don't force her, do you?'

'God no!' he exclaimed, appalled at the thought. 'Of course I don't. Although come to think of it, she hasn't been teeming with enthusiasm recently. But the awful part is, that if she knew that all the time I was making love to her I was wishing with all my might that she were you – then she'd never agree to let me anywhere near her. So it comes down to lying and cheating to get her to have sex, and I feel like a complete shit doing that.'

'You're a nicer person than I am then,' Panda replied, thoughtfully. 'When I'm with Sonchai...'

Teddy clamped his hand over her mouth. 'Don't tell me,' he said, harshly. 'I don't want to know. The only thing I want to hear about you and Sonchai is the date of your divorce.'

John, having coffee with Lisa in the riverside garden of the Oriental Hotel while Leonard played nearby, said, 'You've got a great kid there, you know. Watching him really makes me miss Andy... that's my boy. He's a couple years older but he was about Len's age when I last saw him.'

'Where is he now?' asked Lisa, wondering how anyone

could go so long without seeing their son – especially if it were someone who was as great with children as John was.

'Alaska, I think. Sally, my ex, isn't very good at keeping in touch. You see, she left me for another guy but the thing that hit me the hardest was that she took Andy with her.'

He paused for a moment, as a family hanging out the laundry on a passing houseboat gave him an excuse to look away; then he said, 'I almost never talk about this to anyone. Just thinking about it makes me feel like such a failure.'

'But you shouldn't. Marriages break up all the time and anyway it can't have been all your fault. After all, she was the one who went off with someone else, not you.'

'Well, when I look at it rationally I reckon you're right – but I grew up in kind of an old-fashioned family, where a man who couldn't keep his wife just wasn't a man.'

'That's complete nonsense, if I may say so.'

'I suppose so,' he said, but the lack of conviction in his tone didn't escape Lisa.

'No you don't. You still believe it. I can tell from your voice.'

'Maybe,' he said with a shrug, 'who knows?'

Lisa reached across the table and laced her fingers through his. 'I think your wife was a fool to leave you,' she said softly. 'I don't want to pry, so don't tell me if you don't want to, but I'd like to know what happened. Why did things go wrong?'

'It wasn't any one thing really. You see, Sally was just a freshman at college when I met her. I swear I'd never seen anyone so pretty and adorable in all my life; all blond hair and enthusiasm. She made cheerleader her first semester. I could hardly believe that with all those football playing jocks around she actually liked me – but she seemed to. Well you can be sure I wasn't going to give any of them a chance to snake in on me if I could help it, so we got married that June.'

'She didn't finish college then?'

'No. I got my first job and it was in Charleston so we moved there. Andy was born there a little over a year later. I gave Sally a really rotten deal, there's no denying it.'

'What makes you say that?'

'I took her youth away. You see, she came from one of those real religious families in Tennessee, and they didn't let her go out much in high school. Then, boom! Five minutes after she had managed to get a little freedom and start enjoying life, I came along and saddled her with a husband and a kid. She never had a chance to have any fun. At least, that's what she told me later. I think she made up for it while she was married to me, but I was too dumb to realise it at the time. I'd come home and find the place a mess and Andy would be screaming and she'd say she'd been watching television or playing bridge. I know you'll think I was crazy but I trusted her. I reckoned that when you married someone you were partners; you know – together through thick and thin.'

'When did you realise that wasn't necessarily true?'

'When I got home one day and found that the place was kind of neat and quiet for a change and there was a note on the kitchen table saying that she was going to Alaska – I could hardly believe it – with guy called Chuck. She was taking Andy with her and she wanted a divorce. That was about a year and a half ago and I haven't seen either of them since.'

'Don't you want to see Andy?'

'Desperately.'

'Can't you get custody of him? After all, she was the one who walked out.'

'Maybe, I don't know. In any case, I can't stand the thought of a sordid fight.'

'But to see your son,' protested Lisa.

'The problem is that I wouldn't take him away from his mother even if I could, at least not while he's still small. And this back-and-forth business that some divorced couples put their kids through must be really hard on them. In any case, Charleston North Carolina and Fairbanks Alaska aren't exactly next-door-neighbours. It just wouldn't be feasible.'

'It would be if you only did it once a year. You could

go get him and have him for the summers,' Lisa pointed out – thinking that she would never, ever, relinquish custody of Leonard to Teddy. Then she quickly had to think of something desperately sad – like being told she would never be able to go into toe shoes again – to keep herself from bursting out laughing at the thought of Teddy ever fighting for custody of Leonard.

Unfortunately she wasn't quite quick enough to keep a momentary flicker of amusement from passing across her face; and John, as furious as he was hurt, leapt so quickly that he jarred their table and sent his coffee cup flying across the lawn.

'I knew you'd laugh,' he barked. 'At least, I should have known but I thought maybe you –'

'Oh John! I wasn't laughing at you, I swear I wasn't. How could you think I'd do that?'

Ignoring her, he strode over toward the river and gripped the garden rail as hard as he could.

'I was thinking about the difference between you and Ted,' she said, following him over toward the water's edge. 'How he always wants to have as little to do with Leonard as possible. The very thought of him waging a custody battle – well, it's hilarious.'

'Are you sure about that?'

'I wouldn't say it if I weren't.'

He shook his head gravely. 'I don't see how anyone

could be like that about his own kid,' he said. 'Even an adopted kid. But unless you get a divorce someday, which will probably never happen, I guess I'll just have to take your word for it.'

She was seized with a sudden impulse to shatter the adoption myth and tell him about Leonard's true paternity, but she managed to repress it. After all, she had promised not to tell, hadn't she? And it was a small price to pay for Ted's accepting him. It was just that secrets were awful things when you came down to it – and the more important they were, the worse it was. Not that she had ever particularly wanted to tell anyone until now. Still, the fact remained that they kept you apart from people – didn't let you get really close to them. And in this particular case left her in a situation that was almost funny. She wouldn't feel at all guilty about going to bed with John. Hadn't Ted's behaviour given her a get-out-of-jail-free card for that? But she would feel terribly guilty about breaking her promise and giving away the secret of Leonard's true paternity.

In any case, she wasn't quite sure what John's reaction would be. He had such funny old-fashioned ideas about love and marriage that knowing the whole truth about Leonard's arrival in the world might make him think less of her; and somehow, she didn't want that to happen.

Almost to her own surprise, she found herself blurting out the other secret that was on her mind, one she had made no promise to keep. 'I think Ted is having an affair with…with someone,' she faltered, reluctant to bring Panda into it.

John gaped in astonishment. 'What gives you that idea?'

'I've seen them together. I just know.'

'You seem remarkably calm about it.'

'It's not the first time; there've been others. I'm not sure just how many, probably lots. Women find him very attractive, you see.'

'And you've been able to accept that?' he asked in disbelief. 'I mean, don't you feel that's the ultimate betrayal of trust?'

'Yes, I suppose it is. But the thing is, you can really only be betrayed once. After that the trust is gone. And, without it, there can't be any such thing as betrayal. At least not unless you make a concerted effort to deceive yourself and avoid seeing the obvious. I suppose I was idiotic enough to do that for a while – to try, anyway. But then I woke up.'

'How could you go on living with someone you couldn't trust anymore?' John asked. 'God knows I couldn't have done it; not that I had any choice. Sally walked out and that was that. But you did have a choice – still do, I imagine.'

She nodded. 'Well, at first I stayed with Teddy because

I loved him too much to leave him. And then something happened that... well, it made me feel I owed him something.'

'What could you possibly have owed him?'

Lisa stirred her spoon around in her now empty coffee cup for a moment. Then, her desire not to keep anything from John overcoming her earlier determination not to give away a secret, she told him about her brief romance in Japan and Teddy's extraordinary but amazingly effective way of dealing with Leonard's arrival in their lives.

'I suppose you think I'm guilty of the ultimate betrayal of trust now too,' she ventured, hoping for him to deny it.

He didn't disappoint her. 'No, actually I don't,' he said.

'You don't?'

'No, I don't see how you can be the betrayer and the betrayed at the same time. It has got to be one or the other. I think you dealt with Ted's betrayal in a more positive way than I dealt with Sally's. I just went into what amounted to a grown-up sulking session – although if you wanted to be kind, you could call it depression. But in any case, if I had taken the route you did… Well, men just have it easier because they don't get pregnant, that's all.'

A lovely wave of relief was washing over Lisa when Leonard came running up to them, crying, 'Mommy Mommy! That boy took my fire engine and won't give it back! He says he's going to throw it in the river!'

John, seeing the culprit – a boy a little bigger than Leonard – kicking the shiny toy across the grass, grabbed him by the ear, giving it a sharp twist before repossessing the shiny treasure on Leonard's behalf.

Deafening howls from the boy brought his mother hurrying over in a cloud of fury. 'What did you do to my child?' she cried.

'I just taught him a little bit about helping himself to other people's things,' said John, unrepentant.

If only Leonard had a father like John, Lisa thought, as Leonard looked adoringly at his hero. What a wonderful feeling it was to share a child with a man; and it seemed so natural, after the confidences they had shared. There was only one thing left that they hadn't shared... still, she had promised herself – promised Ted, too – that there wouldn't be any more affairs. But what did that matter now that he was clearly in love with Panda and doubtless having sex with her?

Deciding that he wouldn't even care, she slipped her hand into John's and asked, 'Will you be home tomorrow afternoon?'

'I reckon I could be,' he said, perceiving the suggestion in her voice.

'Then, will you?'

'Yes.'

'I'll come about three then, shall I?'

'I want to come too,' Leonard squeaked.

'No darling, John and I have something we want to do just by ourselves.'

'I won't be in the way,' Leonard protested.

John ruffled the boy's hair and asked, 'Aren't there times when you want your mother all to yourself?'

Leonard nodded.

'Well, that's the way I feel about your mother tomorrow afternoon. I just want her all to myself.'

CHAPTER 14
BANGKOK, 1976

Panda slipped into the dimness of the Temple of the Emerald Buddha, knelt down on a straw mat near the splendid image, pressed her palms together and raised her hands in a deep wai. She hadn't come to pray though, she'd come to think – and it was her favourite place in frenetically active Bangkok to do it.

She couldn't go on, she thought. She had to do something. She had to make up her mind. It was really too bad that Sonchai had come home when he did last night and found her in the bath. They used to have such fun taking baths together, but last night she had just felt she wanted to scream and run away. Then when they – she just couldn't think about it. She had to tell him. Teddy was right. She had to end it.

If they both got divorces and she married Teddy – or even if she just went to America with him – it would mean giving up on everything Thai. After all, at this stage of her life it was Sonchai, not her dad and Christie (and that beast Alexander) that kept her here. Being half Thai wasn't really being Thai at all. It was Sonchai that gave her a place here, drawing her into that fringe of Thai life where he lived.

What made her value the Thai part of herself so much?, she mused. What made her want to stay here and make a place for herself here, when she loved Teddy so desperately, when she would probably be more suited to life in America? Was it childhood memories of sunshine and flowers and Teddy's lizards in the garden, or was it that she had often felt homesick for it all during the long grey days in boarding school?

If only Teddy would stay in Bangkok. He likes it here but he's mad about his work and he'll go wherever it takes him. But did she want to go wherever his work took him? Not really.

She didn't much like the thought of Teddy divorcing Lisa either. She'd feel guilty as hell about messing up her life – much worse than she would about Sonchai's (not that it really would mess his up). He'd be sorry – at least, she hoped so – but he wouldn't be torn apart. He'd just go on painting and taking pictures for the news services like he'd always done. Actually, she wouldn't want him to be devastated or anything. Well – she did. But only for a little while.

Suppose she told Teddy the whole thing was off? Unthinkable – how could she live without him? It would be like being dead when she was still moving around. But if it were really so impossible, why was she sitting here pondering and vacillating?

She knew why. She knew what she really wanted. It was for things to go on as they were, except that Sonchai would go to bars and massage parlours, so their relationship would be totally platonic. That's what she'd like. Teddy would stay here forever and Lisa wouldn't be hurt – except that Teddy wouldn't make love to her anymore. She would have more affairs like the one she had had in Japan and perhaps even have a few more little Leonards if she wanted to. And, knowing Lisa, it even seemed possible that she might turn into one of those women who were so absorbed in their children that they lost interest in sex.

'Why can't it be like that?' she was asking the emerald green figure of the Buddha when she felt the presence of someone behind her.

'Panda.'

'Teddy,' she said, turning toward him, 'what're you doing here?'

'I thought this is where I'd find you.'

'But how did you know?'

'Because I know you and I know you come here when you want to think about things.'

Panda considered this for a moment. It was at once too wonderful and too terrible that anyone should know her so well. And, she decided, a bit too fantastic.

'You're lying,' she said.

'Only a little. I went to your house looking for you and

your maid said you had told a taxi driver to bring you here, so I followed you. I wasn't at all surprised though. It was like you to want to come here.'

'My house,' Panda repeated, not at all sure this was a good idea.

'Yes. I was looking for Lisa.'

'Oh. Sonchai finished painting her ages ago.'

'It can't have been that long –'

'Shhh! People are staring at us. Let's go outside,' she said; and, after making another wai to the image of the Buddha, they crept out of the incense filled dimness of the inner sanctuary.

'Have you told Sonchai yet?' Teddy demanded, when their only audience was a long toothed ogre with a green complexion guarding the temple compound.

'Don't rush me.'

'Why the hell not? You can't keep up this double life. I know you can't. It's simply not you and God knows it's not me either. I go berserk whenever I think about you and Sonchai together.'

'But you haven't told Lisa yet either. Why do I have to be the first?'

'Because I'll tell Lisa the second you tell Sonchai, but I don't trust you to do the same.'

'Thanks for having so much faith in me.'

'I've got as much as you deserve. I'm beginning to think

you like this game of musical sex. Who will it be today, Ted or Sonchai? Whose dick am I in the mood for today?'

Breathing fire, Panda reached up and slapped him as hard as she could across the face. Seizing her hand to prevent a repetition of the attack, he said, 'I must be right if that's the only answer you can think of. Well, let me tell you, the game's over – I'm not playing anymore. I just should have stopped it sooner because it's more than I can stand.'

Then, oblivious of the fascinated stares of the people around them, he dropped her hand and went striding out of the temple compound.

Panda turned and went back into the heavily scented coolness of the inner sanctuary, kneeling down at the feet of the Buddha. Desire was the cause of suffering, he had told his followers. Well, he was certainly right about that. She would be perfectly happy if it weren't for her longing for Teddy. But perhaps he would be as good as his word, and there would never be anything between them again. That would solve everything, wouldn't it? If Teddy would just take his lizards and disappear from her life, she would be happy enough with Sonchai – wouldn't she? She would be able to look down a long vista of peaceful uneventful years with Sonchai in her beloved Thailand, undisturbed by any of the turbulent emotions that Teddy aroused in her. How nice that would be. How nice and how empty and how totally deadening.

Oh God, I've got to end things with Sonchai before I've lost Teddy completely, she told herself. I'll do it tonight. Oh, please dear God – don't let it be too late.

To her surprise, she found Alexander rather than Sonchai in the studio when she got home.

'What evil wind brings you here?' she asked cheerfully.

'I want to see Sonchai.'

'Why?'

'You're not very polite,' he observed. 'Aren't you going to offer me a piece of cake or something?'

'No, there isn't any. You can have some of the gibbon's bananas if you're hungry. Why do you want to see Sonchai anyway?'

'To find out if he really got to do that follow up interview at Khun Sa's camp. You don't happen to know, do you?'

'No, I doubt it though. He hasn't said anything. Why are you so interested in what Sonchai is doing anyway?'

'Because if he's going, I want to go along.'

Panda burst out laughing. 'Don't be such a fathead. It's a dangerous place up there, not a hangout for teenage idiots like you. Khun Sa's got a whole army defending his territory.'

Alexander drew himself up to his full height – which was getting close to five feet – and said, 'I'll have you know I'm older than lots of Khun Sa's soldiers.'

'Well, those soldiers don't have biology tests tomorrow. You do.'

'I don't,' he returned, hotly. 'I don't have one till Monday.'

'Anyway, what makes you think Sonchai's going? It's the first I've heard of it.'

'Lisa's going as far as Chiang Mai with them and she's taking Leonard. I heard her telling Mom about it this afternoon.'

'Who's "them"?'

'Sonchai and that guy John, Sonchai's friend. And maybe some others, I don't know. But if a little brat like Leonard can go as far as Chiang Mai with them, I should be able to go the whole way.'

Panda was about to elaborate on her thoughts about this – all of them negative – when Sonchai rushed in.

'It's all set. We're going,' he cried excitedly. 'It's the chance of a lifetime and I've got about ten minutes to pack.'

'Exactly what's all set?' Panda asked.

'John and I are going back up to Khun Sa's camp with those guys from Tokyo TV.'

'But you just went,' she protested.

'Well, we're going back, and this time it's Khun Sa himself who initiated the contact. Just think, he actually wants to see us.'

'Why?' put in Alexander.

'God knows. I guess he has some point he wants the international press to help him prove and he's going to use us to do it.'

'But you're not going to let him, are you?' cried Panda. 'Use you, I mean?'

Sonchai shrugged. 'What the camera sees, the camera tells,' he said indifferently. 'Unless some interfering bastard takes away the film, that is.'

'But doesn't it bother you to play into the hands of a man like Khun Sa though?' pressed Panda.

'Can't you get it into your head once and for all that journalism is not involvement. If anything, it's just the opposite.'

'But you're the one who said Khun Sa probably wants to use the press for something,' retorted Panda.

'OK, so I did. The truth is that if the devil invited me to take pictures in hell, I'd go like a shot.'

'But that's a perfectly dreadful attitude,' exclaimed Panda, horrified. 'Don't you care at all about the lives Khun Sa is ruining with his drugs?'

'I do actually. But in this case, I think he just wants to tweak his enemies' noses by showing that his position is so secure he can strut around in front of the world press with impunity.'

'What enemies?' asked Alexander.

'Listen,' growled Sonchai, thoroughly exasperated, 'I can't stand here talking. I've got to pack.' And with that he disappeared into the bedroom.

'Can I go with you?' Alexander called after him.

'No way.'

'Why not? I'll be a great help – carry your equipment for you, change your film, all sorts of stuff. I'll be invaluable.'

'Tell me about it when you're old enough to shave,' Sonchai said, taking a small canvas bag out of the top of the closet and stuffing it with shirts and underwear.

'But I already am. Just this morning –'

'Sonchai,' interrupted Panda, following him into the room and not quite shutting the door behind her, said, 'there's something really important I've got to talk to you about before you go.'

Alexander, not wanting to be excluded from a conversation that might prove interesting, trailed after them but he was disappointed when Sonchai's only response was to say, 'Put it on ice. I'll be back in a few days, OK?'

'No, it's not OK,' Panda declared, not noticing that Alexander, his ears on high alert, had followed her into the room. 'It's not the sort of thing that can go on ice.'

'Why's Leonard going with you if I can't go?' persisted Alexander. 'He'll be masses of trouble.'

'Not to me, he won't. In any case, he's not going.'

'Lisa told Mom he was. Lisa's going, too. I heard her say so this afternoon.'

'Get off my back, will you. I've got to get out of here,' exclaimed Sonchai. 'I've got a plane to catch. Lisa and Leonard are going as far as Chiang Mai, that's all.'

'It's a funny time for them to go,' reflected Panda.

'I'm off,' declared Sonchai, swinging the strap of his tripod over his back, his camera case over one shoulder and the canvas bag over the other. 'I've got a taxi waiting outside. I'll be back sometime around the end of the week.'

And to the utter dissatisfaction of both Panda and Alexander, he was gone.

'I bet you're going to be fabulously rich,' declared Alexander, after spending nearly half an hour lounging on the bed and staring at the ceiling. 'I don't know how you're going to spend all that money, so you might as well start by buying me a red Ferrari.'

'I can't imagine what you're talking about,' Panda replied.

'After Khun Sa's cut Sonchai in on one or two big drug deals, the money's going to flow through this place like water.' And, sitting up and looking around, he added, 'In fact, this place's kind of shabby. I think you'd better move.'

'Are you out of your warped little mind? Khun Sa is not cutting Sonchai in on any drug deals. He couldn't even if he wanted to, which I'm sure he doesn't. Sonchai isn't that sort of person. I don't know how you can think for a minute that he is.'

'Smooth your feathers,' returned Alexander coolly. 'I know Sonchai's a saint. He doesn't care about dirty things like money. I'd better be going now. I want to stop by the church and light a candle to Saint Sonchai.'

'Good. The door's in front of you.'

Alexander had nearly reached this hoped-for destination when he remarked, 'You know, you seem somewhat lacking in sisterly affection. You might make up for it by fixing me a sandwich; just one with a little cheese, some ham, a few tomatoes, three or four slices of chicken and a fried egg would do in a pinch.'

'The maid can fix you some fried rice – but if you ever say another word about Sonchai being involved in the drug trade I'll hold you down and pinch the end of your nose so hard that you'll have the biggest, reddest spot in the history of the International School.'

'Fat chance of that,' Alexander said, proudly flexing his arm muscles. 'Can she put a fried egg on the rice?'

'Probably.'

'Then I'll stay and keep you company for a while.'

'I don't remember inviting you.'

'I've noticed you're getting a bit senile these days.'

'And I've noticed you're getting cheekier by the minute.'

'I'm fighting against it,' he said gravely, 'but sometimes it overpowers me.' Then, going back to their former subject, he added, 'Who do you suppose Khun Sa's enemies are? I mean the ones he's using Saint Sonchai to impress.'

'Careful,' warned Panda.

'Is it the Thai police,' he continued, 'or the American Drug Enforcement Agency?'

'Who knows,' Panda replied. 'It could be the Kuomintang –'

'Who are they?'

'The remnants of the old Nationalist Chinese army, you imbecile. Plus there are squillions of other groups up there in the Golden Triangle – mostly on the Burmese side, I think – who are involved in the drug trade.'

'Trying to stamp it out or trying to jump into it?' asked Alexander.

'Probably some of each,' she replied. 'I really don't know too much about it.'

The fried rice arrived, was devoured with enthusiasm and, to Panda's relief, it endowed Alexander with the strength and inclination to go home.

When he had gone she was left to ponder the fact that John had had time to arrange a trip with Lisa and even Leonard, while Sonchai hadn't had time to tell her he was going.

It was, she supposed, the difference between love and marriage.

CHAPTER 15
AROUND THE OPIUM KING, 1976

Don Muang Airport was teeming with people as Lisa, holding Leonard tightly by the hand, looked around for John; spotting him standing with Sonchai and four Japanese reporters in the check-in queue for the Chiang Mai flight, she made her way over to him.

His face lit up when he saw her. 'You came,' he exclaimed, as if he had half-expected her not to.

'Did you think I wouldn't?'

'I was afraid Ted might make it difficult for you.'

'He did seem a bit surprised when I told him I was going – but I don't think he was very interested. You see, that same day a new species of monitor lizard – a smaller relative of the komodos in Indonesia – was brought into the research centre. Apparently it had turned up in one of the southern provinces – Yala, I think. He's been too excited about that to pay much attention to anything else. Anyway, he somehow got the idea that I was going on this trip with Emma – you know, my friend from Leonard's school – and I'm afraid I didn't make much of an effort to correct him.'

What a bastard, thought John, convinced that any man who could find a lizard more interesting than a beautiful woman must have a seriously warped sense of values. Then, turning to the Japanese team, he said, 'This is my wife Lisa and this is Leonard.'

It took a moment or two for her to adjust to this astonishing fabrication; but, as Sonchai was the only one who was in any way surprised by it, she smiled and tried to act as though this was the way she was normally introduced.

'Why did you tell them I was your wife?' Lisa asked, as soon as they finished checking in and found seats a little away from the others in the departure lounge.

'Do you mind?' John countered, a worried expression on his face.

'No, of course not.'

'I often imagine you that way, even though I know it's wishful thinking. But also, Japan is still a country where there're "good girls" and "bad girls" – like Thailand, basically. And if they knew we weren't married, that you were someone else's wife… well, they might get the wrong idea.'

'Does that matter?' Lisa said with a laugh.

'It matters to me,' John replied firmly, 'and in a way it's true, you know.'

'Wait a minute. You lost me there.'

'It's true in the important ways – in the way I love you and in what we've been to each other the past few weeks. I know some people might say that isn't very long, but it's long enough for me to know how I feel. And when the only barrier we face is a temporary one, just a question of a divorce from –'

'Are you asking me to marry you?' Lisa managed to shout over the announcement that their flight was boarding.

'But you must have known I want to marry you.'

'Not really! You never said anything.'

'I've told you I loved you about a thousand times.'

'But you didn't say anything about getting married.'

'I guess it's old-fashioned, but in my book they go together. I was afraid to press you though. Ted's so... well, he's so totally the kind of guy women are attracted to.'

'You mean, a bastard?' she laughed.

'Well, maybe. Anyway, I guess I was basically afraid you'd get bored with me and want to go back to him. But then, seeing you here – going on this trip together, with Leonard making us really a family... I suddenly couldn't resist the temptation to tell everyone you were my wife...'

The appearance of Sonchai put a hasty end to their conversation. 'Are you two just going to sit here and miss the plane?' he demanded. 'Come on, wake up – look alive.' And rounding up Leonard who was playing with another child nearby, he hurried them all through the gate and onto the plane.

Lisa's imagination was very much alive as the plane soared into the evening sky. Divorce Teddy, marry John? Why hadn't she thought about it herself? It seemed so right, so natural that there was almost a quality of inevitability about it. A sense of happiness, security and well-being surged through her, so different from the feelings of tension and nervous uncertainty she so often felt around Teddy. There had always been that deep-seated fear of losing him, a perception on an unconscious level that they would never be right for each other. Why had it taken her so long to realise this, she wondered? John was the one who was right for her, and hopefully she was right for him. He's like me, she thought, not dashing and exciting and theatrical like Teddy – but then neither am I. We're both normal and real. We both want love that lasts and isn't shared with anyone else. And we both want children. Of course, that's sharing love but doing it in a way that's beautiful.

The noise of the engines was making conversation difficult, so Lisa relaxed in her seat and let a sort of dreamy sense of happiness envelope her. Already they were a family of three, the presence of Leonard in the middle seat between them, adding a past to their present relationship and to their plans, barely formed but critically important, for a future together.

By the time they reached their hotel in Chiang Mai it seemed perfectly normal for John to sign the register as Mr. and Mrs. John Smith and son.

'We'd like two connecting rooms for tonight,' he told the desk clerk, 'and then I'll be leaving for a few days so we'll just need one room for my wife and kid.'

'We do not have connecting rooms,' the clerk replied. 'I can give you two rooms next to each other or a junior suite.'

'The junior suite,' John replied, promptly. 'The boy's too young to be off by himself.'

Lisa, suddenly feeling like a naughty teenager checking into a hotel and telling a transparent lie about being married, suppressed a giggle at the thought. Leonard, always quick to catch his mother's mood, joined in the laughter. John, assuming it was the antics of a colourful parrot that was hanging upside down from its perch behind the reception desk that was amusing them, broke out in a big smile too.

Their high spirits persisted as a bellboy picked up their bags and led them to a lift on the other side of the lobby; Leonard, playing monkey and swinging by his arms between them.

Sonchai wondered which of three of them was the greatest lunatic and the hotel clerk, who was convinced that all foreigners were mad, made a mental note to keep a watch on this particular family.

After settling into their new quarters, the three of them went down to the dining room and Leonard began to notice that things weren't quite as he expected.

'My wife will have the chicken peanut curry,' John told the waiter.

'She's not your – ouch,' exclaimed Leonard, as his mother inflicted a swift pinch on his chubby leg. Then, giving her a look of utter astonishment – she had never hurt him before – he burst into tears.

'We're playing a game, darling,' Lisa explained when the waiter had written down their order and left. 'Remember how you were pretending to be King Kong last week? Well, we're pretending that John is your real daddy and the fact that it's just a game will be our secret. It's fun to have a secret, isn't it?'

Leonard considered this for a moment and then asked, 'But is it really a secret if Sonchai knows?'

'Sure it is,' John said. 'He won't tell anyone.'

'I think I'll be King Kong again,' Leonard announced, breaking into simian motions that made his mother blush but sent John and several of the waiters into gales of laughter.

'Darling, you really must stop this,' Lisa said. 'Everyone

is watching.'

Leonard ignored her protests and continued misbehaving until a waiter arrived with their dinner. Seeing that his mother had ordered a plate of pork fried rice for him, he immediately set about scooping everything on it into something that looked like a castle. He was arguing with his mother about whether he should eat it or play with it when Sonchai came over to their table.

'Have you heard the latest?' he asked.

'No, what?' John returned.

'I've just been over to the Chiang Mai Sports Club and word is going around that there was a clash between a bunch of drug people and the DEA this afternoon. Somewhere up near Mae Hong Son.'

'What's the DEA?' Lisa asked.

'The American Drug Enforcement Agency,' Sonchai replied. 'They work with the Thai police and they're Number 4 on Khun Sa's Enemies list.'

'How big was the clash?' asked John.

'Who knows? Rumour has it that a bunch of Khun Sa's guys were killed but nobody has any hard numbers, or can even say for sure they were Khun Sa's people.'

'In any case, you've really got to cancel the rest of your trip now,' Lisa said.

The two men looked at her in amazement.

'That's the last thing we want to do,' Sonchai told her.

'Nobody runs away from a story like this.'

'But you said it might not be big,' she protested. 'It might all be rumour.'

'Maybe, but it sounds like something probably happened. And we're damn lucky to be this close to the action, geared up and ready to go.'

Turning to John, Lisa pleaded, 'You don't have to go too, do you?'

'Good God! This could be the break I've been waiting for all year,' he said. 'The big story, and I'm one of the first ones on the spot. If I got one good by-line out of it, it could make my career – change my whole life. Don't you understand?'

'I suppose so,' she said reluctantly. 'It's just that it's dangerous going up there in the best of times but when there's fighting going on…' She wanted to say more but the look in his eyes told her that any more arguments would be useless.

'The last thing they want to do is shoot reporters,' Sonchai said. 'Think of the bad publicity it would get them.'

'If they cared about bad publicity they wouldn't be dealing in drugs,' retorted Lisa.

'If they weren't dealing in drugs they wouldn't care what publicity they got, good or bad,' Sonchai returned.

Lisa was sure there was a fallacy in this somewhere but

she felt too muddled to figure it out. 'You will be careful though, won't you, both of you?' she said lamely.

They gave her hearty assurances that they would and Leonard helped them out by upsetting his plate – sending grains of rice flying across the table and onto several near-by diners – effectively diverting his mother's attention.

Later that evening when Lisa and John lay in bed together and Leonard, exhausted from the excitement of the day, was sleeping like an angel in the small alcove of their suite, she tried once again to persuade him not to carry on with the planned trip up to Khun Sa's camp but met with no more success than she had earlier. Finally she had to settle for making him promise to come back to her.

'Just try and stop me,' he said.

And she went to sleep with those words ringing in her mind.

Yet in the morning it was John who was seeking assurance. 'You and Leonard will be all right here on your own until I get back, won't you?' he asked, over coffee on the balcony outside their room.

'Of course we will.'

'You're not sorry you came then?'

'Heavens no! I'm glad for a lot of reasons, not just the obvious one.'

'Which is?'

'Being with you of course. But I just had to have a break from Ted. Living with all the deception – not just mine, his too. I'm sure he's seeing Panda and that was really getting to me. And dreading going to bed...well, fortunately he doesn't seem much interested in all that anymore, at least not with me. Still, occasionally in the night... well, I just can't do it. I wanted to get away to think about things but now I know.'

'I know too,' John said. 'There's no way I'll let you go back to him. You've got to come and live with me. You, and Leonard.'

A resounding knock on the door put an end to the topic.

'Get a move on. We're all waiting for you,' Sonchai's voice called through the door.

John took Lisa in his arms for a moment and then he was gone.

The next two days passed in a dream of happiness for Lisa. She took Leonard around in bicycle rickshaws to see the temples and handicrafts of Chiang Mai. The destinations didn't interest him but he loved the rickshaw rides and they didn't stay anywhere beyond the expiration time of his attention span and good behaviour.

On the third morning, as Leonard was creating his usual disturbance in the dining room, he found himself in competition for the 'worst child in the hotel' prize with an only slightly larger boy: one who also happened to be American. Soon the two little hooligans were noisily chasing each other around the tables, making it practically impossible for the other guests to enjoy their breakfasts – and leaving their mothers with no choice but to remove them from the scene.

Both boys were skilful at eluding capture, but eventually they romped ahead of their pursuers into the hotel garden.

'I'm Janice Smith,' the mother of the older boy said.

For a fleeting instant Lisa wondered how she should introduce herself; then, glorying in her first use of John's name, she said, 'I'm Lisa Smith.'

'Isn't that disgusting!' exclaimed Janice. 'I swear to God, half the people in the world are named Smith. I must have really been in love when I got married or I would have found someone with a better name.'

Janice, a large blond friendly woman, seemed to demand only a pair of ears from her listener as she waffled on about the various attributes of her husband that had caused her to overlook the albatross of his name when she had married him.

Lisa replied that she didn't mind the name Smith.

Janice stared at her in astonishment and then suggested, 'Well, maybe your husband has a good first name to make up for it.'

'It's John.'

'Gee whiz! My husband's name is Reginald John Smith. Isn't that the worst name you ever heard in your life? What's your hubby's middle name?'

'I don't actually know.'

'You don't know,' exclaimed Janice. 'How can you sleep in the same bed with a man when you don't know his middle name?'

'It's rather easy,' returned Lisa with a smile.

'You're a cool customer, I'll say that. I told my friends back in LA that just because I was coming to a weird place like this didn't mean I wouldn't meet some real interesting people. I've only been here three weeks and already I've met heaps.'

Janice rambled on about her new friends, the disadvantages of having to stay in a hotel until they found a house, and the numerous problems of bringing up small boys.

The latter was a subject that Lisa could relate to and after they had chatted for a while Janice said, 'My husband is sending the car around this afternoon – with a driver, can you believe that? I want to go out to a Thai silk place some of the consulate people say is the cat's meow, then stop by a dressmaker on the way back so I can get all dolled up for a big bash they're having at the Sport's Club next month. Do you want to come along? It'd give the kids a chance to play together. They seem to hit it off real well.'

Lisa quickly weighed the advantages of providing Leonard with a playmate for the afternoon against listening to Janice's nonstop chatter; the playmate won out.

They met in the lobby after lunch and the excursion proved to be surprisingly enjoyable. The staff in the silk shop was wonderfully tolerant of the boy's antics, laughing and saying how cute they were as they frolicked and romped among the bolts of brightly coloured cloth. Lisa chose three yards of amber coloured silk while Janice selected a piece with blue and yellow checks.

Yet in spite of the indulgent treatment they were receiving, the boys became restive after a while. They were quarrelsome on the way back to town and perfectly horrible at the dressmakers while Janice was being measured for her new finery.

'When it's your turn to be measured, I'll take them out for a walk,' Janice offered.

'Don't worry. I'm only going to be here for a few more days so I might as well wait and have my dress made in Bangkok,' Lisa said.

The dressmaker understood enough English to interpret this as business going out the door. 'Can do,' she hast-ily assured them. 'Two days – can do.'

'Are you sure?' Lisa asked.

Insisting that she could, the woman whipped out her tape measure; and Lisa, eager for a new dress, succumbed to being measured.

'OK boys, how about an ice cream?' Janice said, remembering a place a little way down the street she had noticed on their way into the dressmaker's.

The boy's first response was as enthusiastic as she expected, but as soon as Leonard discovered that his mother wasn't coming too he wasn't so happy. He liked ice cream, especially strawberry, but Janice frightened him a little bit. Plus, everything around him – the crowds surging along the pavement, the noisy motorcycles zipping in and out through the traffic, the enormous buses barrelling their way down the street belching black smoke as they went – seemed strange. He didn't like any of it. And he didn't like the way Janice was gripping his hand so hard that it hurt.

His discomfort had a salutary effect on his behaviour though, and it was a more than usually docile Leonard who ate his coconut ice cream (no one had understood that he wanted strawberry) without even dripping any of it on his shirt.

He felt much better on the walk back to find his moth-er. He saw her coming out of the dressmaker's shop as they approached, so he shook himself loose from Janice's grasp and ran toward her. He saw her face light up for a moment at the sight of him and then, all at once, there was the deafening sound of a gun, a splattering of blood, and his mother fell down on the rough pavement. He didn't notice the sound of one more motorcycle added to the heavy traffic as the gunman vanished into the anonymity provided by horrified crowd.

Leonard just kept running and he didn't stop until he had flung himself on his mother's blood-soaked body. He felt people pulling at him, trying to extricate him from the sodden red embrace, but he held on as hard as he could. He gripped his little hands around his mother's arms with an iron clasp. He kicked, he screamed, he bit. He used every ounce of strength in his sturdy little body to hold onto his mother – but eventually, the adult world triumphed.

The hysterical child, now covered in his mother's blood, was pulled away.

Janice took him in her arms, carried him to the car and ordered the driver to go straight back to the hotel.

Later she told reporters what she thought was the true version of events. Her friend, Lisa Smith, who had been staying in the hotel while her husband was somewhere – she didn't know quite where – had been shot for no reason at all. The gunman had disappeared into the crowd and no one had any idea who he was or where he had gone.

This was the story, along with a blurred picture of Lisa in which only part of the side of her face was visible, that appeared in the next morning's *Bangkok World*.

Panda had a hard time believing that a murder could take place on one of the main streets of Chiang Mai in broad daylight and her father and Christie shared this view. None of them made the association between the dead Lisa Smith in the newspaper and the Lisa Duncanson they knew.

Teddy had no interest in local murders and didn't read the article. He went to work as usual but he hadn't been there long before his phone rang and the American Consul in Chiang Mai told him that his wife's passport had been found. She had, the Consul told him, been rushed to hospital but had been dead on arrival. The doctors agreed that death must have been instantaneous. An American friend of his wife's was taking care of the child but Mr. Duncanson should come to Chiang Mai on the next possible flight as there were numerous formalities to be gone through; and, more immediately urgent, there was the child who would certainly need the only parent he had left. It was hoped that Mr. Duncanson would be able to shed some light on who his wife's murderer might have been.

For the first time in his life Teddy was stunned into silence. Then disbelief rolled over him in a liberating wave.

Those idiots who worked in embassies and consulates were always getting things wrong. Who would have wanted to shoot Lisa? There must have been some terrible mistake.

Barely realizing what he was doing, he found himself picking up the phone and telling Panda about it.

She didn't quite share his confidence that the Consul was making a mistake. She examined the picture again. Yes, it could be Lisa. The only problem was that it seemed too preposterous to be at all believable.

A dazed and bewildered trio – Teddy, William and Christie – took an early afternoon flight to Chiang Mai, William to translate for his nephew and to help him through the byzantine processes of the Thai bureaucracy, Christie to take charge of Leonard – if in fact it proved to be true that the Lisa who had been killed really was their Lisa. Like Teddy, she was almost entirely convinced that some macabre mistake had been made.

Once in Chiang Mai, however, they were forced to come to terms with the fact that there had been no mistake.

'But how could she have been killed like that for no reason at all?' an utterly distraught Teddy exclaimed over and over again.

The Consul, somewhat embarrassed, asked, 'Did you

know that she was registered at the hotel under the name of Mrs. John Smith?'

Teddy looked blank. 'No, why would she have done that?'

The Consul shifted uncomfortably in his chair. 'I'm afraid she checked in with a Mr. John Smith,' he said.

Teddy's usual mental acuity failed him completely. 'That's impossible,' he said. 'She didn't know anyone named John Smith.'

'Have you forgotten Sonchai's friend, John?' Christie asked, gently. 'He came to your house for dinner the night we were there. And you went to the housewarming for his new apartment.'

'Oh,' Teddy recollected dully. 'That moose head.'

'I thought he was rather nice,' Christie said. 'Everybody else seemed to think so too.'

'They couldn't have,' growled Teddy.

'You must try to be reasonable,' Christie said, coaxingly.

Teddy went nuclear at this. 'Why the hell should I be reasonable?' he roared. 'Nobody else is. Some maniac shoots my wife in cold blood and you expect me to be reasonable? Good God, what kind of woman are you?'

'Calm down,' said William testily. 'It wasn't Christie who shot your wife. She's trying her best to help you.'

Teddy's outburst had brought tears to Christie's eyes, but she put an arm around his neck and kissed him gently on the forehead. 'Of course, you're wrought up and none of us are very reasonable right now,' she murmured softly.

'I'm perfectly reasonable,' declared William, 'and I want to get to the bottom of this.'

Turning to the Consul, he asked, 'Do you believe this was a random killing by a maniac?'

'No,' the Consul replied, 'I don't. We haven't any hard evidence but we do have a probable cause.'

'That's impossible,' declared Teddy, 'there can't be any cause.'

'Be quiet, my boy,' said his uncle. 'Let's hear what the man has to say.'

'The DEA, together with the Thai police, raided a heroin processing factory up near the Three Pagodas Pass a few days ago. One of the DEA guys – as a matter of fact, the only one who has his wife here – is a fellow named Reginald John Smith. Well, the factory was burned and a lot of equipment was destroyed, to say nothing of inventories of heroin that must have been worth a king's ransom. Several men were killed, too, although they probably weren't regretted half as much as the inventories. There was a boatload of resin from the poppies ready to go into the works and a breathtaking supply of drugs, all gift wrapped and ready to fly, that will never see the streets of New York or Washington now.'

'I don't see what this –' Teddy began angrily.

'I see,' said William. 'They killed the wrong Mrs. Smith.'

'We think that's what happened,' confirmed the Consul. 'Your wife,' he told Teddy, 'was in the same hotel, the same car, even the same dressmaker's shop as the Mrs. Smith they were looking for. They got mixed up.'

'But I didn't think Khun Sa's people did that sort of thing – revenge killings, I mean. Especially in a place like Chiang Mai against a foreigner,' protested Christie.

'We don't think they do either,' replied the Consul. 'Nothing about this operation bears the signature of Khun Sa. His factory would have been better concealed and better armed, and he would never have brought the spotlight on himself by killing the wife of a foreigner. If it were the wife of one of the less conspicuous people on his enemies list... well then, I don't know. Maybe.'

'Who do you think it was then?' Christie asked.

'My guess is that it was some upstart group trying to cut in on Khun Sa's market. We've been keeping an eye on several of them.' Turning to Teddy, he added sympathetically, 'I wish I could assure you that whoever killed your wife would be found and brought to justice but I'm afraid that's extremely unlikely.'

'Never mind,' said Teddy, in too deep a state of shock to think about things like justice.

For William the next few days of guiding Teddy through the necessary formalities in Chiang Mai were like days of playing nanny to a zombie. Christie's job – trying to bring some light into the eyes of a desolate and inconsolable Leonard – was even harder. By the time they all went back to Bangkok William could at least feel that he had accomplished what he had set out to do. Christie's success with Leonard, even with the willing help of Janice, was more muted.

Leonard stayed with Christie and William while his father took his mother's body home to Vermont. No longer his usual naughty self, he followed Christie around like a silent little shadow.

When Teddy came back three weeks later, Christie assumed that even though he clearly wasn't the greatest dad in the world, he would be eager to see Leonard. So, after giving him a few days to recover from the long flight, she invited him to spend Sunday with them.

Thinking that their shared loss would bring father and son together, she was quite unprepared for the temper tantrum – the first since his mother's death – that followed the suggestion that Leonard could now go and live with Daddy. He bashed his little feet against the floor and flailed his arms in the air and howled until Teddy was convinced that not only he, but all the neighbours and anyone unlucky enough to be within a fifty-mile radius, would be deafened by the atrocious sound.

It was generally agreed that Leonard wasn't quite ready to go back to Daddy.

While Christie was trying to calm Leonard down and get him to go to sleep, Teddy settled down on the veranda for a brandy and a smoke with his uncle. As usual William wasn't feeling terribly talkative and Teddy found his thoughts drifting toward Panda; how could he help it in this achingly familiar house where they had been children together? Then, feeling like the traitor to Lisa he undoubtedly had been, he hastily put those memories – and the grown up thoughts they evoked – out of his mind.

Eventually William and Alexander responded to the call of their respective books. Teddy was left with his brandy – his third or possibly his fourth – and a rare sense of nostalgia. If only he could grab hold of the past, he thought, remembering his lizard collection and the fetid green canal that had run through the garden before they filled it in, and his first man-to-man conversation when a very drunk Uncle William had told him to stay away from women. Damn good advice actually; he should have followed it.

He also remembered how he had felt when he had first come here: how he had hated it; how devastated he had been about his dad and how desperately he had wanted his old life back. Maybe Leonard was feeling kind of like that now, he thought, probably even more so, because he was hardly more than a baby and still needed his mother. Well, thank God for Christie. She'd been an angel.

It wasn't long before a very human Christie, bringing a much needed cup of coffee with her, sank down on a rattan chair beside him and asked him how he was doing.

'I should be asking you that,' Teddy replied, 'you're the one who's been dealing with the raging storm.'

Christie laughed. 'Well, the storm's asleep now,' she said.

'You're a saint,' Teddy declared. 'What Leonard would have done without you – or what I would have done, since Lisa died – I can't begin to think.'

'You know,' Teddy said after a while, 'on that plane going back to the States, I had an overwhelming feeling that I'd killed her. I still feel like that, if you want to know; and it makes me hate myself.'

'Don't be absurd. How could you possibly think that? You had nothing to do with it.'

'Not directly, I know; but I brought her to Thailand, didn't I? I left her alone a lot. I didn't pay much attention to her. I never told her about Panda and me –' He broke off, startled at what he had let slip. But as Christie showed no sign of surprise or outrage, he added, 'maybe you kind of guessed.'

She nodded.

'I think Lisa probably figured it out too. I had no idea we were being so damn obvious, like a couple of stupid teenagers. Anyway, I see now that I did just about everything possible to drive her to Chiang Mai or somewhere – anywhere – with that John Smith bastard.'

'He wasn't actually a bastard, he was very nice,' Christie corrected. 'But you didn't exactly coach her on telling everyone she was Mrs. Smith, did you?'

'Good God, no.'

'And you didn't arrange for her to spend the afternoon with that other Mrs. Smith, did you?'

'Of course I didn't.'

'Was it your idea for her to stay in Chiang Mai while John and Sonchai went on the interview with Khun Sa?'

'You know it wasn't.'

'Then don't you think you're being a little hard on yourself?'

'Thanks,' he said. 'That means more to me than you could possibly know. Being able to love her – love her memory, that is – without being snowed under with guilt. Of course, I never should have married her. I know that now. I shouldn't have married anybody but Panda – but she was still a kid on the far side of an ocean when I started going with Lisa, and I had no idea of the effect she would have on me when she grew up. If I had known, I wouldn't have messed up Lisa's life by marrying her, hurting her... and, however indirectly, killing her the way I did. Panda actually laid into me once about the way I treated Lisa. It made me furious at the time, but now I realise she was right. She saw all the things I never bothered to notice – like how Lisa did about a million things for me and was always there for me.' He paused and gave a short laugh. 'Well, not quite always there for me, I admit, but I'm sure she wouldn't have had that affair in Japan – Leonard wasn't really adopted, you know – or gone off with that idiot, John Smith, if I hadn't driven her to it.'

Christie wasn't sure about that, but she kept her doubts to herself. She had thought for some time that Lisa was a more complicated person than she had appeared at first glance.

'I'm going to forage for another brandy,' Teddy said, getting up and starting inside. 'I'll replenish Uncle William's supply in the morning. Do you want one?'

'No, thanks.'

He disappeared into the house and came back a few minutes later with two glasses.

'You'd better have one' he said, handing her a glass. 'I'm even worse company than Leonard tonight, so you must need it.'

She accepted the glass without protest.

'Damn it,' Teddy exclaimed after a few minutes' silence. 'Why did Lisa have to get herself killed just when she found someone she could have been happy with? With someone she might have married?'

'Perhaps she wasn't as eager to marry him as you think,' suggested Christie.

'If she wasn't, then what was all that Mrs. Smith crap about?'

'I've no idea. Sonchai says John's all broken up about the whole thing though.'

'He's not the only one,' Teddy said; and, holding his empty glass out toward her, he added, 'You wouldn't get me another one, would you?'

She was about to reply that he knew where to find it when, seeing how unhappy he looked, she relented. After refilling his glass she set it on the table beside him.

Noticing that his eyes seemed moist – a bit like Alexander's sometimes were now that he considered himself too old to cry – she reached down and smoothed back a stray lock of hair that had fallen down over his forehead.

The gesture, sympathetic and not at all judgmental, was too much for Teddy. It opened floodgates of emotion; and, for the first time since Lisa's death, he broke out in gut wrenching sobs.

CHAPTER 16
BANGKOK, 1977

'You're back,' Panda exclaimed when she heard Teddy's voice on the phone some ten months later. 'How was Nakorn Sri Thammarad?'

'Not bad. We came across several new lizard species – new to me, anyway – and I had a look at some really exciting monitors. Close cousins of the Komodos in Indonesia.'

'Great! Does Christie know you're back? Leonard will want to see you.'

'Will he? I doubt it.'

'He might. You're his dad, aren't you?'

'You know the answer to that. And given the performance he puts on every time anyone suggests going to live with Daddy... The last time Christie brought it up you could have heard his howls all the way to San Francisco.'

'Well, you can scarcely blame him, you know. You're the worst father on the planet.'

'Thanks a lot.'

'You're welcome. What's happening in your life anyway? Are you going to be around for a while? We've barely had a glimpse of you since... I mean for ages.'

'Capital cities aren't the best places for lizard watching.'

'If you had spent any time in our garden recently you

wouldn't say that. They're romping all over the place there.'

'Well, I'm not about to pay a social call on you and Sonchai.'

'No, of course not. But try Daddy's garden then.'

'I don't need to. I remember it well. You know that.'

She did know and she understood. He had rung her the day after his emotional breakdown in front of Christie and told her that he was going to be in Indonesia for a couple of weeks. Apparently there was some kind of conference in Jakarta he suddenly wanted to go to. And then if he had a chance to nip over to the island of Flores, or maybe even Komodo Island itself – he'd do that while he was in the area. What he hadn't exactly told her, but what had come through loud and clear, was that he couldn't deal with carrying on their relationship for a while. It was all much easier when he was away somewhere but, failing that, it wasn't a good idea for him to hang around places where she was likely to be.

She couldn't have agreed more. After all, he wasn't the only one who had something to feel guilty about. And when, after a week or so back in Bangkok, his Indonesia trip had been followed by a feasibility study for building a herpetology research facility in one of Thailand's four southern-most provinces (lizard heaven according to Teddy), then by repeated stays in Nakorn Sri Thammarad supervising the establishment of the facility, she'd had time to think things through; and, to some extent at least, to come to terms with what had happened.

But now, hearing his voice on the phone – a voice that sounded much like the old Teddy she remembered – she wasn't surprised when he brought up the subject of lunch.

'The Lotus Room at one?' he suggested.

'Let's meet somewhere we've never been before,' she countered.

He thought a minute and then suggested the Golden Dragon on Sukumwit.

'Good idea. I'll be there,' she said.

Teddy cast an approving glance at a large painted dragon scrolling its way up a red pillar at the centre of the restaurant when, a little before one, a waiter showed him to a table. Dragons were close enough to lizards to rank, in his view, as the most interesting mythological animal. Panda, it seemed, had made a good choice of a place for their first meeting alone since...everything that had happened.

She arrived a few minutes later; and, after the waiter had poured them steaming cups of jasmine tea and taken their order, he dived into the prime subject that was on his mind.

'I don't want to talk about this too soon,' he said, 'but

it's getting close to a year since… since the accident. And I want a future I can hang on to. I love you, Panda – and I've got to know that you love me and that you're going to divorce Sonchai and marry me.'

She hesitated.

'You are going to marry me, aren't you?' he said in alarm.

'I'm not sure.'

'What do you mean, you're not sure? You've said all along that it was Lisa, not Sonchai, you really cared about hurting. So now –'

'I know – and I don't mean to be difficult, but it wasn't just Lisa –'

'Sonchai then.'

'Not in the way you mean.'

'If you're thinking of going on having an active marriage – code for having sex – with someone you don't love… all this while you keep me on the string for an occasional naughty afternoon at the Erawan Hotel – you can forget it. You may be sufficiently immoral to think that sounds like a good idea but – surprise, surprise – I take a more choirboy approach.'

'Being so condescending and sarcastic aren't very good ways to get someone to marry you.'

He laughed. 'Point taken,' he said. 'Anyway, if Lisa wasn't the only reason, what were the others? Beside

Sonchai, I mean.'

She nodded. 'Well, it does have something to do with Sonchai, actually. But not in the way you think.'

'In what way then?'

'If I marry you – '

'Not '*if*'. '*When*' you marry me.'

'If I marry you,' she repeated firmly, 'it would mean going to America when your contract here is up. And I'd be forced to come to terms with something I've avoided trying to think about for years.'

'What's that?' he asked, mystified.

'The fact that I don't really belong here. That I'm not really Thai and no matter how often I come back to visit Daddy and Christie and that beast, Alexander – it's just visiting foreigners who happen to live here. It was only with Sonchai that I could feel I really belonged here, because I was his wife and he was a hundred percent Thai in everything except his attitudes toward life. Of course, it was those attitudes that made us suit each other so well, and –'

'That all sounds very cosy,' Teddy interrupted, 'but it doesn't sound like love. At least not a very exciting kind of love. In fact, it sounds about as thrilling as a glass of warm milk and a pair of woolly slippers.'

'I suppose that's about what it was,' she acknowledged, 'although come to think of it, I actually do have something of Thailand in me.'

'Your blood line from your mother's side,' he said helpfully.

'Well, that too. But I was thinking of the fact that Thai women don't glorify being ruled by their heart instead of their head the way women in England and America do. Here people think you're stupid if you give up the life that would be best for you just because you're in love with someone. The love won't last, or so everyone thinks, and then you're left with nothing.'

'But you don't really believe that,' he exclaimed. 'At least, you don't believe it's true for us, do you? Don't answer right away. Think first. I want the real truth.'

'Perhaps it's not entirely true for us,' she said.

'Maybe it's not at all true for us, that's what you mean,' he insisted.

'There's something else too,' said Panda, 'and it has nothing to do with Lisa or with Sonchai or with belonging.'

'Shoot.'

'I don't think it's legal to marry your cousin. Not your first cousin, anyway.'

'What does that matter? You look Thai even if you don't feel it quite a hundred percent. And I promise you that no one in any registry office in America – or wherever we do the deed – is going to wonder whether an exotic beauty named Panida Kaewsonthi, and the blonde oaf she wants to marry, some clown called Theodore Duncanson, are cousins. It would just never to occur to them to ask.'

'But we would know it wasn't really legal.'

'If you try to tell me you shrink from the thought of "living in sin", I won't believe you.'

'Don't be silly, of course it's not like that. It's just that I'd know things weren't quite right. And if we have any children they might be monsters or mental defectives or something.'

'Unlikely. The European royalty and aristocracy have been marrying their cousins for centuries.'

'Yes. And look where most of them are now – driving taxis in Paris,' she laughed.

'Well, if you don't want to give birth to any gruesome little taxi drivers,' Teddy replied, 'it's all right with me. I hate kids. We won't have any. What could be simpler?'

'I suppose it doesn't matter,' Panda said, thoughtfully. 'After all, they might be beasts like Alexander.'

'Or Leonard,' Teddy added.

'Oh, I don't know what I'm talking about or why I'm suddenly seeing difficulties everywhere I look,' Panda cried. 'The truth is that if you didn't want to marry me and take me back to America with you now that you're free I'd – well, I'd feel that the rest of my life was over. I don't care if it's only semi-legal and I don't care about children. Anyway, we'll have Leonard.'

Teddy groaned.

'Remember the monk who told my fortune in the temple that day,' Panda said, thoughtfully.

'Sure, but what does he have to do with our getting married?'

'He said in two years I'd be happy. It will probably take a while for me to get a divorce and by that time the two years will be up.'

'Then there can't be any question about your marrying me,' he exclaimed, triumphantly. 'We've got to make the old boy's prediction come true. I always said he knew what he was talking about.'

'You never said anything of the sort. But I love you terribly, terribly much – and that's the only thing that matters.'

The waiter, a man with a different set of priorities, interrupted their conversation with a clatter of bowls and ivory coloured chopsticks, and the topic of love had to give way to the subject of chicken with cashews and egg-fried rice.

Panda discussed the divorce with Sonchai that evening and, as a result, she called Christie the next morning and asked if she could come home for a while.

Leonard liked Auntie Panda, but not so much that he

would willingly move in with Alexander so she could have her old room back. On learning he was expected to do exactly that, he screamed and shrieked and threw himself on the floor and flailed his arms and legs in the air and generally behaved as though he were about to be thrown into a cage full of wild animals.

Alexander's reaction to the same news was to announce that he was going off to join the mercenaries on the Cambodian border. 'And in any case,' he objected, 'Panda has her own house. Why can't she stay in it?'

'She and Sonchai are breaking up.'

'So Sonchai gets a whole house to himself and I have to share my room – the only little bit of privacy I have – with a howling, blubbering baboon. It's not fair.'

'Leonard's not a baboon and it's only for a little while,' Christie said soothingly. 'He'll want to go back and live with his daddy soon. I'm sure Teddy misses him.'

'No one could miss Leonard,' Alexander argued. 'And if we wait for Ted to miss him he'll be here 'till he's twenty-one.'

This was actually Christie's secret fear, but nonetheless she scolded Alexander for giving voice to it. 'Come on Leonard,' she said, 'let's move your things into Alexander's room because Panda will be here in a little while.'

With Alexander's threat to eat him on his first day in Bangkok still lingering somewhere in his subconscious,

Leonard burst into renewed howls.

'Why can't he stay in there and sleep with Panda and mess up her stuff?' suggested Alexander. 'Why should I be the one to suffer?'

'I'm the one who's suffering,' declared William, coming out of the door of his study. 'Do I have to live in a zoo? There can be no earthly reason for such an infernal noise.'

A taxi sounded its horn in front of the gate and added to the general confusion. William, sensing defeat in his battle against the family hullabaloo, retreated to what now seemed like the relative quiet of his study.

'Alexander, you fathead,' Panda exclaimed as she made her way out of a taxi that was filled to bursting point with boxes and cases, 'don't just stand there like an idiot, help me with all this stuff.'

'Alexander, do this, Alexander do that,' he complained. 'Everyone just uses me when they want something and ignores me when they don't. If there was another servant around here, people would forget about me entirely.'

'A friendly gorilla would be a better substitute,' Panda said.

'I'm afraid some of Leonard's things are still in your room,' Christie said apologetically. 'He's really resisting moving in with Alexander.'

'Who wouldn't?' said Panda. 'It speaks well for his powers of discernment.'

Leonard had no idea what this meant but he liked the sound of it, repeating 'powers of discernment' over to himself three times in a row.

Panda, feeling a bit mean for causing yet another disruption to his life, took the little fellow by the hand and said, 'Come help me unpack.'

Whether Leonard was the sort of child who would inevitably have a mother fixation, or whether this was a result of Lisa's constant attention and Teddy's complete indifference, nobody knew.

What was clear was that after seeing his mother shot and killed before his eyes, he had, with a single-minded intensity, sought the consolation of a new mother figure. Initially Christie filled this role for him; but gradually, beginning with the moment she wanted him to 'help' her unpack, he began to transfer his adoration to Auntie Panda.

Auntie Panda was so beautiful; she wore such pretty bright coloured clothes – mostly blue; and she always seemed to be laughing. Much of the time she wasn't at home, and when she was she didn't play with him or talk to him as much as he would have liked. Still, she always smiled at him and seemed glad to see him when she came in. And when he had frightening dreams about people all covered with blood, she picked him up and carried him into bed with her.

As time went by Leonard began to notice that Daddy liked Auntie Panda, too. This was a nuisance as Daddy sometimes wanted to come along when Auntie Panda took him swimming at Siam Park or for an ice cream at Pan Pan.

'Let's take him to the zoo,' Panda said, one Sunday morning when Teddy came by, ostensibly to see Leonard.

'We took him there just a couple of weeks ago,' Teddy objected.

'That was last month,' Panda pointed out, 'and he says he wants to go again.'

Teddy grimaced.

'Don't you care about him at all?' she demanded.

'Frankly, no. He was always Lisa's kid. I just can't warm up to him.'

'Have you ever tried?'

Teddy shrugged. 'Maybe not. But that sort of thing is supposed to happen naturally, isn't it, or else it doesn't happen at all.'

'Not necessarily. I should think you could help it along a bit if you made any kind of effort.'

Teddy looked sceptical. 'I doubt it. But if you really want me to, I'll try.'

'Good.' Then, changing the subject, she said, 'John Smith was over here yesterday and he looked absolutely terrible. He's really suffered a lot.'

'Spare me the details. What was he doing here anyway?'

'He brought a present for Leonard – a ghastly robot thing that has flashing lights in its eyes and makes all sorts of screaming noises. Daddy hates it but Leonard loves it.'

'I'm with Uncle William on that one. It sounds awful .'

'He was very excited.'

'Who? Leonard or Uncle William?'

'John. One of the American news networks has signed him on.'

'I thought he already worked for one of them.'

'Just as a stringer I think, but now he'll actually get a real salary.'

'What made that happen?'

Panda hesitated a moment and then said, 'I think it was sort of a present from Lisa. I told him that, and it brought tears to his eyes.'

'What the hell are you talking about?'

'It was the story he sent back from that second trip to Khun Sa's camp that got him his first by-line. And then apparently the New York office, or the main office somewhere, really liked his investigative stuff on Khun Sa's enemies and the battles going on up there. If it hadn't been for that, the network would probably never have noticed him. At least, that's what he thinks and I suppose it's probably true.'

'Jesus Christ,' Teddy swore, slamming his fist down on the table. 'I can't stand the thought of that fucking bastard making capital out of Lisa's death.'

'He didn't make capital out of it,' Panda cried. 'He didn't want her to die any more than you did and I dare say he loved her a lot more than you did. He risked his life trying to find out who killed her, that's all. He didn't succeed but if he could write some stories based on what he did find out, I think that's all to the good. I'm glad her death at least did something for someone she loved and you should be, too.'

'Don't tell me what I should and shouldn't feel,' he said angrily. 'I may not have loved her the way I should – the way she deserved – but you're the last person in the world to reproach me for it. And don't forget, I did share a lot of years with her and I'm not as totally devoid of feelings as you might think.'

'All right, we both hurt her; I didn't mean it was only you.' She tried to put her arms around him but, still angry, he shook her off and moved away.

'Leonard,' he called, 'bring that new robot thing in here. I want to see it.'

The little boy, surprised and happy, ran in with his new toy proudly under his arm and held it out toward his father.

Panda caught her breath as Teddy took it from him, thinking he might smash it on the floor. But he didn't; he kept his cool while the red lights flashed in its three eyes (the extra one was in the middle of its forehead) and a deafening screech was emitted from deep in its mysterious interior.

With a burst of laughter, Teddy said, 'You know, I actually like this atrocious thing. Show me how it works.'

Leonard was over the moon at being able to show Daddy something, and it was nearly a quarter of an hour before Teddy looked at his watch, declared that it was late, and put down the mesmerizing toy.

As he was crossing the veranda on the way to his car, Panda held him by the arm and said, 'There is still one thing you can do for Lisa, you know.'

'I can't imagine what.'

'Take good care of her child. And you could start by being a little nicer to him, more like you were tonight.'

'Is that what you're trying to do?'

'That's part of it, I suppose; but then he's a very appealing little fellow.'

'I'm glad you think so,' Teddy replied.

The following evening as the maids were clearing away the last of the rice, green curry, and chicken with cashews, and bringing in plates of pineapple and papaya, William – always a bit slow to catch on where personal relationships were concerned – asked Panda, 'What's going on between you and Teddy? I want to know.'

'We're going to get married when my divorce comes through.'

'You can't marry him,' William growled. 'He's your cousin.'

'We don't care about that.'

'You jolly well should care. I don't think it's legal in America.'

'Nobody's going to know.'

'Of course they'll know. Everyone here knows Teddy's my nephew.'

'This isn't where we'll be living and it isn't the whole world,' said Panda stubbornly.

'It's my world,' he pointed out, 'and it's yours too.'

'We'll get married in America. Nobody there will know we're cousins.'

'Teddy will know, so it will never be a real marriage for him. He'll know he can leave you anytime. And you'll have no recourse, no alimony, and no inheritance rights for any children you might have.'

'And it's dangerous for first cousins to have children,' put in Christie.

'We've talked about that,' said Panda. 'It won't be a problem because we don't want any. We already have Leonard so we won't need any more.'

'Leonard would certainly put you off ever having any,' interposed Alexander.

'I think you'll want your own some day,' Christie predicted.

'I don't see why,' Panda said. 'People already think that Leonard's mine when I take him out places. Some people even say he looks like me.'

'It's not what people think, it's what you know is true that's important,' Christie said.

William, to whom finances were more important than children, said, 'You're making a big mistake if you throw away your youth and beauty on someone who can walk away from you Scot free when you're forty-five.'

'Teddy wouldn't do that,' Panda insisted.

'You just think that because you're in love. Every young fool thinks that some kind of romantic glow is going to go on forever, but it won't. And let me tell you something else about my fine nephew. He's a womanizer. I don't claim to know any details about his personal life – but if he was faithful to Lisa, I'm the King of England.'

'England doesn't have a king,' said Alexander. 'It has a queen.'

'Quiet,' roared William; then, turning his attention back to Panda, he added, 'A womanizer at thirty is a womanizer at fifty, mark my words. You're in for trouble if you throw yourself away on someone like that.'

Christie, who knew the direction Teddy's infidelity had taken, lately anyway, played nervously with her fork but didn't say anything.

'I thought you always liked Teddy,' Panda protested. 'In fact, when we were kids I thought you liked him better than me.'

William, embarrassed because this was true, looked down with sudden interest at the uneaten pineapple on his plate. 'He was a boy, that was all,' he said, gruffly. 'And I do like him. I like him a lot, I always have. But that doesn't mean I want him taking my daughter off to America as nothing more than his mistress.'

'Oh Daddy,' Panda cried impatiently, 'how can you be so old-fashioned? You're hopeless. Nobody uses the word "mistress" any more. It's ridiculous.'

'You chose the word then. I'll use any word you want as long as it illustrates what I mean.'

'Never mind that – can't you understand that I don't want to bind Teddy to me with a million legal chains? They aren't important anyway, because people get divorces all the time. I happen to be getting one at the moment myself, in case you haven't noticed, which you probably haven't. And if Teddy ever should leave me I promise you that getting money from him is the last thing I'll want to do.'

'You better go to America then,' William said calmly. 'You may look Thai like your mother. But, with attitudes like that, you'll never fit in here.'

Panda, going as white and then as red as if her father had slapped her hard across the face, rushed from the table and slammed her bedroom behind her so hard that it woke Leonard.

The little boy had been frightened by the sound of quarrelling and had slipped into her bed, so she cradled him in her arms until she cried herself to sleep.

In the morning Christie heard thumping sounds coming from Panda's room and knocked on the door.

'What are you doing?' she asked, when Panda let her in.

'Packing.'

'Where're you going?'

'To Teddy's.'

'Why?'

'I just can't stay on here with Daddy being so horrible.'

'But you can't go live with Teddy in Lisa's house,' Christie exclaimed.

'Good God, I didn't think of that,' Panda said throwing down the dress she had been folding.

'Your father wasn't very tactful,' Christie went on consolingly, 'but he didn't mean to hurt you.'

'Tactful! He's a dinosaur.'

'You're right, he's a little old-fashioned but he's nearly

sixty-years-old. What can you expect?'

'Lots of older people don't let themselves get sealed into such prehistoric ideas,' Panda said adamantly.

'Lots of older people live in places that are a little more in touch with modern ideas,' Christie replied. 'Bangkok isn't exactly at the centre of social change you know; not European- or American-style change, anyway. Most of the foreigners here, at least the ones who have lived here a long time, are more or less fossilized in the ideas of the country they left twenty or thirty years ago.'

'I suppose you're right,' Panda acknowledged. 'You have a ghastly habit of always being right.'

'Come now! It isn't very fair to put that on me,' Christie said with a laugh.

'Did you ever feel funny about coming to live in my mother's house? What had been her house, I mean.'

'No. She had already left it a couple of years before I met William so it just seemed like his house to me. I hadn't known your mother – and in any case, she hadn't died or anything, so it wasn't at all the same as going to the house where Teddy lived with Lisa. This house just seemed very Thai to me for a place where a foreigner lived and I liked that. I liked the little girl who lived here too. All that rubbish about stepmothers and stepdaughters proved to be just that – rubbish.'

'Well, things got better between Daddy and me after

you came. I used to fight with him all the time when my mother was still here and we had terrible scenes even though I was just a child. Then after she left, Daddy and I just lived in the same house, more amicably than before but without ever talking to each other, at least not in any way that counted. I suppose that was still true after you came but the silence between us wasn't quite so deafening. Of course he was always kind to me, I see that now, so I can't complain too much. But there were times when I used to wish he loved me.'

'Panida,' Christie cried, thoroughly shocked, 'of course, your father loves you. How can you possibly think he doesn't? He's just very reserved about his feelings, that's all.'

'If he has any feelings it would take a Geiger counter to find them.'

'What nonsense,' said Christie. 'Sometimes you're no more reasonable than Alexander. Now let me help you put those clothes back in the closet and then come and have some coffee before you dash off to the office.'

Later that morning Panda rang Teddy and suggested lunch.

'Great, what's up, anything special?'

'Not really. I had a little row with Daddy, that's all. I'll tell you about it.'

'OK, the Lotus Room?'

'I like the Golden Dragon. That's where you asked me to marry you.'

'I don't recall asking you. I thought we were just sorting out the details over lunch that day.'

'Then your memory cells are seriously defective; either that or they've gone on holiday somewhere.'

'Yours are turning somersaults. You'd better stay away from romantic novels. They warp the imagination.'

'I never read them,' she lied. 'The Golden Dragon at one then?'

'If I can remember. My brain cells are busy packing for a vacation in Bali.'

'Beast,' she said and hung up.

'So Uncle William doesn't relish the idea of me as a son-in-law,' Teddy said, after Panda told him about the argument with her father.

'I don't think he'd mind,' she said, 'to tell the truth I think he'd be quite happy about it if it were legal. Christie's upset though at the thought of our not being able to have any children. Any normal ones, that is.'

'Well, there actually are a few things in the world that Christie doesn't understand and that's one of them. The major drawback to marriage is children. Without them, it's a great idea. And as for how legal our marriage will be – old Uncle William hasn't done his homework and your reliable cousin Teddy has.'

'You mean it actually is legal to marry your cousin in America?'

'A little bit.'

'How can something be a little bit legal?'

'It's legal in four states, West Virginia and three others. And a marriage that takes place in any state is legal nationwide. Similarly it's legal here in Thailand and in quite a few other countries, probably including Britain as well; and the United States fully recognizes marriages performed in accordance with the laws of the country in which they were performed. I checked it out with the embassy. And if Uncle William doesn't believe me and still thinks I'm going to carry his daughter off to a life of sin and destitution in America, he can rattle down there in that Neolithic vehicle of his and find out for himself.'

'Well, he'll probably end up doing that. Because I doubt if he'll believe you. When he gets an idea in his head, he's totally pigheaded and stubborn about it.'

'I kind of remember that,' Teddy said, 'but why are you so angry at him? I like him better for not wanting to see you marry a scoundrel like me.'

'He said something awful to me last night.'

'Like what?'

'That I should go to America because I would fit in better there, that I wasn't really Thai. Those weren't his exact words but it was what he meant.'

'He probably had no idea how hard you'd take that,' Teddy observed. 'Most people wouldn't, you know.'

'He's not most people. He's my father.'

'But how well does he really know you?'

'Hardly at all.'

'There you are then. Why pay any attention to an off-the-cuff remark that wasn't meant to be an in depth character analysis?'

'I don't know. I suppose I just can't help it.'

'Now don't get this wrong, I love the aspect of you that's Thai. I don't want to change any part of you. I just think you should stop beating yourself up over this business of being a hundred percent Thai when the fact is — you're not. And I don't like to see you trying to change yourself in a direction that can only lead you away from me. Can you understand that?'

'I think so.'

'Let's go away somewhere to get married,' Teddy suggested, 'get onto neutral territory. You've already been married here once and we don't want a rerun of that memorable occasion. How about getting in touch with your English self again? They've got a lot of that mystical stuff you like there — Druids at Stonehenge, ghosts in country house bedrooms, that sort of thing – don't they? It'll be the perfect atmosphere for a honeymoon.'

'I'm not so sure,' she said with a laugh. 'The ghost of Hamlet's father rattling his chains along some stone parapet isn't quite my idea of a turn-on somehow.'

'Alright, we'll have a "no ghosts allowed" policy on our honeymoon, if that's what you want. In any case, if your divorce comes through before my contract is up,' he went on, 'we'll go together. If not I'll meet you in London. Then we'll go back to California and I'll introduce you to America.'

'You've done that already.'

'Not really. Nantucket and California may be only three thousand miles apart but they're as different as night and day. You'll like California though, especially the Bay area. You get a feeling of freedom there. It's a place where you can pretty much do anything or be anything you want. It'll suit you. I promise.'

'I'm ready to give it a try,' Panda smiled.

CHAPTER 17
CALIFORNIA, 1980

Panda tossed out her bombshell as casually as she could. 'I failed my pregnancy test today,' she said.

Teddy choked on his martini. 'I assume this is some kind of weird joke,' he said.

'A bit of a joke on us I'm afraid.'

'You can't mean you're serious?'

'I told the doctor I didn't think it was possible so he ran the test a second time.'

'But how could it have happened?'

'When little boys and little girls grow up they get married and –'

'I managed to figure out that part,' he said testily. 'But since you're so clever, why don't you explain to me why that little pink pill didn't do what all good little pink pills are supposed to do?'

'I think it was because of the bronchitis. Remember, a couple of months ago when I was really sick?'

'You did seem quite taken with the doctor. I remember you going on about how good-looking he was.'

'Idiot! Well, he did look a lot like Robert Redford – but that had nothing to do with it. Not directly, anyway.'

'Making a baby indirectly can't be much fun.'

'Don't be so horrible,' she said; and then, with a mischievous sparkle in her eye, she added, 'As I recall making this one was quite a lot of fun.'

'Are you sure I want to hear this?'

'I don't know why not.'

'If you need help figuring it out –'

Panda was laughing by this time. 'Stop looking like a thundercloud. I was over the worst of the bronchitis when we went to Hawaii, but I was still taking the antibiotics for it. Apparently they can make the birth control pills ineffective.'

'Good God! Why didn't you tell me?'

'I didn't know. It never occurred to me. I only found out when the doctor told me today. But I do remember we had quite a lot of fun in Hawaii.'

'You mean like that night on the beach when we were so… so intent on what we were doing that we nearly got swept out to sea?'

She laughed at the memory. 'I suppose it pays to take notice of whether the tide is going out or coming in.'

'What could we do though? We had to make up for all the time we had lost when you were sick. Well, at least nobody's overturned Roe vs. Wade yet. It shouldn't be too difficult to get you an abortion.'

'I suppose it shouldn't,' she agreed, her mood of elation somehow evaporating. 'But the thing is, I'm actually not so sure I want one.'

'What the fuck –'

'You shouldn't use bad words, Daddy,' Leonard admonished, coming out onto the balcony with a paper and pencil in his hand. 'Auntie Panda, how do you spell gorilla?'

She told him and then added, 'I thought you were supposed to write about what you want to do when you grow up.'

Teddy doubled over with laughter. 'He wants to be a gorilla?' he explained to Panda between paroxysms of mirth.

'No, I don't,' Leonard replied, looking hurt. 'I want to be a gorilla tamer.'

'That's an appalling choice,' Teddy said, pulling himself together. 'Gorillas should live free and unmolested in the wild, not be tamed for circuses and sideshows.'

'What's unmolested?'

'Unharmed.'

'I wouldn't hurt them. I'd just tame them.'

'Same thing,' said his father.

A thoroughly crestfallen Leonard padded back into the house, leaving his paper and pencil on the table behind him.

'Why do you always have to be so horrible to him?' Panda asked.

Teddy looked at her in astonishment. 'What did I do?'

'You hurt his feelings.'

'Bullshit! All I did was suggest that rounding up one of the world's most endangered species and using them for circus acts wasn't a good idea, and if he can't deal with that – tough.'

'But you must have seen that he didn't mean badly, and he showed a lot more imagination than most seven-year-olds would. Most of them would probably tell you they wanted to be firemen or something like that.'

'At least a fireman performs a useful social function – which is a lot more than you can say for human predators on endangered species.'

'You don't understand any species except lizards,' Panda flung back at him. 'And you certainly weren't cut out to be a father.'

'You're a hundred percent right about that one,' declared Teddy. 'Speaking of which, did the doctor give you a referral for an abortion clinic?'

'Yes, actually,' she said, picking up Leonard's paper and pencil and following him into the apartment.

Panda didn't sleep well that night.

Of course Teddy was absolutely right about not having any children. They had agreed on that and still did. She was enjoying her job at Stanford Publications and there were all sorts of possibilities for interesting promotions. Even more important was the fact that they already had a child. Leonard was a darling, and, because Teddy was such a disaster as a father, he needed more love and attention from her than most children would have. There was really no room for another child in their lives. Even so, there was something terribly disturbing about the thought of plucking out a tiny human being, one that she and Teddy had created together, and throwing it in a bin somewhere.

On the other hand, she told herself, if Teddy had shown any sign of indecision wouldn't she have told him not to be so silly – to remember what they had agreed, what they had promised her father and Christie? Wouldn't she have pointed out how awful it would be to have a child that had some ghastly deformity?' She would surely have said all these things and more besides; things like how utterly impractical the very thought of actually having the baby was.

The next day she made an appointment to have the abortion in two weeks time.

'Why are you waiting so long?' Teddy wanted to know.

'I just can't do it before then.'

'Why not?'

'For starters, Leonard's birthday party is next Saturday

and I have to get everything ready. He's wildly excited about it and I couldn't possibly let him down. Then there's the deadline for the August issue. There's simply no way I can take two or three sick days before that. Anyway, what's the rush? I'll still have lots of time.'

'It seems to me it's better to get it over with as soon as possible,' he protested. 'Well, it doesn't seem that way to me. And I'm the one who's having it,' she declared.

Leonard's birthday passed in a whirlwind of merry chaos and after a frantic ten days of hard work, the deadline for the August issue was met. Panda delayed going home after they closed the office that evening. The air was soft with the gentle warmth of early summer in Palo Alto so she strolled down the main street, bought an ice cream and paused occasionally to look into the windows of shops that interested her. One display in particular, that of a bookstore, caught her attention; she hastily finished her ice cream and went in and asked to see a book called *From Conception to Birth: Your Baby's Journey into Life*. Not only had the title attracted her but she was drawn to the picture on the cover: that of a woman who looked rather like a medieval saint – but who, unusually for a saint, was seven months pregnant.

She thumbed through it, and, on impulse, bought it. It was just a paperback so what did it matter, she thought. She'd stop in a coffee shop, glance through it and then throw it away before she got home.

She hadn't been looking at it very long when she came to a chapter called 'Common fears during pregnancy'. Apparently most women worried about having deformed or mentally handicapped babies but less than 2% of live births involved serious abnormalities. Pregnant women should relax, it said: the statistics were on their side.

Panda's mind flew back to what she had heard about first cousin marriages and tried to remember whether the chance of having an abnormal child was double or quadruple or quintuple that in the average population. Even if it were quintuple, she calculated, there was still a ninety percent chance that everything would be all right. Plus there was that new test here in the States, amnio—something—or—other, that told you whether a baby was going to be normal or not. Why not have that test before taking the irrevocable step of having an abortion?

When she got home and told Teddy what she planned to do, he was stunned. He reminded her of every reason why they should stick to their original decision, insisting that it wasn't just because they were cousins but because children would be such a drag on their lifestyle.

He argued and persuaded and tried in vain to reason with her. He hadn't realised she could be so stubborn, and he considered it a very distressing revelation – but eventually he had no choice but to give in. After all, he couldn't exactly carry a kicking and screaming wife to the abortion clinic. Husbands didn't have any rights at all anymore.

It was an extremely glum and dejected Teddy who paced the waiting room in the maternity ward nearly seven months later. He brightened considerably when the news came that Panda's ordeal was over, but he didn't trouble the nurse with any questions about the baby.

He thought Panda looked very tired when he was taken in to see her, but there was a radiance in her expression that gave her face a kind of loveliness he had never seen before.

He kissed her on the forehead and then sat down on the bed, held her hand and asked, 'Are you all right?'

'Yes. It was pretty awful though. Thank God it's over.'

He ran his hand gently along the side of her face. 'Do you want anything? Can I get you something? That old bat of a nurse isn't going to let me stay very long.'

'Don't you want to see her?'

'The nurse? God, no.'

'No! The baby, you idiot.'

'Oh yes, of course,' he said hastily.

'She's right here,' Panda said, gesturing toward a cot on the other side of her bed. 'Isn't she beautiful?'

Teddy obliged her by looking down at the wrinkled red

little creature Panda seemed to think was so wonderful. He was about to remark that babies barely looked human at this stage, when decided it would be a little tactless and wisely kept his opinion to himself.

'Barely what?' asked Panda.

'Oh nothing, I forgot.'

Then the red and wrinkled creature opened its eyes; and their colour, a misty grey green so like his own, sent an inexplicable feeling of happiness through him when he saw it. Then the baby stirred, stretched one hand out toward him and made a little gurgling sound.

'Look, she knows I'm her dad,' he exclaimed, 'and she's not even an hour old. She must be very intelligent.'

Panda just laughed.

'You know,' he said thoughtfully, 'people always harp on the potentially bad results of first cousin marriages and forget about the possibility of intensifying the good things they bring to the genetic endowment. They're obsessed with morons. They utterly overlook the increased probability of geniuses, assuming at least that the parents have some minimally acceptable IQ.'

'Assuming the parents are as brilliant as we are is what you really mean,' she teased.

'Well, when you put it that way it sounds a little –'

'It sounds a lot like someone is seriously bigheaded,' she said firmly.

The nurse cut off any further discussion of the subject by coming into the room and saying, 'Have we had a good look at our baby now? Isn't she a doll?'

'No,' Teddy said sharply, 'she's not a doll. She's an intelligent human being.'

'Of course she is,' the nurse cooed, her voice sugar-coated. She was used to new fathers (although this one, who hadn't wanted to be in the delivery room with his wife, did seem a little strange). 'But it's time for her mommy to get a little rest.'

Teddy reached down and touched the soft cheek – one that didn't strike him as red or wrinkled anymore. It was a sort of rose petal pink. 'I think I might like her,' he said.

The prediction proved true. As the weeks passed and he gazed into his daughter's pale green eyes and felt the utter trust in her small body as he held her, he decided that maybe being a dad wasn't so bad after all. The only trouble was that she was such a little tyrant, requiring Panda to spend endless hours feeding and bathing and changing her; but he soothed himself with the thought that she would undoubtedly grow out of that phase of her life a lot sooner than most kids.

In April Teddy received a letter from the Wild Life Protection Agency asking if he would be interested in heading up a special team to do research on Komodo dragons and other large lizard species at the Ragunan Zoological Institute in Jakarta. It would be a three-year assignment with a possibility of extension.

'Komodo dragons, the great love of my life, just think of that,' Teddy exclaimed, waving the letter in the air. 'And they're still roaming around free on Komodo Island.'

'There's no such thing as dragons,' declared Leonard.

'You won't say that when one of them has taken a bite out of you,' Teddy told him cheerfully. Then, expecting a more reasonable response from Panda, he said, 'A Komodo project in Indonesia; isn't that the greatest thing you've ever heard?'

Oddly enough, her reaction was rather cold. But he waffled on anyway, 'Just think, not only the biggest but one of the least studied lizard species in the world and they want me to head up the project. Isn't it fantastic!'

'I'm glad you're happy about it,' she said curtly. 'I hear Julie crying. I think she's hungry.'

'Does she have a hollow leg? You just fed her.'

'That was hours ago,' Panda said, and disappeared into the bedroom, leaving Teddy with no one to talk to except Leonard.

'Who told you there was no such thing as dragons?' he demanded.

'My teacher.'

'She just thinks that because she's never been to Komodo Island,' Teddy said dismissively.

'Where's that?'

'In Indonesia,' Teddy explained. 'There're hardly any people on it but it has lots of dragons, big ones, like this,' he said, using his entire arm span to illustrate their size. 'And they have long red tongues and scales and claws – and you can tell your teacher from me that if one of them bites her she'll die in about twenty minutes because of the poisons in their disgusting fetid mouths.'

Leonard was torn between fascination and incredulity. 'Do they breathe fire?' he wanted to know.

'No, they don't need to. They're scary enough as they are.'

'Can I see one?'

'Sure, you can, when we get to Indonesia.'

Leonard wasn't entirely sure he liked the sound of the place. 'Is Auntie Panda going, too?' he asked.

'Of course, she can't wait to get there.'

This surprised Leonard because it didn't seem to him that Auntie Panda wanted to do anything but take care of Julie.

'Is Julie going, too?' he asked, hoping the answer would be no.

'Can you imagine Auntie Panda going anywhere without her?'

Unfortunately Leonard couldn't. He considered this for a moment and then said, 'I don't think Julie will like dragons.'

'Sometimes girls don't,' Teddy explained, recalling Panda's tepid response. 'They're not brave like we are.'

'I want to see the dragons,' Leonard declared, thrilled to be grouped with his father among the brave.

'Good.'

The kid's improving with age, Teddy thought as he went in search of Panda.

As he expected, he found her lying on the bed nursing the baby. 'Can't she eat a little faster?' he asked, irritably.

He wanted to talk to Panda about all the possibilities raised in the letter, but he had discovered that while she was feeding the baby was an extremely poor time to talk to her about anything. She would just say things like 'mmm' and 'yes' and pay almost no attention to what he was telling her. Of course, a beautiful intelligent baby like Julie deserved the best of care, but he was beginning to wonder if it was good for her to spend three quarters of the day and half the night eating. She was beginning to make him think of that butterball turkey Panda had made a valiant attempt, with minimal success, to cook for Thanksgiving dinner.

While he waited for her to finish feeding Teddy wrote a letter back to the Wild Life Protection Agency expressing his enthusiasm for the project and then settled down with a drink and the evening paper. But when Panda finally announced that the baby was asleep he immediately launched into an excited picture of how great it was going to be working on the project.

'Well, have a good time and write often,' she said when she had a chance to squeeze in a word or two.

'What do you mean?' he gasped in astonishment.

'I mean, I think it would be nice if we kept in touch, don't you? Though of course if you –'

'Look here, you've completely misunderstood. We're all going.'

'No, we're not. There's no way I'm taking two children off to some malaria-infested jungle. They're about a thousand places I'd rather go, thank you very much, and if I want to see a giant lizard I'll go to a horror movie.'

'But don't you see –'

'That's the problem: I do see,' she said, and looking pointedly at the letter, she picked it up and tore it into little pieces.

'What the fuck do you think you're doing?' he demanded, grasping both her wrists although there was little left to save.

'It shouldn't be that difficult to figure it out,' she retorted, stomping on the shredded bits of paper that littered the floor.

'That's my future,' he thundered, 'what I want more than anything else in the world.'

'I don't care.'

'Yes, you do care – because it's your future too.'

'Not necessarily.'

'What does that mean?'

'It means I might like to have some control over my life, not have all my decisions made for me by somebody else – not by even you.'

'All right, fair enough. I'll live anywhere you want as long as it has enough interesting lizards and well equipped labs to study them in.'

'That's too bad. Because I want to live in a totally lizard free zone.'

'That rules out Bangkok as well as Jakarta, you know.'

'Bangkok's an exception,' she declared. Then relenting a little, she added, 'Perhaps a place like Jakarta could be too.'

'Then we're on,' he said gleefully. 'Jakarta here we come.'

'When did Jakarta come into the picture?'

'When I opened the letter. The Ragunan Institute is in Jakarta. Didn't I mention that?'

'Not in some revolting reptile swamp?'

'Of course not.'

'Then I might think about it. What's Jakarta like anyway?'

'Not bad. Kind of interesting and it's not all that far from Bangkok, you know. You could pop up there any time you wanted.'

'Any other attractions?'

'Tropical climate, nice people. And foreigners generally live in big houses and are waited on hand and foot by a cast of thousands.'

Noticing that she perked up considerably at this last inducement, he added, 'I've noticed lately that you seem to have lost your bridal enthusiasm for washing dishes and doing laundry, so a housemaid or two around the place might do wonders for your outlook on life.'

'You must be the only husband in America who doesn't do his share of these things.'

'The problem,' he declared loftily, 'is that I don't fully identify with this century. I would have fit in better in the time of Darwin and Wallace when there was more graciousness to life –'

'You would have fit in better in the time of the Neanderthals.'

'I don't think so,' he said in a contemplative manner. 'My intellectual potential would have been stifled in those Palaeolithic caves; my gentlemanly instincts, too.'

'Your what?' cried Panda with a hoot of laughter.

'Don't be rude. I'd think you, of all people, would be

sensitive to some of us having carryovers from a previous incarnation.'

'And I'm sensitive to some people – especially here in California – saying incredibly silly things about going through different incarnations. And I'm putting you in that category.'

Getting on the subject of Panda's mystical ideas was the last thing he wanted to do at the moment, but at least it had gotten her off the crazy idea of his helping with the housework. So it was worth it.

'There's something else about Jakarta that might really suit you,' he said.

'What?'

'It's an Asian city – not Thailand, of course; but still, it's a place where foreigners can sort of make their own accommodation between a local lifestyle and the one they bring with them from their home countries. Some people think that gives them the best of both worlds. And it might be just your thing.'

'Are you sure it doesn't give them the worst of both worlds?' Panda asked with a laugh. 'All the dirt and poverty of Asia and all the plastic and pizza of America?'

'You like pizza,' he reminded her.

'You know what I mean – everything cheap and garish and fast.'

'I don't think Jakarta has much of that,' Teddy said

honestly. 'At least, not that I remember. In any case, if you're really determined to get away from that sort of thing entirely, we'll have to set up housekeeping in Ulan Bator.'

'I might like that,' Panda mused.

'No, you wouldn't. You'd hate it but I really think you might like Jakarta. I can't promise you a lizard free zone around the house, because they have little ones on the walls and in the gardens like they do in Bangkok. But I don't think you'll find any of the bigger varieties wandering into the house looking for breakfast.'

'That's a relief anyway. Just don't start another lizard collection and expect me to feed it,' she said with a laugh that told him everything was going to be all right.

CHAPTER 18
JAKARTA, 1984

'You're Leonard's mother, aren't you?' asked an American woman as she and Panda waited for their drivers on the steps of a supermarket favoured by expats. 'He's one of the nicest most helpful boys in my scout troop.'

'Thank you,' Panda replied, rather surprised. She wondered what Leonard, who had become a bit difficult recently, had done to deserve this praise.

'I'm organizing next year's scouting program,' the woman went on to explain, 'and we need more mothers. I was thinking of you.'

'Good heavens,' exclaimed Panda, aghast. 'Why?'

'Because you have a little boy in the program,' replied the woman, thinking the question was quite unnecessary. 'We're going to be doing some very exciting things and of course working with the boys is a really great experience. All our mothers love it.'

'I doubt if I would. I hate children, especially horrible little boys.'

'But Leonard isn't –' protested the woman, aghast.

'I'm his wicked stepmother, you see, and everything they say about us is true.' And, seeing her driver pull up to the steps, she added, 'I'm afraid I have to dash,' and thankfully escaped.

'I think I need a vacation,' she told Teddy that evening as she finished recounting the incident.

'Why?' he asked. He had been trying to listen to Panda and read the paper at the same time and felt he might have missed a few points.

'I could have avoided the boy scouts without being so atrocious to that poor woman. I think she was really shocked.'

'Do her good, stir her up a bit,' he growled.

'You would think like that,' she exclaimed. 'In fact, it was exactly like something you would have said and really not at all like me. You're a very bad influence. I really do need –'

'Daddy, Daddy!' Julie cried, running into the room with a fluffy stuffed gibbon Panda had bought her that morning. 'Look what I have.'

'Let me see,' Teddy said, folding his paper and lifting her onto his lap.

Panda watched father and daughter together for a few minutes. Teddy's affection for Julie had come as no small surprise; and, given his total opposition to bringing her into the world, it had been a great relief. Even so, she often felt a little sad during times like this. She would think of Leonard and what a stalwart little fellow he was and how – ever since Julie had been born – there was something in his manner that suggested shouldering the burdens of life alone. And the worst of it was that even she, who loved Leonard more than anyone else did, preferred Julie. She couldn't help it. There was something about her little girl that tugged at her heart. Julie was part of her. Leonard was more like a younger nicer version of Alexander. Still, she should make more of an effort.

With this in mind, she slipped out of the room and pushed his door open. 'It's awfully dark in here,' she said. 'Why don't you turn on the desk light?'

The overhead lights in the house, never reliable, were dim at best.

'The bulb went out.'

'Well change it, Helpless.'

'Can't be bothered.'

'Don't you have any homework?'

'Just maths.'

'Why don't you do it before dinner and get it over with?'

'I've already finished it. It was easy.'

Leonard was good in maths.

'What's that?' Panda asked, seeing an envelope protruding from under an empty coke bottle on the desk.

Leonard appeared not to have heard.

Peering at it more closely, she saw that it was addressed to Mr.. and Mrs. Theodore Duncanson. Leonard, she noticed, looked like he wished he were someplace else; and, as he continued to be tongue-tied, she pulled it out, opened it – and read:

Dear Mr. and Mrs. Duncanson,

I am afraid I must ask you to come and see me about Leonard's behaviour as soon as possible. He constantly causes disturbances in class, not only distracting the other children from their work but occasionally becoming an actual menace to their physical well-being.

Today he pulled a chair out from under Jennifer Wheeler just as she was about to sit in it. She fell and cut her head and had to be sent home.

Please telephone me at the school or at home (7692481) for an appointment.

Sincerely,
Margaret Harris

'Your dad's going to go ballistic when he sees this' Panda exclaimed.

Leonard looked glum.

'What's the matter with you anyway?' she demanded. 'Why are you doing all this?'

Leonard looked even gloomier and didn't answer.

'It's not like you,' she continued. 'You've always been relatively human, compared to Alexander anyway. I can't imagine you becoming such a demon all of a sudden. Are you trying to get attention or something?'

'No.'

'If you are,' she said, ignoring his denial, 'you've chosen a pretty idiotic way of going about it.'

'I don't want any attention,' he declared. 'I hate it when people pay attention to me. I just want to be left alone.'

'Do you want me to leave you alone?'

'I don't care,' he said with a shrug. 'You can stay if you want.'

'In that case, why don't we make a plan – figure out what we're going to tell your dad?'

'Does he have to know?' Leonard asked, without much hope.

'Of course he does, you fathead – so we'd better be thinking about what you're going to tell him. Is this teacher some kind of monster who beats kids with a club when they make a mistake?'

'No.'

'Too bad,' sighed Panda. 'Doubly too bad, actually.'

'Why?'

420

'Not only would it be something of an excuse for your slide into wickedness and delinquency, but apparently it's the kind of teacher you deserve.'

'They're not allowed to hit us. They'd get fired if they did.'

'Who put in that stupid rule?'

'I don't know.'

'Listen, I have an idea – sort of.'

'What?' Leonard asked hopefully.

'Your dad's really busy these days. He's got a million things to do, and he's not going to appreciate taking a whole morning or evening – or whatever it is – to see your teacher. In fact he's probably going to be livid about the whole thing.'

The hope faded from Leonard's eyes.

'Now I might be able to save him the trouble,' Panda said. 'I know the teacher wants to see both of us but if I could promise her, absolutely and totally promise her, that you're going to stop being such a trouble-maker... well, she'd probably be satisfied with that.'

Leonard brightened.

'But before I do that,' Panda said sternly, 'you've got to swear to me in blood – well, not actually in blood, but just as solemnly as if it were in blood – that you're going to stop being such a little horror and start behaving like a member of the human race. Do you promise?'

'OK,' he mumbled indifferently.

'Not good enough,' declared Panda. 'I want a solemn promise. One you can't go back on.'

'I solemnly promise,' Leonard said, but his tone was flip and mocking and it infuriated her.

'All right – give me that letter,' she said. 'I'm taking it to your father right now.'

She reached for it but Leonard grabbed it first, and as they struggled they sent the empty coke bottle hurtling toward the tile floor. It broke into half a dozen pieces, one of which landed on Leonard's toe and left it bleeding.

'You don't have some tissues around anywhere, do you?' Panda asked.

'In the top drawer there,' he mumbled, putting his foot up on his desk to slow down the bleeding and indicating a nearby chest of drawers.

Panda found one and, as she dabbed his toe with it, a thought struck her.

'It's a sign,' she gasped.

'A sign of what?'

'A sign that we need to make a blood pact,' she said. And reaching down, she picked up a piece of glass and swiftly made a small cut near the end of the first finger on her left hand. 'If you take a solemn oath that you'll improve your behaviour at school; then I'll promise not to say anything about the letter to your father and we'll do it in real blood so that neither of us can ever, ever go back on it.'

She pressed out a few red drops from her finger; rubbed it against the sticky wetness on Leonard's toe and left her hand there long enough for their blood to mingle.

'Will you swear?' she asked. 'If you want to, that is – and remember, a blood pact ties two people together forever – then say; I swear in this blood...'

Bewildered and a little frightened by this strange ritual, he nodded and solemnly swore: 'I swear in this blood...'

'That I will be polite to the teacher...'

'That I will be polite to the teacher...'

'And stop causing disturbances in class...'

'And stop causing disturbances in class...'

'And generally stop acting like an idiot...'

'And generally stop acting like an idiot...'

'So help me God.'

'So help me God.'

'All right, now we'll burn the letter,' she said. And taking a candle from Leonard's dresser, kept there for when the electricity failed – as it often did – she set it down in the middle of the floor and knelt beside it.

'Here, you sit down here too,' she said, pulling him down beside her; then she struck a match, lit the candle, and held the letter over it.

Leonard had a sense that something very strange and

very important was happening. Mesmerized, he watched the paper turn black, curl up and disappear in a quick burst of flame – one that shone for just an instant in the semi- darkness of the room.

Panda dropped the last edge of it just in time to avoid burning her fingers, scooped up the ashes and then turned her attention back to the candle. Before she blew it out she gave Leonard a final warning. 'Remember,' she said, 'you swore in blood. Anyone who even tries to break a blood pact is lower than the most miserable worm that ever crawled across the ground.'

Leonard was quiet and thoughtful at dinner that night and when he went back to his room he couldn't shake off a queer shivery feeling. He kept looking at the red spot on the floor where his blood, perhaps a bit of Panda's too, had dripped down, and wondered if he really should have agreed to the blood pact. It was going to be kind of embarrassing to start being polite to the teacher and to stop making funny comments in class. At least, he thought they were funny – and the other kids must have too, because they always laughed. Now he'd just have to sit at his desk like all the other dummies and stop doing the things that made the other kids think he was pretty cool. Braving Dad's wrath might have actually been the better alternative, but he didn't have a choice anymore. The pact had been made and there was no way he could break it now.

But would he go back on it now even if he could? No way! A bond with Panda that would last forever –how great was that? Being adopted wasn't so bad – actually it was okay –if you had a blood relationship that was more sacred, more important, more binding than just the ordinary biological one that almost everyone had.

Panda and Teddy, untroubled by such thoughts, lingered over coffee talking about what they had each done that day in their now quite separate lives. Panda silently wondered whose account was the most boring.

Teddy's thoughts didn't run in that direction at all. He had found his day wonderfully stimulating – even exciting at times – and he was sure anyone with any interest in lizards would have agreed with him. As for Panda's day, he would have agreed that it wasn't exactly riveting. She just did the sorts of things that women did, that was all there was to it.

When they finished their coffee they read for a little while, made love briefly, and then Teddy fell asleep. But Panda lay awake for a long time, wondering exactly what was wrong with her life. Nothing really, she decided. She loved Teddy, she loved both children. Life in Jakarta was generally pleasant in spite of a lot of minor aggravations. She wasn't one of those increasingly numerous women who had been brought up to have a career. She had never felt any need to define her identity in a job description or seek self-esteem in a professional hierarchy. That was fortunate – because how could she possibly be married to a nomadic lizard fanatic and have a career at the same time? Nevertheless, she felt there was something missing in her life: some excitement that had been there when she and Teddy had met for secret lunches in Bangkok and spent long sultry afternoons making love in the Erawan Hotel.

A wave of anger at the tedium of her life suddenly flooded over her. It was Teddy's fault, she decided. Teddy had brought her to Jakarta, plunged her into this stifling world of expatriate wives with their frightful boy scouts and then proceeded to abandon her for twelve hours a day while he did went off and did exciting and interesting things (interesting to him, anyway). Furious at the thought, she reached across the bed, pulled the sheet off, and hit him hard in the stomach.

After shooting into the air like a guided missile, he recovered himself and turned on the light. 'What's wrong?' he demanded in alarm. 'Is someone breaking in?'

Panda, lying back laughing, said that she didn't think so.

'What's the matter with you, then? Whatever made you hit me like that and wake me up in the middle of the night?'

'It's not the middle of the night. It's only half past eleven.'

'Doesn't it bother you at all to know that you're being extremely irritating?'

'Not at all; being irritating can be rather fun sometimes. Don't you find that our life has become a bit too placid recently? A little irritation might be good for you, stir you up a bit and make things a little livelier.'

'I'll tell you what isn't good for me. It's being woken up with a thud in the stomach for no reason at all; and it isn't going to be good for you if it happens again.'

'Oh dear, how frightening,' Panda said with a yawn. 'Would you mind turning out the light. I'm getting sleepy.'

Teddy glared at her. He considered leaving the light on just to annoy her, but decided that it would bother him more than it would bother her so he turned it off.

Panda, feeling more relaxed now – there had been something very satisfying about waking Teddy up with a thump in the stomach – drifted into a peaceful dream where she was sauntering happily through a rich tropical rainforest. Then suddenly the dream turned into a nightmare as, sensing danger, she looked around her and saw that black panthers and clouded leopards were peering hungrily at her from the branches of trees. Terrified, she ran into a dark cave; but as her eyes adjusted to the gloom she saw that more and more pairs of eyes – hundreds of them, perhaps millions – surrounded her. Soon it became apparent that the eyes had bodies attached to them, mostly bodies of large predatory animals that gradually began to change into different and evermore alarming forms until, after a while, they began to look almost human but like vicious, demonic humans, all wearing uniforms. That was when she realised she was surrounded by thousands upon thousands of rampaging boy scouts, all bearing down on her through clouds of sticky purple bubble gum.

Desperate for protection, she breathed a sigh of relief when a horde of den mothers sprang into view – but her hopes for deliverance evaporated when she saw that they were really ogresses. Dressed in crocodile skins and gnashing their gleaming fangs as they came charging toward her, they left a trail of bleeding victims, clawed by their razor-sharp talons and covered with greenish slime, behind them.

Where was Teddy, she wondered frantically? If only she could find him, she would be safe. And then suddenly – magically – he was there at the entrance to the cave. She ran toward him and tried to fling herself into his arms, but he didn't welcome her into his embrace and did nothing to help her. Desperate with fear, she did everything she could to break through the wall of his self-satisfied indifference.

'Help me, save me!' she cried, beating on his chest.

'What the hell is going on?' the real life, not-at-all-magical Teddy demanded angrily as he sat up in bed and turned the light back on.

'Oh thank God,' Panda cried, throwing her arms around him, 'it was just the most ghastly awful dream.'

'What are you – why, you're shaking,' he said; and, realizing that she was truly frightened, he held her close, stroked her hair, and soothed her as best he could. 'What could possibly have been so dreadful?'

He listened and tried to keep his lips from twitching as she poured out the story of her nightmare.

'I swear I'll never let the boy scouts get you,' he promised her with all the seriousness he would have feigned if he had been talking to Julie, 'or the den mothers either.'

Then, drawing her back into the adult world, he said, 'Here, let me fix you a scotch and soda. That'll calm you down and make you feel better.'

He brought it to her in bed, along with one for himself and a bowl of cashews.

'What fun,' she exclaimed when he handed them to her. 'I haven't done this in ages.'

'Nonsense, you had a scotch before dinner.'

'No, no, I mean a midnight feast.'

'Like the one we had that night of the water spirits?'

'Sort of, but more like the ones we used to have at boarding school actually. Of course, this,' she said, indicating the whisky, 'would have been totally forbidden so we had to sneak it in – I usually brought airline bottles from the plane when I'd come back from holidays. Some of the other girls, the ones that lived overseas, did that too – but that just made it more fun.'

'Ah,' he said, 'there's your answer then.'

'Answer to what?'

'The boy scout problem, or the girl scout problem or the unisex scout problem or the scouts-looking-for-sex problem. A history of drunken orgies in childhood must be enough to disqualify you in perpetuity from being a den mother to any and all scouts.'

'Do you really think so?' she asked hopefully.

'It's absolutely guaranteed,' he assured her.

CHAPTER 19
JAKARTA, 1984

'Damn,' Panda said to no one in particular; and, after silently cursing whoever was responsible for the Jakarta telephone system, she went down the street to her friend Nani's house in the hope of finding one that wasn't dead as a doornail.

The one good thing about the telephones in Jakarta, she reminded herself, was that their erratic performance had brought about her friendship with Nani. She had appeared at her door one afternoon and asked in fractured English if she could use her phone because her own wasn't working. Not long after that she, Panda, had sought a return of the favour. Cups of tea, accompanied by enjoyable chats, had soon followed these exchanges – and a friendship had grown up between them.

Panda not only liked Nani, she liked going to her house because it was so much like the ones she had gazed into enviously when she was a child. Nani had five children, countless relatives who seemed to be visiting constantly, numerous servants – all of whom had large families tucked away somewhere around the place – and an assorted menagerie of caged birds, scruffy dogs, prolific cats and amusing monkeys. The result was a house that was filled with the same cheerful chaos which had always seemed so inviting to her in Thai homes.

'Yes, I pregnant again,' Nani laughed when they were seated next to a stuffed tiger in the coolness of her dark heavily furnished living room. 'Number six. I think five enough so I take jamu but it not work. You know jamu?'

'You mean traditional Javanese medicine?'

'Yes, very good for many things,' Nani said. 'Keep you look young. But sometimes it not work. You take jamu?'

'No.'

A naughty sparkle came into Nani's eyes. 'You give your husband jamu, keep him strong.'

'I don't think he needs it,' Panda said.

Nani looked sceptical. 'Only two children,' she pointed out. 'You better give him jamu.'

'I'm afraid two are all I can handle,' Panda said, firmly.

'Your husband not want more?'

'No, he's not very fond of children.'

Nani looked shocked.

'Oh, I don't mean his own,' Panda put in hastily. 'He's very fond of them.'

'What birth control you use?' Nani asked with Indonesian forthrightness.

The Thai part of Panda accepted this question as standard but the English part rebelled. After a brief inner struggle she said, 'The pill.'

'Too much dangerous.'

'Not really. It's actually the safest method of all.'

'My cousin, she die from it,' Nani said, 'blood clots.'

'That's very rare.'

'Very what?'

'It doesn't happen very often.'

'Not in your country maybe,' Nani said, unconvinced. 'Better you get IUD.'

Panda said she would think about it.

The conversation drifted on; before Panda left an hour or so later she had heard about the civet cat on Nani's roof, the ghost in her garage, and the diamonds a woman could sew into her navel if she wanted to make a man crazy to have sex with her.

Panda and Teddy had a laugh over the last of these later that evening as they were having over cocktails on the veranda.

Then Teddy grew serious and said, 'I've never heard of anyone dying from the pill.'

'I have,' Panda maintained, 'in Thailand. Thai women, not foreigners though. I wonder if Asian women are more susceptible.'

She considered her own heritage for a moment and then suggested, 'You might have a vasectomy.'

'Good God,' he exclaimed, leaping bolt upright in his chair and spilling his gin and tonic. 'Turn myself into some kind of eunuch. There's no way I'll do any such thing.'

'You wouldn't be a eunuch,' protested Panda. 'If you're a eunuch they cut it off. At least, that's what they used to do to the eunuchs in the Forbidden City in China. I mean just cutting –'

'The answer is no,' said Teddy, firmly.

Julie, who was running onto the veranda at that moment, followed by her ever-vigilant nanny, thought the peremptory word was directed at her. She stopped and her eyes filled with tears.

'Daddy wasn't talking to you, darling,' Panda said, reaching over and pulling her toward her. 'He didn't mean anything.'

Julie leaned against the security of Panda's lap and put her thumb in her mouth.

'You shouldn't let her do that,' Teddy observed.

Panda gently removed the offending thumb, but the moment she let go of Julie's hand the thumb went back in her mouth.

Teddy surveyed them both with displeasure. It was incredible how the feminine mentality was already manifesting itself in Julie even though she was only three, he thought. By the time she was twenty she would be as obstinate and stubborn as Panda and probably have ideas that were just as outlandish. The damndest thing was that they made such a lovely pair, he thought: Panda with her svelte, Eastern beauty and Julie with her pale green eyes and European features. Only Julie's black hair and a hint of the exotic in her cheekbones suggested any connection with her mother. Although on closer inspection, maybe that wasn't all. Wasn't there a similarity in their movements and expressions that linked them together? What he needed was a son: an intelligent, reasonable, good-looking fellow, good at sports, top-notch in math and science, and with a good sense of humour. Of course, there was no doubt that Julie had an IQ somewhere up in the stratosphere. She was fluent in Indonesian, as well as in English, and had never wasted time on that idiotic baby talk. On her first Christmas when toys were spread out for her under the tree the first present she had picked up was a book. He was teaching her her letters himself on evenings when he was at home in time to do it, and her progress was astonishing. But the unfortunate fact remained that Julie was a girl; and because of this – as well as his own busy schedule of course – she was essentially being brought up by her mother. He had already seen Panda pressing Julie's palms together in a wai in front of the bronze Buddha in the hallway. Not that he minded – that sort of thing was all right for a girl. In fact, most of what she would learn from Panda would be fine for a girl; just not for a son. He wouldn't want any of this mystical stuff to rub off on a boy, nor any of this 'feminine logic' which wasn't logic at all. And none of this spoiling of the kid by letting a nanny chase around after him, dish and spoon in hand, trying to persuade the little rajah to have a bite of his dinner. He had frequently protested this sort of treatment for Julie, but had given up as another example of Panda's stubbornness. She flatly refused to make Julie sit down at a table and eat her dinner the way she should, but things would be different for a son. He would insist on it.

He looked around for Panda, didn't see her and decided she had probably taken Julie off to put her to bed. She didn't know about his idea of having a son yet. He'd tell her right away. After all, neither of them was getting any younger.

Teddy brought up the subject as they were having coffee after dinner.

'Surely you must be joking,' Panda laughed.

Hurt and annoyed, he said, 'Of course I'm not joking. I'm completely serious.'

'But you barely tolerate Leonard.'

'That's different. Anyway, I think I'm quite nice to him.'

'And Julie – remember how you wanted me to have an

abortion before she was born?'

'Yes – but that's just it, "before she was born",' he exclaimed. 'I had no idea then what she'd be like. I didn't realise how really great we'd be at making babies. And we are, you know. You've got to admit that Julie is brilliant and beautiful.'

'She's smart and pretty,' conceded Panda, 'but you think she's a genius every time she opens her mouth and says, "Daddy".'

Teddy, perceiving that the conversation wasn't going along the lines he had intended, decided to approach things from a different angle. 'In any case, you must really want a son, don't you?'

'Another one – why should I? We already have Leonard.'

'But Leonard isn't really your son,' Teddy reminded her.

'I feel that he is,' she retorted.

'You've just felt that way in the last five minutes – since I said I wanted a son.'

'That's not true. I've always been fond of him, you know that; and now ever since –' but she couldn't tell him about the blood pact. He would scoff at the whole idea and if she tried to tell him about the effect it seemed to have had on Leonard, or on herself for that matter; well, she didn't think he would listen. If he did he would say it was complete nonsense. Plus there was no way he would understand the pride and happiness that had surged through her the day Leonard had won first prize at the school science fair, nor how acutely she had felt his loneliness during the past year.

She shared Julie with Teddy. Leonard was all her own.

Panda resolutely turned her attention back to what Teddy was saying.

'Just think of a boy who was a combination of you and me. Wouldn't he be great?'

'A combination of you and you is what you really want,' she retorted. 'Why don't you just wait a few years? Then perhaps the genetic engineers will have figured out some way to make babies from clones and we can have lots of adorable little Teddies, a new one every year. Naming them won't be any problem. We'll just call them Teddy One and Teddy Two and Teddy Three and –'

The current Teddy pounded his fist on the table – although at that moment he would have preferred to pound it on Panda's head. 'I can't believe you're making fun of the most reasonable, the most normal, desire in the world – wanting to have a son,' he exclaimed, and emphasized his point by giving the table another pounding. This time his coffee cup leapt an inch or two in its saucer, and a moment later Panda and Teddy were leaping a great deal more than that to avoid the hot black liquid that was splashing over the table and dripping onto their clothes.

Teddy shouted for the maid and Panda retreated to the

bathroom to attack the spots on her dress.

Teddy followed her as far as the bedroom and called through the door, 'Did it ruin your dress?'

'No, I think I got it out in time.'

'Don't put on another one. I want to start making that baby. Somehow your crazy idea about cloning doesn't appeal to me at all.'

'Why not? I'd have thought it would be just your thing.'

'No way! I couldn't stomach the conceited little bastard. I want a baby who's a combination of the two of us.'

'Well, this will be just practice,' Panda said, coming out of the bathroom wearing a towel. 'I'm on the pill, remember.'

'Nasty things, those pills. They cause blood clots.'

Dropping the towel, Panda put her arms around him and bit him sharply on the neck.

'Ouch,' he cried. 'This son of yours is going to be vicious, you know. Probably have a glorious career as an executioner.'

'It doesn't matter; we're only practicing,' she said, drawing him down on the bed.

'For now,' he agreed.

They continued to argue about having another child, and also to 'practice' for several weeks until Teddy, along with several of his colleagues from the Ragunan Institute, went off to Komodo Island for two weeks' observation of the behaviour of the giant lizards in the wild.

Teddy found the trip enormously exhilarating, but it made him realise with a shock how routine his life behind a desk and in the lab at the Institute had become. Darwin and Wallace had been his heroes ever since, as a teenager, he had first read accounts of their journeys. But now, in a wave of mysticism of which he would have thought only Panda capable, he began to see himself as their spiritual heir, taking up their quest for knowledge in the modern world.

When Teddy came back to Jakarta he looked bronzed and fit. He threw his arms around Panda, swung Julie up toward the ceiling in her favourite game of fear and delight and even gave Leonard an affectionate pat on the shoulder.

In the ensuing hours his benevolent attitude toward the boy increased because Leonard was enthralled by every detail of the Komodo adventure. He didn't interrupt, like Panda did, with stories of Julie being stung by a giant spider or the laundry maid getting pregnant by Nani's gardener. The more he talked about Komodo, the more questions Leonard asked and the more expansive on the subject he became.

'What do they eat?' Leonard asked.

'Basically anything that moves. Wild pigs, chickens, you name it. Sometimes they even eat each other.'

'You mean they're cannibals?'

'You bet your arse they are. The first thing a baby Komodo does after it comes out of the egg is run away from daddy. Sometimes even the mother eats the embryos if there's a crack in the shell.'

'How revolting,' Panda said.

'Well, they don't read Dr Spock, that's for sure,' Teddy cheerfully pointed out. 'They feel they've done the motherhood thing by spending the entire gestation period, about nine months, just guarding the eggs. After that the little bastards are on their own.'

'Why do they have to guard them so much?' Leonard wanted to know.

'If they didn't, the males would dig them up and eat them before they hatched.'

Panda shuddered.

'They're not fond of children,' Teddy added, 'except for lunch.'

'Do they eat people?' Leonard asked.

'With enthusiasm, whenever they can get their claws into someone.'

'Does that happen a lot?' Leonard persisted.

'Hard to say. The villagers say that they get hold of a child now and then. Plus there are rumours that a couple of Frenchmen disappeared on the island a few years ago and were never found. There isn't any doubt that they got old Baron Von Reding Biberegg though.'

'Who was he?' Leonard wondered.

'A Swiss fellow. He was a wildlife conservationist before that sort of thing was fashionable. You really have to admire the guy, but sometimes even the brightest people can have a fatal moment of stupidity. That's what happened to him.'

'Why?' Leonard asked. 'What did he do?'

'He broke the most important rule on the island. He left the group he was with – or rather, he let the group go on a bit ahead of him. And when they got back to where they had left him the only things they found were his camera, his hat and one shoe all covered with blood.'

Panda shuddered. 'I hope you were never alone in that place,' she said.

'What kind of fool do you take me for?' Teddy exclaimed.

'A thoroughly demented one to go there at all,' she replied.

Teddy gave her a withering look and wondered briefly why women had such narrow outlooks on life. Even Leonard understood things better than Panda did.

'They put up a wooden cross on the spot where he was eaten,' Teddy went on, turning his attention back to his more appreciative listener. 'It has an inscription that made me feel – well, it's hard to explain. But it really got to me.'

'What does it say?' Leonard wanted to know.

'It says, "He loved nature throughout his life".'

Leonard noticed a softness that he had never seen before come over his father's face; he thought it looked like his eyes were becoming slightly moist.

Panda saw it too and demanded, 'How many drinks have you had?'

'Not enough,' he snapped and poured himself another one.

'Dad, if you go back there again can I go with you?' Leonard asked.

Teddy astonished himself by saying, 'Maybe so.'

Leonard knew that it wasn't anything like a promise; but his father's tone of voice had been so positive, and he had said it so seriously, that he went to bed that night with exciting fantasies of battling prehistoric monsters and making scientific history with his discoveries.

When Teddy and Panda were in their bedroom, Teddy opened his cases and took out a small box that he put in Panda's hand.

'What is it?'

'Open it and see. We stopped in Surabaya on the way back and I picked it up from a Chinese jeweller there.'

Panda opened the box and saw a gold amulet suspended on a chain.

'It's a fertility charm from the Majapahit Kingdom, the one that ruled Java, most of Indonesia I think, in ancient times; at least, that's what the guy who sold it to me claimed.'

Panda gazed at it with decidedly mixed feelings. It was beautiful, but a fertility charm was the last thing she wanted.

'Here put it on, let's see how it looks,' he said fastening it around her neck. 'It suits you, makes you look like a Majapahit princess.' Then to her dismay he added, 'Make me a baby, a son this time.' And, putting his arms around her, he pushed her onto the bed and threw himself down on top of her.

Panda laughed when, passing a mirror, she caught sight of the amulet the next morning. Imagine scientific Teddy bringing me something like this, she thought. Well, it might have worked in Majapahit days – but she couldn't imagine it would be very effective against the pill.

That consideration, along with the undoubted beauty of the amulet, gave her the courage to wear it fairly often, especially over her favourite dress: a deep blue Thai silk one she had had made in Bangkok.

It was what she was wearing the evening before they

left for a long weekend on one of the 'Thousand Islands' off the north coast of Java.

Some of the islands were well fitted out for the tourist trade. Others, such as the one they were going to, had only a few simple bungalows along the beach and a small thatch covered lean-to that served as a restaurant. Teddy had chosen it because he had heard there was a small population of monitor lizards there, some even approaching the size of Komodos, and that made it irresistible for him.

The boat for the three-hour trip to the island was scheduled to leave from Anchol in North Jakarta at eight o'clock in the morning.

'Why on earth do we have to go at such an ungodly hour?' Panda complained over a cup of strong coffee. Had she drunk too much wine the night before, she wondered?

Teddy tried to explain that the boat had to be able to get to the island and back again before the wind and the current changed, but she didn't really listen; Julie was running around excitedly picking up all her toys, declaring that she wanted to take them with her and flying into a rage when she was told she couldn't. Panda was trying to sort her out when Leonard told her that he couldn't find his snorkelling equipment, and then the maid reminded her that she needed money for more soap powder and a new laundry pail. No sooner had she managed to quell these crises than the cook came looking for market money, enough for dinner the day they got back, and the nanny wanted to know whether she should bring cheese and apples along for Julie to eat when they were on the island.

'What's the matter, aren't you ready yet?' demanded Teddy, folding up the *Jakarta Post* and looking pointedly at his watch. 'The boat's going to leave without us if we don't get a move on.'

'Don't worry, we still have time.'

'Not if there's any traffic, we don't.'

'There's always traffic,' she snapped, 'but I'm practically out the door.'

'No, you're not; that's the trouble.'

Mumbling, 'shit' and a few other expletives under her breath, she gave up on doing anything about her own packing or appearance, merely throwing a couple of swimming costumes, three kaftans and a bit of underwear into a case and declaring herself ready.

They were almost at Anchol before it occurred to her that she had been wearing her amulet the previous and it was still around her neck. She wouldn't even be able put it in her handbag for safe-keeping because – shock, horror – in the chaos of departure, she had left it on her writing desk at home.

'My God, we have to go back,' she cried.

'Don't be ridiculous, what for?'

'My handbag – somehow I've gone off without it.'

Teddy just laughed. 'So what?' he said. 'We'll be on a nearly deserted island where you can't possibly need any of that junk you carry around with you.'

'But my makeup; I'll look like the Wicked Witch of the East without it.'

'I'd say more like Cleopatra before breakfast.'

'And my amulet,' she added, suddenly remembering that she was still wearing it. 'I didn't mean to bring that with me.'

'Just keep it around your neck, it'll be OK.'

'Even when I go swimming?'

'Sure, why not? You won't want to leave it lying around. It might tempt the room maid.'

'I'll give it to the room maid. Let her have ten children.'

'Don't you dare.'

Panda, deciding that losing it in the sea might not be such a bad idea, didn't try to argue. Instead she said, 'I suppose we'll barely get to Anchol in time for the boat as it is.'

'Right,' he agreed.

The subject of the amulet didn't come up again until bedtime when Panda was looking for her birth control pills and remembered with a shock where they were: in her handbag back in Jakarta.

Immediately grasping the amulet, she turned to Teddy and cried, 'This is what made me leave the house without them.'

'Don't be silly,' he laughed. 'It's just a piece of jewellery.'

'No, it's not – it's a fertility charm. You said so yourself.'

'I said that a thousand years ago, or whenever those Majapahit dudes were around, it was supposed to be one. I didn't say it actually was one.'

'But it is,' she protested. 'I recognize the shape. It's a yoni.'

'A what?'

'A yoni,' she repeated. 'It's an ancient Hindu symbol for a woman's sexuality– based on the place where she doesn't have what a man has.'

'Jesus,' he exclaimed, able to see that it actually did look a little like that and wondering why he hadn't noticed it sooner; just his pure mind, he expected. 'How do you know all that?'

'Sonchai used a lot of traditional Buddhist and Hindu imagery in his paintings, so I know.'

'Yes, but this is a Moslem country, remember? If it looks kind of like a yo – whatever you said – that's probably just a coincidence.'

'No it's not. Java was Hindu at one point.'

'Well maybe,' he acknowledged, 'but I still think –'

'Never mind what you think,' she interrupted, drawing an imaginary line down the centre of the bed. 'This is my side and that one over there is yours. And if you even think of crossing over, you'll find out that it's not just giant lizards that have teeth and claws.'

'I already know about your teeth,' he reminded her. 'They gave me a nasty bite the first day I met you. Come to think of it, it's a wonder I didn't come down with typhoid, possibly a fatal attack, after that.'

Ignoring this unlikely possibility, she said, 'It would have been what you deserved after throwing that lizard at me.'

'But your claws now,' he continued, 'that would be something new and different; almost as exciting as having a tussle with a particularly fetching monitor lizard.'

'Almost! What do you mean – almost? And how dare you compare me to one of your hideous horrible lizards? And even worse, how dare you have me coming out second?'

'I'm not. I'm comparing you to a hideous horrible one. I'm thinking of a particularly fetching one that arrived at the Institute a couple of weeks ago. I think she kind of fancies me because she flicks her tail in the air in a very sexy way whenever she sees me. Actually you could learn a thing or two from –'

Panda cut this suggestion short by leaping on him and digging her fingernails into his back.

'Hey, I'll get you for that,' he roared, catching hold of her wrists.

'You just try.'

'Say you're sorry,' he ordered, keeping her firmly at arm's length.

'No way!' she retorted, laughing and making clawing motions in the air with her fingers.

'Then I'll make you sorry,' he said – but the sight of blood streaming down his side diverted him. 'Good God, I'm bleeding to death!' he exclaimed. 'Monitor lizards are pussycats compared to you.'

'Idiot! One of your silly mosquito bites got scratched open, that's all.'

'You mean *you* scratched it open.'

'Perhaps I did,' she acknowledged. 'The effect is the same, isn't it?'

'Not for you, it won't be.'

'What's that supposed to mean?'

'Just this,' he said, dropping her wrists, then quickly undoing her sarong and pulling and her knickers down. 'Creatures with teeth and claws don't wear clothes,' he declared, pushing her down on the bed and falling on top of her. 'They just need to be tamed.'

'Do they? And how are you going to do that?'

'Like this,' he said, thrusting his hand firmly between her legs and playing with the small protrusion he found there.

'Stop that,' she cried, trying unsuccessfully to slide out from under him. 'What do you think you're doing?'

'I've just invented a new game, specially designed for playing with humanoid lizards or with lizardoid humans.'

'Meaning?'

'Meaning humans who have lizard-like characteristics.'

'Bollocks, there's no such word.'

'Yes there is. I've just invented it and donated it to the world.'

'You've donated a description of yourself. It fits you perfectly – at least as far as character goes.'

'Good, that settles it then. Lizardoid is an acceptable word.'

He waffled on for a while about other words he was on the point of bestowing on the English-speaking world, all the time letting his fingers continue stroking, petting and fondling the lips and the little button between her legs. Then when her cheeks were flushed, her breath was coming ever faster and he was sure that he had really got her going, he asked, 'What's the matter? You don't seem very interested in my extraordinary word-making talent.'

'I'm not,' she replied brutally. 'And you know exactly what's the matter.'

'Good, that's exactly what I had in mind,' he said; and, taking his hand away, he got up, found his swimming trunks, managed to stretch them over his now hugely enlarged cock and made for the door.

'But where –'

'For a swim.'

'Now? Why ever –'

'I told you I'd get back at you for scratching me like that,' he reminded her with a grin; then he strode out of the room, leaving her, outraged and frustrated, alone on the bed.

But she didn't lie there for long. Instead, she gathered up her discarded sarong, flung it carelessly around her and followed him outside.

A splashing sound from the pool indicated that he was somewhere near the deep end, and the light from a three quarter moon soon revealed that the swimmer was indeed Teddy rather than another hotel guest.

Going over toward him, she called, 'Is this really your idea of a great time for a swim?'

'It's a lot better than a cold shower,' he replied, coming over to the side and treading water.

'You did have other alternatives, or hadn't you noticed?'

'Like putting you out of your misery, you mean? There was no way I was going to do that.'

'Don't be so conceited. I might not have been as miserable as you thought.

'Listen, I know you and I know when you're turned on,

so don't try to tell me you liked being left that way. And it's just retribution for practically draining me of my entire blood supply.'

'It was rather ingenious,' she admitted, 'though in a definitely fiendish sort of way.' And, letting her sarong slip to the ground, she slid into the pool and began treading water next to him. 'At least it might have been agony,' she continued, 'if it hadn't been for the evidence that it was giving you a bit of bother too. That definitely cheered me up.'

'Exactly what evidence did you have in mind?'

'This, of course,' she said sweetly, slipping her hand inside his swimming trunks and taking out his wet cock, 'although some of its exuberance seems to have gone.' After gazing at it sadly for a moment, she put her mouth around the tip and slowly teased her way up the shaft making tickling motions with her tongue as she went. Almost instantly it sprang back to life with all the throbbing intensity it had shown in the bedroom; she made a game of popping it in and out of the water, sucking it and pressing it as it went back and forth – from the water, still warm from the tropical sun, to the air, cooled by the fresh breeze wafting in from the Java Sea. Then when she sensed that he was just seconds away from a Vesuvius-like eruption, she dropped it, turned and swam down to the opposite end of the pool, accidentally kicking water in his face as she went;

and then she climbed out.

Satisfied that she had left him in as dire straits as he had left her, she ran across the beach and flung herself down on the sand, where she let the shallow waves wash over her toes.

Teddy's first reaction after he managed to get the water out of his eyes was one of stunned disbelief. How could Panda – his Panda – who was always as enthusiastic about sex as he was (at least that's what he had thought, until now), do this to him? Well, he'd teach her a thing or two about how a man should be treated – and this time he'd do it properly. He wouldn't walk away until he was absolutely sure that she was turned on like she'd never been turned on before.

With this in mind, he followed her down to the water's edge, lay down half on top of her and, ignoring whatever-it-was she was saying, – something about moonlight shimmering somewhere – he thrust his hand between her legs and deftly inserted his middle finger where a larger part of his anatomy was designed to go.

'I'll get you for running out on me like that,' he vowed.

'Swimming out on you, you mean,' she laughed, delighting in the picture of him being left with a massive erection. 'This love-you-and-leave-you game is one that two can play.'

'That's OK by me – as long as we play by my rules.'

454

'And they are?'

'Rule number one is that I always win.'

'I don't actually like that rule.'

'Never mind, you'll enjoy parts of it before I've finished,' he said, drawing his finger out from inside her and using it to trace figure eights around and over the place most likely to drive her mad with wanting him. Then he brought his other hand into play, putting his thumb into one of her openings and his middle finger into the other, and began moving them in concert with the figure eights.

In terms of driving her crazy, it didn't take him long for him to have reason to congratulate himself on his brilliant strategy. But he had to admit that it did have a downside in that it was sending him into an absolute frenzy as well. There was simply no way he could get up and walk away like he had planned. What's more — far from making her sorry for abandoning him in the pool with a hard-on that would do credit to an elephant — he was giving her every reason to try the same stunt again.

Maybe the best thing he could do at this point, he reasoned, was forget this plan of getting back at her — no more of this nonsense with the fingers — and just get on with fucking her senseless.

Plunging into her, this time with the part of his anatomy perfectly designed for the task, he was beyond noticing that the breeze was getting stronger and the gentle waves were getting larger.

The vagaries of the elements were equally lost on Panda. They were both too wound up to notice that, locked together with her arms and legs wrapped tightly around him, they were rolling down a slight incline toward the water. First Panda, then Teddy, then Panda again, found themselves lying in a few inches of water but they didn't care. Caught up in the fervour of the moment, they could only focus on each other.

Then just as he was streaming into her in a cataclysmic burst of feeling, an unexpectedly huge wave, formed from the wake of a passing ship, came crashing down on his back, leaving him coughing, sputtering, gasping for air and announcing that he had drowned.

Panda was infuriatingly unsympathetic. The pounding wave had sent him rocketing deeper into her than she had ever imagined any man could go; and, after anything as triply fantastic as that, she didn't see that a little coughing and sputtering was anything to bother about.

It wasn't until the next morning that either of them gave a thought to the missing contraceptive tablets.

A few weeks later, when Panda began to suspect she was pregnant, she was convinced that the power of the amulet had made it happen. Unwilling to risk falling under its influence a second time, she secretly gave it to Nani's older sister who had been married for nearly ten years without producing a child.

One of the few good things about being pregnant, Panda decided once she'd resigned herself to the prospect of having another baby, was that it gave her an excuse for an extended stay in Bangkok. After all, why join the general exodus of foreign women to Singapore to have their babies when her old home was waiting for her, only a slightly longer plane ride away?

Therefore two months before the due date she took Julie and set off for Bangkok, leaving a woeful-looking Leonard gazing after their taxi, wishing he didn't have to stay with his dad and go to school.

CHAPTER 20
BANGKOK, 1985

A whimsical feeling that she and Julie were children together swept over Panda as she stepped into her old room. It was beginning to look a little shabby, but she was glad that almost nothing had been done to change it. Her father's salary from Chulalongkorn University was nominal, the sale of his books did little to improve things and inflation had taken its toll on the income he had inherited. The result was that the soaring prosperity of Bangkok had more or less passed him by, and modern luxuries were largely things that he and Christie managed to do without.

Panda and Julie had been there for nearly two weeks when Alexander, who had just finished his freshman year at California State College in Los Angeles, bounced in for the summer holidays.

It wasn't easy for her to reconcile this tall, good-looking boy with her memories of the baby brother who was always on the warpath, attacking her with a squirming mouse or devising some other fiendish and ingenious way of annoying her.

'I must say, you're not nearly as horrible as you used to be,' she told him as they lounged on the veranda together after lunch.

'Yeah, well it just might surprise you to know there're some girls in LA who think I'm pretty cool.'

'I've heard that people in LA have weird tastes.'

'Funny, somebody said the same thing about Jakarta. Maybe that explains why Ted puts up with you. I never understood it before.'

'He's not putting up with me at the moment; you are.'

'Sad but true. How's that beast Leonard doing, anyway?'

'His school reports are fabulous, like he's some kind of budding genius – but he's awfully serious and I'm afraid he's a bit lonely. We've become very close in the past year though.'

'Does Teddy like him any better than he used to?'

'What kind of question is that? Obviously Teddy loves him.'

'It was never obvious to me.'

'You're too much of a fathead to see it, that's all.'

'Liar!'

William, sauntering out on the veranda with the *Bangkok World* under his arm, growled, 'Don't tell me you two kids are quarrelling already?'

Panda, who didn't mind being treated as if she were still ten-years-old – it gave her a feeling of warmth and security – smiled affectionately at him, but Alexander didn't like being treated like a kid and gave his sister a conspiratorial grin as if to say, 'the old man's going dotty'.

Christie, coming out with a tray of coffee, caught his expression and would have given him a reproving scowl if Julie hadn't scampered out, grabbed hold of her leg and very nearly sent the coffee cups flying.

Alexander reached over, picked her up, held her on his lap and demanded, 'How did you and Ted – a nice enough guy but undoubtedly the worst father since the reign of Caligula – ever manage to make an adorable little girl like this?'

'In the usual way, I suppose. When you're old enough I'll tell you how it's done.'

'Too late, my girl, too late; you're talking to the campus champion.'

'Says who?'

'A gentleman doesn't name names. And anyway, the list is too long.'

'Who's the liar now? I thought Teddy had a monumental ego, but yours takes the biscuit.'

Alexander's ego came up for discussion again a few days later when Panda and Julie came back from a swim at the Sports Club and found him sprawled on the sofa with a newspaper and a cold beer.

460

'Where's Christie?' Panda asked.

'At some kind of anthropology thing; Dad was going to drop her off on his way to class.'

'Do you ever think that the time might come when you actually have to get up in the morning and do something useful – like going to work or anything?'

'I hope not,' he said with a shudder. 'But of course I'd probably be head of General Motors or president of the United States or something, where I can pretty much set my own hours and make everybody else do the work.'

'President of the unemployables, more likely.'

'That might suit me better, actually. I don't want to stifle the creative side of my nature – so I'll need plenty of free time.'

'Aren't you ever serious about anything?'

'Not if I can help it.'

'Not even about a girl?'

'Especially not about a girl.'

'Well, I suppose that's a good thing. Still, the next time I ask you, you'll probably have knocked up an American girl and end up staying there. After all that's where the best jobs are, isn't it? And I can just see you in some split-level house in a Californian suburb changing nappies for a set of screaming triplets. You'll be an adorable daddy.'

'Don't be revolting.'

'I'm just reporting what my crystal ball tells me,' she

returned airily.

'Well, it couldn't be more wrong. I'm coming back here about two seconds after graduation. The American economy is in the toilet at the moment, and things are going to get worse before they get better. The so-called Asian dragon countries are the place to be if you want to make some money. And the good news is that I'm in a great position to do exactly that.'

'I fail to see why.'

'That's because you have the business sense of Winnie the Pooh.'

'Thank you very much.'

'I notice you're not denying it. Anyway, look at me –'

'Unfortunately that's exactly what I am doing.'

'I'll ignore that. As I was saying before I was so rudely interrupted: look at me. I'm totally bilingual – which even you, my dear sister, who looks Thai, are not. Your Thai isn't bad but it's not a hundred percent on the mark; mine is. On top of that, I have an American education but I spent the first eighteen years of my life here. I understand the mentality of the people here and know how to make things work in this environment. So you see I'm perfectly positioned to make a killing.'

'God, I never thought Teddy could be surpassed in the ego department; but you run circles around him.'

'Well, I'm not going to spend my life messing around

with a lot of stupid lizards, that's for sure.'

'That's the one good thing about you,' she said affectionately. 'Probably the only thing – but at least it's a start.'

Alexander was about to expand on the subject of his good points when he noticed a cloud crossing Panda's face. 'Something the matter?' he asked.

'Nothing really,' she said, her hand flying to her abdomen, 'just – I don't think it's anything.'

'It'd better not be 'till Mom gets back,' he exclaimed in alarm.

'Don't worry,' she laughed, 'things don't happen that fast. And in any case, the baby's not even due for another six weeks.'

Twenty-two hours later Alexander was the proud uncle of a very small but healthy baby boy who was immediately put in an incubator.

It took a few days for Teddy to be contacted. He had parked Leonard with the family of a school friend and had taken off for one of Indonesia's little-developed eastern islands. But when the news of the addition to his family finally reached him, he made his way to Bangkok as quickly as the limited transportation options in the area allowed.

'I'm so sorry I missed it all,' he said, kissing Panda when he arrived. 'I never meant to, you know.'

'I wish I had missed it,' she said ruefully, 'but the good news is that the doctor says I can never have any more.'

'Was it that bad?'

'Unimaginable.'

Teddy didn't want to imagine it. 'Where's Russell?' he asked, looking around the room for the baby. Ever since the results of the amniocentesis test had shown that it would be a boy, he had been determined to name him after Alfred Russell Wallace, the great naturalist who had spent so many years in the Indonesian rainforest and had come up with a theory of natural selection similar to Darwin's – but who (sadly, in Teddy's opinion) had not quite published first.

'He's in the nursery,' Panda said, getting out of bed. 'Come on, I'll show you.'

'Can you?'

'Of course; they want me to walk around,' she said, leading him out along an open corridor. It surrounded a grassy courtyard dotted with luxuriant flowering trees.

When they reached the nursery on the other side they found two babies in incubators.

'This is Russell, I know it is,' Teddy declared, going straight over to the wrong one.

'That one's a girl,' corrected Panda. 'This one is

Russell.'

Remembering the very first time he had seen Julie – how she had turned to him, opened her eyes and spoken to him in her little baby gurgles – Teddy strode eagerly over to the other incubator. But when he peered down at the tiny form inside it, the only motion he could detect was the newborn's rhythmic breathing.

'Something's wrong,' he exclaimed in alarm.

'Nonsense,' Panda said after taking a look. 'He's just sleeping.'

'Let's wake him up then.'

'He'll wake up when he's hungry, that'll be soon enough. Come back to the room and we'll have the nurse bring us some coffee.'

'You don't suppose they could scare up a whisky and soda, do you?' he asked hopefully.

'I don't know. The room service here is good but it might not be that good.'

As it turned out Teddy had to wait until he was back at the house and could raid his uncle's bar before he could have his whisky – and even then he had to settle for Mekong; but he poured himself a stiff one, nonetheless. Then he followed it by several more, downing them in rapid succession.

'As new fathers go,' Christie observed, 'you don't look like the happiest one I've seen. Is something the matter?'

'No, nothing.'

'Has something gone wrong with the baby?'

'Not really. It's just that he's so small and kind of feeble.'

'That's why he's in an incubator,' Christie said soothingly. 'He'll catch up in a year or two, you'll see.'

'But he doesn't seem to react to anything. He just lies there and sleeps.'

It took a colossal effort for Christie to keep herself from laughing. 'That's what most newborns do,' she assured him, 'and you have to remember – incubator babies like Russell aren't really ready for life yet. But he'll be talking and playing almost as soon as other babies.'

'Not just as soon?'

'Not quite but soon enough.'

This wasn't the answer he wanted, but he had no choice but to accept it.

Teddy spent nearly a week in Bangkok, but Panda and Julie had to wait until the doctor declared Russell strong enough to travel. So he ended up going back to Jakarta by himself.

Nearly two months later Teddy and Leonard met them at the Jakarta airport.

'Excited about seeing Russell?' Teddy asked as their plane came into view.

'Yeah,' Leonard lied. Another baby around the house was something he could definitely do without.

'He's going to be a great kid,' Teddy said confidently.

'Yeah,' Leonard repeated, unconvinced.

As soon as Teddy caught sight of Panda and Julie coming out of the customs area, he rushed over to them.

'Daddy! Daddy!' Julie cried, expecting to be lifted up into his arms, but he didn't hear her. After a quick hug and a light kiss for Panda, he drew the cover away from Russell's face and peered down at him.

An axe murderer embarking on his favourite occupation could not have elicited louder shrieks from his victim than Teddy drew from the startled baby.

Abashed and embarrassed, he jumped back – and unfortunately brought the full force of his weight down on Julie's foot.

She instantly dissolved into screams of pain and anger that resonated through the entire arrivals area of the terminal.

'Jesus, let's get out of here,' exclaimed Teddy, turning and pushing a path through the horrified crowd.

But Panda, still not used to dealing with two hysterical children at the same time, was too flustered to follow him. Instead she thrust the baby at Leonard and said, 'Here, hold him for a minute, will you? Just don't drop him, that's all.' Then, turning to Julie, she bent down and began consoling her.

Leonard felt ten feet tall at being entrusted with the care of this tiny human being. 'It's all right,' he said, looking down at the apoplectic little face, 'everything's going to be all right now.' He had often heard Panda saying that sort of thing to Julie; and, as he couldn't think of anything else, he repeated those two assurances over and over again in a sort of rhythmic cadence.

The effect wasn't instantaneous but Leonard was patient; and, after a few more screams and several hiccups, Russell seemed to feel he was in safe hands. He lay back, closed his eyes – and, by the time Teddy came back to say 'What the hell happened to you? I looked around and you weren't there', he had fallen asleep.

As the weeks went by Teddy had a hard time convincing himself that he wasn't disappointed in Russell. He didn't realise that he had forgotten what Julie was like in the first few months of her life, and that he was comparing him to his daughter as an alert and laughing older baby.

Leonard, on the other hand, was unexpectedly delighted with his baby brother. He had never much liked Julie. She was too good at drawing all the love and attention he would have liked to have had for himself. Now he was too old to want a silly fuss made over him, and he gloried in his role as the one who shared Panda's interest in the baby. Whenever she left Russell in his care for a few minutes, as she did with increasing frequency, Leonard had long serious talks with his new brother about what they would do together when he was older.

'I'll teach you how to snorkel,' Leonard would say, 'and when I get my Master's License in diving I'll teach you how to do that, too. And judo. I've got my Black Belt already, you know. Then if you don't like someone, you can just pick him up and throw him across the room. They tell us in judo class that it's all just for self defence but that's a lot of –' He swallowed the word he was about to use. It wouldn't do to teach Russell bad language at such an early age.

When Leonard said these things, Russell would look up at him as if he thought his big brother was the most magnificent being in the entire world. And by the time he was seven- or eight-months-old, he would break into a happy smile whenever he saw him.

No such delight registered on his face at the sight of his father, however, and Teddy became increasingly irritated by this discrimination. On one occasion he even went so far as to fling some angry words at the baby, with the unfortunate result that for several months Russell cried and reached for Panda or Leonard whenever he caught sight of his father.

When Russell was a little over a year old, Alexander and two of his university friends spent a few days with them in between a few days' surfing in Bali and a trip to Lake Toba in Sumatra.

They were all gathering on the veranda for gin and tonics one evening when Alexander, after studying his new nephew for a few minutes, exclaimed, 'You know, Russell looks a lot like Leonard.'

'That's impossible,' Teddy declared sharply.

'Lots of people say my brother and I look alike,' one of Alexander's friends volunteered, 'although I can't see it myself.'

'That's different,' Teddy said. 'My first wife and I adopted Leonard. He and Russell aren't actually blood relations at all.'

For a moment Leonard felt like he had been cut with a knife. Then he thought about the blood pact, the most sacred bond in the world – something far more important than an ordinary blood tie – and his confidence in his place in the family was restored.

'That doesn't mean they can't look alike,' Alexander pointed out. 'I know it's sort of a coincidence, but I've always thought that Leonard looked like Panda. I told you that years ago, way before you guys were even married.'

Leonard felt even better. This uncle wasn't half as bad

as he remembered. Back in Bangkok he had thought of him as a sort of Genghis Khan and Dracula rolled into one, but he was actually OK.

'It's probably just the Eurasian thing,' Panda explained, 'but Russell couldn't do better than to grow up to look like Leonard.'

'It's a personality thing too,' Alexander continued, blithely unaware of the effect his words were having. 'I think he's going to be sort of introverted and geeky – you know, horn rimmed glasses, green book bag, that sort of thing. The kind of guy who plays chess, not football.'

'I'm in the chess club at school,' Leonard exclaimed, thrilled at this evidence that he and Russell were kindred spirits.

'See, I was right,' Alexander claimed triumphantly.

'You were talking complete nonsense,' Teddy retorted angrily. 'Trying to predict the personality of a kid who's still in diapers is the height of idiocy.' And he indicated his displeasure with his brother-in-law by scooping Julie up; declaring it was her bedtime, overlooking her howls of protest, and promising her a story as he stalked into the house with her.

'It looks like I've offended the master of the house,' Alexander said. 'Sorry about that.'

'Never mind,' Panda said; and, turning to Leonard, she added, 'Will you get Rusty's bottle for me? I think he's hungry.'

A little later when she was alone with Alexander she said, 'You really stirred things up with a stick, you know. Teddy's furious.'

'Still not too fond of Leonard?' queried Alexander.

Panda grimaced. 'Not really,' she confessed, 'but the extraordinary thing is that he doesn't seem to get on very well with the baby either.'

'Not the paternal type, I expect.'

'Well, he's not the sort of daddy who would ever change a nappy – but he adores Julie, as you can see. Sometimes I get absolutely livid at the way he showers love and affection on her and is so awful to the other two – not intentionally, of course, just sort of callous and indifferent.'

'I wouldn't worry about it,' Alexander said, cheerfully. 'Think of Dad. He wasn't one of those "Let's go throw a ball around together" sort of dads. And if he ever saw a diaper – a nappy, as you call it – he probably thought it was something to clean his pipes with. But we didn't go through agonies over it; at least, I didn't – and we both turned out brilliantly.'

'Yes, but there was never any Julie around to make us feel awful about coming in second. And not even a close second; a very long distance one.'

'Well, try not to let it get to you.'

'I can't help it. Teddy is driving me up a tree these days.'

'It's just marriage,' Alexander said, blithely. 'I bet there's nothing like it to put the touch of death to a torrid romance.'

'How ever did a fatheaded idiot like you,' Panda asked affectionately, 'manage to figure out so much at such an early age?'

CHAPTER 21
JAKARTA, 1988

'How would you feel about spending eighteen months on Komodo Island?' Teddy asked Panda, one evening when Russell was three-years-old.

'Have you lost your mind?'

'No, I'm serious. The World Wildlife Organisation wants to set up a small Komodo project where they are actually living in the wild; so what better place than Komodo Island itself?'

'This conversation must be happening in some kind of nightmare,' Panda said, aghast.

'Why?' asked Teddy in genuine surprise.

'I can't believe I'm actually married to anyone demented enough to think that taking his wife and children to live on a God forsaken island crawling with giant man-eating reptiles is a good idea. It's enough to have you certified.'

'No need to be melodramatic. There's a perfectly viable population of about four hundred people who live on the island and don't get eaten. A guy from the University of Florida spent over a year there with his wife and kid not too long ago.'

'Just because he lost his mind doesn't mean I have. The answer is no, no, no, a thousand times no. And I think it's outrageous of you even to suggest it.'

'OK, OK, calm down. You and the kids can stay here in Jakarta if you want. I'll go by myself.'

'Thank you very much; I'll love bringing up three children all alone.'

'You won't be all alone. I'll come home for a long weekend whenever I can. And with a cook and a maid and a nanny, plus the gardener and the driver, you won't exactly be alone.'

'Servants aren't the same thing as a husband.'

'Clever of you to have noticed the difference.'

'A half-blind mole crawling around the garden would see the difference between people who are relatively sane and reliable – I refer of course to the servants – and someone who cares more about lizards than he does about his own children.'

'Now you're making me into some kind of monster; that's totally unfair.'

'No, it isn't. I swear you've spent so much time with your horrible reptiles you're just as cold-blooded as they are. You must have been a lizard in a previous life; that's why you're so interested in them. It's just unfortunate that you've been born into this life with all your old characteristics.'

'Now you're just being silly.'

'No, I'm not! And if you hadn't closed your mind

to any worldview apart from your own Judeo-Christian one, you'd see that I'm simply expressing my thoughts in Buddhist terms.'

'Buddhism or no Buddhism, I don't like being set up as some kind of ogre who's about to feed his children to the komodos. People live on that island. Tourists go there. They have bungalows where people who work for the government stay and where we'll have our project. Sure, if you let a kid run out in the open grasslands by himself it would be dangerous; but if you let a child run out in the street in Jakarta that would be dangerous too. Nobody's perfectly safe anywhere – but as long as you behave sensibly, you'll probably be all right.'

'That sounds really wonderful. As long as I close myself up in some gruesome little bungalow and bring up three illiterate children on an island where there's no school for them to go to and no safe place for them to play, everything will be fine.'

'Nonsense. It would be kind of a rough life, I admit – but you could teach Julie at home and Rusty's too young for school anyway. Leonard could go to Singapore. There's a good boarding school there.'

'Don't even begin to talk about it,' Panda cried. 'You always twist everything around and around until somehow I find myself doing things I never wanted to do.'

'When did I ever do that?'

'You do it constantly. And even if there wasn't any danger –'

'There isn't if you're halfway sensible.'

'Even if you're right – and I don't think you are – I don't want to go to Komodo. I'd hate living on some remote island surrounded by a lot of hideous lizards, to say nothing of being far away from everything that's fun and interesting.'

'Is that what it would be like for you, even if we were together?'

'Yes,' Panda cried, 'yes it would.' And even as she said this she thought about how little time had passed – perhaps three or four short years – since it would never have occurred to her to say such a thing.

Teddy must have been thinking something similar, she realised, because he looked like he had just been slapped in the face.

'If that's the way you feel –' he began, but was interrupted by the phone.

'Hello,' he said, picking up the receiver. 'No, that's OK. I was just having a little chat with my wife... Tomorrow morning, terrific. Listen, if you can get in touch with Eti, tell her she should be there too... No, she'll be coming under University of Indonesia auspices, not World Wildlife... Yes, get Pak Harsono and Pak Mardani too. That way the minister can meet the whole team. If we get the nod from him we can aim for a start-up date in about four months... Any faxes for me? Phone calls? ... Tell him I died... OK, see you in the morning.'

'Hurray, the Minister of the Environment is going to see us tomorrow,' Teddy told Panda when he had put down the phone.

'About Komodo?' she asked tremulously.

'Yeah. It sounds like it's in the bag.'

'Then you're definitely going?'

'It looks like it.'

'How I feel about it doesn't matter at all then?'

'It matters a lot. I'd be much happier if you were coming with me.'

'But it doesn't matter enough to keep you from going?'

'Look Panda, you've got to try to understand what this means to me. A chance to study komodos in their home territory like this doesn't come every day, and it's something I just can't pass up. Think about it for a minute: the largest lizards in the entire world and nobody's done a real study of them in their natural habitat yet. It would absolutely make my career. I'd be famous! ... In certain circles, at least.'

'Oh, that's all right then,' Panda scoffed. 'Never mind having your children torn limb from limb by a horde of carnivorous monsters. Let's have a chorus of "Hail to the Lizard King". Or perhaps, I should say, "The King of the

478

Lizards".'

'Say what you like, get it off your chest – only try to be a little more reasonable.'

'I am being perfectly reasonable,' she insisted, but her protest was drowned out by an ear-splitting shriek from Julie.

'There's a centipede on my bed,' she cried, shooting out of her room like a guided missile, 'a great big enormous one.'

Panda called the gardener, oversaw to the removal of the creepy-crawly and asked herself what else could go wrong today. She found out when she discovered Russell spoiling his dinner with a box of sweet rice cakes. She delivered a few stern words to the miscreant and then she returned to Teddy.

To her surprise, she found him deep in conversation with Leonard, who was telling him about the class project he was doing on orangutans. Wildlife seemed to be the one interest they had in common; glad they had at least that, she left them to it and didn't intrude. Instead she went into the kitchen for dishes of rice and fresh fruit to place in front of the Buddha image she had brought with her from Thailand.

She did this every day, but today she was startled by Julie, who came up behind her and asked, 'Why do you give the Buddha food when he doesn't really eat it?'

'He inhales the essence of it,' Panda explained, 'that's what's important. And he knows we're thinking about him and offering him something.'

Julie, impressed, gazed at the image with new interest and asked, 'Is it made of real gold?'

'No, bronze.'

'How does he know we're offering him something when he's just made of... what was that you said?'

'Bronze; he knows because when an image of Lord Buddha is made, a tiny bit of his spirit goes into it and gives it power. Then he can give us help when we need it. But we must do our part too and make offerings in return.'

Julie considered this for a moment and then wondered, 'is it nearly dinnertime yet? I'm hungry.'

'Almost,' Panda said fondly, 'but we'll show our respect for the Lord Buddha before we go find Cook.' And pressing the palms of Julie's hands together in a wai, she lifted them to the child's forehead, then lit a candle and a stick of incense, said a brief prayer, and made a wai of her own.

'What is that for?' said Julie, fascinated by the trail of sandalwood scented smoke that wafted toward the ceiling from the incense; she jumped up and tried to catch some of it in her hand.

'It's to carry my prayer to heaven.'

'I didn't see you pray.'

'Prayers aren't something you see. Come on now – let's

go find out what Cook is making us for dinner.'

Panda felt better after her brief prayer and later that evening told Teddy over coffee, 'I think I'll go to Bangkok for a few weeks before your horrid project starts up. That way you'll still be here for the kids.'

'Me,' he exclaimed in alarm.

'Why not? I'll take Russell with me if you think dealing with all three of them would be a bit much; but Nanny can see about Julie after school and Leonard will more or less take care of himself. He won't be any problem.'

'How about me?' he demanded, appalled at her cavalier attitude. 'Who's going to look after me?'

'As you pointed out earlier,' Panda replied, trying not to laugh, 'there's a cook and a maid and a nanny and –'

'OK, OK, I get it.'

'Good.'

'But I'll miss you.'

'Good,' she said again.

'If I admit to being an insensitive rat and beat my chest a few times, will you change your mind and stay?'

'No. But I'll enjoy the performance, just the same.'

Ten days later Panda and Russell were on the Thai International flight to Bangkok; they were only going to be gone for two or three weeks (somehow she hadn't wanted to commit herself to an exact date to come back; she'd rather wait and see how things went), but it was a bit disconcerting to think that the prospect of a holiday away from Teddy could feel so good.

Of course, it probably wouldn't take her long to start missing him. That was usually what happened when he was away on his 'lizarding' excursions in the eastern islands. She wondered if he bothered to miss her when he was the one who was away. He said he did, but she wasn't at all sure she believed him.

She had to admit there was a funny side to it, actually – feeling neglected because her husband was off chasing lizards. Her friends in Bangkok worried about their husbands going off with other women, but at least those bargirl temptresses – or 'minor wife' mistresses – were human. Being abandoned for a lizard was really hard on the self-esteem.

Alexander met them at the airport in a shiny blue Toyota Corona.

'Not a bad heap you're driving there days,' Panda commented, as she settled Rusty on her lap. 'Life must be treating you well.'

'I picked it up second-hand. I regard it as the first step toward a Mercedes.'

'How are Daddy and Christie?'

'Dad's getting on you know – pushing seventy. But he's

as stubborn as ever, maybe more so. He absolutely refuses to get a new car; says he wants one that rattles more than he does. Still, all things considered, he's not doing badly.'

'And Christie?'

'She never changes, thank God.'

'I hear you have your own place now.'

'Yeah, a great little pad, strictly bachelor style. Come over tomorrow and give it a squint.'

'Thanks, I'll do that,' she said, glancing out the window as they passed a colourful temple with spires that pointed toward the sky.

With horrible darling Alexander on one side of her and the quintessential structure of a world she understood on the other, Panda felt she had come home.

She had been there for a number of days when Christie, whose comments seldom fell far from the mark, said, 'I don't want to pry but are things all right between you and Teddy?'

'Oh yes,' Panda answered casually; then, seeing that Christie didn't believe her, she added, 'well, mostly all right. I mean things are never a hundred percent all right in a marriage, are they?'

'I don't suppose so,' she replied; then she waited quietly to see if Panda wanted to tell her anything more.

After a few minutes Panda did.

'Everything seems so very one sided though,' she said. 'Every time Teddy wants something that I don't, he goes on and on about it until he wears me down and eventually I give in. I keep telling myself that I'm not going to let that happen again but somehow it always does –'

'I'm really surprised. You always struck me as being very strong willed.'

'Well, I'm going to be strong willed on the Komodo Island thing, I'll tell you that. But he'll just charge ahead and go anyway and leave me in Jakarta with the kids; I know he will.'

'That won't be much fun for you.'

'No, but of course it's not the end of the world either. I suppose it's just being married and middle-aged and responsible and bound to a family that gets to me. There are times when I feel like someone's tied me up with a rope. I want to be young and free and half in love all my life.'

'Only half?'

'Absolutely. Being totally in love can be agony – tear you apart, make you a slave. I never want any part of that again, thank you very much. But being half in love is different. It's fun – rather like a glass of champagne at a summer picnic – and gives a lovely magical quality to practically everything. It never ties you in knots or makes you suffer. After all these years of having Teddy dominate my life, that's the kind of love I want now.'

'Don't you think that might be a bit dangerous at this point?'

'More than a bit,' Panda acknowledged. 'At least, the rational part of me knows that; but sadly I'm not all that rational. You know, I used to hate my mother for leaving me and running off with that Swiss fellow, but now I'm beginning to understand how she must have felt. And the curious thing was that in spite of how much I thought I hated her, I wanted more than anything to be like her. You probably remember that. Well, perhaps I resemble her more than is good for me.'

'You sound like a cautionary tale about being careful what you wish for,' Christie said, trying not to seem alarmed at Panda's revelations. 'But I must say I can't imagine Teddy being left with three children.'

They both broke out laughing at the thought and didn't stop until William came into the room said, 'What's all this nonsense about? I thought we were going to the Polo Club.'

'We are,' said Christie assured him. 'I'll be ready in a minute.'

An hour later Panda was having a swim – sort of – with

Rusty at one end of the enormous swimming pool at the Polo Club; but the water was too deep for a child his age and she had to hold him constantly. As there was no baby pool and Christie and William were immersed in a tennis game, she was glad when Rusty seemed ready to get out and have the ice cream she had promised him.

She found a table at the poolside café, ordered a vanilla cone for Rusty and a cup of tea for herself and settled back to watch the swimmers.

There was something vaguely familiar, she thought, about a spherical head with thick black hair that was doing laps up and down the pool – and when it finally paused for breath, she saw that it not only possessed a moustache but actually belonged to her old friend, Thanit.

She was just on the point of calling out 'hello' when he disappeared under water. By the time he surfaced again he was well out of hearing so she concentrated her attention on seeing that Rusty didn't drip more than half his ice cream on the table or on himself.

After a while Thanit also got out of the pool, shook himself once or twice in a half-hearted effort to get dry and came toward her table. Just as she was about to make another stab at saying hello, Rusty turned what was left of his ice cream upside down, burst into tears, and effectively sabotaged any prospect of a reunion.

Thanit, watching his step to avoid treading in the sticky

mess, walked by without glancing in Panda's direction.

More annoyed with herself than with her old friend, she ordered another ice cream for Rusty and tried to resign herself to the fact that she had aged beyond recognition.

A few minutes later Thanit, now dry and wearing his glasses, came over to the table and said, 'Panida, what a surprise! I heard you married your American cousin and went to the States. Are you just here on a visit?'

After giving him a brief account of what she had been doing during the past few years, she asked about him. 'Did you go into business with your dad? That's what you were thinking about doing, wasn't it?'

'You have a good memory,' he said, sitting down at the table.

'And marry the daughter of your father's business partner?'

'I'd better be careful what I tell you,' he said, laughing. 'It's like having it carved in stone. But yes, we've been married for twelve years now.'

'Any children?'

'Four; three boys and a girl. Actually my wife knows an old friend of yours.'

'Oh, who?'

'Khun Suchida. I think she lived on the same compound you did when you were married to your first husband.'

'What ever happened to her? I always meant to write to her but I'm afraid I never actually did it.'

'She has two children now and has opened an antique shop in Siam Centre.'

'Is she still married?'

Thanit looked rather shocked. 'Of course,' he said.

'I only ask because, she didn't seem very happy,' Panda said hastily.

'You didn't ask whether she was happy; you asked if she was still married. This is Bangkok, remember.'

'I know but I can't help thinking that sticking out life with someone you don't love must be hell. I couldn't do it.'

'You want a perpetual honeymoon then?' he asked, only half teasing.

'Don't you?' she laughed.

'I'm not sure I do actually.'

'Why ever not?'

'Unless it was with the right person –'

'Of course, with the right person; that goes without saying.'

'And if the right person is married to somebody else by now?'

'You mean the Scottish girl?'

'You really do remember everything.'

'Only the interesting things – and too often not even those.'

By this time Russell had eaten all the ice cream he wanted and was dripping the melted remains over anything or anyone within reach. Thanit, not eager to be the next victim, looked at his watch and said, 'I've got to be running – but it's been fun seeing you again. Are you by any chance free for dinner tomorrow night?'

'Yes. It will be lovely to meet your wife.'

'Actually, the two of us lead separate lives – except for family things, of course. But it would just be dinner with an old friend – nothing you couldn't tell your husband about.'

'To tell you the truth, I wasn't thinking about Teddy. I was thinking about… Oh, never mind.'

'We're on then?'

'We're on,' she confirmed.

She should have just gone ahead and told him that it was Christie, not Teddy, who was on her mind, she thought after he had gone. Still, he would have had no way of knowing that Christie would have viewed the evening in the light of all the things she had said about marriage that afternoon. She decided not to think about it.

It was fun to wash her hair and think about what she would wear and, in general, be like a young girl getting ready for an evening out again.

Christie didn't say anything, but Panda saw the disapproval in her eyes and felt quite naughty as a result. It was fun though – rather like being back at boarding school again and trying to put something over on the housemistress.

She met Thanit in the lobby of the Oriental Hotel at eight o'clock and they went up to the Normandie Grill on the top floor. The headwaiter showed them to a table overlooking the river, now a darkened mirror reflecting the lights of Thonburi on the opposite bank.

They ordered drinks and Thanit had told her a bit about his business.

'It sounds like you're very successful,' Panda remarked.

'No credit to me, I'm afraid. My father and uncles already had everything on track when I got back from England. My father-in-law's a very clever chap too, and there's no arguing with the fact that he's got all the right connections. The business is growing and we have several joint enterprises now.'

Panda's tried to keep her mind on what he was saying, but it kept flying back to that long ago conversation they had had about marriage. 'I know I shouldn't ask this,' she began, 'but do you ever regret the choices you made?

'The choices?'

'Giving up your Scottish girlfriend and marrying the

daughter of your father's business partner?'

'Regrets,' he mused. 'Possibly – but only in the way you would regret that a dream was over after you woke up. Real life for me is here, and there is no way she could have been a part of it.'

'Are you sure about that?'

'Very. The family would never have accepted her. She would have been miserable; she probably would have hated me after five years and divorced me after six.'

Panda looked unconvinced. 'I don't think love – deep passionate love I mean – can ever really turn to hate.'

'I wouldn't know,' he said. 'I left Fiona while I still loved her and after that... Well, marriage is a practical affair with us, an arrangement between families. It's very stable though. We don't let a lot of emotional gymnastics send us running into the divorce court, and that makes it better for the children than marriages in Western countries.'

'Is that what love is to you then – just some emotional gymnastics?'

'Rather tepid ones recently.'

He said this with a laugh, but at the sight of Panda's face, added, 'Don't get the wrong idea – I'm not a robot. I just don't think romantic love is something that lasts. I was in love once and it was great – it's what youth is all about – but once is all anybody can ask in life. After that it's time to grow up and get on with important things like family responsibilities.'

'And making money,' Panda added.

'And making money,' he agreed, 'doing the best you can to fulfil the hopes of your parents and provide for the future of your children.'

'Of course, you never enjoy any of the money yourself,' Panda said sarcastically.

'It would be rather absurd not to, don't you think?'

The arrival of a waiter to take their dinner order prevented any response to this question, and after his retreat the conversation turned towards other things.

The delicious dinner was followed by drinks and dancing at a new club on the top of Siam Centre; and, when she said goodnight to him at the end of the evening, she couldn't help wondering what sex with him would be like.

She flirted with the idea as she got undressed. It might be rather fun, she thought, but once she was in bed she changed her mind. When Thanit talked about his attitude toward life it seemed so reasonable, so sensible, yet so cold and empty; it would surely take the most of the pleasure out of it. Of course he was probably right; love didn't last – not that kind of love, anyway. Still, she couldn't imagine Teddy saying such things and she would be absolutely devastated if he did.

Teddy – she dreamed about him when at last she fell into a fitful sleep. They were on the beach in Nantucket with the rain beating down on them and the wind swirling round them and the waves pounding up on the shore, but all that mattered was how desperately they wanted each other. And then the dream began to change; the wind died down, the stars came out and the lovers on the beach were older... yet still in the throes of an intense passion, they were engrossed in making a baby. Then, in the curious way of dreams, Teddy wasn't Teddy anymore but Thanit – and for a fleeting moment he lay there in her arms before voices, all speaking Thai, began calling him away. 'This is all that life offers,' he told her before he too faded away, leaving her alone and desolate on the shore.

'I'm going back to Jakarta tomorrow,' Panda told Christie over lunch the next day. 'I went to Thai International and booked my return flight this morning.'

CHAPTER 22
JAKARTA, 1988

It's going to be a wonderful homecoming, Panda thought when she saw Teddy waiting for her at the airport; a moment later she was throwing herself into his arms as if they had been separated for a hundred years.

'Hey, don't rape me here,' he said, pleased but pretending to be shocked at her enthusiasm. 'Wait till we get home, at least.'

'What a conventional old bear you are,' she chided.

Laughing, he turned to Rusty and with almost as much affection as he might have shown toward Julie; swept the little fellow up toward the ceiling, swung him around and asked, 'How are you doing, old sport? Glad to see your dad?'

Rusty, unlike Julie who had adored being lifted to these thrilling heights, let out a shriek of terror and burst into tears.

Teddy grimaced, set him down and settled for putting an arm around Panda instead.

'As for the Komodo project,' he said when they were in the car. 'It should be starting up in about three months and I think you'll like the way I've set it up. I've –'

'What! I can't believe I'm hearing this.'

'Don't get upset,' he said hastily. 'I've designed it specifically so that I'll have to be back here for a few days every six or eight weeks. That way we can have plenty of long weekends together. And I promise you whenever you feel like raping a lizard enthusiast –'

'A reptile in human form, you mean,' she retorted, too outraged to discuss anything rationally.

He ignored this and went on unphased. 'And we can have a weekend in Bali together whenever you feel like it. Did you know that the Batak people in Sumatra say that a house without a lizard is a house without happiness?'

'No, I didn't and I hope I never hear it again.'

'Anyway,' he said, refusing to take her reaction seriously, 'I heard if from Eti.'

'Who's he?'

'She,' he corrected. 'She's the graduate student – or postgraduate, as you would say – from the University of Indonesia who's going to be working with us on the project. I'm sure I must have mentioned her before; she's doing her thesis on Komodos. You'll like her. She's a Batak and has lots of stories about ghosts and spirits – just your sort of thing.'

Then, seeing that Panda wasn't reacting well to anything connected with the Komodo project, he managed to put on the subject on hold, and asked how things had been in Bangkok instead.

Leonard and Julie were waiting for them on the veranda when they pulled up in front of the house.

'Mummy! Mummy! Mummy!' Julie called, running out to the car and throwing her arms around Panda.

Leonard's greeting was considerably more restrained, but she suspected that he was the one who had missed her the most.

The cook brought out tea and biscuits, and the two children vied with each other for Panda's attention as they told her all their latest news. Then Julie darted into her room and came back out wearing a tiger mask and making ferocious roaring sounds.

'What's this all about?' Panda asked, laughing. 'Where did you get that?'

'At the zoo. Eti got it for me.'

'We had to put in a couple of weekends' work,' Teddy explained hastily, 'to get the project design done on time.'

'At the zoo?'

'Of course not at the zoo – here, at the house. But last Sunday we got to a point where we needed a break so we took Julie to the zoo. It was fun wasn't it?' he asked, turning to his daughter.

'Sort of,' she replied without enthusiasm.

'Sort of?' Teddy repeated, surprised. 'I thought it was a

great time.'

'I liked the animals but –'

'But what?' Teddy demanded testily.

'I don't like Eti.'

'Why not? She really likes you.'

Julie looked stubborn but didn't say anything.

'She has a silly giggle,' Leonard explained, agreeing with Julie for once.

'And she's always eating sweets,' added Julie, who knew her mother had strong views on this subject.

'Sesame sweets,' Leonard added as if this made them particularly abhorrent.

'You kids just don't appreciate how intelligent she is,' Teddy said, not troubling to hide his irritation, 'and you don't understand how important it is to have Indonesians involved in the project.'

'Is she going to Komodo Island, too?' Julie asked.

'Of course she is,' he snapped. 'We've got three Indonesian researchers on board so it should be a good team.'

'I wish you'd let me come with you, Dad,' Leonard said.

'Don't be ridiculous. You've got school.'

'I could come during the summer holidays.'

'Accommodation's going to be tight,' Teddy said tersely, and was relieved when the unexpected arrival of Nani cut off any further discussion on the subject.

'You come back,' Nani exclaimed, surprised to see

Panda.

'Of course I came back. I just went for a visit with my family.'

'Can I try your telephone? Mine is no good today.'

'You know where it is,' Panda said. 'I hope it's working for a change.'

Miraculously it was. Nani made her call and then sat down for a cup of tea and a chat – but as neither Teddy nor the children were interested in hearing about her family, her profusion of relatives, or her servants, they soon drifted away.

When they had gone Nani dropped her voice and said, 'Better you watch your husband.'

'I don't know what you mean,' Panda said defensively, although she knew exactly what her friend was trying to tell her.

'No good to leave man alone,' Nani explained. 'Your husband good man. But you leave man alone, trouble comes.'

'I'll try to remember that,' Panda replied, concealing her annoyance with difficulty and steering the conversation firmly back to Nani's concerns.

Between Nani's vaguely disconcerting warning and the news that Teddy was really going ahead with the Komodo project, this 'wonderful homecoming' was fast turning into the homecoming from hell; at least, this was what Panda thought as she watched her neighbour set off back down the street to her own house. At least the children had been touchingly glad to see her; so she spent the rest of the afternoon first playing with Julie and then having a long conversation with Leonard.

It was shortly before dinner when she went into the bedroom to unpack. The electricity was low (typical, she thought; really – Jakarta was a hundred years behind Bangkok) and it was a bit dark in the room, so she went over and lit the oil lamp they always kept on the bedside table for emergencies. She was just turning up the wick when she noticed a crumpled packet of something beside it. Thinking she would put it in the bin, she picked it up, then glanced down at it to see why it was so sticky (she didn't want anything that might attract ants in the bedroom). Then she felt herself go cold all over.

It was a nearly empty packet of sesame sweets.

For a moment all she could do was stare at it as her emotions gyrated between rising fury and disbelief, but gradually the ice in her veins gave a wintry clarity to her thoughts. A vivid image, not of Teddy but of Thanit, took form in her mind.

He understands what life was about, she thought. He wouldn't waste time pursuing fairytales like romantic love.

'Fulfil the expectations of your parents and secure the future of your children,' she could almost hear him saying. Those were the important things in life – the things that gave it meaning, the things that were real. Intelligent, mature and rational adults didn't let childish fantasies of a love that lasted forever blur their vision or govern their lives.

In the milli-second it took for her to associate the sesame seeds with Eti, her school girl fantasies about romantic love evaporated and by the time she heard Teddy coming into the room behind her, she had grown up.

Fighting back a sudden wave of nausea, she spoke without turning around. 'I didn't know you liked Indonesian sweets,' she said.

'I don't, they're nothing but coloured sugar and some sort of sickening flavourings injected into them – probably the reason why Indonesian kids have such rotten teeth.'

With a supreme effort Panda kept herself from trembling. 'In that case, I suppose you'll want to give these back to their rightful owner,' she said, turning to face him and handing him the crumpled packet.

Teddy looked blank for a moment and then said, 'Oh – they must be Eti's.'

'I expect they are,' Panda returned. Her face had gone white and her voice was edged in steel.

'Hey, wait a minute,' he cried. 'You've got it all wrong!'

'That's a bit difficult to believe, actually.'

'Listen, it's not what you think. Eti was just taking a shower here – taking it in our bathroom, I mean – after we got back from the zoo. She got up too close to the rhino pen and got splattered with mud so she was desperate for a shower. She had to take it somewhere and the hot water heater in the kid's bathroom was on the blink.'

'And of course she took the sesame sweets into the shower with her. Everybody likes a little snack between drops.'

'How the hell do I know what she likes in the shower? Listen, do you really think that if I were interested in another woman – which by the way, I'm emphatically not – that I'd bring her here and have sex with her in our bed?'

'I admit it surpasses anything I would have thought you were capable of.'

'Listen, you can't think –'

'Daddy warned me something like this would happen if I married you. I should have paid attention.'

'Oh, did he? Well thanks a lot, Uncle William. I really appreciate that. What a nice guy!'

'I'm not talking about being nice. I'm talking about being right.'

'So that's what you think.'

'Of course it's what I think. Do you expect me to believe those sesame sweets jumped onto the bedside table by themselves?'

'I expect you to believe a sensible explanation like –'

'Like what?'

'Like maybe the maid put them there when she was cleaning, I don't know.'

'Let's just say the tooth fairy brought them,' Panda suggested; and, picking up her still unopened case from Bangkok, she started for the door.

'Hey, wait a minute,' he cried. 'Where are you going?'

'To a hotel; sorry if you need the car. If you do, I suggest you find a taxi.'

She drove straight to the nicest hotel in Jakarta (well, it was her favourite anyway). With its red and gold lobby ceiling, it always gave her the feeling that she was stepping into an ancient Javanese palace and entering another world was exactly what she needed right now.

A traditional Javanese orchestra was filling the air with the plaintive strains of its music as she checked in; gave firm instructions that she didn't want any phone calls, and emphasized that she didn't want her room number given out to anyone.

Yes, this was the right place to come, she thought as the music wrought its soothing magic, its five tone scale taking her momentarily back to sounds of the Erawan Shrine; the right place to try to pull herself together after the horrendous blow Teddy had delivered.

She felt that she was regaining control of her life as the porter picked up her case and showed her to her room. But once she was there, deprived of the uplifting power of the music, her mood changed. She was only aware of how desolate and alone she was, and how completely at the mercy of events outside herself. For lack of any better alternative, she wandered over to the window and looked down on the lush green garden and azure blue swimming pool below, but they barely registered on her consciousness.

All she saw was a vision of Lisa, translucent in the evening dusk, hovering just outside the window... Lisa — lovely, ethereal and crying.

'Oh God, is this how you felt when Teddy and I —' Panda murmured, almost out loud. 'I didn't think about you the way I should have. I didn't understand how you must have suffered. Sonchai played around; at least, I think he did — I'm almost sure of it, actually — but it barely hurt at all. It was just something men did and I didn't care that much. That's the secret, isn't it — not to care too much? Then when they betray you, it's more like a mosquito bite than a dagger to the heart. Did you care too much? I think perhaps you did. In spite of John Smith or that time in Japan, I can't help believing you weren't the sort of person who loved lightly. I think Teddy must have driven you into the affair with Leonard's dad, with John too, just like he is going to drive me into bed with – I'm not quite sure who – Thanit, perhaps. But it won't be the same though, because he won't be Teddy. And that's the awful thing; nobody else will be Teddy.'

She turned away from the window and mixed herself a drink from the mini bar; downing it down in less than five minutes, she mixed herself another and went back to the window. Lisa was no longer in the garden and she felt almost disappointed not to see her there – as if the only one who understood her had gone away.

She picked up the room service menu, made an effort to interest herself in its contents, chose what she wanted and then forgot to order it. Instead she turned on the television. A Bollywood movie was playing and she sat down to watch it without noticing that she didn't understand a word of it.

Teddy had betrayed her; nothing else mattered.

For a while it was only variations on the theme of 'how could he have done it?' that raced in circles through her mind. Then a variety of different circumstances took hold of her imagination.

If it had just been a one-night-stand with someone he would never see again, of course she would forgive him, she told herself. Then she thought of the well-known penchant of Thai women for greeting an erring husband with a knife and slashing off the offending part of his anatomy. One of the Bangkok hospitals even had a special unit devoted to sewing it back on... at least, if the victim got there quickly enough and brought the severed appendage with him. The idea made her laugh. Damn it, she thought, she wished she had done that; the problem was – exactly how? Teddy would either have had to have been very very drunk, which he hadn't been (not when she had found out anyway), or she would have had to have waited until he was asleep. The trouble was, she didn't think she could go through with a premeditated crime. It would have to be a crime of passion or no crime at all.

She let other possibilities drift through her mind. If Teddy had a brief affair with someone while she was away, or even when she wasn't away, it would be hard to forgive him – harder than she would have realised even twenty four hours ago. But she could probably manage it (that is, if the affair were with someone who would conveniently disappear from their lives). But this girl – woman, vampire, whatever she was – was about to spend eighteen months on some God forsaken island full of rampaging giant lizards with him, and unless one of the filthy beasts decided to eat her for lunch – too much to hope for – she was likely to be around for a while.

But did that really have to happen, Panda asked herself. Teddy was head of the project; surely he could get her taken off it if he really wanted to. Or alternatively he could drop out of it himself. She thought of all the objections he would undoubtedly make to either of these possibilities, but what would they matter if she held firm? It would be a test; if he cared more about this girl or about the project than he did about her, then perhaps now was the time to find out. And if she had to put Teddy out of her life, wasn't it better to do it while she was still young enough to make a new life for herself? On the other hand, if he promised not to see this female reptile anymore, could she just go home and could they take up their lives where they had left them off before her trip to Bangkok?

She didn't think so. A tendency toward promiscuity might be inherent in the human male; but marriage, she had discovered, involved more than just sex. It was sharing a life together, trusting each other. And Teddy had brought this creature into their home, had sex with her in their bed, and shared their child and their life with her. That made it all something quite different. It was horrible, sickening; it made her want to throw up. She might be able to close her eyes to a passing indiscretion, but this was something she could never forgive.

She undressed, turned off the light and slipped into the comfort of the soft bed. Was it an American mattress, she wondered? It felt like it. The fact that she had made a decision about the future relaxed her a little, and she managed to sleep for two or three hours.

It was still dark when she woke up; she turned on a light, ordered coffee from room service and tried to keep the future from impinging on her thoughts. It didn't work though. She couldn't keep herself from wondering what it held.

What could she do? She wasn't really all that young anymore, and she certainly wasn't free. She had three children and she didn't even have the option – not that she would have taken it – of leaving them with Teddy, because he was going off to spend eighteen months with a bunch of voracious lizards. He had told her they sometimes came into the village and got a goat or a child. She shivered with horror at the thought. Anyway she didn't want to leave the children. They were her children – even Leonard – and she loved them and wanted to keep them. And you couldn't leave children with someone like Teddy very long, even if he were staying in civilization. The idea was ludicrous.

If she just had money of her own she could take the children to Bangkok, rent a house, put them in school and look around and see what she wanted to do with her life. She could even go back to England or perhaps to America after a while, if she decided the career prospects weren't good enough in Bangkok. But she didn't have money of her own, that was the awful thing, and she couldn't just descend on her father and Christie with three children and say, 'Here we are, for God knows how long. You won't mind a little noise and chaos and crowding, will you?'

There didn't seem to be any good solution, and after a while the room which she had hoped would be such a good place to think in became desperately claustrophobic. It was getting light by then so she put on her swimming costume, tied a sarong over it and went down to the pool. Several businessmen, intent on getting their daily exercise before the start of work, were already there; they eyed her svelte beauty appreciatively as she approached. Ordinarily she would have considered this mild lechery slightly annoying – if she had noticed it at all – but this morning it was different. The fact that one of them was a bit round in the middle and had cheeks like a chipmunk; that the second one was long-nosed, lean and predatory looking; and that the third was so hairy he would scarcely have needed a costume to impersonate a gorilla, didn't matter at all. She had no desire to get to know any member of this menagerie any better: it was just that Teddy's behaviour had seemed like such a rejection that she welcomed the idea of any male of any species finding her attractive again. With her ego ever so slightly buoyed up, at least for the moment, she plunged into the water and raced up and down the length of the pool, only stopping when she was out of thoroughly out of breath and exhausted.

When at last she climbed out of the water, she was greeted by the tantalizing aroma of freshly brewed coffee. A waiter was bringing it to the gorilla and it reminded her that she hadn't eaten anything since her lunch on the plane the day before; so she changed out of her swimming things and went in search of food.

Finding an enormous breakfast buffet laid out in the restaurant, she went in and piled a plate high with its scrumptious looking offerings. After all, why should she let herself die of starvation just because Teddy was a womanizing cheating rat, she asked herself, as she settled down to enjoy the delicious fare and polished it off with several cups of coffee.

'Mrs. Duncanson,' the manager called to her as she passed the reception desk on her way back to her room, 'there have been many telephone calls for you. And,' he added, looking embarrassed, 'Mr. Duncanson has been here three times now asking for you. I am sorry to have to say this but the last time he really became quite difficult. The security guards had to be called.' Then, as if to make up for reporting this unfortunate news, he pressed a dozen or so message slips into her hand.

She thanked him, went around the corner to the lift, and dropped them unread in the bin.

Back in her room, she took several sheets of stationary

from the desk; wrote a note to each of the children, and finally one to Teddy.

November 17, 1988

Dear Teddy,

It's over. I can never live with you again after what you've done and I don't want to see you or talk to you.

I'm going back to Bangkok; and, as I need to be free to look for a job and find a place to live without putting too much of a burden on Daddy and Christie, I'm leaving the children with you for a little while. But don't panic, I'll come back for them – for Julie and Russell, anyway – before you go to Komodo. I know I have no real claim on Leonard but I can't help thinking of him as my own and I don't believe you will object or stand in my way on that score. I have mentioned the idea of boarding school to him as he is now at an age where he might enjoy it and I think it would do him good. If he feels that England or America would be too far from home, he could go to Singapore. There is a very good school there that has boarding and he would be able to spend his holidays with whichever one of us he chooses.

Panda

CHAPTER 23
BANGKOK, 1990

'All men are bastards,' Panda declared over a lunch of spicy fried noodles with Suchida, and was surprised when her friend didn't seem to share this view. Hadn't she been frightfully torn up when her husband started going to massage parlours and brothels? Then Panda remembered that Suchida had learned most of her English from the Victorian novels she loved and was probably taking the word 'bastards' literally.

'I admit we have to keep a few around,' Panda continued after sorting Suchida out on modern usage, 'some of the less atrocious specimens anyway, to provide donations at sperm banks – but that's absolutely all. We don't need them for anything else anymore and our lives would definitely be better without them.'

'What about Thanit?' Suchida asked, mischievously. 'Would your life be better without him?'

'He's mostly just a friend.'

'And what does 'mostly' mean – in modern usage?'

Panda laughed. 'It means a friend you don't spend the whole night with.'

'But you do,' Suchida pointed out.

'Never the whole night,' Panda said with a laugh. 'I

always get up and come home afterwards.'

'Why?'

'Because of the children — mostly.'

'It's a very useful word — mostly,' Suchida said with mock seriousness.

Well, Julie's old enough now; the kids at the International School are so precocious, she might figure out what was going on and I don't want that to happen. But I admit it's also for me. I want to make a new life for myself, a completely independent one that doesn't revolve around a relationship with any man. Can you understand that?'

Suchida not only nodded but looked rather envious. 'You are very lucky,' she said, 'your husband does not try to take your children away from you or —'

Panda tried not to laugh but she couldn't help it. 'Not only that,' she said, 'when we actually get around to getting our divorce, Teddy's going to give the judge the shock of his life. He's going to give me custody — well shared custody, anyway — of his son from his first marriage.'

Suchida, unable to take this in, was convinced she must have misunderstood.

'Anyway Leonard's a darling,' Panda continued. 'And he's seventeen now so he pretty much does his own thing. The only problem is that my apartment is so small, it's a bit of a squeeze fitting everybody in during the school holidays; but then he's in Singapore during term time so we manage. And you know what Bangkok rents are like; even with the child support I get from Teddy, my salary won't stretch to anything bigger.'

'Without a job that pays international salary,' Suchida pointed out, 'and that's very difficult to find –'

'Don't I know it,' agreed Panda emphatically. 'I wouldn't even have the job I do if Daddy hadn't known the man in charge of publications at AIT.'

'AIT?' queried Suchida; then, embarrassed to have let it slip her mind, she quickly said, 'The Asian Institute of Technology. You are very lucky to be working there.'

I wouldn't say that. The pay is pathetic and it's getting very boring.'

'I thought you liked it very much.'

'I did at the beginning, but it's getting awfully repetitious now. In fact, if my boss doesn't move up or out fairly soon – and believe me, he's not someone to keep around for the sperm bank – so that I can get his job, then I'm going to look for something else.' Glancing down at her watch, she added, 'Oops, I've got to go. There just aren't enough Saturdays in my life and I want to do some shopping before I pick up the kids. Fortunately they're both playing at friends' houses today. Then I'm meeting Thanit for dinner.'

'It doesn't sound to me like you hate men so very

513

'much,' Suchida reminded her with an affectionate laugh.

'I suppose they have their moments,' Panda conceded and joined in her friend's mirth.

Thanit liked to start off his evenings with Panda in a European restaurant rather than a Thai or a Chinese one because he felt the atmosphere was more suited to their sort of relationship. Tonight they were meeting at Charlie's on Sathorn Road and then they might go dancing at the new disco in Siam Square. After that they could move on the nightclub at the Dusit Thani Hotel, where he had taken a room for the night.

Their evenings together usually followed this pattern and they would end by making love with the slow deliberateness of experienced lovers, sitting up in bed and drinking gin and tonics and eating little packets of salty, spicy peanuts from the minibar afterwards. Then Panda would invariably insist that she had to go.

Sometimes he would protest, saying that it t would be so much nicer if they just spent the night there, but in truth, the arrangement suited him very well.

Of course she always claimed that she didn't like to leave the children alone with the maid all night, but it was really just an excuse. In reality it was that the thought of spending the night with Thanit didn't appeal to her.

Having sex with him was one thing; but actually sleeping with him, waking up in the morning with him, involved more intimacy than she wanted and so Thanit, after feigning reluctance, would get up and see her home in a taxi. Then he would go back to his wife.

The maid, only half awake, opened the door for Panda when she got home, and then hastily went back to bed.

The two children were asleep; Julie with one arm around a large furry green crocodile Teddy had sent her from Singapore, Rusty clutching his favourite dog, an animal that had once been fluffy and blue but was now showing distinct signs of wear. His father had sent him a crocodile like Julie's but it had met with considerably less appreciation than hers. Panda, seeing its tail protruding from behind the toy chest, picked it up, dusted it off and made up her mind to give it to the night watchman's little boy, since Rusty would have nothing to do with it. In the last few months he had developed what amounted to a phobia about lizards. Even the little translucent ones on the walls of every house in Bangkok seemed to give him the horrors, sometimes sending him into paroxysms of screaming. Of course, it was just a childish phase; he would get over it, she knew – but living in a city where lizards far outnumbered people was a bit hard on the poor little fellow. That he had a father who was obsessed with the larger relatives of the harmless little creatures didn't bear thinking about, so she turned out the light and went into her own room.

She had just finished getting undressed when the phone rang; she recognized a slightly blurred version of Teddy's voice.

'Do you realise it's nearly three in the morning?' she demanded.

'I didn't call you to talk about the time,' he returned testily. 'I called to find out exactly when you're going to come to your senses and get back here.'

'I came to my senses over a year ago; that's why I left.'

'Your senses didn't come into it. You went berserk over something that never amounted to anything except in your depraved and warped little mind.'

'Thanks – you do say the sweetest things. I'd love to hear more except that you're keeping me up. It's late and I want to go to bed.'

'Why so eager? Who have you got waiting there, may I ask?'

'No, you may not ask.'

'Then you do have someone there.'

'Yes, if you want to know,' she lied. 'I do.'

'Well I don't want to know,' he said vehemently and hung up. Then he kicked the telephone table and, after massaging his big toe, poured himself another drink.

Fuck, he thought, Jakarta's hell these days and I've got a whole week of it ahead of me before I go back to Komodo.

The trouble with this house was that just about everything in it made him think of Panda. It was her tenacity that outraged him. All right, he shouldn't have had sex with Eti; and, most of all, he shouldn't have had it here. It was stupid of him – but it had happened well over a year ago, and it was damn vindictive of her not to forgive him by now. If she would just give him a chance, he could explain that while Eti was a nice girl, an intelligent colleague and one who admittedly didn't exactly hurt the eyes, she was too shy and sweet to be very exciting as a woman. But how could he tell her anything when she wouldn't even talk to him? And why the hell did it take a genuine card-carrying witch like Panda to give some zest to life anyway? Life was so God damn fucking unfair. Here he was being a model husband, not even screwing Eti since she got engaged to that microbiologist in Yogyakarta, spending weeks at a time on a lonely island with nothing to chase but a bunch of prehistoric reptiles and barely speaking to another woman except about monitor lizards – and what happens? His wife takes off and starts fucking some creep in Bangkok. The injustice of it all was beyond his comprehension, but all he could do about it at the moment was pour himself another drink. Then, starting tomorrow, he'd try to work up a modicum of interest in some woman other than Panda. The problem was that it was damn difficult.

'Where're you going, Mummy?' Julie asked a few days later as Panda was dressing to go out. 'Can I come too?'

'No, darling; you stay here with Rusty and Khun Siriporn. I'm meeting Granddad and Grandma at the Foreign Correspondent's Club and you would just have to sit quietly through a lot of grown up talk. You wouldn't like it – not now, anyway– but you can come when you're older.'

'Why do I have to be older for everything nice?'

'You don't, not for everything.'

'Do you like being older?'

'Not particularly.'

'Do you miss Daddy?'

'No, never. Do you?'

'Sometimes.' Julie fell silent for a moment and then she asked, 'Mummy, what makes people stop loving each other?'

Panda put down her mascara. 'I don't think they really do, darling. I mean, if it seems as if they stop loving each other – well, it probably means they never actually did.'

Julie looked perplexed so Panda tried again. 'I mean

it's easy to think you love someone because they are good looking or pretty or fun to be with or something like that, but you can be terribly wrong.'

'How do you know if you're wrong?'

'Sometimes it takes a long time to find out but if it is really love, I believe it goes on forever. Nothing can ever destroy it. If you have it – and I hope you will, darling, with a husband you can trust – you have the most important thing in the whole world. And if you don't, well...' She trailed off, wondering how much Julie would understand.

'Will you stop loving me?'

'Oh, my darling – no, never ever,' Panda exclaimed, devastated at the anxieties she had raised in the child. 'I could never stop loving you or Rusty or Leonard; that kind of love will last forever and ever, no matter what.'

'And Granddad and Grandma?'

'Of course,' Panda assured her.

'Then why not Daddy? Why did you stop loving him?'

'Oh God, Panda thought, sitting down and drawing Julie onto her lap, this is going to be a long conversation.

She was very late for the Foreign Correspondent's Club but William and Christie were even later (odd really, because, in spite of living in Thailand since the age of the dinosaurs, William was usually very punctual). So she went ahead and sat down at the table William always reserved for the Wednesday evening buffets and programs.

Alexander, who sometimes came along to these evenings, unglued himself from the long bar when he saw her and came over to the table. 'You aren't looking altogether repulsive this evening,' he said looking her up and down. 'Apparently the swinging singles life suits you.'

'You seem to be enjoying it, I'll say that. Where's the beautiful Miss Thailand – or aren't you seeing her anymore?'

'She wasn't Miss Thailand. Due to a grave miscarriage of justice she only made it as far as Miss Songkhla. We did have a little difference of opinion though.'

'Over whether or not she should go to bed with you?'

'It shocks me to the very core,' he said, trying but failing to suit his expression to his words, 'to think my dear sister would credit me with such base and immoral intentions.'

'Your dear sister suspects the wicked wolf could take lessons from you.'

'You wound me deeply. By the way do you have any interest in knowing that I ran into your ex downstairs?'

'You mean Sonchai?'

'How many other exes do you have, here in Bangkok anyway? I thought you might like a little warning – just in case he wanders up here.'

'Not particularly. We have a very civilized relationship,

you know. I've even met his new wife, remember?'

'I can't say I do; what's she like?'

'An art student, rather delicate and sensitive looking.'

'Not my type then. I like a woman who won't break apart when I – never mind, actually. Why doesn't he ever bring her here I wonder?'

'She doesn't speak enough English to understand the programs. And I don't think she's mature enough to be interested in them, anyway.'

'Meow, meow,' laughed Alexander. 'Do I detect a little note of jealousy?'

'No, you do not.'

The arrival of Christie and William put an end to the subject.

'Sorry to be so late,' Christie said as they sat down at the table. 'Your dad had a hard time getting the car started.'

'It's a miracle that it started at all,' said Alexander. 'It should be in a museum.'

'It was built in the days when things were made to last,' William declared.

'Like you, Daddy,' Panda said affectionately.

'Have you heard anything from Leonard recently?' Christie asked. She knew it annoyed William when Alexander ribbed him about the car.

'Only once since Christmas,' Panda replied, 'and he

doesn't seem to be doing as well as usual this term. He said that one of the masters had just had a real go at him for messing up on his chemistry project.'

'I must say that doesn't sound at all like Leonard,' said Christie.

'I know,' Panda agreed. 'It makes me wonder if perhaps he has a girlfriend or something and that's what's distracting him.'

'I wouldn't be surprised,' replied Christie. 'With his looks, I imagine the girls must be flocking around him.'

'Yeah, he takes after me,' announced Alexander.

'God help him then,' groaned William.

'Pssst,' Alexander told Panda in a stage whisper, 'there's your Mr. Ex over there at the bar. Are you going to say hello to him?'

'Of course, if he comes over here. But I'm not going to rush madly over there.

A few minutes later Sonchai not only came over but pulled up a chair next to Panda; turning to Christie, he asked, 'Do you mind if I sit down for a minute?'

'Of course not,' she replied. 'How are you?'

'Not too bad, actually. I've got an exhibition coming up at Siam Centre. It opens next week.'

They all congratulated him and William ordered him a drink.

'I thought you might want to hear what happened to

John Smith,' Sonchai said.

'Who's he?' asked Alexander who was constitutionally incapable of staying out of any conversation within earshot.

'The man Lisa was with when she was shot, you dolt,' Panda reminded him. 'Everybody in Bangkok knows the story.'

'And everybody who's over a hundred remembers it,' retorted Alexander.

'Just ignore him,' Panda told Sonchai. 'What about John?'

'He was killed up in the tribal areas of Burma. He was doing a piece on the Shan states for CBS News and you know how the Burmese government feels about reporters, or anyone for that matter, nosing around up there. So the bastards got him. It wasn't very pretty.'

'Oh how awful! I'm really sorry,' Panda said.

'Yeah, he was a great guy,' Sonchai said; after a moment, he added, 'and he certainly changed our lives.'

'Do you think so?'

'Don't you?'

'No, I don't actually. I think things would have worked out the same way for us even if there hadn't been any John Smith and if Lisa had lived. It would have taken a little longer, that's all. We weren't really suited to each other, you and I, you know that. Neither were Teddy and Lisa. Of course, the truth is that Teddy isn't suited to anyone apart from a card-carrying masochist.'

'Well, maybe we would have made it together and maybe we wouldn't; who knows?' Sonchai said with a shrug. 'In any case, it's silly to waste time on "what if's".' And, standing up, he thanked William for the drink, muttered something about some friends waiting for him, and turned to go.

'Wait a minute,' Panda said, putting a hand on his arm. 'Did John ever marry?'

'No,' Sonchai told her; then, without saying anymore, he left.

When Panda went to bed that night she couldn't get Lisa out of her mind and after a while a sense of her presence in the room became so strong it was almost palpable.

'I'm glad John never married,' Panda told her ghostly visitor, 'because I think it means he never stopped loving you. I hope so anyway. After everything Teddy must have put you through, you deserve that kind of love. And if you hate me for the part I played in it all, I'll understand. Thanks to Eti, I realise things now that I was too much of an idiot to understand before – like the fact that how much it hurts depends on how much you care.'

'And did you care desperately,' Panda went on to ask,

'or had Teddy sufficiently trampled on your feelings with his infidelities by that time so that you weren't as torn up as you might have been? Had you already done your suffering and built up some imperviousness to the pain of it all, an immunity that set you free to love John; or doesn't it work that way?'

'It seems strange that both you and John met violent deaths,' she continued. 'Neither of you would have struck me as likely people for that sort of thing. Did you recognize some quality in John, an adventure-seeking spirit, that wasn't readily apparent to other people; and did he detect something similar in you? Is that what initially drew you to each other, but later got you into such violent situations? Of course, that adventurous spirit was responsible for wonderful things too, like drawing you into the fling in Japan that resulted in Leonard. Whatever was responsible for that, I'm glad it happened. Sometimes I think that of the three children, he's the one I love the most. He's going to be a scientist like Teddy – just as smart but much nicer. He's sensitive and thoughtful and kind and, in spite of messing up on a chemistry project recently, he's doing well in Singapore. You can be very proud of him. We both can.'

CHAPTER 24
SINGAPORE AND INDONESIA, 1990

Leonard was, in fact, doing even better than Panda knew; he was totally, wildly, gloriously happy. He had had no idea what love was like until Colette Chen's test tube had exploded in the middle of chemistry class and he had helped put out the small fire that resulted.

Several weeks of despair had followed when he had been sure that no one as beautiful as Colette could ever be interested in him. Then one evening she had actually asked him to help her study for a chemistry test and they had discovered that they had a thousand things in common. They both had messed up families; both were Eurasians who had grown up in South East Asia; and both were convinced that when it came to dancing, there wasn't any music like Prince. It was the basis for becoming best friends – right up until that incredible night just before the Christmas holidays, when they had become so much more to each other. He had discovered that she loved him in the same way he loved her: romantically, sensuously, completely.

The two months after Christmas were the happiest he had ever known; but expressing their love wasn't easy in a boarding school in straight-laced Singapore, and early in March the inevitable happened. They were caught having sex.

It was the last night of Teddy's week in Jakarta and he was just going out the door with an evening in a Chinese nightclub in mind when the phone rang.

He immediately recognized Leonard's voice on the other end.

'Dad, I'm coming home tomorrow afternoon.'

'No, you're not. I'm taking off for Komodo at two fifteen in the afternoon.'

'I've got to, Dad. I've been expelled.'

'What the fuck for?'

'Colette and I were caught… well, you might say "together".'

'Can you manage a complete sentence or has your expensive education been a total waste?'

'Colette and I were caught making love. The headmaster's calling you in a few minutes but I thought I'd better tell you myself first. He's already booked my flight to Jakarta tomorrow.'

'For God's sake, can't you keep it in your –'

'I love her, Dad,' interrupted Leonard, cutting off what he didn't want to hear.

'Bullshit, you're only a kid. You don't know what you're

talking about.'

       'I'll be eighteen in a few months.'

'That's my point. Where is this headmaster anyway? If I can talk to him maybe I can get him to see reason and cancel that ticket.'

'They're pretty puritanical here in Singapore,' Leonard warned. 'But I'll get off the phone so you can try.'

'OK. I'll deal with you later.'

'But Dad –'

'What?'

'If he won't let me carry on here, I'd really like to go to Komodo with you for a while. I'll bring books along and study, I promise.'

'Can't you go stay with Panda,' Teddy asked hopefully. 'That is, until we can find a school for sex maniacs that will take you?'

'The thing is, her place is really small. I'd have to bunk in with Julie and Russell.'

'A pretty dire prospect, I admit, but you can regard it as part of your punishment.'

'But I'm planning to do my A level thesis on Komodos, remember? The biology master here gave me the go ahead for it, so hopefully the next school will approve it too. And think what a brilliant chance this could be to do the research.'

'Maybe you're not such a fool after all. You've been

pretty quick to figure out what the two most interesting things in life are: lizards and women, in that order.'

'Is it OK then? Can I come to Komodo?' asked Leonard, deciding this was not a time to quibble about the order.

'God knows, I don't know what else to do with you. It doesn't seem fair to inflict you on Panda if she's that pressed for space. I didn't realise it was that crowded when you were there. If I can't change the old bastard's mind about expelling you, I guess you'll have to come. I'll meet you at the airport and we'll catch a late afternoon flight.'

'You idiot,' Teddy said when he saw Leonard the next afternoon.

'I know. I'm sorry, Dad.'

'Well, hurry up. We don't want to miss our flight.'

'To Bali?' Leonard asked in surprise as Teddy turned toward the departure gate for the holiday island.

'Don't get the wrong idea; there'll be no fun and frolics on Kuta Beach for you. We're going to catch an early morning flight from there to Flores, have a hell of a long drive over to the tip of the island, and arrange for a boat to take us over to Komodo Island from there.'

'Sounds OK to me,' Leonard replied, picking up his duffle bag and flinging it over his shoulder. 'I left most of my gear – all the stuff I wouldn't need on Komodo – with a day boy at school.'

'Good move,' said Teddy, pausing at a kiosk to buy copies of *The Herald Tribune*, *The Asian Wall Street Journal*, *Newsweek* and *The Economist*. He handed the latter to Leonard.

Then, well-armed with reading material, they boarded the plane – and Teddy was spared the necessity of having to say very much to Leonard until they were sitting across a table from each other at a little restaurant in Kuta (where he always went on these stopovers).

Much to his surprise, he found that Leonard was actually a rather good companion. He was genuinely interested in the Komodos, in the other species such as flying foxes on the island too, and actually knew a surprising amount about reptiles... well, more than you'd expect from a kid anyway. It was all the encouragement Teddy needed to sit back over coffee and wax eloquent on his favourite subject.

The restaurant was closing by the time he remembered that he really should be playing the heavy father, chewing Leonard out for what he had done. But he just couldn't see himself climbing up on a high moral plane; especially when the subject in question was sex.

He finally settled the matter by leaning back in his chair and saying, 'I should be giving you hell, you know, instead of going on about Komodos. But I don't see that there's much point in it now. It was pretty God damn stupid of you to get caught with your pants down like that. But you could have done worse.'

'How?' Leonard wondered.

'You could have gotten kicked out for something like stealing or cheating that would have made me really ashamed of you. If you've to get the boot, a minor sex crime's the right thing to get it for.'

Leonard nearly objected to his father calling anything in connection with Colette a crime, but decided that he was getting off more easily than he had expected so he let it go.

It was late afternoon the next day by the time their boat docked at a tiny village that clung to the edge of the island.

'How do these people live here?' Leonard wondered as they went ashore. 'Aren't they afraid of being mauled or eaten or something?'

'I guess they are. To a degree, anyway. That's why they build their houses on stilts with just those rickety ladders going up to them. And the people don't venture out beyond the village unless they've got a damn good reason.'

'Don't the Komodos come in?'

'Apparently not very often,' Teddy said as they made their way down a sandy narrow street between rows of flimsy houses crowned with soaring thatch roofs. 'Although the locals do take the precaution of keeping their goats on a nearby island.' Then, seeing that Leonard was too busy returning the stares of the sarong clad men and women and the naked children along the way to watch his step, he added, 'Hey – look out! Don't tread on tonight's dinner.'

Leonard looked down and hastily diverted his steps from a large mat, one of many that had been strewn about, spread with squid that had been set to dry in the sun.

'It's also tomorrow's breakfast and lunch for these poor bastards,' Teddy said, indicating the villagers. 'I swear you'll be so sick of them by the time you leave here, you'll never want to eat another one.'

When they reached the end of the street they found half a dozen small brown men holding long, forked sticks waiting for them in front of a little mosque.

'They're our beaters,' Teddy explained, 'at least, that's what I call them. They go with us whenever we leave the project bungalow. And you're not ever, under any circumstances, to go out without them. Is that understood?'

'You can't mean those under-nourished little guys with their pathetic sticks are going to be all that'll stand between us and a bunch of voracious lizards?' gasped Leonard.

'You got it.'

Leonard hoped his face wasn't turning green.

'You can't have researchers on a World Wildlife funded

project carrying guns around and shooting endangered species,' Teddy pointed out.

'OK… But how about tranquilizing darts or something?'

'Only in very special circumstances. Komodos are cannibals, you know. Knock one of them out with a dart and his friends and relatives come and have him as a mid-morning snack while he's sleeping it off.'

'Suppose the special circumstance is to keep one of them from eating me alive?' Leonard suggested.

'If you keep your wits about you, that won't happen. Anyway, these guys are tougher than they look; and they know what they're doing. The Komodos have an Achilles' heel – sort of, although it's at the opposite end of the anatomy. They've got super sensitive noses, and these guys you seem to think are so ineffectual know just how to bash them in the nostrils and get them to beat a swift retreat. So you see, we don't need a supply of darts.'

A feeling of adventure, along with a newfound sense of companionship with his father, tingled in Leonard's veins as they trudged over the rolling hills of arid grasslands (dotted here and there with lontar palms and tamarind trees) to the project bungalow together.

This kid's not too bad, Teddy thought, as they followed the beaters along. Having him around might not be such a drag after all.

In the succeeding weeks Panda often wondered how Leonard was getting on with his dad, but his brief letters were mostly about the Komodos – a subject she could well do without. She hoped Teddy appreciated having a son who so enthusiastically shared his interests, but she rated it as highly unlikely.

On the morning of her fortieth birthday she woke up thinking about Leonard because of a nightmare she had had about him. He was a little boy in the dream and she was reading him a story, when suddenly a host of dragons rose up out of the book and rushed toward them with tongues of fire streaming from their hungry jaws. The biggest dragon of all turned out to be Teddy in disguise; and then, with a pounding heart and gasping breath, she had woken up.

When she turned on the light she saw that it was only ten minutes after five, but she got up anyway – her mother had taught her that she must offer special food to the monks on her birthday. They always came by shortly after dawn, so a birthday lie-in was out of the question.

The maid had already cooked the rice when Panda arrived in the kitchen to bundle it up – along with two different curries – in banana leaves, and have it all ready for the monks by the time they arrived. They didn't thank her when she deposited these offerings in their black bowls.

Instead she made a wai and thanked them for giving her this opportunity to make merit.

At noon she gathered up Julie and Rusty and went to her old home, where Christie had promised her a cake.

Alexander sang out 'Happy birthday' as she walked through the door, then added, 'You're looking great – not a day over seventy-three.'

'It's about time you got here,' William growled. 'I was beginning to think that I wasn't going to have any gin left by the time Alexander finished celebrating your birthday.'

'Happy birthday, darling,' said Christie, adding her voice to the general chorus. 'A bit of gin for you too? And how about the children; what would they like?'

'What's that?' asked Panda, freezing at the sight of a bunch of newly delivered roses – all white except for one red one in the middle – tied up with a shiny pink ribbon.

White roses; dead love. Oh Teddy, she thought, how could you?

'Who're they from?' Julie asked.

'I dare say the card will provide a clue,' advised William.

'It's addressed to you, Panda,' Christie said, detaching the envelope from the pink ribbon and looking at it.

'They're an award for longevity,' suggested Alexander.

'I'll read the card for you, Mummy,' cried Julie.

'They're from Sonchai,' announced Alexander, reading over his niece's shoulder.

'How adorable of him,' Panda exclaimed, relief flooding over her.

'I don't see what's so adorable about it,' Alexander replied. 'White roses are a super polite way of giving someone the royal heave-ho.'

'It's a little late for the heave-ho,' Panda pointed out. 'We've been divorced for twelve years. And anyway, the red one in the middle makes it lovely.'

'The artist's touch,' observed Christie.

'I'm hungry,' whined Russell, who felt that nobody was noticing him.

'We'll have lunch soon,' Christie promised. 'In the meantime, come help me put the candles on the cake; you too, Julie. It's in my room.'

'What's it doing in a bedroom?' Julie asked.

'It's too hot for it in the kitchen,' Christie explained. 'The icing would melt and run off and the candles would fall down, so I took it into the air conditioning.'

'One of the advantages of my bachelor pad,' Alexander declared as his mother disappeared into the bedroom with the children, 'is that the kitchen is approximately the temperature of the North Pole. Of course, nobody ever cooks anything in it except breakfast for visitors. I'm the world master of the scrambled egg on toast, you see.'

'How much longer are you going to be a free floating menace to the female population of Bangkok?' Panda wanted to know.

'Until some lucky girl comes along and catches me. But I have to make my fortune first before I can let some female start spending it for me.'

'You better work hard then, because whoever marries you deserves to do a lot of shopping.'

'Hard work doesn't do it. That's a fairy tale you picked up in America. The world's full of benighted bastards who work like the devil just to fill the old rice bowl and often they don't even manage to do that. No, it's the three Cs – contacts, cleverness and chance – that count when the bank balance is finally added up.'

'Chance being luck in this case,' Panda assumed.

'Right but CCL doesn't sound as good as CCC.'

'Never mind how it sounds: let's just hope you have it,' his heartless sister remarked.

Alexander looked pained. 'What you don't seem to realise,' he said grandly, 'is that it's that I've got the first two sewn up.'

'I can think of a few teachers at the International School who'd be surprised to hear it,' Panda said, 'and as far as the contacts go; that's certainly news to me.'

'Well it shouldn't be; not if you kept your eyes open. You know Kamala, the girl I play tennis with at the Polo Club?'

Panda nodded.

'Well, her dad has money coming out of his ears and he's always looking for places to put it.'

'That doesn't mean he'd be idiotic enough to let your grubby little paws get anywhere near it.'

'It wouldn't be idiotic. I've got some serious plans. And he's not only got money, he's got contacts – namely, a brother in law in the provincial government in Haad Yai. So that means getting building permits and that sort of thing wouldn't be any problem.'

'Building what?' William wanted to know.

'Hotels, beach resorts, that sort of thing.'

'And what does that have to do with you?' William asked.

'A lot.'

'I fail to see why,' his father said.

'Two reasons; the first is that I understand how foreign tourists see things, what they are looking for and…' he trailed off, casting an eye uncertainly toward the room where his mother had gone with Julie and Rusty.

'And?' prompted Panda.

'Well, it's not quite definite yet, that's why I haven't said anything to Mom – but I just might marry his daughter.'

'Kamala?'

'Who else?'

'You rat,' Panda exclaimed, horrified.

'What's the matter with Kamala?' he demanded. 'She's

beautiful, she's intelligent, she comes from a good family –
and to top it off, she plays a wicked game of tennis.'

'But you don't love her. You're just marrying her for her
father's money and I think that's a rotten thing to do.'

'My dear sister, what country did you grow up in?'

'England. During term time, anyway.'

'And for your information, when a guy thinks about
marrying a girl who looks like Kamala, money's not the
only thing on his mind.'

'How about love?'

'Funny you should say that – love didn't quite work out
according to plan for you, did it?'

'Don't you ever think about anything except making
money and seducing women?' interrupted William.

'Sure I do; I was thinking about food all the way over
here,' he replied cheerfully, 'although right now the main
thing on my mind is another drink.'

'I swear, the nurses at the Bangkok Nursing Home must
have mixed up the babies,' William groaned. 'That's the
only possible explanation.'

'Do you suppose they mixed up the babies when Rusty
was born?' asked Julie, bounding into the room. 'I'm sure
they did, so we'd better take him back.'

'I don't want to go back,' cried Rusty, running to his
mother.

Everyone set about reassuring Rusty and scolding Julie,

but without much effect. It was as difficult to depress her spirits for long as it was to alter her brother's perception of the world as a place filled with menace and gloom.

After a lunch that Rusty wouldn't eat because he didn't like it and a cake that he barely touched because he wasn't hungry; Julie piped up with, 'Don't worry, Granny, he never likes anything.'

'He has a sensitive palate,' asserted Alexander. 'That makes him a natural gourmet, like me.'

A roar of laughter went up around the table.

'Mummy says you used to be a walking talking rubbish bin when you were a little boy,' Julie told her uncle.

'You're going to be sorry for that remark, young lady,' declared Alexander. 'I'm going to beat you at Animal Snap like you've never been beaten before. Come on – our young gourmet here can play, too.'

'Does he have to?' objected Julie. 'He'll spoil it.'

'Don't worry, kid,' Alexander told his nephew, 'my sister used to be horrible to me too, still is in fact. Sisters are like that.'

'You lot all belong in the zoo,' declared William. 'I'm going to take a nap.'

Panda and Christie took their coffee out on the veranda and after they had talked about William's rheumatism (getting worse), Alexander's future (if any), and whether Russell would ever out grow his tendency to be a wet blanket, Panda brought up the subject of Thanit.

'Did you know that we are sort of having an affair?' Panda asked.

Christie nodded. 'Not for sure, but I sort of suspected you were.'

'You always figure everything out,' Panda laughed.

'Not always.'

'Well, I thought it would be good, possibly really great. Because after all, I've always liked him. ... But somehow it isn't. I just don't like him that much, at least not in that way. I don't mean that it's a disaster or anything – just a bit disappointing; so I've let the relationship continue. I keep telling myself that I had ridiculous expectations of what it would be like. After all, I haven't had an affair with anyone since before I married Sonchai.'

'Then what would you call the relationship you had with Teddy while you were still married to Sonchai if it wasn't an affair?' she asked.

'Well, I wouldn't call it an affair,' Panda protested.

'Why not?'

'An affair is light and fun; a kind of grown up playtime, a fling.'

'And what was it with Teddy then?'

Panda thought for a moment and then said, 'I suppose you could call it love if you really wanted to but –'

'But you don't?'

Panda shook her head. 'People use that word for so many trivial, stupid, passing relationships in their lives that I just can't use it for what Teddy and I had together. It was – well, it was what my life was all about.'

'I beat him, I beat him,' cried Julie, sprinting out onto the veranda. 'I won the most games.'

'I'll get you next time; just you wait and see,' declared Alexander, following close behind her. 'Rusty and I are going to combine forces and we're going to pulverize you.'

'In the meantime,' he added, turning to his mother and Panda, 'I'm off to hit the jazz scene down on Pat Pong.'

Russell sidled over to Panda. 'I want to go home,' he whined.

'All right,' she said reluctantly, 'I suppose it's time. It's going on six.'

'You want a lift?' Alexander offered.

'It's way out of your way. Why don't you just drop us off at the Erawan corner. We can get a taxi from there.'

'OK, you're on.'

Music was drifting out over the crowd around the Erawan

shrine when Alexander dropped them off.

'Oh Mummy, look – there're dancers. Can we go in and watch them, please, please, please?' cried Julie.

Panda, conscious that Rusty was tired and irritable, started to say no – but somehow, she found herself saying 'yes'. And, after pausing on the pavement to buy the usual gifts for Phra Bhram, they wound their way through the passing throng and into the sandalwood scented enclosure.

Julie loved the cloudy mystery of shrines and temples, often going to them with her mother, so she had no need of special coaching in temple etiquette. Russell, unlike his sister, had to be shown what to do; but for once, possibly because he felt an eerie sense of power radiating from the gilded god, he didn't complain.

When the dance was over and their offerings had been carefully placed in front of the image, Panda pressed Russell's palms together in a wai. Then she and Julie each made a wai of their own and were turning to leave when an evening breeze wafting over the saffron coloured candles caused their tiny flames to flicker; this in turn made Phra Bhram's nearest face appear to change expression.

Russell was too terror-stricken to whine about going home; Julie was enthralled... and Panda viewed it as a sign from the god that he was listening to her heart.

'Please,' she implored, 'please bring Teddy back to me. I don't care what he's done. I haven't been perfect either.

The thing with Eti mattered so terribly when it happened but now when I look back on it... well, it doesn't seem so important anymore. If Teddy can forget her, so can I. Other men are just cardboard cut-outs as far as I'm concerned. They have no reality for me at all. Only Teddy counts. I can't just live for my children or through my children the way some women can. I'm not that sort of person. And a career won't give me any real reason to be alive either. Only Teddy will ever give me that. Oh Phra Bhram, don't let him go farther and farther away beyond my reach. I asked you to bring him back to me once before and you did, remember? It was on the day before Teddy had to go back to America; I was still a little girl then. Please, please, please... hear my prayer now and bring him back to me again.'

'Mommy, are you about to cry?' Julie asked.

'No, darling. It's a bit smoky in here: it's making my eyes water, that's all. Let's go.' And taking a child by each hand, she hurried out onto the crowded pavement.

Julie was unusually quiet as they settled into a taxi; but after a while she said, 'You know, I was thinking about Daddy when we were in the shrine.'

'Oh, were you, darling?' Panda replied vaguely.

'Do you suppose he ever thinks about us?'

'I'm sure he thinks about you and Rusty.'

'And Leonard?'

'Of course, Leonard too.'

'Is Eti there on Komodo Island with him?'

'I imagine so.'

Panda's imagination did not take account of the Idul Fitri holiday, the most important time of the year for family gatherings in Indonesia. Eti and the three other Muslim researchers had gone back to their homes in Jakarta and Sumatra and had left Teddy to carry on the work of the project and write the quarterly report as best he could.

The morning after they left, Teddy had breakfast on the veranda of the government bungalow, contemplating the ten days that lay ahead of him with something little short of amazement. Here he was, faced with nearly two weeks of no one but Leonard to talk to – the beater's English was even worse than his Indonesian – and he actually didn't mind. The kid had proved to be quite human. He wondered why he had never noticed that before. Not only did he have an alert mind and the makings of a first rate scientist, but he was a born naturalist whom it was a pleasure to teach. As a result, Teddy had involved him more in the work of the project than he would ever have thought possible and the kid had actually proved to be quite useful. Even so, he'd have to take some time off work pretty soon and see about getting him back into school somewhere.

He mustn't leave it to Panda; she wouldn't know a good science program from a mediocre one. And the thing he was still having trouble getting his head around was that he would actually miss the young delinquent when it came to opening a beer or two after work.

At the thought of the social life – if such it could be called – on the island, his mind turned to Eti. He frowned slightly. It was going to be a relief to have her out of the picture for a few days. He deeply regretted the role their relationship – it had been little more than a fling actually; and he had been a middle-aged fool, flattered by the admiration of an attractive young woman – had played in the breakup of his marriage. In any case their little group of researchers was too small and too close knit, all living together in the one bungalow the way they did, for any sex to go unnoticed; and Eti had told him that she had a reputation to think of. He hadn't really minded, but somehow he no longer felt comfortable around her in any situation that wasn't a hundred percent professional. And when one of the Indonesian scientists had said something about an engagement ceremony being planned for her while she was at home for the holiday, he hoped it was really true.

His thoughts were interrupted by Leonard, a water flask over his shoulder and a beater's stick in his hand, coming out on the veranda.

'Are you ready?' he asked.

'Be right with you,' Teddy said, gulping down the last of his coffee before picking up his notebook and stick and summoning the usual complement of beaters.

It was extremely hot that morning and most of the Komodos, rendered slothful by the tyrannical sun, had sought shelter in the miserly shade of an occasional kapok tree or in the shallow protection of the tall grass. As a result Teddy and Leonard were able to make very few sightings of the giant lizards.

'What do you say we bag it for the day?' suggested Teddy, after trudging across the arid terrain for several hours. 'I think we're wasting our time today. The bastards just aren't coming out.'

'I'd kill for a cold beer right now,' Leonard admitted.

'You and me both,' Teddy agreed. 'Better tell the beaters we're giving up for the day and heading back to the bungalow.'

Leonard, whose Indonesian was much better than Teddy's, was relaying this information when he broke off in mid-sentence. A scaly head was popping up out of the grass a few meters away and the creature it belonged to had apparently singled him out as the tastiest thing on the menu. It rose up to its full height; fixed him with its cold steady gaze, then flicked its long flame coloured tongue directly at him – but Leonard, confident the beaters would rally round and do their stuff, kept his cool.

The beaters didn't disappoint him. True to form, they silently gathered around and waited until a barely discernable tensing of the dragon's muscles signalled the onset of a predatory forward rush. Only then did they bash the giant reptile on its sensitive nose and drive it away.

'Great sighting,' Teddy exclaimed, taking out his notebook and jotting down his observations. 'The day hasn't been a total waste after all.'

They were almost ready to start back when there was a rustling sound in the dry grass and seven or eight of the huge scaly lizards darted out of their shelter, and came charging toward them at high speed.

The unexpected size of the group galvanized the beaters into immediate action and they formed a semicircle of protection in front of Teddy and Leonard. The Komodos, sensing the presence of a formidable adversary, froze. They waited and watched, their only movement being the flicking of their forked tongues as they licked the air, permeating the atmosphere with the putrid stench of their foul breath. Then the beaters went on the attack; in a perfectly choreographed manoeuvre they started whacking the huge reptiles on their noses, sending them retreating in confused disarray.

Just one thing went wrong.

In the ensuing turmoil, no one noticed one of the gigantic lizards running off to the side of the group.

An instant later it rushed at Teddy from behind, thrashed him across the back of his legs with its steely tail, and sent him sprawling on the ground. Leonard, who was standing next to him, hit at the creature with his stick. Unfortunately, he lacked the skill of the beaters; he only succeeded in thumping the animal on the side of the head and grazing its nose – but it was enough to alter its trajectory. The giant teeth were only able to sink into their victim's leg, grinding it off at the knee, before the beaters drove it away. Teddy's foot was dangling out of its mouth as it disappeared into the tall dry grass.

Leonard instantly tore off his shirt to make a hasty tourniquet; then he reinforced it with strips from the stronger material of his blue jeans before the beaters managed to carry an unconscious Teddy back toward the bungalow.

As soon as the house came into view Leonard raced ahead; he turned on the single-sideband radio and got the Jakarta Emergency Medical Services.

'We've got to have a helicopter right away,' he gasped.

The night crawled by with agonizing slowness. The painkillers in their medical kit were completely inadequate for the situation and Teddy alternated between periods of screaming delirium and unconsciousness. As his fever mounted, the remaining part of his leg began to swell and turn ghastly shades of purple. By the time the first signs of dawn began to lighten the night sky, Leonard doubted that his father would live to reach a hospital. Yet all he could do was continue to press cool compresses on the burning forehead and keep checking the tourniquet to be sure it was holding fast.

Long before it was possible for the helicopter to arrive, he began scanning the horizon for a sign of its appearance. When it finally bounced down in the grass a few yards from the bungalow, Leonard saw a doctor emerge, followed by two assistants carrying a stretcher, and a bag that he hoped was filled with things like bandages and syringes. Try as he would, he couldn't stop the embarrassing tears of relief that were pouring down his face.

Yet there was no time for emotional indulgence. Within minutes Teddy was bundled into the helicopter and Leonard climbed in after him, for the trip to a tiny airfield on the tip of Flores. There they transferred to a small jet for the flight to Singapore.

Leonard almost immediately fell into an exhausted sleep; he didn't wake up until the plane was beginning its descent more than three hours later – but as soon as he opened his eyes he knew he had to pull himself together. He wasn't a child anymore. There was no one else to take responsibility for his Dad.

Teddy regained consciousness for a while as they took

him off the plane; he was vaguely aware of Leonard's presence in the ambulance with him, but he was utterly confused about where he was and what had happened. He started to ask but decided he didn't care enough to make the effort. Oblivion overcame him once again.

An instant later – or so it seemed to Teddy – tubes were attached to him and he was being wheeled down long white corridors.

The next thing he knew he felt like he was floating somewhere up near the ceiling of a very white room. If he wanted to, he could look down and see his body lying on a table, but he didn't want to look. It almost seemed like someone else's body – and anyway, something was wrong with it. Half of one leg was missing and people in white coats and masks were doing something to the half that was still there. He watched them without pain and with little interest. The masked people kept taking readings from machines that were hooked up to almost every part of that body. They seemed to be trying to bring him back down from the pleasant place where he was drifting high above it all, to put him back into that body... but he didn't really want to go. He liked being where he was. Moreover he sensed, rather than saw, the presence of a golden light just beyond the closed door; he wanted to go to it, but as he started to move in its direction he heard a voice – Panda's voice – calling to him to come back.

When Panda learned what had happened to him that day and discovered that his out-of-body experience had taken place about the time she was at the Erawan Shrine, she was convinced that Phra Bhram had been answering her prayer to bring him back to her.

Teddy refused to believe the timing was anything but coincidence.

CHAPTER 25
JAKARTA, 1993

Teddy's limp was only a minor impediment to his progress as he strode out onto the veranda with a freshly opened letter in his hand. 'The Rainforest Wildlife Organisation is starting a Threatened Species Protection Program in Irian Jaya,' he exclaimed, 'and they want me to head it up.'

Panda and Russell looked up from the maths review paper they were working on.

'Oh God,' she said with a laugh. 'I know what's coming.'

'Do you really think it would be all that bad,' Teddy said, sitting down where he could stretch his artificial leg out in front of him. 'Jayapura's supposed to be a beautiful city; at least, that's what I've heard. Would you mind it terribly?'

'Is it for very long?'

'Two years for a start.'

'Good God, what about the children? They have to go to school, you know.'

'You could teach Rusty at home. You're doing a lot of that already and –'

'That's just extra help,' she objected. 'It's not really teaching.'

Teddy frowned. Julie had never needed extra help; neither had Leonard.

'Anyway,' he continued, pushing the comparison out of his mind, 'Julie could go to school in Singapore or even Australia.'

'She's only twelve,' Panda said doubtfully.

'You were about that age when you went to England, weren't you?' he reminded her, but he couldn't keep his mind off the topic at hand for long. 'Lizard adaptation in the marsupial area would be a damn exciting thing to get into,' he said eagerly.

'What if a lizard bites your other leg off, Daddy?' Russell asked.

'Let's not think about things like that,' his mother told him with a shudder.

'Don't worry,' Teddy assured him, 'that's not going to happen. None of the lizards in Irian Jaya would dare.'

Russell looked like he didn't believe this. 'I don't want to move to a new place. I want to stay here.'

'Where's your sense of adventure, darling?' Panda asked reproachfully.

'He lost it in the birth canal,' Teddy muttered, giving his son a look of mild disdain. 'He should try to be more like Leonard.'

At that moment a car pulled up in front of the gate and Julie clambered out amidst noisy goodbyes from her friends.

'I came top in maths today,' she said dropping onto the sofa beside her mother.

'Again?' Panda asked although she wasn't really surprised. 'That's wonderful.'

'Not bad,' Teddy acknowledged gruffly; inwardly, he glowed with pride in the intelligence of his beautiful daughter – and it showed in his eyes.

'How's the leg, Daddy?' she asked.

'In mid-season form today; I'll be climbing trees before you know it.'

'Just like Leonard,' Julie said, laughing at the mental picture of her dad in a tree. 'He's not going to spend the whole summer holiday at that orangutan rehabilitation project, and not come and see us at all, is he?'

'If he wrote a little more often,' Teddy grumbled, 'I might be able to answer that. God only knows when we last heard from him.'

'It was just a few weeks ago,' Julie pointed out. 'Ouch!'

The exclamation was provoked by a small leopard cat that had just leapt down onto Julie's shoulder from the back of her chair, and was steadying itself by digging its claws into her.

'Oh, she must be hungry, poor darling,' Julie said. 'You know how she expects a treat when I come home from school.' And holding the little animal up against her shoulder like a baby, she headed for the kitchen.

Russell followed at a safe distance. He was afraid of the diminutive leopard but wanted to get out of doing any more maths.

'We'll go find you a lovely snack,' Julie told the cat. 'How about a delicious bowl of fish and rice?'

'Remember, no more wild animals as pets,' Teddy called after them.

'Yes Daddy, I know,' replied Julie, who had a well-established habit of saying 'yes Daddy' and then doing exactly as she pleased.

The acquisition of the little leopard cat had been one such situation. She had rescued it from a horrid little cage in the pet market, even though she had known her father would go ballistic – and he had. He was vehemently against giving any kind of encouragement to wild animal dealers and a battle of earthshaking proportions had resulted. To help her remember never to deal with people like that again, he had ordered her to give the little beast away. She had, with difficulty, managed to look penitent and say, 'Yes Daddy,' but had hastily devised a two-pronged strategy for keeping it. The first of these involved banishing it to the maids' quarters whenever he was at home and never mentioning it in front of him (but only for a while); the second prong consisted not only of going to him for advice on her science project, but actually following it. It had worked and the cat was still in residence.

With the two children out of hearing, an uncharacteristic silence fell over the veranda. Both Panda and Teddy tried to ignore the letter about Irian Jaya, simply letting it lie like a large question mark on the table between them.

Then, unable to bear the tension in the air, Teddy picked it up, tore it in half and then tore it in two again. Then he crumpled up the scraps and threw them back down on the table. 'I won't go anywhere you won't be happy,' he said.

'And I won't stand in the way of something you really want to do,' she said, 'at least, I won't as long as you're willing to give it up for me.' Then pausing for a moment to study his face, she added, 'so I'll just get some cello tape, shall I, and we can put that letter back together?'

His face lit up; he caught her hand as she started to go into the house. 'You mean you'll go?' he asked eagerly. 'You won't go berserk on a jungle island like that?'

'I don't need a jungle island to drive me berserk,' she said, as he drew her down onto his lap. 'Just living with you should do it.'

CHAPTER 26
THAILAND, 2004

Alexander pulled his new red Ferrari to a stop in the car park of Phuket Airport on the southwest coast of Thailand. Notwithstanding the fact that he was an extremely successful businessman, married and a father of three, he retained something of his teenage self in his tastes and pastimes. Flashy cars, flashy women to ride around in them and flashy business deals (to provide the necessary wherewithal to sustain the first two) were his stock in trade; but, underneath all the bling, he was basically generous and good-hearted.

His presence at Phuket Airport today was due to the double celebration he had in the works: a birthday bash for his mother's seventieth birthday – although it wouldn't exactly be a bash. It was too soon after losing his Dad for that, so it would be just a family party with Panda and her tribe flying in for it. Then, three days later, he would have the official opening of the spectacular new hotel that would be the flagship of his rapidly expanding chain.

His own tribe – comprising his mother, his wife, Kamala and the three kids – were already ensconced in his private suite at the top of the hotel. It was on the top floor, had four guest bedrooms plus two maids' rooms and a view from the terrace that took your breath away. You could see up and down the coast for miles, and the same was true for the slightly smaller three-bedroom Royal Orchid Suite next door. He was planning to put Panda and Teddy and their family in there, but he wasn't entirely happy with that arrangement. His mother had heard from Panda that Teddy practically foamed at the mouth when there was any mention of Julie's boyfriend – but the hotel was going to be packed to the gills during the Grand Opening, and was pretty well booked up for Christmas a few days later, so he hoped Teddy would manage to keep a handle on his temper. Fortunately Leonard was coming out for the double celebration; hopefully he would be a stabilizing influence. It was great about his new job at that National Institute of Health place in Washington, although geneticists never made much money wherever they were. Still, he'd bet old Leonard was getting a hell of a lot more than he'd been making in the UK. Pity about his divorce though; it was a damn shame that women never seemed to go for the really nice guys.

Ever practical, his mind soon reverted to the preparations for the upcoming reunion. Maybe he'd do Julie a favour and give her and her boyfriend a room in his suite (if Kamala bunged the baby in with the other two kids, there'd still be a bedroom for his mother and as well as their usual one for himself and Kamala); and it would put a little space between Julie and her dad.

Then there was Rusty; poor guy, he was always sort of forgettable, but he could be slotted in somewhere. It wasn't going to be easy though. Coming from that college of his, some small place in southern California, he was going to be the last of the lot to arrive.

The announcement of Panda and Teddy's flight cut his ruminations short. A few minutes later he was exchanging insults with his sister and shaking hands with his brother-in-law as if they had never been away. Some things never changed, and he liked the feeling of solidarity and continuity that gave him.

'How's Christie getting along?' Panda asked when they were in the car.

'She's not too bad,' Alexander said, 'but you can tell she misses Dad like crazy. I try to look in on her as often as I can, and Kamala's very good about that sort of thing. Mom's great with the kids of course and they adore her. Plus she's got her friends and the stuff she does for the museum. So, what with one thing and another, she'll be OK.'

'It's hard to imagine her living in a modern air conditioned apartment instead of our old house though,' Panda replied sadly.

'I know, but it was practically falling down around her ears. Even the maids were complaining about all the leaks in the roof, so I finally managed to persuade her to make a change and I think it's cheered her up. She has a great little pad in one of Kamala's dad's buildings now, complete with elevator and swimming pool and every modern convenience known to man. She claims not to know how to work half of them but that's Mom for you – stubborn as ever.'

'You can't talk about stubborn,' Panda objected. 'You win the championship there.'

Teddy stayed out of their inevitable teasing banter; thinking instead about how incredible it was that this brash and boastful kid brother of Panda's could have grown into such a phenomenally successful businessman. It made him wonder, not for the first time, just how much Alexander's marriage to Kamala had to do with it. Just about everything, he suspected, although he and Panda disagreed on whether the money had inspired the marriage or whether it had been the other way around.

Panda, with what he thought was extraordinary naiveté, was convinced that Alexander had just happened to fall in love with a girl from a fantastically rich and well-connected family; and that his father-in-law had showered them with goodies – mostly monetary – out of concern for the happiness and well-being of his daughter. And Alexander, not quite as much of an idiot as he sometimes seemed, had used the money to make some surprisingly good, or perhaps just lucky, investments.

Teddy was sure that was total bullshit, or most of it was anyway. After all,

Alexander had always been a kid with an eye for the main chance. Knowing that he wasn't going to get any seed money for his business deals from William, he had decided to marry it. And what better choice could he have made than Kamala? Rich, attractive and possessed of a doting father who wanted his little girl to have every luxury – she was perfect for him. And the icing on the cake was that for some unfathomable reason, she seemed to have fallen for him in a big way; big enough to persuade her father to let her marry a foreigner, albeit one who knew Thailand very well and looked like he would be spending the rest of his life there.

The truth of the matter actually lay somewhere in between, and involved the former night watchman at the old house – a Sikh named Kanwarjit – who had slept on a string bed in front of the house when Alexander was a boy and who had taught him how to play chess.

Kanwarjit had disappeared suddenly one day when Alexander was nine or ten; but, to the surprise of each, they had run into each other one afternoon in the lobby of a friend's apartment building a decade or so later. No longer looking like someone who would even think of sleeping on a string bed, Kanwarjit was well dressed and striding through the lobby as if he owned the place – which, in fact, he did. Partly, anyway.

During Bangkok's phenomenal property boom, when apartment buildings were springing up like weeds in the Sukumwit area, it had been the night-watchmen who were the best placed to know which houses were to be sold and where one might be obtained at a rock bottom price (and quickly resold to a developer). Family ties were strong amongst these watchmen; so was the desire to get ahead in life. Brothers, uncles and cousins had readily pooled their meagre resources, keeping the spending of their respective households down to a bare minimum and borrowing up to the hilt to get enough money together for down payments on desirable properties. At first they held them only as long as necessary to turn them over, so they could re-invest the profits in their next deal; but, as time passed, they began to hold onto their properties and lease them to developers. That was when the big profits really began to flow in – and of course, when they were no longer desperate for the money, the banks were eager to lend to them.

Kanwarjit and his family consortium prospered.

On the afternoon of his unexpected reunion with Alexander, Kanwarjit had just lost an argument with his older brother about whether or not to buy a great property he had spotted off Soi Asoke. His brother had declared that it wasn't worth taking on more debt for, not at this time anyway, but Kanwarjit was convinced that it was. And, since the prospect of a lost business deal was weighing heavily on his mind, he found himself telling Alexander about it – and, on a whim, asking, 'How are you fixed for money these days; any chance you could invest in something like this? I could probably get about half the cash we'd need for the deposit together if you could put in the other half.'

Alexander, always interested in any proposition that involved making money, said that he might like to have a look at the place. But then, glancing down at his watch, he had remembered that he had a tennis date with Kamala at the Polo Club and had to hurry. He was almost tempted to give it a miss and call her up and apologize afterwards, send her flowers, that sort of thing, but he figured she might not be that much of a forgiving angel; in fact, he strongly suspected she wouldn't. And he didn't want to lose her just because of some hair brained scheme of Kanwarjit's. Nevertheless he kept in touch with him.

The traffic was terrible, even worse than usual that day, and Kamala and her dad were already on the court by the time he got there. Her sister, dressed in tennis clothes, was watching from a nearby bench, so the four of them ended up playing doubles and then having fresh lime juice at the terrace cafe together afterwards.

It was there that the idea that would change his life had

occurred to him.

Why not, he thought, she's a beautiful girl and an ace tennis player and I'll probably want to get married sometime anyway... so why not to Kamala? What's the matter with having a family that's super-rich and well connected? I bet a word or two from her dad would be an open-sesame for financing the sort of property deals Kanwarjit was talking about. And what the fuck, she's just the sort girl I would go for anyway. The only problem now is getting her to fall for me. Oh, and one other problem – getting her family to agree. They probably won't be overjoyed to have her marry a foreigner.

They weren't, but Alexander turned on the charm in a big way, Kamala fell in love – and a combination of persistence and patience on his part brought about the desired results. By the time the wedding day arrived, Alexander truly wouldn't have wanted to be marrying anybody else.

Of course things didn't happen fast enough for the deal on the property near Soi Asoke to become a reality, but other possibilities came up from time to time. And, when they did, a few phone calls from his father-in-law to various banking friends usually liberated the required funds.

After a few successful ventures in the Bangkok property market, Alexander began applying Kanwarjit's strategy to the purchase of land for hotels in the burgeoning seaside resorts along the southwest coast of Thailand; and, as tourism there had taken off in a big way, so had his fortunes. They had soared to the point where he could invite his whole family to celebrate his mother's birthday in his fabulous new hotel – and he could even meet them at the airport in his longed for red Ferrari. How great was that?

He didn't actually meet Julie and her boyfriend when they arrived the next day, though. A small fire in the kitchen of the seafood restaurant at the far end of the garden caused a hasty change of plan, and Panda went with a driver to meet them instead.

'Hello Daddy,' Julie said casually when she came across him lounging by the pool, her restraint in marked contrast to the enthusiasm with which she usually greeted him.

Chafing at the lack of an affectionate hug, he looked up from his newspaper and said, 'So you finally got here. I suppose your loathsome lover is with you, or have you parked him out of sight for a while? Perhaps in a suitable swamp somewhere?'

'Really Daddy, you have no cause to talk about him like that.'

'No cause?' he exclaimed, scarcely able to believe his ears. 'I have every cause. When some slimy idiot convinces my otherwise intelligent daughter to give up on a postgraduate degree in mathematics in order to chase after a career as a starving actress – '

'I don't have that degree yet; I'm still miles from it, so

I'm not giving up anything.'

'You'll get it if you give yourself half a chance, you know you will, but if you –'

'And anyway,' she continued heatedly, 'Tom had nothing to do with my decision to go into the theatre. That was totally my own.'

'Oh? And the fact that he fancies himself the undiscovered genius of the stage and screen is sheer coincidence, is it? It was really the God damn Easter Bunny that gave you the idea?'

'Teddy, will you please stop talking to Julie like that,' Panda said, coming over to them and spreading a towel down on a deckchair. 'She's twenty-three; she's entitled to make her own decisions, even if you don't agree with them.'

'Whose side are you on anyway?' he demanded, glaring at her.

'Julie's side, of course,' said Alexander, coming within earshot and answering for her. 'You can bet on that. Hello gorgeous, great to see you. Sorry I couldn't make it to the airport. I hope you haven't unpacked yet because I've managed to free up the honeymoon suite for you and John.'

'Tom,' she corrected.

'A rampant case of pre-mature senility,' Panda explained, indicating her brother.

After thumping her between the shoulder blades, he

went on, 'It's a bit down the hall from the rest of us, but it's still on the top floor – great views and all that, so it should be OK.'

Julie threw her arms around him, half-smothering him in the affectionate hug she would have given Teddy if he weren't being so horrible about Tom.

'You know,' Panda told Teddy when they were back in their room, 'you can thoroughly spoil this holiday for me as well as for Julie if you want to.'

'I don't want to spoil anybody's holiday,' he returned sulkily. 'Well, not yours or Julie's anyway. I wouldn't mind giving that reptilian Romeo a few bad moments.'

'Well, try to repress the feeling. Concentrate on the fact that Julie is as likely as not to have a different boyfriend the next time we see her. Remember how you were complaining about her having a new one every five minutes?'

Teddy laughed and admitted defeat. 'OK, OK, I'll be nice – to Julie, anyway. And if I remind myself about the five-minute changeover every time I see the boyfriend, I might just manage to be civil.'

He did manage it and Christmas day was full of fun. There were presents under a tree in Kamala's and Alexander's suite in the morning, swimming and sunbathing in the afternoon, plus a lovely turkey dinner that none of them had to bother about cooking in the evening. It appeared as if by magic, sent up from one of the kitchens and accompanied by a selection of the wine steward's delicious recommendations.

Panda partook heavily of these and as a result woke up feeling a little rocky on Boxing Day. A swim was what she needed to sort herself out, she decided; so, getting up quietly to avoid disturbing Teddy, she slipped into her bathing things and went downstairs. Crossing the terrace cafe where some of the hotel guests were having breakfast, she started across the manicured lawn toward the beach.

That was when she blinked her eyes and asked herself whether she was still drunk from the night before, or was having some sort of weird hallucination.

What else could explain the fact that the sea wasn't where it had been on Christmas Day? It was farther away – much farther – and the beach was much wider. But until quite recently the ocean had been where she thought it was. She could tell because the sand was still wet, although now lots of excited children were running around playing on it, picking up shells and stranded sea creatures. One of them looked like Sawat – Alexander's eldest – and she started to wave to him; but then he came closer, and she saw that it was someone else.

The tide here must be really strong, she thought, and was surprised Alexander hadn't warned her. She would suggest putting a notice about it in all the guest rooms. In the meantime, she didn't fancy a long hot walk down to the water. She'd just have a quick splash in the pool instead.

'I hope you won't regret this when you find out what a seriously bad player I am,' Leonard told Alexander as they trudged up the hill to the golf course behind the hotel.

'Don't worry about that. The point is just to get a little exercise before it gets too hot. Kamala says I'm getting fat.' Alexander patted his middle, which had indeed outgrown its youthful slimness; now, it was an indicator of a fondness for good food, good beer and good living. 'And you've really got to take in the view from the first few holes; it's spectacular.'

'Better than the view from my balcony?'

'Much better; it's quite a lot higher so you can see for miles up and down the coast.'

'Great!'

'Look, Mummy, look Granny,' Alexander's daughter, Deng cried, running in from the balcony of their suite, 'the sea has gone away.'

'Don't be silly, darling,' Kamala said absently. She was

nursing the baby and simply couldn't deal with all three children at once. Where was Nanny, anyway?

'The sea doesn't go away just like that,' Sawat, who was two years older than Deng, said, scornfully. 'The tide goes in and out, that's all. Honestly, girls are so stupid.'

'You'll like them better when you're older,' Christie predicted. Then, taking Deng by the hand, she said, 'Show me what happened to the water. I want to see.'

'Good heavens,' she exclaimed when she looked out over the balcony rail and saw the hugely widened beach.

'Can we go down and make a castle while the sand's still wet?' Deng asked. 'That's when it's best.'

Christie frowned; for some reason she wasn't quite happy with that idea.

Tom, his hand between Julie's legs, was still asleep. But whenever she stirred, as she did from time to time, he would wake just enough to readjust the position of his hand, sometimes slipping a finger or two inside her, and then go back to a night of the most incredible dreams.

Rusty, who liked early mornings by the sea and who really hadn't done justice to his uncle's Christmas wines, was taking a solitary walk and wondering what he wanted to do with his life. He wished he had some overwhelming interest in life like his father had, or was just good at everything like his sister. It wasn't fair that he didn't seem to be good at anything. Even his mother sometimes seemed to patronize him – and, he was sure, look down on him. A wave of anger at the world welled up in him. He kicked at a rock that was in his path, but even that went wrong for him. His big toe took the brunt of the encounter and started hurting like crazy. He wondered if maybe he had broken it. Shit, he could hardly walk. Shit, shit, shit.

The same word was running through Teddy's mind as he woke up to a raging thirst, a pounding headache and a vaguely queasy feeling in his stomach. Damn it, he shouldn't have drunk so much. It was all that brandy he had had after dinner; that and the gin and tonics he had had to start with, to say nothing of all those great wines: a light white one for the fish, a dry full bodied red one with the turkey followed by an ever so slightly sweet one to complement the Christmas pudding. He had done justice to all of them. He had to say that Alexander really knew how to lay on a feast.

He wondered if Panda felt as God-awful as he did. Where was she anyway? He staggered out onto the balcony to see if he could see her by the pool or in the garden anywhere.

'Jesus Christ,' he exclaimed to no one in particular, his hangover symptoms forgotten when he saw the vastly widened beach. Receding water on a scale like that could mean only one thing – an imminent tsunami. There had been one on Flores when he was there once on his way to Komodo Island. Fortunately he hadn't actually been on the coast at the time, but everybody had talked about the outgoing rush of water that had lured so many people to their death, thinking it would be a great chance to pick up fish that had been caught unawares and beached.

To his horror he saw that Panda was just climbing out of the pool.

Dashing back into the room, he threw on his swimming trunks and raced down the stairs as fast as his artificial leg would allow but by the time he got to the garden, several feet of water was rushing toward the hotel.

The next thing he knew, Panda – who had looked like she had been about to towel herself dry – was no longer visible. He had no way of knowing whether she had simply been knocked down by the force of the wave, hit and possibly wounded; or knocked unconscious by the debris that was now being tossed about in the swirling water; or – but he couldn't think about that. She simply had to be somewhere where he could find her.

Fishing boats, Royal Navy Patrol boats and pleasure

boats that had been bobbing up and down in the ocean a few minutes earlier were now reduced to planks and splinters and scattered across the hotel grounds. Chairs and tables around the pool and in the garden restaurant had met a similar fate. Jet skis went shooting like missiles through the turbulent water, oblivious of the snakes, centipedes and various unpleasant insects that must have been washed from their chosen hideouts. But he didn't see Panda anywhere.

'Don't go out there, you idiot,' he heard somebody call to him as he plunged into the swirling water but it wasn't a question of choice. Panda had to be out there somewhere, and he couldn't just stand there and do nothing.

Battling his way against the force of the tide, he headed toward the place where he had last seen her, but he wasn't even half way there – his artificial leg wasn't helping by sinking into the sodden ground with almost every step – when he began to hear cries of 'coming again, coming again' and 'run, run' followed by tremendous crunching and breaking sounds as a second wave, many times larger than the first, rushed toward him. Realizing that no one, not even someone with two good legs, would be able to outrun the onslaught of water coming toward him he did the only thing he could. He grabbed on to a low hanging palm frond and swung himself up into a tree, high enough, he hoped, for the water to do no more than merely graze his feet.

Then he looked around for Panda but all he could see were throngs of terrified people, running, screaming and then disappearing as they were encompassed by the relentless wave. Oh God, he thought, Panda had to be among them. Where else could she be? Nevertheless he clung to the hope, a hope his rational self told him was slim at best, that since he hadn't actually spotted her in the panic stricken crowd, she had somehow managed to get to safety; but safety where? And Julie and Leonard and Rusty – where were they? Oh God, what could he do for any of them? It was all too awful to think about.

Leonard and Alexander were also incapable of rational thought as, from their vantage point on the hill behind the hotel, they could only watch in horrified disbelief as the first and then the second wave of the tsunami came rolling like a monstrous juggernaut, across the garden below them, engulfing everything in its path. Too shocked to say anything, too stunned to take in what they were seeing, too afraid to ask the terrible questions about the people they loved – they simply stood near the first hole staring at the devastation.

They had no idea how much time passed before the hotel helicopter, acquired in case of swimming or boating accidents, appeared; hovering like some kind of beneficent insect overhead, it winched them both back to the hotel.

Once there, a glance at the lobby floor covered with blood-soaked victims (of collisions with wayward planks, broken branches and loosened metal parts from boats and kitchen equipment, and God-only-knew what else) convinced them that their time as onlookers was over. They immediately set to work moving debris to clear passages between the wounded, so the few doctors and nurses amongst the hotel guests could get to those who needed them. They tore up sheets to make bandages and tourniquets; learned how to dress wounds; helped fit emergency splints; brought water to thirsty patients – and in general worked like coolies, doing anything that needed to be done. Nor were they alone in their efforts; virtually all the able bodied survivors pitched in, wherever they could be of help.

Christie and Kamala left the children in the care of the nanny and took up the task of trying to reunite lost and desperate members of separated families with each other while at the same time searching for the missing members of their own. They hadn't seen Panda, Teddy, Julie or Rusty since before the wave hit; and, as the morning droned on and more and more dead bodies were dragged out of the relentless sun, their feelings of pessimism grew.

Christie was trying to console a little girl who couldn't

find her mother when she heard a boy with an American accent say, 'Hey Mom, look, there's man up in that tree! Way up high, see?'

Without thinking, Christie let her eyes follow the direction of the child's gesture; and, to her delight, she saw Teddy there.

She hastily gave the little girl over to a nearby woman, ran out into garden – it was knee-deep in mud since the wave had receded – and called up to him, 'My God, I'm glad to see you. How did you get way up there?'

'The question is, how the hell am I going to get down?' he called back. 'Unless you know a friendly fire department that's got a very long ladder, I'm pretty much stuck here for the duration.'

'Don't worry – I'm sure there's one in the town. Alexander might even have one around here somewhere.'

'Is he OK?' Teddy asked, suddenly too afraid to broach the question he really wanted to ask. Then pulling himself together, he asked, 'And the others?'

'Leonard's fine, so are Alexandra and Kamala and the children but –'

Teddy felt his blood run cold. 'But?'

'We don't know yet.'

He came close to breathing a sigh of relief. It wasn't good news but at least it wasn't the worst.

Christie quickly turned away to hide the expression

on her face. She was virtually torn apart by fear that they weren't all going to come through this alive. For one thing, she knew that Rusty liked to go for walks along the beach in the mornings, searching for shells, watching birds, stopping at one of the lean-to restaurants for a bowl of noodles, that sort of thing; and she had seen him set out on one of these strolls an hour or so before the first wave began to suck the water out. No one on the beach could have survived, she was sure of that.

Christie knew what Teddy was thinking because the same sorts of things were going through her mind but she forced herself to be practical. 'Wait here,' she said before realizing how stupid that was, 'I'll go see if I can get my hands on a ladder.'

'Make it a long one,' he called after her as she hurried away. 'I'll probably still be here when you get back.'

It wasn't easy in the chaos but eventually she found a ladder that had been used to replace some broken tiles on the roof of the garden restaurant, as well as two men to carry it over to Teddy's tree and set it up.

When – stiff, sore and with his artificial leg dragging at an awkward angle – he was down on the ground once more, she greeted him with such an enormous hug that she practically knocked him off his one good leg.

This was partly out of genuine relief; she had always been fond of him – well, almost always – and partly because it delayed dealing with the questions she knew he would ask.

One of those questions was answered very shortly when Rusty trickled in, unaccountably followed by a scruffy little white dog (although in all fairness, the creature looked like it might be quite fluffy and appealing if anyone ever gave it a bath and dried it off) and greeted her with a casual, 'Hello Gran'. Then before she had a chance to ask him anything, much less get any answers, he sauntered off in the direction of the kitchen with the animal at his heels.

She was left torn between happiness that, however he had managed to do it, he had survived and a strong desire to strangle him.

Later she would find out – he always found it easier to talk to her than to his mother or his dad, especially his dad – that while the horrendous waters had been swirling around beneath him, he had been doing some serious thinking on the roof of a beach front cafe, the little dog beside him.

He hadn't really been able to explain just why he had taken to the little fellow the way he had. He had never been crazy about animals the way Julie was, but this one had looked so alone and so frightened with its wet fur plastered down against its body and a sort of quizzical expression in its soulful brown eyes that he hadn't been able to resist the impulse to scoop it up, tuck it under his arm and climb up onto a railing with it. From there he had managed to get them both up onto a ledge and finally to the safety (relative safety, anyway) of a roof.

The truth was that he had seen his own feelings reflected in the little animal's eyes; and, as they had sat on the roof together with the powerful forces of the ocean churning around beneath them, his conviction that there was an important bond between them had increased. The little fellow's utter trust in him made him feel strong: almost like the man his father wanted him to be; almost like the man his brother Leonard was; almost like a man who could take control of his life and change what he didn't like about it.

There wasn't actually much about his life that he did like. For a start, he didn't like college in the States. He didn't want to go back to it and he wasn't going to do it no matter what his dad said, and that was that.

The problem was that what he really wanted to do was just to go on and on here on this roof forever, isolated from the world with the little dog. But even he could see that that wasn't exactly doable.

When the sea had finally appeared calm again, he had reluctantly started back to the hotel, and was thrilled to see that the little dog was following him. And that was when a plan began to take shape in his mind.

By the time he had retraced his steps and turned into the mud and debris-filled garden of his uncle's hotel, his ideas had turned into a full-fledged rebellion. He wasn't going to go back to college. He wasn't going to go back to America or to Indonesia either. He wasn't even going up to Bangkok. He was going to stay here and work in the hotel and keep the little dog. He was sure that Uncle Alex, one of the few people he actually liked, would give him a job. After all, his uncle had always been kind to him and never made him feel bad about all the things he wasn't very good at. He would work really hard for him and perhaps even be allowed to work his way up to manager in one of his smaller hostelries someday.

'How would you like to live here and be my dog?' he had asked his soon-to-be-clean-and-fluffy companion – and took it as a resounding yes when the little fellow perked up its ears and wagged its tail.

It was an hour or so later that one of the cooks found Panda, barely conscious and wedged between a trellis and one of the walls of the kitchen garden on the inland side of the hotel. She was covered with blood and purple bruises, and so many scratches that she looked like she had been clawed by a lion; her appearance was made even more alarming by a very angry looking swelling on her face. She barely stirred as two men lifted her onto a makeshift stretcher and carried her into the lobby.

After one look at her, Teddy made a dreadful scene in an effort to convince one of the overworked doctors that

Panda was more important than anyone else who needed medical care. But her condition proved to be less dire than it first seemed, and it wasn't long before she was sufficiently cognizant of what was going on to ask the question Christie didn't want to answer – 'the children?'

She quickly reassured her about Leonard and Rusty but stumbled over what she could say about Julie and the silence that served as an answer cut her like a knife.

'Don't worry,' Teddy and Christie and Alexander told her more or less in unison. They pointed out that the place was in chaos and nobody could be sure where anybody was but Panda wasn't soothed.

'She'll turn up though, you wait and see,' Alexander said with a heartiness he didn't feel and Teddy had job of it restraining her from getting up and starting to search on her own.

Panda, drawing on a source of strength that seemed little short of magical in the circumstances, managed to break away from him but when she tried to stand, her head started whirling around; the floor seemed to come up to meet her and her legs gave way beneath her so she agreed to let Christie and Kamala conduct a search instead.

Once she was settled back down on a straw mat again, the horrible whirling sensation inside her head started to go away and after a while her mind was clear enough for her to give a fairly lucid account of what had happened.

'The first wave was terrifying enough,' she was able to tell Teddy, Leonard, and Alexander, 'with everybody trying desperately to run away from it, but most of them not getting very far before they were caught in it. I knew I wouldn't stand a chance if I tried to outrun it so I climbed up on one of the tables around the pool but then the table, with me on it, got picked up by the wave and went shooting through the water and all I could do was hold on for dear life. I was scared out of my mind and to make matters worse all sorts of awful things – broken up boards, some of them with nails in them – kept bumping into me. That must be how I got all these scratches. Anyway it was all such a nightmare that when the table finally came to a stop and everything seemed to be over, I was too shaken and too exhausted to do anything but lie there.'

'You dingbat,' exclaimed Alexander, 'if you'd wanted to drown in the next wave, that would have been a good way to do it.'

'Who ever thought there would be a second wave? I didn't and I can't imagine that you did either.'

He had to admit, he hadn't.

'It's amazing you came through as well as you did,' Leonard said, pressing a cold compress on Panda's forehead.

'It was an incredible stroke of luck actually. The first wave carried me around the side of the hotel, nearly out to the street and swirled me around until I felt like some kind of spinning top. But then when it began to go out again, the main building of the hotel was between the ocean and me – and I suppose that's what stopped me from being sucked back out to sea.'

'And of course you didn't think of getting up and going into the hotel,' Alexander said incredulously. 'Talk about dippy!'

'At that stage I wasn't thinking about anything,' she shot back at him, 'I was so out of it I couldn't have told you who I was or where I was. But looking back on it now I think the hotel building must have broken the force of the second wave, so that only a little of it trickled around to where I was. But then something – I don't know what – came crashing down on me and I don't remember anything after that... not until I woke up on the lobby floor and Teddy was having a go at the doctor.'

'How did you get that nasty thing on your face?' Sawat, asked.

'I don't actually know. The doctor thinks it might have been a centipede bite. Does it look too dreadful?'

Sawat nodded and pointed out ominously, 'People can die from centipede bites.'

'Shut up, you little horror,' Alexander told his tactless son, 'Auntie Panda is going to live. We all are, the whole family. You wait and see.'

584

Reckless as the assertion was when he made it, it proved to be true.

Julie and Tom were found.

High in their third floor suite and even higher on some great ganja they had picked up in Bangkok, they were having fabulous sex – and missed the whole thing.

END

END